# Praise for *The Mistletoe Countess*

"In *The Mistletoe Countess*, author Pepper Bash[...]perfection. Grace is the most adorable heroine ever written[...]red spirit. And Frederick? Readers need to keep a fan or fai[...]ge. Grace's imaginative but genuine heart, Freddie's swoonil[...]and a few mysteries afoot will keep you enthralled from b[...]

–Carrie Schmidt, reviewer & blogger, ReadingIsMySuperPower.org

"With her trademark wit and whimsy, Pepper Basham has written a thoroughly charming story. *The Mistletoe Countess*, with its adorably quirky, mystery-loving heroine and dashing hero, pays homage to well-loved classic literature while also delighting modern readers. This marriage of convenience romance will make you wish for Christmas, mistletoe, and the magic of a kiss."

–Kimberly Duffy, author of *A Mosaic of Wings* and *A Tapestry of Light*

"Charming and delightfully amusing, Pepper Basham has once again penned a story that will leave readers smiling long after the last page is turned".

—Jen Turano, USA Today Bestselling Author

Delightfully witty and full of vivacity, *The Mistletoe Countess* proves that Pepper Basham is not only the queen of romance, she's also the grande dame of characterization. Grace's quirky innocence and plucky spirit will remind readers of another beloved literary redhead from North America, and the story will thrill readers from the meet cute to the daring (albeit somewhat bumbling) rescue. Destined to be a Christmas favorite for years to come. Keep a cold compress handy for the characters' (and author's) abject devotion to that foreshadowing in the title--*mistletoe.*

—Chautona Havig, author of *Deepest Roots of the Heart* and the Aggie Series.

A festive Christmas read, *The Mistletoe Countess* will really put you into the holiday spirit! Spunky heroine Gracelynn Ferguson is the perfect match for Lord Astley—too bad, though, that it's her sister who's supposed to marry him. There are so many fun twists and turns to this story that there's just no stopping a huge grin as you read. Grab a hot chocolate and nestle down with a blankie for this winner!

—Michelle Griep, Christy Award-winning author of *Once Upon a Dickens Christmas*

Set in 1913, *The Mistletoe Countess* combines the energy of a new century with the formality of the British nobility. When Gracelynn Ferguson is made a substitute in her sister's arranged marriage, bewildered Frederick Percy, Earl of Astley, gets more than he bargained for. While Grace's unorthodox American behavior ruffles aristocratic feathers, the new couple soon learns that the biggest threat to their happiness isn't their differences but a murderer hunting for the earl. A laugh on every page and a swoon-inciting encounter in every chapter, you don't want to get caught under the mistletoe without this thrilling book.

—Regina Jennings, author of *Courting Misfortune* and *Proposing Mischief*

*The Mistletoe Countess* is a must-read for all romantics. Basham delivers an evocative story that feathers the heart with humor and stirs the soul with moving prose. The witty dialogue, sparky romance, and clever antics of a memorable heroine will captivate readers from start to finish.

—Rachel Scott McDaniel, award-winning author of *Undercurrent of Secrets*

A richly romantic literary romp, *The Mistletoe Countess* sweeps you into the embrace of irrepressible Grace and her far from fictional English earl. Overflowing with hope, heart, and hilarity, Pepper Basham crafts a sigh-worthy love story for every season, a melding of two people on different paths into an unforgettable, faith-filled whole that will make your own heart skip a beat. Beautiful!

—Laura Frantz, Christy Award-winning author of *A Heart Adrift*

*The Mistletoe Countess* ©2021 by Pepper Basham

Print ISBN 978-1-64352-986-8

eBook Editions:
Adobe Digital Edition (.epub) 978-1-64352-988-2
Kindle and MobiPocket Edition (.prc) 978-1-64352-987-5

All scripture quotations, unless otherwise noted, are taken from the King James Version of the Bible.

This book is a work of fiction. Names, characters, places, and incidents are either products of the author's imagination or used fictitiously. Any similarity to actual people, organizations, and/or events is purely coincidental.

Cover image © Greg Jackson, Thinkpen Design

Published by Barbour Publishing, Inc., 1810 Barbour Drive, Uhrichsville, Ohio 44683, www. barbourbooks.com

*Our mission is to inspire the world with the life-changing message of the Bible.*

Member of the
Evangelical Christian
Publishers Association

Printed in the United States of America

# The
# MISTLETOE
# COUNTESS

# PEPPER
# BASHAM

BARBOUR
PUBLISHING

# Dedication

To my daughter, Lydia, who listened to me read scenes from
this book as I wrote them and responded with giddy laughter
and "I think Grace is your best character yet, Mama".

Thank you for being excited for me, my imaginary friends,
and these crazy stories, girlie.

And for thinking a mom who writes
"kissing books" isn't TOO embarrassing.

Love you BIG!

# Acknowledgements

This was simply one of the most fun books I've ever written! And, of course, while writing and after writing, I had to share it with a multitude of people because Grace danced off the page an into my heart! Shouldn't others experience her too? And so, I shared her with folks who helped encourage me to bring Grace and Freddie to the published page. There is no way I'll remember everyone, but here are a few of the lovely people who have made this story extra special.

Thank you to Courtney Clark, Courtney Cole, Jennifer Kracht, Susan Snodgrass, Rebecca Maney, Nicole Fremmerlid, Kara Grant, Marisa Stockley, Carol Moncado, Dawn Crandall, Katie Donovan, (and probably a dozen more I'm forgetting), who read an early copy of this book and shared their thoughts and love for it. It really does take a village to help me get over my insecurities sometimes! LOL

Carrie, Rachel Dixon, Beth Erin, and Joy, you guys have been unending in your love for me and this story. I couldn't wait to share new ideas and "quotes from Grace" with you all. But more than that, I appreciate how you encourage me through this writing process so that I keep writing and keep loving stories.

Thank you Debb Hackett, who made sure my British-ese was on point. You are such a fantastic encourager.

Laura Frantz, I love you. That is all.

Thank you to the fabulous Kim Duffy, Jen Turano, Michelle Griep, Rachel McDaniel, Carrie Booth Schmidt, Chautona Having, and Regina Jennings for your time it took to read TMC and your endorsements!

Becky Germany, thank you for taking this story and bringing it to the printed page! I'm so glad that you can put up with all my story excitement so well ☺ #graphics Plus, thanks for encouraging me to turn it into a Christmas book ☺

# Chapter One

November 25, 1913
Willow, Virginia

*Every fairy tale needed an appropriate castle.*

Gracelynn Ferguson gripped the Model T's window frame and leaned forward, breath caught in a suppressed gasp. An unexpectedly warm November breeze brushed against her heated cheeks, inciting a thrill of anticipation. As if two black curtains rolled back on a stage, a pair of ornate iron gates stood on either side of the drive, welcoming the car forward.

Grace angled farther, waiting for the great unveiling and holding her hat in place against the wind.

One turn around a hedgerow of braided vines showcased this hidden gem of the Blue Ridge Mountains. The palace of the Shenandoah.

Whitlock.

Framed by blue-tipped mountains and rolling green hills, the Italian-style mansion stood as an edifice of white marble and colonnades, with two dazzling towers at each corner gleaming in the late morning sunlight. Yes, it was indeed very castle-like and the perfect place for her sister and the Earl of Astley to begin their lifelong romance.

"Good heavens, Grace, sit back before the servants see you hanging your head out the window like a dog." Lillias's reprimand sliced into Grace's whimsical admiration, but Grace shrugged off her sister's rebuke with a deep breath of. . .pine.

Ah, country life suited her sensibilities much more than their stuffy

Richmond town house. And Whitlock? Her favorite place in all the world, with a labyrinth of familiar passageways and spaces to explore or hide in from stuff-shirted wedding guests, as the case may be.

"Really, Grace. The wind is loosening your hair from its pins." Her sister's voice pinched tight. "I'll not have my future husband embarrassed at the sight of you showing up in such a state."

"No one will notice me when you're near." Grace pushed her loose strands from her face and twisted her neck to appreciate how Whitlock's snowy towers contrasted against the azure sky. The towers served as excellent hiding spots too.

"They'll certainly notice if a ginger-headed wildling enters the house instead of the refined young lady you are *supposed* to be." Lillias's volume hovered on the edge of unladylike. "And Mr. and Mrs. Whitlock were so kind to offer their home for the house party. Would you wish to embarrass them too?"

Grace pulled her head inside so quickly she almost hit her cloche hat on the frame. The last thing she'd ever wish was to bring pain to Whitlock's magnanimous master and mistress. Though she couldn't quite understand how her unruly hairstyle would shame the Whitlocks. If anything tempted trouble, it was her scandalous red hair, whatever its coiffure.

"Grace." Her father's deep voice melted into the conversation, a soft familiar rumble. "It's a mercy that you're not the one marrying an English earl, or the poor man would have a job on his hands."

Her grin perked at her father's gentle teasing. "Which is why I'm particularly glad my sister bears the burden of marrying for circumstance, so that I can engage myself to some insignificant farmer and live in obscurity with my garden, books, and passel of rambunctious children."

"Oh, good heavens," Lillias pressed her fingers into her forehead and shrank back into the black leather seat. "You say the most ridiculous things."

"Besides, I don't plan to think of marriage until I'm forced to by circumstances, will, or heart."

"Our Grace has too many adventures to be had with her Sherlock Holmes, I'd say?"

Grace sighed at her father's mention of the detective and his thrilling escapades. "Indeed, Father dear, I prefer my current, delightful predicament of being wholly unattached—except to my fictional heroes, of course. It's a perfect occupation for watching Lillias's romantic story unfold without having to delve into it myself."

"This is a business transaction, Grace. Don't try to romanticize it." Her sister groaned. "And please refrain from your book discussions when Lord Astley is present, won't you? Half of the time I can't tell which people are real and which are fictional."

Lillias looked positively exhausted, and with thoughts of her impending marriage being a business transaction, no wonder. Grace marveled at her sister's ability to keep her emotions so well-controlled—and with training from the hawk-nosed tutor Father had hired to prepare Lillias for life in the British aristocracy, it made sense—but the past few weeks, her sister's well-honed control had appeared a bit more frayed than usual. "I'll only speak of all your many attributes to ensure Lord Astley falls in love with you before the week's end so this business transaction will prove more about hearts than money and titles."

"You read too many books, Grace." Lillias sighed, her pale eyes suddenly older than they ought to be. "Love isn't necessary. Money is."

Grace's entire soul revolted against the idea. "But I'm certain it's helpful, particularly related to marriage."

"How little you understand the world."

"You could seek one and gain both," Father added, his eyes velvety with memory of their mother—a woman of substantial means in her own right before their father, with his new money, wooed her into matrimony. . .and then love.

But marrying someone you didn't find the least bit fascinating? Grace shrugged off the incomprehensible possibility. "Even though you only met Lord Astley's mother on your last trip to London, it doesn't mean your groom isn't going to give you his heart as soon as he sees you. Who wouldn't? He'll hardly be able to wait a week to make you his bride."

"Don't marry me off so quickly, Sister dear." Lillias's sharp look stilled Grace's smile. "Be sure, I intend to make wise use of the *full* week I still have as Lillias Ferguson, and despite his dowager mother's many accolades of her son and initiation of this entire arrangement, we are still strangers." She offered a weak laugh, a distraction, if Grace knew her sister at all. "Besides, I wouldn't wish to leave my family too soon, you understand."

A twinge of something indefinable pricked Grace's mind, and she gave her sister another lingering stare, studying the shifting of her gaze, the dip in her brow. Grace turned her attention back to the house. If Lillias did express more "high emotions," as her father called them, who could blame her? Marrying a complete stranger for a title? Any thoughtful woman should flinch at the very idea!

But something else pearled beneath the surface of her sister's moodiness. Or else Grace's imagination had taken another indulgent turn. Of course Lillias had always wanted a grand and glorious life, so perhaps it would be worth the cost to her. She'd never been the sort to jettison an audience of admirers. Grace almost cringed. An audience of admirers? How positively dreadful!

"I'm certain you'll find Lord Astley quite agreeable, Lillias." Father tapped the cane he held between his knees. "Distinguished man. Most distinguished. A proper gentleman with an excellent understanding of landscapes."

Grace caught her chuckle in her gloved hand. Landscapes. The very pinnacle of romance. Her smile paused. Romance and marriage proved such daunting prospects in reality, but hidden within the pages of her beloved books, their appeal sparkled with magic and mystery. She sighed up at the familiar mansion, her attention drifting to the floor-to-ceiling windows of the library on the far left of the house.

Books were so much safer.

Their car rolled to a stop in front of a portico, where a few servants waited to greet them in their usual style. Ivy strung across the front, and red bows dotted at perfect intervals to create a lovely contrast against the bleached stone. Christmas at Whitlock! A house built by a besotted husband in honor of his beloved wife. Truly, how could Lillias and Lord Astley not fall in love at such a romantic house during such a romantic time of year?

With the customary welcome and care of Mrs. Evangeline Whitlock herself, Grace and Lillias were shown to their rooms. And as usual, the estate mistress placed Grace in the bedroom closest to the back library stairway—easy access to thousands of books and wonderfully far from the rest of the house. Grace had barely removed her cape before her feet turned in the direction of her heart.

"Don't even think about it, Grace." Lillias snatched Grace by the arm. "I saw your face when Mrs. Whitlock mentioned the most recent additions to the library. We meet Lord Astley in less than three hours, and I'll not have you missing it all because of some book."

But what a book! *Fire in Stubble*! Grace's face warmed to the memory. Oh, roguish Michael. . . "If you'd read the book you'd understand."

Lillias's eyes wilted closed. "No I would not, because I recognize books for what they are. Pretty words, paper, and binding."

Lillias really shouldn't refer to books in such a dismissive way, and Grace would have said so if she'd thought it would have made a difference. Grace tossed a lingering look to the secret stairway and released a sigh. Social engagements interfered with the most delightful bookish discoveries.

"I need you with me."

The sudden quaver in the timbre of Lillias's voice pulled Grace's attention away from the coveted library doorway and into her sister's pale gaze. Something uncommonly vulnerable flashed in those eyes, tugging Grace a step closer. "You don't have to go through with this, Lillias. Are you so desperate for a title?"

Lillias opened her mouth as if to speak but snapped her lips closed, her expression stilling to placid. "I've become accustomed to a certain lifestyle and expectations. This marriage provides both and will only succeed in bringing our family into the best circles."

"Can't you wait? Spend a few more weeks getting to know your future husband?"

"No." Lillias's attention shifted away, and she dropped her hold on Grace's arm. "There's no need to wait."

An undercurrent of something uncertain rippled through Grace. She touched Lillias's cheek until her sister met her gaze. "He will fall in love with you, Lillias. I am sure of it. What man could do less?"

"I'm not concerned about *his* heart." Lillias pulled away and walked toward the door, her whisper so soft Grace wasn't certain she heard clearly. "Not his."

⁕

The riffling of book pages hushed through the silent library, pulling Grace from the delights of *Jane Eyre*. She hadn't been able to locate *Fire in Stubble,* so she'd settled for a beloved favorite, determined to get in a few pages before the social tornado began. Had someone else eluded the cacophony of arriving guests too? Not that there was a scheduled event yet. Everyone planned to gather for the party and then dinner, but still, the expectation of mingling hovered in the air like Great-Aunt Eloise's potent perfume.

Grace shuddered and pulled the book into her chest, peering over the balcony to the library's lower level in search of another stealthy rebel. Not one burgundy seat stood occupied. A sound creaked from behind her in the direction of the guest bedrooms through the secret stairs.

Grace bit her bottom lip and froze—waiting—until the sound dissipated.

Oh, if Lillias found out she was in the library instead of taking a bath, she'd never hear the end of it. But who wouldn't delay bubbles for a conversation featuring the dastardly Mr. Rochester?

With quiet steps, she tucked her book beneath her arm and hurried down the winding staircase toward the secluded window seat of the Mahogany Room—and ran directly into the chest of someone ascending. A strong someone, whose arms wrapped around her to keep her from tipping over the stair railing in an indecorous heap of blue velvet and Irish lace. The faintest hints of leather and amber teased her senses deeper into the sturdy embrace to ensure proper identification of the aromas. *Yes, decidedly amber.* She smiled her appreciation. Such a delightful scent.

"Pardon me."

*English?*

Grace looked up from her cocooned place within the man's arms and met a pair of eyes so dark they reminded her of chocolate. The bronze hues of his skin gave off a toffee glow. Oh heavens! A man who reminded her of chocolate-covered English toffee. Wouldn't Lillias adore him! She loved toffee!

"You're English!"

He tilted his head, examining her with a most intense stare. "I am."

"I'm so sorry. Not that you're English, of course. But that I nearly derailed you off the stairs." She shifted back a little to get a better look at him. "You see, I was reading up on the balcony and thought I heard someone." She gestured toward him. "And you must be that someone. How delightful to meet you."

A quizzical look crossed his features. "And you are?"

"Oh, of course. Introductions." Grace righted herself—as much as the tiny stairs allowed—and offered her hand. "Miss Ferguson."

"*You're* Miss Ferguson?" His dark brows rose almost to his hairline, and Grace realized her mistake with a laugh.

"No, I'm not *that* Miss Ferguson. I'm her younger sister, Grace."

His expression softened a little, and he backed down the stairs, taking her hand until her feet settled firmly on the floor. "It's a pleasure to make your acquaintance, Miss Grace Ferguson."

"And you, Lord Astley." She curtsied, her mind buzzing with a million questions for this future brother-in-law of hers, but first things first. "How do you like Whitlock's library?"

His lips made as if to smile but stopped before giving the room a steady look of appreciation. He stood at least four inches taller than Grace, wearing his gray sack coat and matching trousers with a sense of refinement her father failed to accomplish. "It's an excellent library."

Grace decided she liked him quite well.

"Almost as large as mine at Havensbrooke."

"*Almost* as large?" Her bottom lip came unhinged, and every envious bone in her body stiffened.

His attention dropped to the book in her hand, one dark brow darting skyward. "I suppose you are an avid reader?"

"Oh, I devour books." She tugged the novel against her chest. "It's a disastrous habit for being productive, I'm afraid."

Humor lit the darkness of his eyes and made him a little less imposing. "And is that the extent of your vices, Miss Grace?"

"I'm afraid, Lord Astley, my vices are too many to name, only one of which is a proclivity for disappearing from large crowds at the first availability. My sister, however, has very few vices and only ones I feel certain you will find endearing."

"The dutiful, indulgent younger sister, I see."

He did have fascinating eyes. Dark and alive. Lillias was sure to like them. "Indulgent, yes, but I fail quite miserably at dutiful. You see, if I was truly dutiful, I wouldn't be hiding in the library." She lowered her voice to a whisper and gestured toward her book. "Trying to uncover the mystery in Mr. Rochester's attic."

His brows rose.

"But instead, I'd be upstairs helping my extravagantly beautiful sister prepare to meet you."

One corner of his lips twitched. "Extravagantly beautiful?"

"Oh yes! We look nothing alike. She has an Athena profile and the most exquisite golden curls." She sobered, holding his gaze to add solemn reassurance. "Nothing as red and terrifying as mine."

"Terrifying?" His dark gaze examined her hair with such concentration, her head started to tingle. "Red is unique."

She twisted a loose lock through her fingers, peering down at it with a sigh of resignation. "Well, unique is a much better word than what some of my governesses called it. The sixth one said I was nothing more than a—"

"Sixth?" The word burst out on something remarkably close to a laugh. "Sixth governess?"

Wasn't an earl supposed to be aloof and somewhat disgruntled? Perhaps fiction didn't always get it right. "I'd blame my imagination, but that would imply I don't take responsibility for my actions. Unfortunately, governesses—or at least the ones I've known—are terribly short on imagination and could never understand how I'd find myself inside attic chests or up trees or swimming in the—"

"Gracelynn Amelia Ferguson!" A harsh whisper burst from the corridor through the secret stairway. "If you're in the library instead of the bath, you'd better have an excellent excuse."

Grace gasped and met Lord Astley's wide eyes.

"You told her you were taking a bath?" The brooding earl blinked a few times in quick succession as both sides of his lips tipped in unison. A bit crookedly, but it suited him.

Grace offered a helpless shrug and backed toward the winding staircase, holding up her book as leverage. "I got distracted on the way, you see. Honest mistake." She made it halfway up the stairs before she turned. "If you enjoy Charles Dickens, Mr. Whitlock has a full collection on that shelf." She reached the top and grinned back down at him with a shrug.

"Grace!"

Grace jumped at the increased edge in her sister's voice and slipped a few more steps toward the secret corridor. "Oh, and there is a fabulous selection of architectural and landscape books on the other side of the fireplace."

He stood below her, by the mantel, hands on his hips, everything about him boasting refinement and excellent grooming. His smile was probably devastating. She'd read about a devastating smile once in a three-volume novel and thought it a wonderful description for a roguish sort of man in a smart gray suit with eyes the color of chocolate truffles.

Oh, wouldn't he and Lillias make a fabulous couple! Her imagination indulged for a moment as her feet faltered in her retreat.

"Grace Ferguson," Lord Astley's deep voice pulled her attention.

She peered over the balcony railing, pushing back a rebel strand of hair. "Yes, my lord."

"It was a pleasure to meet you."

"Oh yes, my pleasure as well." She grinned and started to disappear toward the secret stair but then turned back to him. "Please don't tell Lillias I met you first. It's not every day a woman meets her future husband."

# Chapter Two

Marrying for money left a sour taste. Frederick Percy, Earl of Astley, had pursued every option other than a marriage contract, but nothing else served to save his future with such expediency. His mother had arranged it all, after an unexpected introduction in London between both sets of parents led to a speedy decision of the perfect match. Frederick reined in a sigh.

His family's legacy hinged on a respectable exchange. His title. Her dowry.

*Respectable.* He stayed the grimace waiting to curl behind his smile. The agreement had sounded simple enough two months ago when an ocean separated him from the reality of it, but now, with the signatures' ink still wet on the contract and a mere week until the wedding, the decision weighed upon him with treacherous foreboding. Was this truly the only way to make amends for his past and save his family's estate? And what of the girl?

He glanced down at the woman in his arms as they danced together across Whitlock's marble floors, the glow of Christmas lights casting an otherworldly hue against the soft folds of her golden hair and glimmering off the silver-blue headband set like a crown among her curls. Her gown matched the headband, a sleek display of the latest fashion, or so that is what Frederick presumed. Cinched at the waist, slim skirt, and an open neckline above a beaded bodice to reveal an ample amount of her milky skin.

Lillias Ferguson met every requirement on his mother's extensive list, and her father's money met every necessity on Frederick's.

Appearance? Almost angelic. Demeanor? Aloof. Affections? Tempered. Carriage? Flawless. Conversation? As expected, a command of the weather, local news, and the art of diversion from herself. Miss Ferguson presented as the very portrait the Countess of Astley ought to depict.

In fact, she exerted such control over her emotions and facial features, Frederick felt as though she'd arrived with prescript discourse down to the very breath. Perhaps she was nervous. What woman wouldn't be at the prospect of marrying an utter stranger? They'd barely had two conversations before Mr. Ferguson produced the contract and sealed their fates.

Frederick gave a mental shake to dislodge his unease as he moved with Miss Ferguson in graceful unison across the Music Room floor. The space teemed with at least two dozen of the Fergusons' party guests, some sitting in conversations while a few chose to dance, the holiday festivities encouraging more gaiety than Frederick could muster, though he was well equipped to play the part. He met Blake's gaze through the expanse of enthusiastic dance partners, as his cousin waltzed with a woman twice his age. A Mrs. Seaton, was it? Frederick almost grinned. Stephen Blake and his avoidance of matrimony had become almost legendary. Ah, the liberty of being the third son of a baron. The very idea nearly vaulted Frederick into a foul mood. His days of liberty had ended six months ago when his older brother suddenly died, leaving Frederick as the sole rescuer of an entire legacy.

He stiffened his resolve. There was nothing else to be done. And he would see it through.

He returned his attention to the lovely inducement in his arms, her countenance as controlled as his. They both knew their roles and—God help them—the consequences.

"Is it true, Lord Astley, that you were almost overrun by an autocar in the village upon your arrival today?"

A most unfortunate introduction, for certain. Frederick forced a smile. "A simple case of someone mishandling their new automobile, I'd imagine. Finicky machines, they are."

Instead of being appeased, she blanched, her hand tightening against his shoulder. "When I overheard Father speaking about it only a few moments ago, it sounded terrifying. It's lucky you were not injured or worse. After all the plans and expectations. . ." Her brow furrowed for an

17

instant and cleared so quickly he wondered if he'd imagined the tightening around her eyes, the fear trembling over her countenance. "For your dear Havensbrooke, of course."

His stomach clenched at her subtle shift. He searched her face a moment longer to no avail. Nerves most likely. Blast his own suspicious nature! The poor woman didn't deserve it.

Despite his best efforts, his gaze sought Blake's, as if the man could overhear their conversation above the exuberant thrums of the piano. His cousin was already on edge about the entire affair with the autocar, and Frederick half wondered if Blake had been hidden among the shrubberies of the gardens earlier while Frederick took Miss Ferguson on a private stroll.

*"This was not an accident, Freddie. And neither was the docks."*

Blake's words cast a shadow over the festive evening with its Christmas lights and cheerful holiday decor. A residual throb from Frederick's sore shoulder provided the tactile memory of barely dodging a falling tower of freight upon disembarking their steamer in New York. Had it not been for Blake's quick movements by slamming his body against Frederick's. . .

"Yes, Havensbrooke." Best navigate the discussion away from uncontrolled autocars and his possible demise. "I understand you enjoyed your most recent visit to England. September, wasn't it?" And the catalyst for this choice.

Her gaze flickered to his, golden brow arched as if perfectly aware of his careful topic shift. "Yes. The countryside was beautiful."

A response without feeling but perfectly executed. It's exactly what Frederick needed and should have desired. No scandal. Low attention. "Were there any places you particularly enjoyed visiting?"

"We spent two weeks in London, and it was thrilling. I adore the exciting opportunities the city provides, don't you?"

London! His least favorite place in all of England. "It is most diverting."

"Father said that your estate of Havensbrooke is in Derbyshire." Her smile clung to her lips but failed to surface in her eyes. "We passed through that region on the train. It's lovely but. . .rather remote."

Remote? The word brought unvoiced criticism with it. "We are only a few hours from London by rail, and there is an estate village with all the necessary comforts."

"Ah, that's good news." Her body stiffened ever so slightly, but otherwise nothing changed. "And does Havensbrooke have telephones? Electricity? I've heard from my great-aunt who married an earl some ten years ago that she moved into an estate house that had been nearly untouched for a hundred years."

Frederick's stance tightened along with hers. If her expectations for Havensbrooke matched the modern elegance of Whitlock, Miss Ferguson was doomed for disappointment. "Part of the house has electricity, a new feature in the past year." His brother's addition, despite depleting funds for the estate. "As well as a telephone. And I do have a townhome in London."

"A townhome?" Her gaze shot back to his, brightening. "That is good news."

He felt his defenses rally. "And once we're married, I would appreciate your involvement in deciding how to best improve Havensbrooke, to see it modernized for our benefit as well as the next generation's."

She studied him, her delicate chin tipping in assent. "I am no architect, but I have studied some of the more modern conveniences and, of course, will delight in hosting your parties."

"*Our* parties."

Her gaze darted away and back, her smile not quite right. "Yes, of course."

Oh, this was a disaster. God help him. God help them both.

Another sweep of silence stilted their dialogue. Frederick raked his thoughts for further questions. "Are the gardens at your Rutledge House of similar style as those here at Whitlock?"

"They are much smaller. We haven't the grounds as Whitlock, of course, but Mother took painstaking care to ensure Rutledge's beauty, so Father has made it his purpose to maintain them to the highest standard to preserve her memory."

A tender sentiment. "And do you have a hand in designing them?"

"Heavens, no." She laughed, shaking her head, her periwinkle gaze meeting his. She did have the most engaging eyes when she smiled. "I enjoy their beauty for as long as it lasts, but attempt to sort them out? That's for the gardener, don't you think? Their work and our pleasure, so to speak."

"Yes, of course." Despite being second-born, the love for his land forked into his very nature, braiding through his bloodline. He lived for country air and open vistas, dirtying his hands alongside the gardeners at times to feel the earth of Havensbrooke beneath his fingers. He steadied his breath and gave another try. Surely there had to be some interest they shared. "And what do you enjoy, Miss Ferguson?"

Her manner maintained a tempered expectation. There was nothing for which to find fault, yet Frederick, who had no false fancies of romance, had hoped for something. . .more.

"I'm quite fond of music and dancing." She tilted her head as a gesture toward their current movements, her expression the most animated he'd witnessed thus far in their acquaintance. "And fashion, of course. I'm rather adept at it."

Fashion and dancing? Perhaps benevolent indifference was to be their lot in life. "You and my mother will have a great deal to discuss. She was quite the expert in her day."

The strains from the piano took a more turbulent turn, snagging Frederick's attention. Grace Ferguson—dark green evening gown spilling around her—sat poring over the keys in a fury, eyes closed, brow clenched in concentration. Frederick tightened his lips against a growing grin. The poor girl had no reserve whatsoever.

"Your sister plays with a great deal of. . .energy."

"Energy?" A welcome glow warmed the social veneer of Miss Ferguson's expression as she followed Frederick's gaze. "I'm afraid my sister isn't meant for a life of refinement, and there's no training her. Father and I have tried without much luck."

"She appears quite lively of mind and spirit."

"That is a very kind way to speak of her. She is the most generous-hearted person." Miss Ferguson's entire countenance gentled. "Though among our social circles, she's a disaster."

"I believe she's found a way to live above such disappointment."

Miss Ferguson laughed, a light airy sound, and her entire face bloomed with a beautiful genuineness. Frederick's chest expanded. Perhaps this relationship only wanted time and understanding.

"She truly is one of the dearest creatures in all the world, but her mind overflows with innumerable ideas and impossible stories. She's been well protected from the trials of convention, as is evident in her passionate playing for all the world to see. Such. . .freedom." As quickly as the brightness appeared, her countenance clouded. "Yet there is something to envy in her lack of concern for others' opinions or expectations, don't you think?"

"Pardon?"

She stared toward the piano as if lost in thought. "But she's young yet."

"Miss Ferguson?"

"Speaking of my untamed sister." She blinked back to him, as if rallying from a dream, and smiled too brightly. "I'm certain she would enjoy a dance with you. She's spoken of little else than becoming better acquainted. Excuse me."

Without warning, she left his arms and approached the piano. The sudden alteration of her mood from adoring sister to—what was it? melancholy?—unsettled him. As desperate as he was to save Havensbrooke, a worst decision would be to marry a woman who became embittered by her choice or, worse, sought intimate companionship outside their marriage. A knife of memory stabbed against his determination. No, he must avoid another scandal at all cost. Hadn't he done enough to his family? Yet he had no choice. He'd signed the contract.

Blast his heart! Following the unpredictability of his affections had led to every past calamity of his life. He steadied his expression and chilled his own feelings. He'd mastered his emotions in the past. He'd master them again.

This was a business transaction. Her money. His title. His future happiness couldn't matter.

Within a few seconds, Lillias ushered a reluctant Grace toward him and returned to the piano, beginning a waltz by Chopin.

As he took Grace into his arms, her ready smile melted the tension from his shoulders. "You play with great. . .feeling, Miss Grace."

Her countenance dropped with an exaggerated sigh. "I was hoping I played so wildly they'd ask me to leave the room, but alas, everyone enjoyed dancing too much to find offense."

A laugh nearly shot from him, but he muted it into a cough. "So is it that you don't enjoy playing or dancing?"

"I'm fond of both, but I'd prefer to do them in a smaller company." Her grin tipped. "Perhaps even by myself."

"You enjoy your own company, is it?"

"As an enthusiastic reader, Lord Astley, I'm never really alone." Her voice lilted with easy kinship. "There are myriad book creations to share my mental space. I've danced with princes, and fought a few too. I've even swung through the jungles with Tarzan. Breathtaking!" Before he could react to her divergence into fictional raptures, she leaned closer and lowered her voice to a whisper, those sapphire eyes as alive as her sister's were distant. "Did you know that Mr. Rochester already has a wife and tried to marry Jane anyway?"

He took a mental inventory of the invitation list in search of the scandalous Mr. Rochester without upturning the name, but he'd heard it before. Where? He studied the young woman and the answer emerged, along with a desire to grin. "You'd rather be reading."

"Wouldn't you? Or at least having tea and cake with a party of no more than four?" She worried her bottom lip and nodded toward her sister. "I don't know how Lillias can love these parties so much, and hours on end too." She sighed, a small smile returning. "But she does look exquisite at the piano, and you should hear her sing. Heaven's angels and all that."

He glanced toward his future bride where she sat poised as perfect as any debutante, more beautiful than most. She played the waltz well, commanding attention from the tilt of her chin to the charismatic glint in her eyes. Another rise of caution squeezed his chest, but he stiffened against the uncertainty. *Duty over heart.* "Indeed."

"Isn't she immaculate? Always so poised and in control," Grace whispered, the woodsy scent of rosemary accompanying her nearness. The fragrance suited her, rather sprite-like. "And she's brilliant too. Well, if that's important to you. I realize not all men care about a woman's brain, but you seem the good sort."

His smile teased up on one side against his bidding. "Do you say everything that pops into your head, Miss Grace?"

"Oh goodness, not everything." Her eyes rounded to saucers, but she didn't lose one step in the dance. "If I said everything, I'd leave many more horrified expressions in my wake. But at times my feelings are so large, they must burst out into words. Don't you ever have that happen?"

"I cannot think of any particular time." Except when Celia ruined his family, and not even his strict upbringing controlled him in the wake of his wounds. Another instance of bowing to heart instead of head. "But I do hope I am the good sort, for I believe a wife with a brain is much better than the alternative."

It took her only a second to recognize his jest, and that infectious laugh of hers bubbled forward without reserve. "Unless you're writing some Gothic horror novel, and then they provide all sorts of glorious mischief."

After the stilted reserve of Lillias Ferguson, Miss Grace's authenticity slipped through his guardedness like wind through spring trees. Of course he needn't feel as cautious with her. She wasn't the one to save his estate and restore the honor of the Percy name. Miss Grace, however, would certainly add colorful dialogue when she visited Havensbrooke. His mother would be absolutely appalled.

"I see your brain is in good shape too." Her chin dipped in assent as if he'd passed some test. "We're going to get along quite nicely, I believe."

"I'm pleased to meet with your approval."

"I have very high standards, Lord Astley." Her brows darted northward with a playful intensity. "I read fiction."

He resisted the compulsion to laugh, shocked by its sudden arrival again. "What is it you find so appealing about fiction?"

"Where do I begin? Exploring new places, escaping into history." She sighed as if her thoughts plundered some previous novel. "I've been on treasure hunts, solved mysteries, been captured by pirates, but my favorite stories are romances."

"Of course you'd choose something as predictable as romance."

"You say that like it's second rate." She wrinkled her nose, a tiny spray of freckles across the bridge momentarily distracting him. "But romance has to be worth something if people throughout all time have spent years, money, risk, and a whole host of daydreams in finding it."

He studied her, his lips tempted into another grin. Hmm. . .young but quick-witted and thoughtful. He'd have to reevaluate his initial thoughts on her simplicity. "I stand corrected in my opinion."

"Though I have to say I've never experienced *real* romance." A rush of pink brought out the glow in her eyes. "Lillias raves about it—all the swooning and pining. She says men rarely think of much else when the conquest of a woman is involved."

"Does she?" Not a very flattering thought to his general sex. His gaze shot to the pianist. And how would Lillias know? Had she been pining over someone? Did she still?

"But I'd rather keep my head while losing my heart, wouldn't you?" She continued, oblivious to the utter inappropriateness of her divulgement. "A thoughtful romance makes much more sense for a lifetime friendship, even if kisses change things."

He choked out the words. "Kisses change things?"

"That's what Lillias says, anyway." She studied his lips with such intensity, they warmed beneath her perusal. "But I've not sorted out how placing one's mouth on someone else's could render a person witless." Mercifully, her gaze flitted back to his, no worse for the wear in the irregular turn of their conversation. "I suppose I'll understand one day."

He cleared his throat. "Indeed."

"Oh dear, I've gone down the dark road of impropriety again, haven't I?" Her bottom lip jutted out into a pout. Paired with the kissing talk, he couldn't seem to pull his attention away fast enough. "I can keep my conversation dull and proper, if I put my mind to it. Truly. And you never need worry about Lillias speaking so scandalously. She's the very model of decorum."

Yet what Grace had said about Lillias's statements lent doubt to how untouched Lillias Ferguson's heart was, a fact Frederick had to uncover. Failing that, he must find a way to securely transfer her affections to him.

❦

Frederick lowered his head to his hands at the desk in his bedroom and exhaled a shaking breath. This was never meant to be his lot. He was the *second* son—not the bearer of the family's extensive legacy—but here he sat, shouldering a position that his heart and head felt utterly ill-equipped to bear. He squeezed his eyes closed against a lingering ache.

*Please, help this choice be the right one for Havensbrooke. . .and for me.* He'd prayed for months. Pleaded. Offered his entire self for the remaking of his inheritance. Only God could work things to the good at this point. But couldn't he at the least pray for his own heart too, even if he couldn't be guided by it?

"I believe I shall enjoy my bit of American charm, Freddie. Indeed, this place is remarkable."

Frederick slid a look to the doorway where Stephen Blake leaned against the frame, pale hair tousled in typical disarray and lackadaisical grin set in place, though the expression never fooled Frederick. Blake had the unnerving ability to keep a steady head while playing the part of a leisurely gentleman. If only Frederick held such expert skill.

But there was little to be done for Blake, and no better friend in all the world. Frederick's home had always been one of gravity and expectation, but Blake's existence provided an almost necessary levity.

Always had.

"Remarkable indeed," came Frederick's slow reply. Yet the word seemed a flimsy descriptor for the opulent country estate. The drive in from the train depot featured pristine landscaping and manicured lawns, all framed by a sea of purplish-blue mountains. Then the house? An Italian revivalist villa of white marble and updated features: en suite lavatories, electricity, even a lift!

He focused back on his cousin, his gaze dropping to Blake's bandaged hand. "How are you?"

Blake shrugged a shoulder, his grin taking a turn. "A mere flesh wound."

Frederick shook his head and held to the levity of Blake's response. If it hadn't been for Blake, the car in the village would have hit Frederick head on, and Blake had already been nursing a hand wound from the disaster at the docks. A hollowed-out feeling reverberated in his stomach. No! Let the accidents keep Blake on edge. Frederick had enough to busy his mind.

"Thank you for being here, Blake."

"It's good to keep an extra set of eyes about." Blake held to his smile, but his gaze sobered with an unspoken camaraderie. "I'm happy to provide them."

Frederick attempted to ignore the steely weight Blake's words set on his chest, but they took up residence anyway. "You should endeavor to enjoy yourself while you're here, instead of worrying over a few accidents."

"Accidents?" He raised a brow and waved away Frederick's excuse. "You're here to become a married man, and I'm here to see that the new Earl of Astley lives a great many years yet. You don't have to agree with my concerns or methods, but I'll not be dissuaded." Blake's smile vanished. "I didn't like how your brother's death was handled, and I'm not about to take a lazy approach to his successor taking up a mantle under which the previous two earls died unexpectedly. Something doesn't sit right about all your *accidents*." He spat the word. "And until I feel satisfied, I won't settle."

Frederick twitched at the mention of his brother's and father's deaths, but he refused to be teased into another argument about it. "I fear spending time with your detective-cousin has sent you looking for invisible fiends, Blake."

His cousin shoved his hands in his pockets and turned to the nearby window, promptly ignoring Frederick.

Frederick joined his cousin at the window. An afternoon fog cloaked the distant mountains in a ghostly shroud. "I shouldn't have been so hasty to sign the contract."

Blake released a slow sigh before turning. "Cold feet or. . .worse?"

Frederick thrust a hand through his hair, replaying various scenes from his time with Lillias Ferguson over the past two days. "After all that happened with Celia, perhaps I'm too cautious, too concerned about the slightest change of interest or turn of attention." He groaned and dropped down into the nearest chair. "I. . .I cannot bring such disgrace on my family again, Blake."

"Freddie, you fell in love with a social-climbing predator. You can't take the blame for Celia's depravity."

"But my response didn't help."

"If you're speaking of your mother, stop there. You know as well as I that her happiness and goodwill are as predictable as my sister's fashion sense."

"I shouldn't have challenged her in front of a crowded room."

Blake winced, and Frederick sunk back into the chair, sighing, his memory fresh from the sting of shame and betrayal. "Miss Ferguson is nothing like Celia, Freddie. Mark my words. She hasn't the malicious air."

"Perhaps not malicious, but some of the comments Miss Grace shared about her sister inadvertently suggest. . .unpredictable."

"And you don't think the youngest Ferguson is prone to exaggeration?"

"Indeed." Frederick almost grinned. "Which is why I didn't take much heed, but after my interactions with Lillias today, I'm beginning to wonder how untouched my future bride's heart is."

"What do you mean?"

"Today, as we engaged in a more personal and private conversation, she seemed to become friendlier. Before I left her, I took her hand and placed a rather intimate kiss to her wrist, and there was no response. No intake of breath. No shock at the touch. Not even a recoil, but quite indifferent." Frederick ran a hand down his face. "As if. . ."

"She had experienced such liberties before."

"I'm not naive enough to expect love, Blake." Frederick shook his head. "She wants the social catapult, and I need the financial salvation. At best, I hope for camaraderie, and at worst, benevolent indifference.

But anything more?" He rubbed at his chest as the ache ground deeper. "It is a commodity I cannot afford, even if I wish it."

This decision was about redeeming his past and securing the future of Havensbrooke, not of his heart. Frederick raised his gaze, the weight on his shoulders doubling. "I know it seems small, maybe even a slight paranoia, but it's my future, and I cannot take my family through another scandal."

Blake shook his head, his lip curling into a frown. "This is one of those rare moments when I'm exceptionally grateful you're the son of an earl and I'm not."

Frederick shot him a weak glare. "You're the son of a baron."

"The third son of a baron, so I feel quite safe in my position of irresponsibility." Blake sobered and took a seat near Frederick. "You can't back out now. You'd lose a third of Havensbrooke based on the contract."

"It's a sad world indeed if my two options are either financial ruin or possible scandal."

"Isn't that the very definition of an aristocratic life?"

"Are you supposed to be helping me?"

Blake snapped his fingers, his smile spreading with too much mischief for Frederick's peace of mind. "I have an idea, Freddie."

"We change situations?"

"Not on your life. And certainly not on mine." Blake slid into an opposing chair and leaned forward, an unsettling glint in his pale eyes. Frederick had a sudden memory of the time the two of them had bet on riding one of the new horses in the stables at Havensbrooke. Frederick had lost—and ended up with a broken arm. "But since you've already agreed to marry the girl, the only recourse is to kiss her."

Frederick's head shot up. "What?" All this kissing talk was unnerving. First Grace and now Blake?

"Come on, Freddie, you're not as thick as all that. A woman who is used to being kissed kisses much differently than one who isn't. If it allays your fears, then what is the trouble? I'd expect you'll be doing quite a bit of kissing within a week at any rate."

"You can't be serious."

His palm came up to temper Frederick's reaction. "She's practically your bride already, so show her your commitment with a good kiss. For one, it could encourage a transfer of her wayward affections, so to speak, and for the other, it may provide a gauge for how entrenched your fiancée's heart and emotions are. Then you can plan any drastic measures accordingly."

"You say the most ridiculous things."

Blake shrugged. "I can't say I ever shy away from a good kiss now and then."

"I'm beginning to understand all the more which one of us took after Grandfather's sensibilities."

"Which means I must have taken after Grandmother's charm." Blake grinned. "So I should age like an excellent wine."

Blake's levity eased some of Frederick's angst about the entire affair. He couldn't change his decision, but Lillias Ferguson was not Celia Blackmore. He would do all in his power, with God's help, to make his future much better than the mistakes of his past, and that process started with wooing his fiancée's heart.

# Chapter Three

Frederick marched toward the Music Room for another night of festivities, determined to make his engagement and marriage to Lillias Ferguson work. True, they were not as well suited as he'd hoped, nor was he certain of her heart being untouched, but as he'd learned firsthand, many times the past attached weights to the future if he let it.

He would not. The die had been cast.

The thick green curtain separating the massive room from the rest of the house was pulled to a close, keeping in heat and blocking his view of the guests. If he remembered rightly, card playing and games were the menu of the evening.

He paused and drew in a breath before entering, but a glimmer of dark purple peeking from beneath the corner of the curtain caught his attention. A shoe? He slowed his steps and examined further, his smile crooked up in revelation.

Gracelynn Ferguson stood mostly hidden within the folds of the curtain, book raised to almost touch her nose, attention intent on the story. Her ginger hair topped her head in a rain of curls, much the same style as her sister's, but every expression of her downturned face bloomed with authenticity.

"Aren't you supposed to be with the party?"

Her head raised, eyes wide, and she drew the book to her chest. "Well, I. . ." She looked to the curtained door and back to him, her pink lips twisted into an impish grin. "Aren't *you*? A guest of honor, even?"

There she went again, almost unraveling his smile in a most unnerving way. "I have an impeccable excuse. My valet twisted his ankle, and I went to see how his recovery was coming along."

"How very chivalrous of you." The conversation paused for a moment, and her gaze slid back to the curtain then to him. "Yet a feat you could have entertained earlier in the day, I imagine." Her eyes shimmered with an unvoiced laugh. "You don't like house parties, either, do you?"

She was a clever one. Her innocence and vibrancy dripped with a contagion, luring Frederick's former carefree nature to resurface. "I find smaller gatherings more meaningful, as a rule."

"You seemed the sort." She nodded. "I'm glad to hear it, for opposites attract, I understand, and my sister adores socializing." She sighed. "Yet I do envy your advantage over mine."

"And what advantage is that?"

"Everyone expects you to sweep my sister into your arms and have whatever conversations you like. I, on the other hand, must make do with some of the dreariest rhetoric with whoever pins me into a corner. What is so interesting about the weather, a certain breed of cattle, or a person's social status, I have no idea! One is so obvious it seems redundant; the second is. . ." She rolled her eyes to the ceiling. "I cannot find a comment, and the third is relatively meaningless to the real stuff of a person."

"Spoken like a true philosopher."

She snapped her book closed and stepped forward, sapphire orbs alight. "You tease me, but I have an inkling you know I'm right."

"And I'm enjoying the dialogue."

She rewarded him with a full smile. "Well, we can continue this conversation as long as you like. Besides it being one of the best I've had this week, I can also blame you for my tardiness, and everyone will forgive me because you are an earl."

"Surely it hasn't been so bad, Miss Grace." He studied her, working hard to keep his lips steady. "We've only had two nights of dancing. Last night was games and conversations."

"And I was stuck at the card table with Father's business associate Mr. Douglas Porter, who talked for half an hour about the differences between the climate of Virginia as opposed to your home in Derbyshire. A half hour?" One of her ginger brows rose. "In case you weren't aware, my dear Lord Astley, let me sum it up for you. Your environment is decidedly wetter than mine."

He lost the fight against his smile. "Indeed."

Her expression bloomed, as if she'd solved some great mystery. "You *do* have a devastating smile."

He gestured toward the book in her hand and ignored the warmth rising up his neck. "That sounds suspiciously like something an author would write about a hero."

"And why not?" She laughed. "Don't you know? You are the hero of your own story."

"Me?" The response spoken so carelessly took surprising root. A swell of purpose straightened him to his full height. "A hero?"

But he'd always been the black sheep—second best, the one passed over. What would it be like to view himself as a hero? Of his own life? He shook the thought away, too sensible to be drawn into one of Miss Grace's fictions.

"God has given you a life, and you're the only one who can decide how to write it." Her eyes grew wide. "Daring adventure?" Her gaze slipped to the curtain with a wiggle of her brows. "Grand romance? Your choices all factor into the novel of your life. So do you plan to be a hero, Lord Astley?" Her eyes narrowed, playfully baiting him. "I have no doubt you are capable."

Her question followed by her ready confidence pierced deep, gripping at his core to such an extent he almost lost control of his emotions as readily as his smile. Could he become much more than a victim of his circumstances? The challenge settled, secured. He could certainly try. Starting now. He drew in a deep breath and offered his arm. "At the moment, my plan is to escort you into the dreaded house party."

She exaggerated her sigh and took his offering. "I suppose we must." She leaned close, lowering her voice to a whisper. "But thank you for the repartee. I shall be much better prepared to face the tedious meteorological conversations in my future, knowing I had at least one tête-à-tête of interest."

They slipped through the curtain, and Frederick's gaze searched the room until it landed on his bride. She sat at a table near the piano, a look of unbridled pleasure on her face as she stared over at her partner, a man Frederick hadn't been introduced to as yet.

Frederick's newfound peace plummeted. Miss Ferguson clearly possessed a great deal of feeling, but how could Frederick win such looks from her? Gain her trust and heart? At least her allegiance. Blake's kissing idea emerged unbidden, but Frederick shoved it to the back of his mind.

Lillias's gaze met his across the room, and her smile stilled. She stood, expression trained to cool welcome as she approached. "We wondered where you'd disappeared, but I see my sister monopolized you, Lord Astley."

"Oh yes, Sister dear." Miss Grace released his arm and offered a mock-sober expression. "I was practicing the art of conversing, just as you suggested."

"That sounds. . .entertaining?" Her expression softened and the concern faded. "But now that you are back, I should like some of my own conversation with my future husband, though I doubt my discourse will sparkle as brilliantly as yours."

Grace offered a wrinkle-nosed grin at the compliment. "I have no doubt yours will be less shocking, and thus more to Lord Astley's tastes."

"Not at all." He held on to the joy in her eyes, hoping his sincerity nudged away her doubts. Oh for the days when he'd lived in the carefree world of the second-born! Though suffice it to say, he'd never worn *carefree* as brilliantly as the younger Ferguson.

"Miss Grace, I was wondering where you'd got off to," Mr. Porter called from across the room, his pudgy face filled with ruddy animation.

"Ah, Mr. Porter, you are just the person I was hoping to see." Grace shot a helpless look over her shoulder before her countenance stiffened with resilience. "Have you any idea of the weather patterns in Italy? I hear it's rather dry."

Frederick swallowed his laugh and turned his attention back to the beauty on his arm. The cobalt gown trimming each part of her figure brought out the brilliant color of her eyes. A dazzling beauty. The savior of Havensbrooke.

"She is hopeless, yet one cannot help but love her."

"Indeed, Miss Ferguson." His heart softened to the compassion gentling Lillias's features. "Your sister will certainly make an impact on Havensbrooke's gray world, as will you."

Frederick had never been the charmer. Too direct for some. Too reticent for others. Women usually supposed he was standoffish because of some darker turn of thoughts, but in all honesty, he remained inept at the wooing game. Blake wore the gift like the clothes on his back, placing his words and his smiles in perfect synchrony to capture women with his charms, but the constraints of "proper" dialogue hung like a noose over most conversations Frederick experienced with women.

Except Grace Ferguson. But her youth afforded an uncommon ease and authenticity.

Celia had ruined him to simple trust, even in himself. Her deceit had torn his world apart and ripped him of the closeness he'd once known with his brother. Frederick looked down at Lillias. But she was not Celia, and he desperately needed to give Lillias the benefit of the doubt. After all, he was the greater beneficiary of this bargain. Her massive dowry.

The conversation with Lillias took its usual superficial course. She was the sort of woman who kept her ideas close and her emotions beautifully manicured for the purposes at hand. A well-trained and strategic skill designed by the upper class, which left men in frustrated confusion at the true personality of the woman of interest. Frederick preferred some help in the grand scheme of marriage, if he could find it.

"Did you enjoy your afternoon with your friends?" His gaze darted back to the man at the table she'd left. "I can only imagine the difficulties of leaving your home."

"Oh yes, and you have been gracious in allowing me time to spend with them." She swayed closer to him, teasing with a little of the coy attitude she'd given earlier in the day. "But in the evenings, I'm all yours."

Her palm smoothed up his chest to rest against his shoulder, the touch inciting heat from his neck to his temples. Yes, she knew the way the world worked, didn't she, but why the sudden display?

"I mean to lessen the sting of this transition as much as I am able. And I do wish for your happiness." He drew in a deep breath, his directness not exactly in tune with romantic sonnets. He worked her name onto his lips. "Lillias."

"I believe you do." Her eyes took on a vulnerable look before she glanced away. "Having Grace join me for a few months will ease the sting, I'm sure. Thank you for your forbearance with her. She lives life too authentically for anyone's good."

His gaze locked with hers. "Authenticity can be seen as a virtue in many instances."

Lillias's attention flickered away, her cheeks darkening. They took a turn about the room as people enjoyed various sorts of card or board games. A few women flittered about with wedding talk on their tongues. "My world is very different than yours, yes, and you will face disappointments in it, but I'd like for this to be a true match, Lillias." He tried her name again. Not as difficult the second time. "A true commitment, if possible. Hopeful for both of us."

Her gaze came up to his, a shadow passing over her expression. "I want that as well."

He released the breath he didn't realize he'd held. "With Mother's connections, I imagine you will be able to make new friendships rather quickly." He swallowed to wet his dry throat. "New. . .attachments, I hope."

She gave the slightest hitch of breath, diverting her attention to the corner of the room where a few of her friends stood in conversation, along with the man Lillias had shared the table with earlier. Something flickered between them. Frederick's stomach clenched.

He took her arm and turned her to face him. "You don't have to do this, Lillias." He lowered his voice, drawing her closer. "Not unless you're certain. For both our sakes, I'd rather you decide now than uncover any pretense later."

"There is no pretense, I assure you." Her eyes widened, uncertainty wavering over her expression. "I. . .I am determined."

"There's no need to act rashly." He searched her face. "We can extend the engagement period if you have doubts—"

"No!" Her abrupt response silenced him. She fixed her focus on him with such determination, almost desperation, he couldn't look away. "I would be lying if I told you I didn't harbor grief and regrets at leaving those I've known and. . ." Her words stalled. "Those I. . .love. But despite the trial ahead, I am a woman of my word and dedicated to improving my family's interests as well as yours. I don't need more time."

She searched his eyes, her expression solemn, and—God help him—he wanted to believe her. "Once we are wed, you will have my complete allegiance and my unreserved affections." Her expression softened, imploring with those engaging round eyes of hers. "I don't want to prolong anything. But do allow me these last few days to enjoy the life I've always known before I must embrace a new one."

She felt the weight of the game, as he did. The sacrifice. The freedoms they both aborted once the wedding rings wrapped around their fingers. Yet upon further inspection of her beautiful face, her apparent dedication, perhaps there was hope for more than a contract.

"I would be honored with your allegiance and affections, Miss

Ferguson, and I sincerely hope to lessen your regrets. Take as much freedom in these last days as you need."

"You are very kind, Lord Astley." A faint sheen of tears glistened in her eyes. "Very kind."

"Oh my goodness, Lillias, look where you're standing!"

Frederick turned from his spot with Lillias to find Grace approaching on her father's arm, her grin stretched as wide as possible, it seemed.

"You're under a Christmas kissing ball." Grace's announcement lilted. "How romantic."

Frederick raised his gaze to the doorframe above to find a small orb of greenery wrapped in twine and ribbon hanging above his head.

"They have mistletoe inside them, Lillias." Grace's whole expression brightened like the electric lights on the tree nearby. "You know what that means!"

Frederick looked over at Lillias, whose entire face had paled.

"What a charming idea, Grace." Lillias breathed out the comment, her gaze flickering around the room. "But I prefer to keep my affection for Lord Astley to a more private venue."

Grace rolled her eyes and then paused, her gaze fixed on something nearby. "Good night, Mr. Dixon, you're wearing quite a severe expression for a card party. Did you lose to Mr. Cole again?"

Frederick followed Grace's exclamation to see the man from earlier standing nearby, his tall, lean frame poised not too far from the doorway where they stood. His suit shone of a lesser fineness than Frederick's or Blake's. Dixon? Was he a family friend?

The man flicked his gaze from Frederick to Grace, his expression stiffening.

"Grace, dear, you know how Mr. Dixon despises having attention brought to him," Lillias offered, her voice low.

Grace tilted her head, her gaze shifting between Mr. Dixon, Lillias, and Frederick, those intelligent eyes making some sort of examination, if Frederick knew anything. What did she see? The unhappy conclusions Frederick drew resurrected his doubt with a fury.

"I'm so sorry, Tony." Grace touched the man's arm, and his body relaxed. "You know I never mean to make people uncomfortable. I just have an uncanny ability to do so, and"—her voice dropped to a whisper—"Mr. Cole isn't the most straight-and-narrow sort, so I'd check beneath the table if I were you."

Frederick couldn't help grinning at her generosity mixed with such—well, he wasn't quite sure what to call it. Genuineness?

Grace looked back to the kissing ball. "But why hang such a lovely invention in public at all, if it's only meant to inspire *private* affection? That seems rather ruthless, if you ask me."

"Grace, dear, they're tradition." This from Mr. Ferguson.

Grace tightened her hold on her father and grinned up at him. "Well then, Father dear, we shall not let the tradition be wasted." And she bounced up on tiptoe and pressed a kiss to her father's cheek. "Besides, I always feel a bit merrier after sharing affection with someone I love, don't you?"

"Indeed, my dear girl."

Frederick watched them walk away, a smile lingering in his mind at the unfettered display of fondness. Miss Grace left nothing in doubt, did she? Frederick couldn't even fathom having a woman love with such boundless, and somewhat terrifying, sincerity. Her future husband would need a steady head and a solid sense of humor, but—the idea pricked at his conscience—he'd no doubt find joy woven through the unexpected.

"I'm afraid I've caused you to doubt my earnestness. Perhaps Grace is right." Lillias's raspy voice drew his attention back to her face. She moved closer to him, entwined their arms. "A little show of affection might be just what each of us needs to ease the uncertainty of the next few days."

"Lillias?"

She shifted her body, pressing close, her rosewater scent filling his lungs like an aphrodisiac. "Perhaps. . .I can assure you of our compatibility. Of my ready willingness." Her gaze dropped to his lips again, her words smooth, enticing. "It would not be improper for an engaged couple to show certain affections to one another." She searched his face as if trying to convince herself as much as him. "Test the waters, so to speak?"

"I don't know that—"

"Meet me in half an hour in the Mahogany Room," she whispered, placing her hand over his. "It is vacant and will provide a perfect hideaway." And with that, she slipped away to join her group of friends on the other side of the room. His gaze followed her movements, her figure made to admire.

Frederick glanced back to the kissing ball above, his mind warring with his will. Whatever her connections, he had to at least attempt to transfer her feelings to him, for the good of Havensbrooke's future as well as his own.

Perhaps a kiss *would* make a difference.

# Chapter Four

Frederick walked across the loggia, breathing in the scent of pine and winter on the chilled air. Voices and laughter emerged from inside as he took his time crossing the less-traveled path from the party to the Mahogany Room. He wasn't certain when Lillias had disappeared from the Music Room, but he'd waited an appropriate amount of time before slipping away himself.

He'd never imagined something as simple as a kiss could feel like a precipice for his future, but perhaps Blake was right. If a kiss, or the proper type of kiss and freely given, could encourage affection, he'd ensure he'd do his best, if skill and sincerity had the power to do so.

The door to the Mahogany Room stood partially open—an invitation—so Frederick slipped in without a sound. His pulse hammered up a notch. A dying fire provided the only light in the expansive room, its soft glow casting deep shadows across furniture and carpet up to the wall of windows. His breath caught. Outlined by a large arched window and haloed in moonlight stood the silhouette of his bride-to-be.

She was beautiful. Dazzling, even. The entire ambience of the setting brewed with the amber hues of a dream. He eased his approach, waiting for her to turn, but she appeared lost in thought—gaze trained toward the dark outline of the distant mountains. Her shadowed profile intrigued him most of all. There was a gentleness to her thoughtful features that tugged his heart more than his desires. He'd witnessed her compassion toward her sister and father. She'd softened at the idea of having caused him to doubt her sincerity. Yet here, in this intimate moment, he'd never anticipated Lillias Ferguson to look almost hallowed, basking in moonlight and dusk. Seductive? Yes. Intriguing? Perhaps. But angelic? Innocent even?

On a whim, he swept his arm around her slim waist and pulled her against him, catching her gasp with his lips. An immediate jolt shot through his body at the connection. A first kiss often gave away many hints, but this one surprised him. She tasted of strawberries and smelled like mint and rosemary. A tremor shook from her body into his, as if this kiss was wholly unexpected, but just as he thought to pull away, she relaxed. Her pliable, warm mouth contoured to his in such a tantalizing way, it encouraged him to linger. He tightened his hold, confirming his intentions without reservation.

Her soft curves melted against him and a gentle moan purred up from her throat like a request for more. He gladly complied. Her cool fingers slipped up his chest to graze his cheek. The gentle touch—more curious than seductive—sent an almost maddening battle to his raw emotions. She felt so small in his arms, so perfectly fitted. A sudden rush of protectiveness gripped him. There was an indefinable sweetness in her caress, and her almost innocent response wrung his heart with tenderness. Hope.

Was this the woman she hid from the public? This moonlit creature?

In the quiet of their intimate moment—this first kiss—he vowed to endeavor to win her, if he could. Even if it meant staying in London more than he wished or hosting more parties than he cared for. He had to try.

With the slightest hesitation and a sigh from his beautiful companion, he drew back, the full glow of the moon lighting her face.

But it wasn't Lillias Ferguson he'd kissed with such devotion.

Staring back at him, bright eyes as wide as saucers and lips swollen from his thorough assault, stood Gracelynn Ferguson—his bride's sister.

❧

That was singly the most invigorating moment Grace had ever known. Her entire body hummed alive, warmed by some internal light radiating heat through every fiber of skin.

Her eyes fluttered open and met Lord Astley's somewhat horrified expression. The moonlight gave him a mysterious, vampire-like appearance, which reminded her to reread *Dracula* at her earliest convenience.

She blinked a few more times to clear her head, then glanced around the room, her imagination pulling all the pieces together. He'd meant to meet her sister here.

A clandestine meeting? A shiver incited gooseflesh at the enticing thought. How romantic!

She raised her fingers to her lips, investigating their reaction to her first kiss as her breath continued to pulse in halts and stops. "You. . .you didn't mean to do that, I don't think."

He shook his head a solid five seconds before any words emerged. "Indeed no."

"You thought. . .I was my sister?"

"Yes." His answer scratched through ragged breaths like hers. So perhaps the intensity of the reaction was normal.

Her gaze dropped back to his lips, and hers tingled afresh. Kisses told a tale of Lord Astley she'd not anticipated. Tenderness, passion. Her breath grew short again as something in her awakened to the awareness of their intimate encounter. Not nervous, exactly. She pressed her hand against her stomach, her face warming. "Well, I would convey your message to her, but I don't believe it would have the same impact."

A shaft of air burst from his lips, a sound between a cough and a laugh. "You are positively unexpected."

"Obviously." She attempted a grin, but her lips tingled so much she wasn't sure of the effect. Oh my, what a glorious endeavor. "But a secret rendezvous is a perfectly amorous undertaking. I didn't take you as the sort."

"The. . .the sort?" He still seemed utterly discombobulated.

"To indulge with such determined passion and spontaneity. Not that I'm complaining, you understand. I'm certain Lillias will find every bit of it breathtaking."

"Are you not disarmed in the least by this turn of events?" He narrowed those dark eyes of his and surveyed her from top to bottom as if she'd gone mad.

Ridiculous man! He was the one who'd kissed the wrong woman, not her.

"I kissed you as if you were my fiancée!" He pinched his eyes closed and shook his head. "My sister would have puddled to the floor in a mortified heap if such an exchange happened to her."

"Well, it was quite a shock!" Her lips still prickled in appreciation.

"But why waste such a beautiful blunder on mortification? And what an unpleasant word that is. *Mortification.* No wonder the preacher says it with a scowl on his face. Oh no, I would never place the word *mortification* and your lovely kiss into the same sphere, let alone the same sentence."

"I mistakenly kiss you in a dark room in a way to possibly ruin your reputation and you're concerned about the word *mortification?*" His brow furrowed and he raised his hands in exasperation. "You really are the most peculiar creature."

Well, that certainly wasn't the first time she'd been called peculiar, but the way his deep tones spoke the word, in slight fascination, didn't make it sound as unkind as how others had used it. "Come now, my lord, it was an honest mistake, and I was just pondering how the dastardly Mr. Rochester must have kissed Jane Eyre when he declared his love for her, so when you came out of the darkness and swept me into your arms, I was fairly certain my imagination had gotten away with me, which isn't an uncommon occurrence, you understand, but never quite so"—she slid her finger over her lips again—"tactile. I'd always considered a kiss to be an extraordinary thing. I'm so glad you proved me right."

"I offer my sincerest apologies." He released a slow breath and took a step back. "I would never have presumed. . . Wait. This was your first kiss?"

"Well of course! You don't suppose I'm off kissing men on a regular basis, do you? Fantasy and reality are not the same thing, and despite my love of fiction, I don't confuse them. Often." Her attention drifted back to his mouth. A well-formed mouth, now that she thought about it. "We shouldn't tell Lillias about this. Even though it was an honest mistake, she'd find the idea—"

"Intolerable."

"I was going to say *uncomfortable*, but *intolerable* may be better, or perhaps even such a delightful sounding word as *reprehensible.*"

He stared at her to the point his very strong chin slacked a bit.

"Please don't look so distraught. I'm unharmed, as you see." She gave his arm a stiff pat. "If it's any consolation, I can tell you with certainty my sister will enjoy your kisses. I can't think of one woman who wouldn't, but I suppose we shouldn't be caught in this dark room alone."

He blinked to attention. "Indeed." He took her by the arm and gently guided her to the doorway. "Perhaps you should rejoin the party first?"

Grace shook her head. "I can sneak through the breakfast room and then the servants' corridor, and return to the party without anyone seeing us together."

"Please accept my most ardent apologies, Miss Grace." His dark gaze found hers again, so filled with remorse she gave his arm another touch, less stiff this time.

"No harm done, my lord, but do promise me one thing."

He nodded.

"Make certain all of your other kisses are reserved for your bride, won't you?"

His very nice lips crooked to one side. "I can assure you, Miss Grace, I will make quite certain the next woman I kiss is the right one."

# Chapter Five

How on earth had he kissed the wrong woman? When he returned to the Music Room and found Lillias at a table with her father and friends, he wondered if his mistaken encounter with the little fairy Ferguson could have been a dream—he'd hoped it had been a dream.

Then the scene rushed back to his mind with every touch magnified, every scent of rosemary and soap, and the heat of his rash choice burned a bright trail through his chest and into his throat.

Lillias later apologized for missing their meeting, explaining that her friends had kept her engaged and she was unable to get away.

And Grace? She'd returned to the room a full fifteen minutes after their inadvertent rendezvous as if nothing was amiss, though she touched her lips too often.

He didn't sleep one wink the entire night, tossing between the memory of Grace's warm mouth against his and the utter humiliation of his mistake. By dawn he was in the saddle of one of Whitlock's white stallions, pouring his energy into a fierce ride across the countryside.

The morning mist wet his face and hair, but he drove the stallion harder, farther away from the house. Before his brother died, he might have dismissed the mistake as easily as Grace—oh good heavens, he kept referring to her by her first name—but he couldn't seem to help it. Her lack of pretense left little room for ceremony. He'd never met anyone like her.

Young, yes. Much too outspoken. And wholly unspoiled, which his mother would find positively atrocious, yet she *lived* every moment with a joy and curiosity that almost made him smile, even in his agitated state of mind.

And she kissed with the same enthusiasm.

Good night! He had to erase his thoughts or he'd never look at Grace Ferguson as Lillias's younger, almost childish sister again.

The sunrise made a failed attempt against the dark clouds in the distance—only enough to splice the gray and crown the deep purple mountains with amber strokes. The scene proved to distract his mental derailment with a sense of wonder at such divinely crafted beauty. How long had it been since he'd appreciated such a scene? Certainly not in the last six months, if not longer. Edward's unexpected death—deepened by Blake's doubts at the cause—shifted everything in Frederick's future and thrust him into the role of savior for a flailing estate he loved and rescuer of a long-lived legacy.

A single sunray split through the distant clouds and fell to earth in resplendent magnificence, transforming a river in the distance to liquid gold. Frederick drew in a long breath and closed his eyes. The man he used to be would have stopped and pondered the ineffable artwork of the Almighty, but the new Earl of Astley could not afford such luxuries.

The wind against his ears voiced a protest. *Where was God if not in everything?*

The awareness grated against his choices, against the helplessness in his situation. Didn't Frederick deserve to pay for his ill choices from the past by sacrificing his future? Isn't that how the game of life worked?

His heart pulsed in objection, but he pushed the stallion forward, as if to outrun the past, the future, and every other sour decision in between. All of a sudden, the trail took a sharp turn, catching Frederick off guard. The horse slid against the damp earth. Frederick moved his body with the beast, but the saddle turned beneath him in an unusual shift. He grappled for the reins, but they slipped over his damp gloves as his body flew in one direction and the horse turned in the other. In slow motion, Frederick flew through the air, turning his body so his shoulder might take the brunt of the fall, but somewhere along the way his foot twisted free too late from the stirrup. A sharp pang shot from his ankle up his leg.

The grass provided a merciful pillow for his landing but failed to dampen the ache in his ankle or the thud his shoulder took against the cold earth. He hadn't fallen from a horse in years.

Frederick clenched his teeth against the pain and pushed himself to a sitting position in time to see his steed race back toward the house, following instinct instead of the needs of his rider. This part of the trail hovered on the edge of a steep drop down to a roaring riverbed, perfect for an excellent prospect of the horizon but not for a riding accident. If he'd fallen any closer to the edge. . .

His gaze shifted back to the house. Another accident?

He caught a last glimpse of his horse disappearing into the wood and a prickling of warning raised the hair on the back of his neck. His fingers slipped down to his boot, skimming the hilt of his dagger to ensure its position. He kept his attention fixed on the wood's edge as he pushed to stand.

A swell of pain wilted him back to the earth. A severe sprain. He frowned. He wouldn't be walking back to the house until the pain lessened.

Whitlock's towers rose above the tree line in the distance. He groaned his displeasure. He'd ridden much farther than he'd planned, proving distraction a very unhealthy traveling companion in an unfamiliar place.

Casting a glance heavenward, he raised his brow. What sort of plans did the Almighty have in store for him with this wretched beginning? Surely the fall was nothing more than God's disapproval at Frederick's impulsiveness last evening.

With a series of painful moves, he made his way to a nearby tree that afforded him a better prospect of the house as well as a prop for his back.

All he could do was wait until the pain eased a little or someone came looking for him.

His gaze shifted back to the view. The dark clouds had snuffed out the sunbeams, leaving little of the molten sunrise on the horizon. What if—like his grandmother often said—God used everything as a building tool of character? And if God was the Father he'd always heard his grandparents profess, the *loving* Father, would he love Frederick enough to mold his character, even after so many mistakes? *I've fallen so far.* A sad grin tilted his smile as he reviewed his current predicament. *But I want to do right. You know I do.* He leaned his head back against the tree. *Help me become the man I'm meant to be.* He paused, doubt plaguing his prayer—guilt pausing his request. *And would You help with this marriage too?*

His happiness was a luxury he couldn't afford. He knew, yet so did God, and the mental assent gave some relief in the truth that Frederick wasn't alone. God could help Frederick cultivate a solid relationship with

Lillias Ferguson, couldn't he? The foundations of a better future for his children than the one he'd known?

A sudden movement from the direction of the house caught his attention and had him reaching for his dagger again. He used the tree as a crutch to rise to his full height, despite the stabs of pain coursing up his leg. Over the hillside glided a black horse, moving at a fantastic pace with his horseman. An experienced rider—at ease astride the midnight animal—moved near enough to perhaps hear Frederick's call.

He waved and finally succeeded in gaining the rider's attention. Could it be one of the guests from the house party? The formal riding uniform suggested such.

The horseman was barely a slip of a person. Lithe. Petite. Who from the party fit such a description?

"Oh, my dear Lord Astley." The voice coming from the rider sounded oddly familiar—and not at all like a young gentleman. Heat rushed from his body as the stranger swished off the riding cap, releasing a bountiful swath of fiery hair.

Grace Ferguson! His mind drew a complete blank in response.

"What sort of mess have you gotten yourself into this morning?" Her breath puffed into the cool air.

She rode closer, examining him from her perch. All thoughts of her being a young man fled his mind at the sight of her fitted riding suit. "What are you doing all the way out here on foot?" Her gaze widened, and she slipped from the horse. "Oh dear, are you hurt?" Her riding breeches offered a view of her slender legs as she approached. Frederick's mouth went dry. He averted his gaze.

*Grace Ferguson is not Lillias. Grace Ferguson is not Lillias.*

"Of course I'm not my sister. She hates riding."

Had he spoken aloud? Clearly, he was going mad. "You're. . .you're riding astride?"

"Mr. and Mrs. Whitlock know my bad habits, but like the best of people, they keep my secrets safely hidden from my father." Her grin crinkled her nose. "He finds the whole idea of riding unsavory. I'm not sure why. It's one of the most exhilarating experiences in the whole world."

His mind shot directly back to their kiss. He cleared his throat. "How is it that you are out so early?"

She gestured toward her breeches, an invitation his wayward gaze didn't need. "As I said, to truly ride the way I love best, I must do so early enough not to humiliate my family, so as you see, here I am." He attempted to stand up straighter as she approached, but the shift in weight produced a wince.

"You *are* hurt." She rushed forward but came to a stop just before touching him. He could tell she wanted to, not as a romantic reaction, but in complete abandon to assist. The woman kept him in as much uncertainty of the next action as a feral horse in training.

"I'll ride to the house for help and be back in half an hour."

He pressed a hand to his head in a vain attempt to recollect himself. "You can't get to the house and back in half an hour."

Her grin took such a playful turn it almost inspired his. "I'll bet all your pocket change I can."

He shouldn't indulge her, but the glimmer in those eyes teased him into action. "I'll take that wager, Miss Grace."

She rewarded him with her dazzling smile, pushed the hat back on her head, and with the ease of familiarity—and the assistance of a nearby tree trunk—swung herself back on the horse.

"I shall wait under the shelter of this tree, in the instance the storm arrives before you return."

She followed his gesture to the horizon, and her face paled. "Oh dear. I. . .I hate storms, especially thunderstorms." A flicker of worry puckered her brow. "And it's coming rather quickly, isn't it?"

"I'll be fine with a little rain." *Frozen rain, more like.*

"I'm sure *you* will." She slid from her mount and marched over to him, lips pierced with purpose. "But *I* won't, because then I'll worry about you. So let's ride back together."

"Ride together?" And his thoughts plummeted to holding her in his arms again. He shook his head. "I don't think that would leave the best impression with your sister."

Grace glanced back to the house, her teeth nibbling at her bottom lip. He could almost see her mind working up a solution. She liked solving things, which could be either an asset. . .or utterly terrifying. "We'll take the forest trail all the way to the stables." She tipped a smile over her shoulder. "Besides, why would she ever be jealous of me?"

The poor girl really didn't see herself as viable competition at all, but with a kiss between them, her presence took up much more residence in his thoughts than it ought. No, she wasn't as exquisite as her elder sister, but there was a prettiness about her, an intelligence in her expression—and those eyes? They nearly sparkled with, well, he wasn't certain, but whatever it was, it drew him toward her.

She moved to assist him onto the horse.

"I can mount on my own, Miss Ferguson." He growled out the words. The very idea of her pushing on any part of his person in assistance made him want to attempt to hop all the way to the house on one leg in escape. He gentled his voice. "If you'll bring the horse around."

Gritting his teeth to keep from moaning, he placed the weight on his good leg and slung the painful one over the horse. He gave his throbbing ankle time to settle by adjusting himself in the saddle, and then he turned to his companion, offering his hand. She grinned up at him with such unfurled joy, his lips responded quite helplessly.

With a firm tug, he brought her up to sit in front of him. Wafts of rosemary and mint hinted from her hair, and he almost leaned into the scent, but that meant he'd squeeze even closer to her, and the intimacy of their situation was already nigh unbearable.

"Would you like to take the reins or"—her light voice flittered on the breeze—"I can take the reins and you can. . .um. . .hold on to me."

The very idea of putting his arms around her small waist had him nearly inching off the backside of the horse. "I'll take the reins."

She sighed, keeping hold of them as if she hadn't heard him.

"Miss Grace?"

"Oh! I'm sorry." Her body straightened, and she turned just enough for him to see her profile, handing him the reins. "I was quite distracted by your wonderful scent of amber."

He squeezed his eyes closed. The girl's directness was positively maddening. With a forced swallow and a deep breath, his arms hemmed her in on either side as she relaxed back against him.

"Ah. Now we're snug." Her pitch slid up an octave, hiding nothing.

His throat nearly sealed altogether as the full fragrance of her hair assaulted his senses. All the world conspired against his good intentions.

He pinched his eyes closed, a laugh waiting to explode from the entire ridiculousness of the scene. After playing the social game for so long, Grace's evident inability to do so offered a comical, and somewhat disconcerting, change.

They followed a trail through the wood, trees filtering morning light across the path ahead as they moved in silence. The tickle of laughter waited, itching for release, until Frederick forced dialogue into the stillness. "I suppose you were afraid you'd lose the bet, so you compromised with this decision."

She shook her head sending more mint his way. "I couldn't lose."

"You couldn't lose?" The woman was baffling. "And why is that?"

"I have no pockets, thus no pocket money." Her laugh lilted, as if at home in this morning wonderland as any fairy's.

"That isn't quite fair, Miss Grace."

Her shoulders slumped from the truth, and his grin teased for release. "You're right, and I considered what I could give you if you won." She turned slightly, lips tipped. "Which you wouldn't have, because I'm a very good rider."

Watching her glide across the countryside confirmed it. She might even best him. His grin won. What a fun competition it would be to race her!

He shook the vision from his head. "In the instance you'd lost, what would you have offered?"

"Well, I was going to offer a chaste kiss." Her smile slid wide from her profile. "But that seemed fairly anticlimactic after last night."

He grunted a response and pulled his attention away from her lips and toward the path ahead. Five years ago, he'd have been her equal in lively sparring and hopeful optimism, but too many losses and betrayals marred his vision.

"Ever since our book discussion last evening, I've been curious about what you enjoy reading, Lord Astley."

His gaze dropped to her hair as it spilled over his arms in an unruly and fascinating way. He cleared his throat and attempted to distract his wayward musings.

"Oh wait. Let me guess." She sat a little taller, quite proud of herself. He could almost envision the pixie glint in those eyes.

"Biographies?"

His brow twitched. "I do enjoy a good biography."

"And histories, I should think."

His smile faded. "Occasionally."

"Occasionally?" She snorted her laugh and then covered her mouth with one hand. "Come now, what else? Landscaping? Geography?"

*Yes and yes.* His grimace deepened. He was much too predictable, but then he knew how to tempt her. "Actually, I've discovered a particular interest in adventure stories of late, and mysteries."

Her gasp of delight hit him square in the chest. He'd surprised her. Why did that feel so pleasant? "Fiction?"

"*The Count of Monte Cristo* and *King Solomon's Mines*, anything by Sir Arthur Conan Doyle."

She nearly turned all the way around in the saddle, eyes dancing. "*The Count of Monte Cristo* was fabulous but horribly sad, and I've never read *King Solomon's Mines*, but I've heard it's positively delightful. And Sherlock?" She turned back around and giggled. "Oh, I'm so glad you read fiction too. That makes you even more interesting."

And unfortunately, with every conversation she too became more so. *Lord, help him!* Gracelynn Ferguson didn't come with the dowry to save Havensbrooke. Lillias Ferguson did—and she was his future bride.

He needed to confirm his mental assessment with a strong enough kiss to wipe the memory of Grace's from his mind. . .before he lost all sense and kissed the wrong sister again.

"Lord Astley!"

The call came from ahead on the trail. A boy, one of the stable hands, dashed toward them with Elliott at the lad's heels. Frederick straightened to alert. He'd never seen his valet move so quickly in all the years he'd known him.

"You. . .you"—Elliott paused to bend at the waist, panting—"are all right, sir?"

"He has a hurt ankle," Grace replied before he could respond.

"The horse came back without you, sir." The boy rushed forward, barely getting the words out between breaths. "And your saddle. I didn't know, sir. You have to believe me. I didn't know about what happened to your saddle."

"Know?" Frederick looked from the boy back to Elliott. "My saddle?"

"Sir, it seems your saddle was not in the best condition for riding." Elliott tipped his head toward Grace, brow raised in question.

Heat seeped from Frederick's face. "Ah, I see." He shifted his hold on Grace's waist. "Elliott, would you mind escorting Miss Grace to the house while I return her horse to the stables? I'm certain she'd like to get out of the chill."

"Escort me to the—" She turned on him, ginger hair flying around her shoulders as she did. "I think I'd like to know what is going on." Those intelligent eyes examined each face before landing on the weakest link. "Cam, what were you saying about the saddle?"

"That's right, Miss Grace. The saddle. If I'd knowed it was—"

"Come now, Miss Grace." Frederick held Elliott's gaze, and his valet took the hint, stepping to the side of the horse just as Frederick lifted her from the seat. With Elliot's help, she was on the ground before she could protest. "The house will be awake soon enough, and Miss Grace will be missed."

She turned back toward him, rebel brow raised in challenge, pink lips set. "You're the guest of honor, my lord. Perhaps *you* should go on to the house, have your ankle tended, and *I* can see to this mess about your saddle."

"Very thoughtful of you." How could he possibly be fighting a smile? "But I believe this situation requires my immediate attention, and I'd prefer you find your way safely back to the house. I feel certain your sister would agree."

"My sister? Of course." She shot Frederick an impressive, though powerless, glare before slipping her arm through Elliott's and pushing on a smile that resembled nothing like the genuine ones he'd seen before. "Lead the way, dear Elliott. What would a young woman know of saddles and mysteries after all?"

"No one said anything about mysteries, miss," Elliott replied with a gentle smile.

She sent a look over her shoulder at Lord Astley, their gazes meeting in an unspoken battle. "Of course not, Elliott," she said, her voice hiding nothing as Frederick rode the horse past her. "No mysteries at all."

# Chapter Six

Dismissed? Grace pinched her arm more tightly around the perfectly postured valet as they finished their walk up the trail. If she hadn't liked Lord Astley so much, she'd have been tempted to think very bad thoughts about him. Thoughts of Gothic horror proportions. But he really was much too nice for Gothic horror. Perhaps murder mystery? Her grin tipped. Yes. He could be the handsome inspector who was always proven wrong by the lady detective.

She sighed in resignation. Oh well, not *always* proven wrong. She did want the inspector to have some wits about him. It made for a much more balanced story.

But in all honesty, why did everyone think she couldn't manage distressing news? With the amount of fiction she consumed, she would likely be the least shocked of anyone.

Something was amiss. Something about the saddle and Lord Astley's fall.

The tingling of a mystery pricked at her scalp, even as she was relegated to safety in the house. Ridiculous men! She *had* to learn the truth.

"I do hope Lord Astley's ankle is quickly mended." She glanced in her periphery at the valet, who seemed much too young and handsome for his job. Why had she supposed English valets were old and disgruntled as a rule?

"It was fortunate you were out early enough to find him so quickly."

Best create friendly dialogue to throw the good valet off her sleuthing scent. "Well, it's the only time I can ride astride without offending half of the women at the house party and unnerving half the men. You know, it really doesn't make sense to get ourselves nearly killed for some ill-placed sense of propriety. I feel certain you wouldn't want to ride sidesaddle if you were a woman, would you, Elliott?"

He kept his gaze appropriately diverted, but his lips pinched in the strangest way. "I really can't give an informed opinion on the matter, miss."

"No, I suppose you can't." Grace's laugh bubbled out. "But what a valiant attempt you're making at not being horrified by my question. I can already tell you are the excellent sort."

"I should like to think so, miss."

A little chink in his well-honed demeanor teased her curiosity. "You know I'm to escort my sister to England after the wedding, don't you?"

"Indeed, miss."

"As you can imagine, I have little to no idea of how to behave in an English country house with a sister who will be *lady* of the manor."

He dipped his head again, looking unsure how to respond. "It is a change, miss."

"I'd be ever so grateful for your guidance in any way you see I might unwittingly embarrass Lord Astley or his mother, or. . .well, the entire household. Because to be perfectly candid, Elliott, I'm well aware enough of my defects to know that my good intentions rarely show how good they are in public."

Both his brows rose to his hairline.

"In all honesty"—she lowered her voice, as if anyone were near enough to hear—"they're no good in private either, but fewer people witness the horrid effects."

He pinched his lips into almost a smile. "I shall endeavor to do what I can, miss.

"Thank you. I'll feel such relief knowing I have a friend on the inside of Havensbrooke."

The man cleared his throat. "Pardon me, Miss Grace, but Lord Astley will be there for you and your sister. He isn't one of the usual sorts to go off clubbing and on hunting parties, as is want of most of the gentry. He means to take good care of his estate and tenants, as his grandfather before him."

Oh! Did Elliott believe she and Lord Astley might become friends? Her finger trailed to her smile, reliving a rather decadent moment of mistaken identity. She blinked away from the thought. Good heavens! "I'm glad to hear it, Elliott, for I should like to be friends with Lord Astley, for my sister's sake if nothing else."

The sound of voices up ahead as they approached the stables turned her mind back to the mystery at hand. Her thoughts spun through what she knew. She slid another glance to the good valet at her side—now more relaxed than before—and dared a little sleuthing. "It is such a shame that Lord Astley fell from his horse only days before the wedding. I was under the impression he rode regularly and quite well."

"He's been an excellent horseman since childhood, miss. This is certainly uncharacteristic."

She steadied her expression, even studied some of the ornate carvings on the stable walls as they passed. "Then perhaps a turn in the trail. He's unfamiliar with the paths here, I'd say."

Elliott shook his head. "He took the usual route he'd taken the past three mornings."

Ah, then there was certainly something unusual going on.

The *clip-clop* of a horse coming into the stables ahead alerted her to Lord Astley's arrival. Mr. Whitlock rushed through the archway of the courtyard, the stately man arriving in an abnormal dash.

"Is he injured?" Mr. Whitlock asked as he passed Elliott. "I've telephoned the doctor."

"Thank you, sir," Elliott responded. "It appears to be a sprain."

"Thank heavens." The master of the house rushed past, and Grace turned to Elliott with her sweetest smile, or at least she hoped it was her sweetest. Her mind was too busy to really focus on the perfect tilt.

"Well, Mr. Elliott, thank you for escorting me." She released her hold on his arm. "But I can make it the rest of the way on my own. I feel certain Lord Astley will require your immediate assistance."

He tucked his head. "Yes, miss."

As soon as Elliott turned the corner into the stables, Grace scanned the courtyard and then dashed through the arched doorway of the servants' entry. An advantage of visiting this house every summer for ten years meant she knew all the secret hiding places.

With silent steps, she rounded the back of the stables, nearing the male voices.

"The saddle strap, sir. It was tampered with." Cam's voice quaked.

Poor boy. He likely feared losing his job, and his widowed mother counted on his income.

"And you didn't notice when you saddled the horse." This from Mr. Whitlock.

"N–no, sir. It was one of the new saddles, and it went on for Lord Astley as it had every morning for his ride."

A ladder to the nearest loft caught her attention. Certainly it would afford her a better view of the scene. She quietly shimmied up and crawled closer to the voices, peering through the cracks in the old wooden loft. Down below, Cam stood, a saddle at his feet, his head bent and hat in hand. Lord Astley leaned against Elliott on one side while Lord Astley's friend Mr. Blake, Mr. Whitlock, and the stable manager, Cooks, formed a half circle on the other side of the saddle.

"How could you not have known, boy?" Mr. Whitlock offered an uncustomary growl. The man rarely raised his voice, even for tea. "The strap is cut clean through. How it stayed on the animal as long as it did is a miracle."

"Were there any strangers in the vicinity? Unfamiliar faces?" This from Mr. Blake, who had knelt to examine the saddle.

"None other than the guests and their servants, sir," Cooks answered. "And we keep a sharp eye out where the animals are concerned. Had a couple stolen not four months ago."

"And I inspected the saddle before setting it in place, Mr. Whitlock, just as Mr. Cooks taught me," Cam offered.

"So whoever tampered with the saddle must have done so just this morning, between the time you inspected it and I rode off." Lord Astley replied, his low voice a rumble of consonants and wonderfully English vowels.

Her neck tingled from the memory of his riding behind her up the trail. Heaven and earth, what a glorious feeling to have a massive, strong man who smelled of amber so close. Romance definitely had become more relatable over the last twenty-four hours.

Grace flipped her mind back to the present with a little shake of her head. Whoever tampered with the saddle must have been familiar with the stables enough to know which saddle would have been chosen for Lord Astley. The servants wouldn't have any reason to sabotage Lord Astley's saddle, but would a guest?

She slid closer to the edge of the loft, the wood bending beneath her weight. She'd read in one mystery book or another about something similar happening when the strap wasn't cut through, only partially. As the rider took on more speed and added more stress to the straps, the saddle would break, making an apparent accident take place long after the actual crime had been committed. So very clever. She squinted to try and make out the saddle strap.

"After the incident at the train depot, now this?" Mr. Whitlock shook his frosty head. "It sounds rather suspicious, Frederick."

"Why would anyone from our party wish to cause me harm?" Lord Astley's quick, deep response reverberated among the group. He did have a remarkably pleasant voice, and that counted in Grace's book. Words meant a great deal and spoken in his velvety tones, only made her crave chocolate for some reason.

"Until we're certain, we should all keep our eyes open." Mr. Blake shot his friend a look. Ah, Mr. Blake had a solid head on his shoulders.

Two incidents? And aimed at Lord Astley? Highly suspicious.

"We'll have the grounds searched." Mr. Whitlock gestured toward Cooks. "And I must decide what to do with Cam."

Grace caught her gasp in her hand. Cam wasn't the culprit. The stable boy never was. No, no, no. Hadn't these men read their fiction? Her movement incited the strangest sounds from the board on which she lay, but before she could scoot away from the edge, the wood beneath her made a resounding crack. In one massive crash, Grace fell through the loft floor and into a pile of hay below.

"What in heaven's name!"

"Is it the rogue?"

"I say!"

Well, if she was going to fall into a bed of hay in front of a group of men, at least she was wearing breeches instead of a gown. Another argument in favor of breeches.

She sat up and once she'd brushed straw and hair from her face, found herself looking up into a group of unhappy men. Cooks even had a pitchfork in hand, pointed at her.

"Grace?" called Mr. Whitlock.

"Miss Grace!" Elliott's polished accent lilted.

"Grace Ferguson." This from Lord Astley, who didn't sound surprised at all.

Grace opened her mouth to respond then closed it again, attempting to work up a logical reason she'd just fallen from the stable loft during a private discussion about scandal. "A haystack, how fortunate." That sounded noncommittal enough.

With a quirk to his lips, Mr. Blake offered a hand. "A new reading spot, Miss Ferguson?"

"Not as effective without a book, Mr. Blake." She wiped her hand against her breeches and placed it in his with a smile, as he raised her to her feet. "Though a possible daydreaming nook, I should think, once the boards are mended."

"Curiosity will be your downfall, dear girl." Mr. Whitlock lost some of the bite in his reprimand. "I've always told you that. You are forever finding yourself in places you shouldn't be."

"Quite literally my downfall this morning, wouldn't you say?" She dusted off her breeches and sent a smile to her audience, her gaze finally landing on Lord Astley. "Perhaps Lillias shouldn't hear of my latest escapade. She'd be mortified."

A very appropriate use of the word at this point.

"You shouldn't be here." Lord Astley narrowed his eyes, staring down at her from his towering height.

"It's a good thing I am, or you might have made a grave mistake on poor Cam's part." She held her head high and walked to the saddle.

"A mistake? What could you possibly know about this?"

Mr. Whitlock waved away Lord Astley's exclamation. "Not to contradict you, Frederick, but Grace is quite the amateur sleuth. Those horses that were stolen?" He gestured toward her. "She's the one who found a clue to the thieves, just with a little bit of her snooping about and that unrelenting imagination of hers."

"Unnerving to have such a busybody about, if you ask me." Cooks sniffed.

*Well, no one did, Mr. Grumpy Goose.* But Grace kept the response inside, all the more determined to prove her point. "One only needs to look a little closer." She knelt by the saddle and examined the strap. Aha, exactly as she'd thought it would look from the evidence in one of her mystery books. Slit and then ripped.

"I appreciate Miss Ferguson's youthful and inventive mind, but you can't really suppose she'd—"

"Lord Astley." She broke into his doubt with a glare. "If you will note, the saddle strap was not sliced all the way through. Only part of the way." She turned the strap around for the men to view. "The smooth section suggests the work of the knife, but this more ragged, stretched part?"

"The cut working its way out as Freddie rode the horse."

"Yes." She nodded to Blake. "It's exactly how the Duke of Darber was murdered to make it appear like an accident."

"Who on earth?" Mr. Whitlock scratched his head. "Is he someone you knew from across the pond, Frederick?"

"Fiction." Lord Astley added, holding Grace's gaze. "*The Duke's Dissent.*"

All annoyance for the dashing earl dissipated into utter appreciation. Any man who spoke in fiction was certainly worth forgiving. "Exactly." She rewarded his excellent deduction with a smile and turned her attention back to Mr. Whitlock. "And it's perfect because the actual crime can happen hours before the results, so the perpetrator has plenty of time to disappear from the scene, which is likely what happened here and will cause a nuisance in uncovering the truth."

"I should be concerned about the workings of that mind of yours, Miss Grace, if I didn't know you had such a sweet heart." Mr. Whitlock shook his head. "But you're right. I see it now."

"That does narrow down the possible suspects, don't you think?" She stood and pushed back her hair, her fingers pricking on a few pieces of hay. "It would have to be someone who knew Lord Astley's morning routine *and* had ready access to the stables without causing suspicion."

"Cooks, come with me. We'll start a list and give notice for certain servants to keep watch." Mr. Whitlock turned to Lord Astley. "You need to see to your ankle."

"I'll take a ride about," Blake offered. "Though, if Miss Ferguson's conjectures hold true, our suspect has had plenty of time to disappear."

It felt rather nice to be taken somewhat seriously now and again. "Not to add concern, but perhaps someone should subtly interview the guests."

"The guests?" Mr. Whitlock's bushy brows took flight.

"She's right." Blake sent her a nod. "They would have access, but it's going to take subtle investigating. Might I offer my skills in that instance?"

"Blake is rather proficient at getting information from people without them even knowing," Lord Astley added.

"Very well. I'd be grateful for any help in the matter," came Mr. Whitlock's reply.

Grace sent a curtsy to the group and stepped back toward the stable doors, locking eyes with the earl. "Well now, as Lord Astley has so kindly reminded me, I must return to the house before I'm missed."

She veered to leave.

"Miss Ferguson."

Grace paused and pivoted back to Lord Astley. "Yes, my lord?"

"I would appreciate you keeping this bit of information to yourself." His dark eyes narrowed, intense. "We wouldn't wish to cause any undue concern without proof."

"You have nothing to worry about, my lord. Lillias isn't fond of mysteries." She pinched her hands together with purpose. "And I have every intention of keeping your wedding on schedule and your bride happy. Surely nothing worse could happen than a possible murder attempt."

❧

Grace scanned the bookshelves, glancing through her favorite titles. What would he like? Oh! Jules Verne's *Michael Strogoff*, but it was in French. She tilted her head and examined the binding. Well, of course an earl would know French.

She moved down the row of bookshelves. Aha! *The Riddle of the Sands* by Erskine Childers. Espionage. Perfect. And perhaps it would encourage his own solution to his current mysterious plot. She placed the second book on top of the first and quickly slipped up the winding staircase to the library balcony in search of the Arthur Conan Doyle selections. Was *The Earl of Notham* in Mr. Whitlock's collection? Several people attempted to kill that particular earl, and he outsmarted them all. Definitely a good choice for Lord Astley's self-preservation.

"The hall is clear," a harsh whisper—female—slit the ominous silence from the direction of the secret stair.

Grace's body stilled. Was that Lillias's voice?

"Hurry. You can't be seen."

Grace slipped closer, listening into the darkness of the stairway entry.

"Come tonight, Lillias." A male voice emerged next, urgent.

Who on earth could he be? Not Father, from the youthfulness in the man's tone. And what single man would dare tread in the women's bedroom hallway? Mr. and Mrs. Whitlock ensured single men and women were judiciously separated on opposite sides of the house to keep from impropriety, as Father explained it. Though Grace still wasn't fully aware of all the shades of such impropriety to which he referred.

"You're asking too much, my dear." Her sister's voice staggered with pitiful sobs.

Grace rushed to the shadows of the secret stairs to help, but the male voice halted her in her steps. "We have only days to make a lifetime of memories. Please, come to my room again tonight."

His room? Again! Grace's palm flew to her mouth, barely catching her gasp. Lillias visited this man in his room? At night?

That wasn't appropriate by any standard she'd ever read, unless for illness, birth, or when someone's bed was on fire.

"I don't know if I can." The plea in her sister's voice drew Grace a step closer.

"You found a way last night and the night before, and even this afternoon."

Grace nearly dropped the books in her hands. Lillias was supposed to be in town visiting a friend this afternoon before dinner with Lord Astley.

*Lord Astley!* Her eyes grew wide. Her sister was marrying Lord Astley in a few days and spending the night with. . . Whom? She knew his voice. Her mind grasped for a face to match.

"I have loved you for years, Lillias. Give me these last hours! If we must live an ocean apart, I'll not make you quit us so easily."

For years? The voice clicked into place, and Grace dropped back against the wall to catch her weight. Anthony Dixon, their neighbor in Richmond.

"Easily?" The word tore from her sister with such agony Grace reached for her own throat in empathetic pain. "I leave my soul here with you when I go. I must do this for my family. For us. It's the only way."

Grace shook her head, trying to make sense of it. If Lillias loved Anthony Dixon, why would she agree to marry Lord Astley? Surely a title wasn't worth this subterfuge and heartache.

"For us?" His tenor trembled like Grace's ragged breaths. "How can your choice to marry another man be for us?"

Silence greeted his question, followed by the sound of a muffled sob. "I'm with child, Tony."

Air stopped in Grace's throat.

"No one can know. If Father breaks the contract with Lord Astley, he'll be ruined. There's no other way. I have to marry as soon as possible so no one will ever know."

Grace's stomach coiled until she bent from the pain. Poor Lillias. Poor Anthony. She squeezed the books to her chest. Poor Lord Astley.

"How. . .how could you do this?"

"I was going to back out of the agreement last month, but then I discovered. . .my situation. Father needs this alignment to solidify some of his business dealings, but I need it to keep from ruining my family's reputation. If I don't marry Lord Astley soon, he'll know the baby isn't his."

A baby? Grace's vision glossed over with a rush of tears. A lie?

"Lillias, you're carrying *my* child and my heart." Anthony's voice grated with raspy emotion. "You're choosing to separate us forever."

Grace squeezed her eyes closed, quelling a whimper. *No, no, no. This wasn't supposed to happen. Lord Astley and Lillias were supposed to live a fairy-tale future.* Grace sent a look to the ceiling, the magnificent library painting of curious onlookers peered down to her from their lofty spot above, and she closed her eyes against their blank perusal. The only answer came from divine intervention beyond the painted ceiling, and Grace prayed that God would unleash a way of escape. *God, whatever it takes, please make a way to redeem this broken thing. For Lillias, Tony. . .and for Lord Astley.*

# Chapter Seven

"Whatever happened to you at dinner last evening, Grace?"

Grace had avoided everyone until the next afternoon, strolling through the gardens and crying out for heavenly wisdom for this very earthly catastrophe. It seemed like a travail too large for even the assistance of fictional characters, though she did attempt a cursory view of *Tess of the d'Urbervilles*, which only left her feeling worse.

Her stomach twisted in nauseating knots, swinging her determination between keeping the secret for the sake of her sister and bringing out the truth for the sake of Lord Astley. By all accounts, he was a good man. He didn't deserve this deception, but what would happen to Lillias if the truth surfaced? To her father? Lillias had said Father would be ruined.

Grace had never known such a dilemma in all her life. Her poor book of Psalms looked much more worn for the wear, and the pages in her prayer book crinkled from the unavoidable dripping of tears.

She'd always tried to do the right thing, even if she'd bumbled it. Truth and goodness gave a great deal of hope to the world. But how on earth could God mend such a broken situation? Was there even a way without irreparable damage? She knew He was in the business of healing hearts and situations, but this seemed a monstrous task by every human account. It was all very well and good to kill giants with stones and rain fire from heaven, but earls and fortunes and middle-class businessmen were terribly absent in the Bible. *Please help me, Lord. Show me how to make things right.*

Her heart squeezed within her chest as she looked across the room at her sister. There was nothing else to do but for Grace to relinquish her fight. "I know, Lillias."

Truth won. It had to.

"Know?" Lillias continued applying powder to her face from her dressing table.

"About Anthony Dixon." Grace forced volume into her words.

Lillias's gaze flashed to Grace through the mirror's reflection. Something flickered in her eyes. "What in heaven do you mean?"

"I know about Anthony and the deception."

Her sister stared at her for a second longer, and her steady expression melted. "I knew it was bound to come out at some point." She pressed her fingers into her crinkled forehead as she leaned forward against the dressing table. "He didn't truly want to hurt anyone. He's not the sort. He was jealous, you see."

Grace paused her forward motion. Jealous? What was Lillias—

"If he'd been in his right mind, he'd never have considered it at all, Grace. You must understand. He even attempted to dispatch the saddle altogether, but one of the stable hands came in before he could hide it, and there you go." Her gaze came up, pleading. "I was going to leave him in less than a week. Forever. He was trying to create more time for us, because it's all we have left. He would never have wanted to kill Lord Astley. And he tried to make things right. You have to believe me."

Mr. Dixon was the man who tampered with Lord Astley's saddle! Grace stepped closer, redirecting the conversation from her previous plan. "And did Mr. Dixon try to run Lord Astley over in the village too?"

"What? Of course not. He had no idea who Lord Astley was before meeting him here, and if you recall, Anthony arrived a day later than everyone else. So he couldn't have." She turned from her mirror, her eyes red-rimmed. "As I told you, jealousy got the best of him with the saddle. It was a one-time offense, and he attempted to make things right. We must keep this to ourselves, Grace."

"His jealousy could have cost a man his life. If Lord Astley hadn't been such an avid rider or as strong of build, things could have turned out much worse."

"I know. It's such a horrible thing." Lillias pinched her eyes closed and brought out her handkerchief. "Poor Anthony. Poor Lord Astley."

"You cannot marry Lord Astley, Lillias. Not with these feelings you have for Mr. Dixon."

"I must." Lillias straightened in the chair, chin up. "It is the right thing to do for Father and for me."

"But what about Lord Astley? What about Mr. Dixon's heart?"

"So I should undo everything Father has planned just because of Anthony's lapse in judgment?" Lillias stood, this time with fire in her eyes. "Really, Grace, you are too pious for your own—"

"I know about the baby, Lillias." Grace's throat burned, but she continued. "Mr. Dixon's baby."

"What?" Lillias blinked and released a puff of air from her parted lips as if she'd been hit in the stomach. "What on earth are you talking about, you ridiculous girl?"

"Stop it." Grace marched forward, her voice shaking. "Stop lying and trying to justify your wrongdoing." The same tears that had threatened her eyes all morning rose to the surface. "You can't go through with this wedding. It isn't right."

Lillias's plastered smile descended into a snarl. "It isn't right?" Her laugh took an uncharacteristically sardonic turn. "No, none of it is *right*, but it must be done. I don't live in your fairy world, Grace." She pressed her finger against her chest. "I am the eldest. Raised to marry a man who will advance our family. I'm not allowed to have love. Or dreams. Or a happily-ever-after. Because I must forfeit it to save—"

"Your reputation and Lord Astley's title are not worth this."

Lillias turned her head away and walked to the nearby desk. "Someone of our standing has little else but her status and reputation."

Grace shrank down on the bed. "There must be something we can do."

"Don't you think I would have thought of it, if there was another way? I cannot salvage my reputation and Father's finances without this. The cost is too great." She snatched a paper from the desk and slapped it onto the bed beside Grace. "Besides, everything's already announced. There's no going back."

Grace stared down at the headline on the local paper: "One of the Illustrious Ferguson Daughters to Wed English Aristocracy."

"Plans can change, Lillias." Grace trailed her fingers over the words, emotions raking her voice to a whisper. "They *must*, reputation or not." Her fingers curled into a fist. "Surely in your new situation, you will want to be with Mr. Dixon. After all, he should have some say about his own child, don't you think?"

"I was not meant to be a middle-class businessman's wife, Grace."

"Then you shouldn't have joined Mr. Dixon in his bed."

The declaration came out so quickly, it shocked Grace as much as Lillias. She wasn't quite sure what happened between a man and a woman in bed, but it clearly produced a child, along with all sorts of other mischief. Grace reined in her distracted thoughts and released a sigh. "Frederick Astley probably doesn't wish to marry a woman who is carrying another man's child either."

"You know nothing of these matters."

"I know enough to tell what is right and wrong." Grace stood, bringing the paper with her. "You should never have brought Lord Astley into this. . .this sleeping arrangement." She waved the paper toward her. "Mr. Dixon didn't force himself on you, did he?"

Lillias rose from the bed, eyes narrowed. "Of course not!"

"Then you've already made your choice, Lillias." The truth knifed deeper. "You must let Lord Astley and his title go."

"You're such a child. You can't understand." She rolled her gaze away from Grace and walked toward the window, running her trembling fingers over her forehead. "There is no other way."

"There has to be another way."

Lillias sat down on the bed, diverting her gaze away, her fingers slipping over a document with signatures. "If Father breaks the contract, he forfeits a substantial amount of money, funds that are currently made up of stocks and such. Father could lose everything." Her gaze shot back to Grace's. "Then. . .then it will impact Father's name all over the business world, which, in finance, would be detrimental."

Grace didn't fully understand, but she certainly believed in honor and keeping promises. Lillias had forfeited both. "So Father must keep his promise."

"Without a doubt."

Grace took the papers from Lillias's hands and skimmed over them. The sum of money nearly took Grace's breath. She'd never been involved in much of the financial discussions of home, but she enjoyed helping her father come up with innovative ideas. He always asked her opinion about things such as automobile style or where to build a new factory or how to beautify their garden. Creativity inspired her. Money? Not so much.

But there had to be another option.

Grace stilled. Option? She read over the agreement again and halted on a sentence. "Lillias?" She reread the words: *A daughter of Henry T. Ferguson will marry Lord Frederick D. Astley.* "It doesn't mention your name."

"What does it matter?" Lillias groaned into her palm. "Everyone knows the intention."

*One of the Illustrious Ferguson Daughters. . .*

Grace stared at her sister, an idea swirling from the fog. Worry lines creased Lillias's porcelain brow, her pale eyes watery. Grace's gaze dropped to Lillias's middle. A baby. Her niece or nephew.

Grace wouldn't condone Lillias's behavior. Her "perfect" sister had the potential to ruin several people's lives in one fell swoop. Their father's reputation? Lord Astley's financial needs? Anthony Dixon's heart? Her own happiness?

One decision could fix everything. One choice.

Grace pushed herself to a stand. The words squeezed through her throat. "I'll do it."

"What?" Her sister growled, rubbing her forehead and sparing a weary glance in Grace's general direction. "Grace, the truth will only cause bigger problems in this situa—"

"I'll marry Lord Astley."

Lillias froze and then slowly dropped both hands from her face, eyes narrowing. "What did you say?"

"It's either that, or I tell everyone the truth." She shook her head, tears blurring her vision. Her pulse pounded in her ears. "I can't condone this lie, Lillias, not even for you. Perhaps especially not for you. I love you more than that. If you disappear, someone will have to take your place, and since the agreement doesn't stipulate a name—"

"You. . .you would take my place?"

Grace's knees began to tremble, but she continued as the plan became clearer, the conviction deepening. "Neither your Mr. Dixon nor Lord Astley deserve a future built on deception. Our father's name will remain trustworthy. Lord Astley will receive his money, and I"—where, oh where, was that silver lining?—"I will get a real-life adventure."

Though marriage wasn't how she'd envisioned her adventures. Captured by pirates? Maybe. Dazzling the world with her renowned wit as she toured Italy? Perhaps. But giving up her freedom to rescue her sister's heart? Never. Grace pinched her eyes shut, closing off the dreams she'd had for the future. She'd just forfeited her expectations and taken on a role she'd never planned to play, so now. . .now she had to see it through.

*God, help me.*

"But. . .but you're. . .you. . ." Lillias stared, eyes widening.

*Lord, change these circumstances before I make a mistake. I cannot turn back now.*

Grace stood a little taller, pulling from a confidence she didn't feel. "And I'll have to be enough."

Grace tried to keep her breath steady as everyone sat in the grand dining hall for dinner, all surrounded by the Christmas beauties of Whitlock, but her mind refused to settle. Mr. Whitlock had spoken with her earlier in the day to share their lack of evidence in the saddle-slicing incident, and it took every ounce of Grace's self-control to keep the truth lodged deep—though she did attempt to soften the accusations a little.

She'd fought against melancholy with all her might, even pulled out some of Oscar Wilde's more humorous plays for medicinal purposes, but her heart ached with the sinking reality of what she'd given up and. . . what she'd chosen.

Grace's gaze traveled the length of the table and settled on the man seated next to Mrs. Whitlock. Frederick Percy, Lord of Astley. Perhaps thinking of good things would help.

For instance, what did she know of this future husband of hers?

As far as husbands went, he had an excellent list of attributes to recommend himself. Handsome, in a dark, mysterious sort of way. A thrill of warmth splashed over her skin at the very idea. Of course, looks weren't everything, but they certainly made staring much easier.

She cleared her throat and diverted her rather unruly inner assessment.

He enjoyed reading fiction—a definite benefit where she was concerned.

He appreciated a woman's mind, or so he'd said, which only proved to highlight his own.

His sense of humor seemed a bit lacking, but in all honesty, she'd caught him at the worst possible times. A mistaken kiss. Falling off a horse. Murder attempt.

He enjoyed the outdoors. Her grin bit into her face at the memory of them riding Nightshade together. And he'd been kind to everyone he'd met at Whitlock.

Her smile softened. Kindness was a most attractive feature, especially for a husband, she imagined. And somehow the idea made him a little handsomer.

Her gaze dropped to his lips as he took a drink from his glass. He kissed like a rogue. Her fingers flew to her own lips. Well, Grace assumed he did, but since she'd no experience kissing rogues—or anyone else for that matter—Lord Astley kissed exactly the way she imagined a rogue should kiss, which then inspired all sorts of curiosities about how very roguish he might be in other ways.

Perhaps reading *The Mysteries of Udolpho* before bed proved detrimental to her ladylike sensibilities.

"Grace, dear, are you feeling well?"

Grace snapped her attention to Mrs. Whitlock, the woman's acute perception not helping Grace's plight at all. "Excuse me? Yes."

"You look flushed, dear."

"Ah. . .um," Grace's gaze slid back to Lord Astley, who studied her. She should add fascinating eyes to his list of attributes. Her face blushed hot. "Actually, I am feeling a bit warm. Perhaps it was all the walking I did today in your lovely gardens. Too much sun." She cleared away the tickle in her throat, but it returned.

"The gardener said you gave him some excellent suggestions on arrangements." Lady Whitlock smiled her appreciation. "You've always had a clever head." Mrs. Whitlock turned to Lord Astley. "I should think she'd enjoy your grounds at Havensbrooke when she travels next week, Lord Astley. She's forever coming up with ideas for them."

Lord Astley's attention fastened on her so intently she felt sure he'd read every thought in her head, including the roguish ones.

"You enjoy gardens, do you?"

"Clearly, too much enjoyment of them today." Grace's face grew warmer, her breath shorter.

"Rest is what you need, dear girl." Her father chimed in with his usual charisma. "You mustn't become ill before the wedding."

The wildest urge to laugh scratched at the back of her throat. She shot to her feet and placed her napkin on the table. "Very true, Father." She met Lillias's wide eyes, and her throat constricted with another tickle. "Excuse me."

The sooner Tony and Lillias disappeared, the sooner she could get this secret out in the open. She loved her sister, but she couldn't avoid a group of thirtysome people in a house for much longer without confessing everything she knew.

Lillias was gone.

She'd left a letter and her trousseau, but somewhere in the early morning, she and Mr. Dixon must have disappeared into their future together. Grace closed the letter and stared out the bedroom window at the vast view of morning mountains on the horizon. Reality sobered her to the core, and her eyes fogged with a sheen of tears.

How did everything get so muddled? Her? A countess? Or even a wife?

What did *she* know of marriage? The slips of memories of her parents gave little to go on. Grace barely remembered her mother. Her portraits showed an extravagant beauty with the same unruly red hair as Grace.

Her father's recollections waxed with sweet sentimentality, and of course Grace enjoyed romanticizing it all, but her parents had *created* a romance together, not fallen into one. They'd married because of prestige and money, not moonlit walks and romantic prose.

Which gave Grace a great deal of hope.

Her mother came from the nouveau riche and her father excelled in the business world—a combination of affluence, the right connections, and two amiable personalities that turned into a true partnership. But having lost her mother so early, Grace couldn't recall what the actual everyday life of their marriage looked like. Had they teased one another? Held hands? Secluded themselves in the garden to kiss?

Had they discussed books or passionately argued? Doubtful, since her father rarely seemed to hold a strong conviction for long before acquiescing to the other party. And fiction wasn't any help at all in deciphering the quandary of married life, since most heroines appeared to be orphaned.

Her gaze flipped heavenward. *I certainly hope You know what You're doing—especially for the future of an entire English estate and generations to come.*

She pinched her eyes closed. Generations to come?

The clock struck ten. Lord Astley and her father had planned breakfasting together to discuss some of the final arrangements of the contract. It was the perfect time to face the inevitable.

With a quick prayer to add to the many she'd said through the night and a dash away of a single tear on her cheek, Grace took the grand staircase down to the Morning Room.

Once she stepped through the doorway, her future, her dreams would change forever.

She paused with a hand on the slender, curved door handle. Had Gaskell's Margaret felt this weight of decision when her future swirled into uncertain territory after her parents died and she was left to face the world alone? Without even the good thoughts of John Thornton to sustain her?

Grace's forward momentum faltered. She would leave everything she'd known to marry a man who didn't love her. Was she brave enough now as the moment hovered a threshold away? She firmed her shoulders and shook off her fear. She *had* to be brave enough. Her father needed her to be brave enough.

Besides, there were so many things to look forward to instead of regret. Regret seemed a terrible waste of mental energy with no real outcome besides a headache. Traveling abroad to a large, crumbling manor house in England. A sickly, reclusive mother keeping watch on her progeny. A mysterious, handsome young lord recently inheriting the responsibilities of his elder brother.

It all sounded very much like one of the novels Grace loved so well. She grinned despite the terrible storm in her stomach as she heard her father and Frederick's voices beyond the door.

With a deep breath, she pushed the door open and offered her broadest smile, pleased to see the room empty except for Lord Astley and her father. She'd considered several ways to broach the subject of her sister's elopement, pregnancy, and subsequent running away with her beloved, who had sabotaged Lord Astley's saddle, but what actually came out of her mouth was nothing like what she'd planned.

"You know, I heard the most curious news as I walked through the library the other day."

Her father placed his cup in the saucer with a clink. "Grace, what a way to enter a room, girl."

She forced down the fear tempting her to flee back up the stairs and instead fixed her full attention on Lord Astley, accepting her fate, as any good heroine should do. "It's quite life-changing news. Surprising, even." She cleared her throat and continued. "You do like surprises, don't you, Lord Astley?"

Lord Astley's subtle smile slipped slowly from his handsome face.

"Grace, child, what are you talking about?"

She swallowed through her dry throat and tilted her chin up. Might as well just say it outright. "I'm going to be an aunt." Her voice quavered. All right, that wasn't as direct as she'd planned. "Isn't that a fabulous surprise?"

Lord Astley stood, slowly, awareness dawning in his expression. Grace reached for the back of the nearest chair for support.

"I think your celebration is a bit premature, Grace." Father laughed. "Your sister isn't even married yet."

A painfully obvious truth. "I'm afraid it's going to be much sooner than any of us anticipated. . .and not with our dear Lord Astley."

Her father began to catch on, rising from his chair, but Grace couldn't take her eyes from the man most impacted by this news. "I'm so sorry, my lord. Her actions were not against you, though I'm certain it feels personal. She. . .she was frightened and—"

"Grace, you can't be serious." Father's voice penetrated her focus on Lord Astley's darkening expression, and she turned to him, his wide eyes frantically searching hers. "Bring Lillias to me at once so we can clear up this misunderstanding."

"She's gone, Father." Grace's heart ached from the pain creasing her father's face. The betrayal he felt. Oh, this was much more difficult than she'd imagined, and that was saying something. Her eyes burned, but she refused to give in to the tears. Someone needed to keep their head in the middle of this maddening moment. "She left a note."

"Dixon." Lord Astley didn't ask. He knew.

Grace should add *perceptive* to her quality husband list.

"Dixon? Anthony Dixon?" Her father took Grace by the shoulders. "The man's a banker."

"She loves him, Father. It seems she's loved him for a long time." Grace looked over her father's shoulder to Lord Astley. "And I couldn't bear the thought of her marrying you while carrying his child, so I confronted her—"

"She planned to carry on with the marriage?" His voice boomed across the room.

Oh dear. Grace shouldn't have disclosed so much. Now she'd damaged her sister's character even more. "Of course, she changed her mind once she saw reason. She'd never really want to hurt you."

"Only deceive me."

The entire conversation had turned out so much better in her head.

"How could she do this to us?" Father released Grace's shoulders and stumbled back, bent and shaken. "We're. . .we're ruined."

Lord Astley replaced him, a mountain of seething fury towering over her. "How long have you kept her secret?"

"Kept her secret?" Grace's bottom lip dropped. "I only discovered it two evenings ago, quite by accident."

"That's why you retired early," he murmured, eyes narrowed at her as if *she* was the sneaky one. "At dinner."

"I only kept the information to myself until she decided what she would do. If she'd planned to carry on with the engagement, I would have told Father immediately, but I'd hoped she'd do the right thing on her own."

"So she's left you to bear the brunt of her escape. How very magnanimous of her." His voice ground low and deep, as close to a growl as she'd ever heard from human lips. But no wonder. She had hit him with quite the blow.

He turned and prowled the length of the rug toward her father. "You know what this means, Mr. Ferguson. Your daughter forfeited the agreement. Per our contract, you have a sum to procure."

Her father withered into a chair, looking frail and ten years older.

"No one has forfeited the agreement."

Lord Astley spun around to face her. "I will not marry a woman who is carrying another man's child."

Grace failed to recoil. In fact, his grumpiness just fueled her determination. "You still have a Ferguson bride."

"How do you propose—" His jaw unhinged, and he studied her

from brow to toe, eyes widening. "You?"

"Me." She tilted her chin even higher, mostly because he stood so close. "The contract listed a daughter of Henry T. Ferguson to marry the honorable Lord Astley."

"No, you were not a part—"

"If you were willing to marry a stranger for money yesterday, how is today any different? The same stipulations apply." This part of the conversation in her head emerged beautifully. "The same exchange. *You* can choose to forfeit at your own cost, but Father's end of the bargain remains intact."

"You mean to take her place?" His scowl fell into a look of astonishment, which suited him much better. He backed away, shaking his head a few times before running a hand through his hair. "This is preposterous."

That was *not* what she'd heard him say in her head. She'd hoped he'd find her choice mesmerizingly attractive. Not preposterous. "That it may be, but it still fits within the constructs of the contract."

He blinked over at her, a look of complete bewilderment softening the angles of his face. "You. . .you can't want that."

"Sweet child," her father gasped.

"I'll be your wife." Speaking it aloud drove the decision deeper, even though she choked a little on the word *wife*, but maybe Lord Astley didn't notice. "I've considered my future and how this will benefit me, my family, and at some point, maybe even you." She offered a helpless shrug in the hopes he saw some of her virtues beneath her many vices. "I will not change my mind."

Lord Astley crossed the floor back to her, his eyes narrowed slits of pure skepticism. "You're certain you'll marry me, are you?"

She refused to cower from the fierceness radiating off him. "I am."

His dark gaze surveyed her, peering deep. Was he looking for her courage as much as she was? He'd have to search much longer because her knees were beginning to tremble. She braced against the fear with a silent prayer and an inner visual of Lizzie Bennet for backbone.

"But there's still a problem, Miss Ferguson." His expression softened a little. "I am not certain *I* will marry *you*."

# Chapter Eight

"Not certain?" Grace's eyes met his, unwavering, wounded. And the sight hit him like a blow to the stomach. "You'd risk losing your home instead of marrying me?"

"It's not about you. It's about this farce of a decision." He stepped back, distancing himself from the way her emotions set him off-balance, the way her choice affected him. "A deceptive bride is a worthy reason to flee from marriage."

Her gaze flared with a sudden fury. "You do not have a deceptive bride *now*."

She was sincere, if misdirected. Confident to a fault. He shook his head. How could he view her as a bride? She was practically a child! "You have no idea what you're saying."

"Then let me see if I have it right." She stepped closer, one ginger brow peaked high, the challenge in her eyes unyielding. "Do you, or do you not, still need money to save Havensbrooke and the Astley legacy?"

He squinted, the truth stinging afresh. "I do."

"And do you or do you not have an agreement to marry a *daughter* of Henry T. Ferguson, which states that if you refuse, you will have a sum of money to procure at your precious estate's expense?"

He almost growled. "I do."

Her other eyebrow edged up to join the first, proud of her interrogation. "And don't you think it makes logical sense for both parties to receive what they agreed upon without any wasted time or funds?"

"I do."

"See?" A faint light glimmered in her eyes as her pink lips slipped crooked. "You say those words quite well. Just in time for a wedding ceremony."

Her humor nearly derailed his annoyance. "You're young."

"I'm almost nineteen. On Christmas Eve, in fact."

"You were born on Christma—" He shook his head against the distraction, attempting to sort through this catastrophe. "And. . .and we barely know one another."

"How many more conversations could you really have had with my sister?" She waved toward him with her hand. "We have some similar interests, can participate in successful, if not even enjoyable, dialogue, and have working minds, even if one has thoughts that wander unchecked at times. I think we could be compatible, at least."

She was right on all accounts, so why was he fighting her? Lillias understood the world she entered. Grace? She had no idea. A house haunted by his brother's death. His mother's bitterness seeping through the halls like a poison. A crumbling manor house and an earl with a sullied past, not to mention centuries of aristocratic expectations. She didn't deserve to feel the brunt of what he knew. To have that joy stolen. There had to be another way. "Youth isn't always defined by age, but experience."

"Which you can give me. Unless you haven't the courage."

"Courage has nothing to do with it. I'm actually thinking of you. My life, my world, is not one to enter unprepared."

"And I'm thinking of you and your dear Havensbrooke." She brought her palms together and graced him with a pseudo-angelic smile. "How very generous we both are already! What an excellent start for matrimony."

He didn't know whether to laugh or scoff.

"Come now." She stepped forward, her expression pleading with him. "In all honesty, Lord Astley, just imagine how much worse you could have it."

Those eyes, as bright and distracting as her hair, challenged him. Indeed he could have it much worse. In fact, he nearly did. Her honesty and her courage humbled him. She had more strength than he'd realized.

"I believe you underestimate me a great deal. Loving fiction, having an overactive imagination, and skirting along the edge of propriety at times does not make me weak. In fact, I may be prepared for many things no one else is."

He squeezed his eyes closed for a second, then leveled her with a look. "We are two very different people."

"As most are." Her smile faded, and he immediately felt the loss. She lowered her gaze. "If you're worried about my lack of qualifications at elegance, then I could understand your hesitancy, though I am teachable and—"

"Grace." Her name slipped out so easily, too familiar. He waited for her gaze to meet his, and then his voice tempered to a whisper. "You shouldn't feel forced into this."

"I know what I'm agreeing to by my own will."

"No, you don't."

"Now you are questioning my intelligence as well as my maturity?" She placed her hands on her hips, her eyes narrowed into slits. He certainly preferred her ire over her hurt. "I may be young, Lord Astley, but I am neither dimwitted nor oblivious. Choosing not to focus on certain things does not mean I do not see them."

Her statement nearly derailed his train of thought again. Did she choose to see the good, even in the middle of this disaster? "Your compassion is admirable. Your zeal may be to your detriment in this case, however."

"*My* detriment!" Her posture shot pencil straight. "Stubborn man, you seem bound to lose an entire estate."

"Stubborn?" That was a bit of the pot calling the kettle.

She released a massive sigh and pinned on a glare just for his benefit. "No bride should have this much trouble convincing a groom to marry her."

He almost laughed out loud. The woman was maddening. "Within the past few minutes, I've learned that my previous bride planned to marry me as a ruse for her involvement with her longtime lover, and her younger sister has offered herself as a substitute to save her father's future." He sent a look to pale-faced Mr. Ferguson, by all accounts as surprised. No, this seemed a rash decision on Lillias Ferguson's part, which left the rest of the family piecing the situation together—especially Grace. "So I beg your pardon if I seem indecisive or abrupt."

His mind spun, unbalanced. He needed some distance and a level-headed conversation with Blake for perspective. "I will give an answer by this evening, and then we can make plans accordingly."

"I won't change my mind, if that's what you're worried about." Her brow tilted in challenge, her sapphire gaze following him as he moved toward the door. "Another one of my many vices, Lord Astley, but I've found reason for it to be a virtue as well. I'm terribly good at solving problems, and this"—she waved a hand between them—"doesn't have to become one."

He stared at her, unable to muster a reply. His need for justice warred with his desire for compassion. She'd never been a part of the plan, nor did she deserve such a fate. But Havensbrooke had to come first. The decision clawed a raw ache through his middle.

There really was no choice.

❦

Frederick found Blake in one of the three spots his cousin had occupied since arriving at Whitlock. The bowling alley. Blake's life was looking more and more appealing with each passing catastrophe. Perhaps they could switch places as easily as Grace had with her sister.

He groaned and slowed his pace as he entered the long corridor, the clash of ball and pins welcoming him. No, it couldn't have been an easy decision for her. What woman would wish for another woman's intended?

Blake took in the news with nothing more than a quizzical brow, even as Frederick divulged the entire affair to his friend, complete with the possible scandal in the papers when the bride's name changed.

"I really think you ought to add a bowling alley to your improvements of Havensbrooke, Freddie. A jolly good way to spend a rainy day, if you ask me."

Frederick pinched the bridge of his nose and released a long-suffering sigh. "Blake, have you heard one word I've said? My former fiancée has eloped with the father of her unborn child, and her younger and much less experienced sister has offered to take her place as the Countess of Astley." Frederick shoved a hand through his hair and paced from the scoreboard on the wall to the window on the opposite side. "When I told Lillias Ferguson to enjoy the remnants of her freedom, I had no idea she'd take my well wishes so liberally."

"Pass that ball, will you?" Blake gestured toward the bowling ball the servant brought forward, without one hint of concern. "It was certainly a poor choice on her part, though she didn't quite seem your type."

"What? Monogamous?" Frederick grabbed the heavy white ball and shoved it into Blake's stomach. "How can you take all of this so lightly? Everything has changed."

"Your circumstances, despite the shock, have not altered all that much." He rolled another ball toward the pins and took down all but one. "You will still gain a dowry and a bride."

"A child bride."

"As far as I can see, she has all the alluring female accoutrements of her sister." His grin quirked with his infernal shrug. "In what way a child?"

"Her. . .her exuberance and authenticity." Frederick groaned. "Her joy."

Blake leveled him with a frown. "It is a sad commentary, Freddie, that you only relate joy with the behavior of a child. Understandable from your parents' atrocious actions toward you, but sad all the same. I do not believe Miss Grace has suffered a similar childhood, which would likely be a benefit for you and your offspring."

Frederick's shoulders wilted with a groan. "A benefit?"

"Her exuberance, as you call it, makes her appear more youthful than she is, and the fact she was your former bride's younger sister secured that mental assertion, but a woman with such generosity and selflessness cannot be all bad." Blake's forehead creased. "And should I remind you that your sister was eighteen when she married?"

"My sister is an English woman raised in an earl's house. She grew up knowing the conventions and expectations. And that's beside the point. There are a million things Grace Ferguson doesn't begin to understand about being a countess."

"Is the woman smart? From my limited conversations with her, she appears intelligent. An amateur sleuth, as I recall."

Frederick growled as he rolled the ball down the lane and missed the entire lot of pins, Grace's repartee from only a half hour before still ringing with clarity and wit. "Yes, she is."

"Kind? Agreeable? Which, to my mind, are more important than knowing what dish to order for a dinner party." Blake made a solid strike. Frederick was starting to think the game was trying to make as much of a point as his cousin.

"She certainly appears so, though my judgment may—"

"Weren't there similar interests the two of you shared? Reading? Riding?"

"That is not the point."

"I don't understand your argument." Blake waved a palm in the air, as if the decision was simple. "If she is so young, then you have time to shape her into the lady you think she needs to be. I'm certain your mother will be more than willing to take her in hand."

Frederick cringed at the very idea of placing Grace at the mercy of his mother.

"No, wait, you're right. I like Miss Ferguson too much to send her into a home with your tyrant mother and the unsolved mystery of your brother's death lingering over the house like a cloud."

"Edward's death is not a mystery. The doctor said—"

"Come now, Freddie." Blake shook his head and took another ball. "Edward, the model of health, dies within the house on the very day you arrive back from India?"

"Of a heart attack."

Blake narrowed his eyes, unconvinced, the suspicion knocking like an unfinished story in the back of Frederick's mind.

"And your mother has no idea of ever writing a letter to request you return home? No wonder the whole town refers to it as the Astley curse."

Astley curse? His fist tightened at his side. Frederick could not contemplate another scandal. Not again. Even if Blake's doubts needled with unanswered questions. Salvaging his family's estate remained his first priority. "We are not speaking of my brother. We are speaking of Miss Ferguson and an impossible match."

"Impossible? How so? If the girl has no objections and you have no qualms about ushering her into the disaster which is your family, I don't see why this should change your mind about the arrangement at all. And let's not forget that she *chose* to take her sister's place, a decision that speaks a great deal to her character." He raised a brow before turning back to the task of besting Frederick at bowling. "Imagine that, Freddie. A woman of character on your side? Something you've never experienced, I should remind you."

Frederick squeezed the bowling ball between his hands.

Blake spoke truth, so why did the very idea of marrying Grace Ferguson leave him in a dither? He rolled the ball and knocked down six pins. What was he afraid of? Was he concerned she'd breach the wall around his heart, and he'd only disappoint her as he'd done everyone else?

"I know you're thinking of your mother's reaction."

*Not exactly.*

"But in all honesty, Freddie, you're the one marrying the girl. Shouldn't your primary concern be *your* ability to get on with her, not your mother's?" He took another ball and turned back to his friend. "She's made sport of managing people's affairs and done a poor job of it. This is *your* future. *Your* bride."

Frederick looked down at the ball. The weight of his own past when compared to Grace's genuine innocence pressed upon his shoulders like a heavy black cloak. "To be honest, Blake, I. . .I don't deserve someone like her. Not with the fool I've been. But for Grace Ferguson's convictions, I'd have walked directly into a deception very similar to what I left years ago."

Blake's blond brows rose. "But for Grace Ferguson?" He held Frederick's attention with a look to drive his point home. "It seems to me that Grace Ferguson is a providentially provided answer." He grinned. "I'll admit she's a bit odd, but some of the best people are, you know? Just think of Aunt Lavenia."

Frederick almost grinned. His aunt was certainly one of a kind.

"What if you took this whole situation for what it appears to be? A new beginning? If I'm not mistaken, you've been searching for such an opportunity for over two years now."

"Yes, but—"

"Then why are you suddenly surprised when the Almighty gives you what you asked? If I recall from what sermons I've attended to, God is known for lavishing love on His children. Grace, I believe it's called?" His brows winged high again. "Why not shower Him with thanksgiving and take the gift He's placed before you? I would hazard a guess that gratitude is never a bad start for any relationship."

Frederick stared at his friend, the truth sinking in. A new beginning? Could it be possible, right before him? He dared not believe it. "You're very smart for a single man with no responsibilities."

"Plenty of time to contemplate others' futures, I suppose."

Gratitude? Could this one choice set in motion a future to redeem his past? Frederick rolled the ball forward and produced the sharp crash of a strike. A tiny shaft of hope slipped beneath his fear. Could God really offer a solution for his heart and legacy? "I believe I've regained my focus, good man."

"I'm glad to see it." Blake nodded. "You're horrible company when you're pensive."

Frederick walked toward the doorway, a lighter step to his gait. "I hope you'll see less of it in the future."

If God was offering a new beginning, Frederick had every plan to take it—if the woman he'd rejected would still have him.

⚬≶⚬

Rejection left an unsavory flavor.

Grace had offered Lord Astley a solid proposition, yet he seemed less than interested in the proposal—or her. Was she really that horrible of an option? It was true that in light of Lillias's many attributes, Grace fell terribly short, but honesty and a dash of creative wit had to count for something in the grand scheme of things, didn't it? And she'd gotten much better at talking about dull things without yawning.

An uncommonly hollow feeling branched out through her chest and made her think of reading something morose like *Wuthering Heights*, but the haloed glow of sunset kept her from delving too severely into disappointment. The golden-orange hues deepened as the shadowed mountains cradled the sun's fading light. A smile warmed her face.

God always seemed to send a cheerful something at the most opportune times.

The chilly breeze from her position on the Whitlocks' back terrace brushed against her warm cheeks and offered a sweet caress. She embraced her solitude to tend her wounds, taking the opportunity to sneak away from the other guests, especially the unnerving eyes of her would-be fiancé. Or rather, "wouldn't be" fiancé.

He'd watched her during supper with that piercing gaze of his, an inscrutable expression on his face. What did he see when he looked at her? Likely anything but a countess.

Grace sighed and pressed her palms into the rough cement of the terrace wall. What had she done wrong? She'd witnessed a few of her father's business conversations—mostly from the safe distance of a crack in the door—and her offer to the reluctant earl held as many solid arguments as any of those. Even more than some.

Yet he'd refused her.

Though she wasn't as socially equipped as her sister, surely she came with a few virtues of her own. She couldn't really help her hair color, and she wouldn't apologize for her vigorous imagination—it had proven indispensable on many occasions. But she did come with a great deal of money, which seemed more important than her penchant for speaking before thinking and riding astride.

She held her shoulders a bit straighter. And she was quite pleased with her own eyes. They were like her mother's, a fact she clung to with gratitude. Her gaze lingered on the halo of gold still gripping daylight.

Perhaps Lord Astley's rejection was for the best. Being married for one's money instead of oneself couldn't be the best start to a lifelong romance.

She raised her eyes to the growing splattering of stars, vast and innumerable in the fading night. "Dear Lord, what do You want from me? I'll happily oblige, if You'll let me know. I understand asking for an overt sign feels rather faithless, but I'd be content with a shooting star or a voice from heaven or even a message scrawled on a wall as long as it didn't mar the beauty of Whitlock's marble walls. Something fairly obvious, if You please, because I'm quite a distractible creature, as You well know, and. . .I only want to do the right thing, whatever that right thing may be."

"Is talking to yourself one of your vices as well, Miss Ferguson?"

She spun around to find Lord Astley approaching from the Music Room doors, the lights framing his silhouette like a shadow from a dream.

"Actually, I do talk to myself quite often, but in this particular instance I was praying aloud, so unless you're one of the growing number of atheists in the world, you were interrupting a quite honest conversation for guidance."

"I'm acutely aware of my need for divine intervention, and I do hope the Almighty will forgive my interruption."

She couldn't make out his expression with the light behind him, so she turned back toward the horizon. A pleasant tingle skittered up her spine at his nearness in the dark. No, no. She shouldn't like his presence. He'd rejected her, even with her dowry, her ready smile, and her somewhat average beauty. "He's known for being slow to anger, from what I understand."

Lord Astley slipped up beside her, his amber scent not far enough behind to keep her from turning to breathe it in. Rebel senses. No man should smell good enough to eat, especially one who refused to marry quite marriageable ladies.

"Abounding in love too, I believe is the way of it."

She looked up at his profile, attempting to make out his approach. Was he trying to dismiss her gently? Reject her in a kind way on a lanterned terrace surrounded by mountains and starlight at Christmas? That was too cruel. Clearly, he'd been reading all the wrong books.

"Well, it's good someone is abounding in love." She clenched her hands in front of her and noted a few moonlit clouds passing in the darkening sky. "Generous hearted, willing to take the quite shameless overtures of a sweet young lady without dismissing her outright."

He chuckled. *Chuckled.* "You are simply the most unique woman I've ever met."

She glared at him, and his expression sobered.

"I'm sorry to have offended you, especially since you have also borne the burden of this broken situation. And I do mean unique in the most delightful of ways."

She sighed out her frustration. A heartfelt apology killed her anger every time. "I'm sorry for my sister's selfishness." Her gaze returned to the sunset, which had almost flickered into night, the weight of her sister's guilt, her thoughtless actions, swimming in the same heart pool as Grace's wounded pride. "After this horrible fiasco, it's no wonder you wish to end the entire arrangement. You expected a refined and elegant lady. Not me."

"No, I never expected you." His voice brewed over the night air, warm and enticing.

Oh, the comparison between her and her sister was too awful to imagine. Poor Lord Astley. No wonder he'd rejected her. "And instead of the excellent conversationalist that my sister is, you're offered someone who rattles off about the silliest things and has a tendency to talk to fictional persons."

"Grace." There was a smile in his voice when he said her name, and the sweetness of the sound almost distracted her from her defense *against* herself.

"And you're right, I'm not the best candidate to be an earl's wife. In fact, I'm probably the worst option as a whole." She sighed forward, the case against her building to mind-numbing proportions. "What does an earl need with a bookish chatterbox who rides astride when no one is looking?"

"Grace." He took a step closer, and she turned to him, tilting her head to make out some of his features.

"But I feel certain I can learn to be the wife you need." She shrugged and pinned on a smile. "There have to be books about it somewhere."

With a gentle move, he gathered one of her hands into his warm ones, drawing her close enough to wrap her breath in delicious amber. "You forget, I've never been a husband before. We both may need to locate the proper books."

"Well, you have an enormous library, I'm sure—" What had he said? Her attention shot to his. "What did you say?"

"Miss Gracelyn Ferguson, will you do me the honor of becoming my wife?" His gaze, as black as the night, stroked her face with an expression she couldn't decipher but very nearly brought her to tears.

A lantern-lit terrace probably helped matters a little.

"Oh, it sounds very different when you say it." The words slipped out, her breath lodged around any reply. The tenderness of the request housed in such a baritone blend swept any response clear from her head. She kept staring, replaying the lingering sound of his voice in her mind. Amber and that voice? A cello in a fragrant wood.

Proposals were very romantic things when done properly.

"This is the part where you give me an answer, Grace."

"Oh," she laughed, and her cheeks bloomed with enough heat to make her eyes water. "An answer." She looked down at their hands, braided together in the night as if. . .as if they belonged. Could he learn to love her for more than money? Even if he didn't, holding hands with a man who smelled of amber, looked like a dashing villain, and kissed like a rogue couldn't be the worst of futures. "Yes, I'll marry you."

She felt his devastating smile all the way to her heart.

"But remember, I've been sure to list off my many vices, so whatever awaits us, prepare yourself for the need of a great deal of fortitude."

He raised his brows and squeezed her fingers, his expression creasing with a little uncertainty. "I'm looking forward to the journey."

The man was delusional, and the very thought made her like him even more. Perfect and dashing caused too much intimidation, but delusional and dashing? She could fit into a world with a man like that—maybe—if she could just figure out what exactly a countess was supposed to do.

# Chapter Nine

Her father had wept when he learned of the engagement.

Wept and apologized while holding her within an embrace Grace had known her whole life. It had all seemed rather lovely last evening on the terrace, but now, in daylight? The truth settled with finality over her heart. All the plans she'd made for her future, all her daydreams, plummeted into a monotony of social expectations and fashionable conversations. What about her own adventures? Her passion for becoming a daring heroine in possible life-threatening situations?

She wiped a hand over her damp cheeks and dropped down at her bedroom window seat to rest her forehead against the cold pane. The horizon of mountains and sky beckoned her heart to trust in One who weaved the patterns of life and death and adventures and romances together in the tapestry of eternity. Would He work this decision out for good? He knew she had done it all for the right reasons.

She breathed out a long breath and sat up. She'd made her decision, and crying didn't help. But the ache reverberating through her chest found no other release except through her eyes. *God, help me.*

"I see reality is settling in, my dear." Grace looked up to find Mrs. Whitlock entering the room, her salt-and-pepper hair pulled back in a becoming way.

The illustrious mistress of the manor offered a gentle smile and took a seat beside Grace. The Whitlocks had been one of the few in the wedding party who'd learned the whole truth of Lillias's situation. Otherwise, the simple narrative had been shared that Frederick's affections had transferred to the younger Ferguson daughter and an amiable transition had taken place for the wedding. It had sounded so simple and, in many ways, true. Lord Astley desired a wife who didn't already belong body and soul to someone else, but the lingering awareness that love was nowhere in the decision weighed upon Grace.

She wiped her face with the back of her hand and then groaned at forgetting to use her handkerchief *like a lady*. "I don't know if I can do this."

Mrs. Whitlock tipped her chin in a thoughtful manner. "And why do you suppose you can't?"

Grace stared at the dear woman as if she'd lost her mind. "I know little about what life is like as an earl's wife. I'm not worldly and elegant and witty. What if I ruin his entire legacy?"

"I have known you your whole life, Grace." Mrs. Whitlock chuckled. "And I don't believe you have the ability to bring down the entire Percy family."

Grace sighed with a sudden sense of relief. If Mrs. Whitlock said so, it had to be true. She'd been raised among the aristocracy.

"You don't recognize it, my dear"—she took Grace's hand, her smile kind—"but you already possess the tools within you not only to survive but to thrive in this choice, perhaps even more so than your sister."

Mrs. Whitlock spoke with such confidence that there had to be a semblance of truth somewhere in her optimistic ravings, and Grace adored optimism in any form.

"How can that be? Lillias had training to *become* a countess. I can't even remember which fork to use at dinner."

"My dear Grace." Mrs. Whitlock's gentle countenance smoothed away even more of Grace's worry. "Embrace his world as your own, and in doing so, you will find your place."

"What do you mean?"

"Despite your misgivings, you make a fine match. Your optimism suits his reserve. His thoughtfulness compliments your action. The pairing is far from hopeless." Her brow rose. "But as is true of any marriage, you will have to work for your happily-ever-after. Noblemen carry a burden far beyond themselves, so to win his favor, you must learn to love his land, his home."

"Havensbrooke?"

"He shoulders the weight of generations. It is a heavy burden, so if you support him—love his world as freely and fully as you love so many other things—he will respond to you." Her smile softened. "With as full a heart, if I am any judge of men."

"So by caring for Havensbrooke, I could nurture a friendship with Lord Astley?"

"I have every faith you'll nurture much more than friendship." She raised a finger in warning. "But it's no easy feat, my dear. You will be faced with trials from a dowager mother who, by all accounts, is not even-tempered and has had her way with the place for years now. The servants may be rigid in their ability to see you as their mistress, and Lord Astley will feel the pull of conventions and expectations of his rank and station. His world will be very different than yours. But you are strong, brave, and filled with imagination. Remember who you are and what you believe. You were *made* for this moment, Grace."

Mrs. Whitlock's smile offered such tender encouragement that Grace almost started crying again. The woman had witnessed Grace's childish misadventures and triumphs and had watched her grow into the distracted, whimsical young lady she'd become. And being from England herself, Mrs. Whitlock brought a unique view into a world Grace had only glimpsed through the pages of books. Could dear Mrs. Whitlock be right?

Despite a tremor in her chest, Grace smiled. If God chose her for this task and knew she stepped into it with all the best intentions, wouldn't He also provide everything she needed to fulfill it?

"You've never been the pampered, indulgent sort. And you have an amenable and adaptable demeanor, which will prove indispensable to your and Lord Astley's happiness. So many of the less successful American brides in the past failed to reach beyond their differences and disappointments or failed to employ their imaginations to assist them in the transition from our world to Britain. Continue in your kindness, even when it's not returned. Sprinkle your very special type of joy on the shadowed parts of his world, and you will glean more than I think even *you* can imagine, my dear girl."

Grace wiped away the remnants of tears from her cheeks and sat a little taller at the compliment. Why, if what Mrs. Whitlock said was true, Grace had plenty of resources from which to draw at least an adequate amount of courage. "More than *I* can imagine? It sounds like an adventure worth the risks."

"Indeed it does." Mrs. Whitlock squeezed Grace's hand and offered a smile that somehow held power enough to evoke a great deal of confidence. "You hold to the same faith as I, but even more than that, your Creator holds to you. No matter where you go or what the expectations are, you are not alone. Remember who you are, and you will not only survive, but you will flourish."

With the flurry of transition in plans and only one day until a wedding, Grace had few opportunities to spend time with Lord Astley more than meals and one turn around the garden with a party of six. He'd remained polite and pleasant enough, keeping his conversation well-honed except for a rather stimulating discussion about their mutual pleasure in reading *The Mystery of Innisworth*—he'd liked it as much as her, by all accounts— and an enthralling discussion about Havensbrooke and his desire to restore it. Mrs. Whitlock's words settled deeper into Grace's spirit. *Love his world and win his heart.*

Oh, to win her husband's heart! Wouldn't that be a lovely adventure?

Grace was just contemplating those words on her way to the Music Room for a final evening of conversations and games, when someone grabbed her hand and pulled her into the shadows of the Mahogany Room. Strong arms wrapped around her to keep her from stumbling, and the sudden scent of amber hinted of the identity of her assailant.

"I apologize for startling you." Lord Astley's deep voice pearled a delicious warmth around her as inviting as his scent. "But it is nearly impossible to find some privacy in this house, and I mean to speak with you before tomorrow."

She looked up from the cocoon of his arms, his face half hidden in shadow. "Our sudden transfer of affections for one another has caused quite a stir."

"Yes, that." His grin tipped. "I'm afraid it was Blake's idea to circumvent a scandal."

"I doubt anyone who really knows Lillias or me believes it." She shook her head, slipping back a step from him. "The very notion that you would choose me over Lillias is beyond imagination, Lord Astley, and I am a great proponent of imagination."

"Frederick," his voice swooped low in a tingle-down-her-neck sort of way. Oh, was this marvelous response attraction? She liked it a great deal. Very magical. "In private you may call me Frederick."

Frederick? It sounded lovely in her head. She worked the syllables over her tongue as amber shrouded her in a tantalizing hue. "Frederick. . .is a very nice name."

"I believe Grace is nicer." His gaze softened, watching her in a most curious way. What was he thinking? Did he find her pretty doused in moonlight? It probably gave her hair a much less fiery glow.

"You don't seem quite so aloof when we are alone." She swallowed against the sudden knot in her throat at his nearness. "Not that we've been alone a great deal, but the few times we have, you've been more. . .approachable."

"I want you to feel as though you may always approach me."

The quiet room paired with his nearness left her uncharacteristically speechless. She was marrying him in the morning. Surely she could usher up something to say, especially since he was encouraging her freedom to speak and all of that. Her throat tightened around another whiff of amber.

"Mrs. Whitlock said that you've been poring over architecture books in your leisure hours the past two days."

"Oh yes! In one of our earlier conversations you had mentioned that you'd welcome my help with Havensbrooke's improvements."

"Indeed I would." He studied her, his face unreadable in the dark, but then he wrapped his hand around hers and led her to a nearby couch, settling beside her. "My grandmother was an integral part of the estate business with my grandfather." He had positioned himself so that the firelight played across his strong, angled features and his eyes glowed amber gold. "I should like a similar partnership between us. Something, if you'll forgive me, your sister would not have offered, I don't believe. But I hope, perhaps, we can find such an alliance."

Was he complimenting her? Even over Lillias? No one had ever done that except her grandfather. She'd flattered herself that she was her grandfather's favorite, if favorites were to be had, but he was a bit of a troublemaker too. "I find the entire thought of reworking a house or designing gardens enthralling, like an adventure of sorts. A puzzle to be solved, you know? There are quite a few innovations related to hydraulic-powered fountains. Have you heard of them?"

A shock of a laugh burst from him. "You do fix yourself to something quite passionately, don't you?"

She looked down at her lap, fidgeting with her gloves as a swell of heat rose up her neck. "Another vice to add to the list, I'm afraid."

"Or virtue?"

Yes, he did keep growing handsomer, especially when he spoke sweetly. Amazing how kind words could impact one's appearance. "Please hold to that interpretation as long as you can. Then perhaps I won't become such a nuisance."

He chuckled, a warm sound that awakened wonderful tingles across her shoulders. "I can be rather gruff at times, and Havensbrooke hasn't afforded many happy memories for me, I'm afraid, but I'll endeavor not to bring such shadows into your life, if I can."

She studied his profile. He carried a heaviness she could almost see. She had the greatest urge to cover his hand with her own. It waited on the cushion between them. Was it proper for a fiancée to take such liberties? She had no idea! She sighed. This attraction and marriage business was mentally taxing. "I can become cross when I'm stuck indoors for too long."

His grin crooked. "Is that so?"

She traced a finger along the cushion nearest his hand, trying to work up the courage to touch him. He had such nice hands. Strong with long fingers. "My father used to call me his fairy child because I was drawn to nature like a creature of the forest." Her attention came back to his face, searching his unreadable expression. "But I will try my best to learn what I must for Havensbrooke. . .and for you. I do so want you to like me for more than my money."

His smile flashed for a second before he quelled it. "And I should hope you'll like me for more than my title."

"I don't know a great deal about titles, so you're already at an advantage."

He turned toward her, close, studying her face with such intensity she thought. . .maybe. . .he'd kiss her again. If she was prepared this time, she'd do a much better job of responding in kind. She'd imagined a second chance over and over and felt certain she'd sorted out where her hands should go.

"Grace." Her name radiated across the inches between them, somehow touching her pulse. How had her simple name suddenly taken on feeling? "I want this marriage to be more than an exchange of money and titles. We've both been thrust into positions we were never meant to fill, and I don't take your choice lightly."

She stared at the bowed head of this dashing man and, paired with little glimpses and phrases he'd mentioned of a childhood much less happy than her own, some untouched part of her heart opened to him. What would it be like to really feel loved by him? And to love him in return? If she looked close, beyond the grand earl and all of those connections, she had the slightest inclination Frederick Percy was in as much search of happiness as she. With a timid hand, she slid her fingers across the cushion to wrap around his.

His gaze shot to hers, the faintest hint of a smile touching his eyes, and without breaking his focus on her face, he turned his hand to envelop hers. Sparks erupted in her chest at the warm touch of his skin against hers.

"I'm certain it will take all of my money to match your forbearance, but I assure you, when I stumble it will be from the very best intentions to do right by you." His thumb moved across her knuckles, and she nearly forgot what she was saying. "I. . .fumble often but almost always from good intentions."

"Almost?" His dark brow rose, his question a mere whisper.

"I have red hair." She unleashed her smile. "You can't expect me to have perfect intentions all of the time."

His grin flashed as if he wanted to laugh, and then a tenderness fell over his features, somehow drawing her closer to him. Or was he moving toward her?

His fingers tightened around hers, and he brushed a palm against her cheek. Air whooshed from her lips at the unexpected touch. With a trembling breath, she copied his movement, pressing her hand against his face, the angle of his strong jaw fitted inside her palm. In an achingly slow approach, his mouth found hers. Gentle, a whisper of a touch, but it shook through her, pooling a warmth in her chest and dispersing it in waves through her body. His free palm slid to curl around the back of her neck, his thumb grazing her ear. Nothing in any novel ever described such a delicacy as this. A sudden sense of belonging washed through her.

Oh heavens! If this was a foretaste of marriage to Frederick Percy, then bring on the wedding bells.

He pulled back, and she blinked open her eyes, a surprising sheen of tears invading her vision of his face. "Thank you, Lord Astley."

His breath quivered slightly, as his palm slipped over her cheek. "And to what do I owe your gratitude?"

"For that lovely kiss."

"I've kissed you before, if you remember." He studied her, his thumb trailing to her chin, brow raised. "And more thoroughly."

"But this time you knew who you were kissing and continued to do so anyway."

His lips tipped ever so slightly, and he gave her hand another squeeze. "My dear Grace, it seems that my mistaken kiss wasn't so mistaken after all."

# Chapter Ten

"This isn't like showing up late at Lord & Taylor for a fitting, Grace." Her father's face flared red above his tight, fitted shirt collar as he ushered her into the Model T with a huff. "It's your own wedding! And to an earl!"

She cringed at the accusation in his voice and nodded to Ellie, her lady's maid, as the rosy-cheeked woman pushed a warm cloth into Grace's hand and disappeared to take her place in the following carriage. "Not too late. Only a little. I had no idea there were so many plant varieties in the Peak District of England, Father, or I never would have started the conversation with Mr. Leeds to begin with."

"You know better, Grace. The Whitlocks' gardener is many things, but succinct is not one of them, and hours before your wedding? Most women wouldn't even have left their rooms. What time did you descend into the gardens to find him? Eight o'clock?"

She took the cloth and scrubbed at the remaining dirt beneath her fingers that a quick bath hadn't removed. "Or seven."

"Seven? Good grief, girl. You are about to become a countess. You cannot keep flittering about like a country schoolgirl." His eyes nearly bulged. "Don't you understand? You will become Countess of Astley this very day. You must at least *attempt* to be a lady."

Grace sat up straighter and pushed back the nuisance of a veil as it kept tangling against her attempts to clean her hands. "Mr. Leeds is from Derbyshire, Father."

Surely that would help him understand, but he only stared at her with eyes growing increasingly wider.

"He's from the same area as Lord Astley." She spoke more slowly to help with comprehension, since her father appeared bewildered beyond intelligent conversation. "So of course I had to try and talk to him about gardens, and this morning was my last chance."

Father groaned back against the leather seat, his head in his hands. If Lord Astley wanted her insights for Havensbrooke—and if loving his land led to his heart—then Grace very well planned to douse the poor man with ideas, and she had to start somewhere.

With a sigh, she moved to Father's side, twining her arm through his and settling close. The dress gleamed in white satin decorated with a beautiful lace inset at the knee to the floor. A matching sash cinched Grace's waist, pinned in by Ellie's expert handiwork to fit a very different bride than intended.

She fought against the resurrection of doubt knotting her stomach, her father's words tightening the pinch. How much would she have to change to "become" the grand Lady Astley? If looks transformed anyone, perhaps she could play the part. Grace had barely recognized herself in the mirror before leaving her room. Ellie had set her hair in a pompadour-style bun, very much the Gibson girl, leaving a few extra strands of auburn curls unfastened around her face. An immaculately embroidered veil framed her from head to toe. Oh, she'd looked lost among the fabric and expectations of this day.

But God would give her strength. He promised.

Grace closed her eyes to memorize the feel of her father's warmth at her side, the sweet smell of cigar. As driven and gregarious as he was, leaving for months to undertake another grand and glorious business venture, he'd always surrounded her with such happy love and many times had indulged her unconventional whims. Even now his fit of frustration smoldered with more smoke than fire.

And they weren't going to be terribly late. Brooks, the chauffeur, took remarkable liberties at the wheel of the car to make up any lost time.

"You know I shall write you so many letters you won't feel I'm gone at all."

He nodded, casting her a glance, his lips pressed so tight his chin puckered. Her heart broke at the sight, and she ignored every rule about disrupting her veil or the orange-blossom wreath wrapped around her head, and lowered her cheek to her father's broad shoulder. "I love you, Father."

He sniffled and continued to nod, placing his hand over hers against his arm. "You've always been such a good girl. Such a joy."

She squeezed in close to him, offering him a smile despite the rush of tears to her eyes. "It's much more polite to agree with someone else's assessment than admit it oneself, you know."

His smile held a ghost of some unvoiced grievance, "My girls will be looked after. No father could wish for anything more."

"Of course we will." She patted his arm.

He reached over and touched her face, pressing the veil into her cheek with a gentle brush. "I've never wanted to change your eccentric ways. You've always been authentically. . .you. So much like your mother, and I'm proud of you."

⌦

Frederick stood in complete control before the small crowd of strangers at St. Michael's Episcopal Church. Poised on one of the large steps of the altar, he waited through yet another classical interlude from the organ, Blake at his side.

He refused to look at his watch, though he could tell by some of the glances among the guests that something wasn't right. He'd set his mind to this choice, even convinced himself after last night that Grace Ferguson could very well be someone with whom he might share his heart as well as his future. But now? Was she nothing more than another woman to choose something or someone else besides him?

He cast a look to Blake, who only raised a brow.

Suddenly a hush fell over the room and the organ music shifted to the bridal march. Frederick released his clenched breath and turned. The crowd stood, and everything faded into the periphery. Walking toward him down the long aisle came Mr. Ferguson and Grace, his bride. Despite his expert attempts at training his expression, his chest squeezed.

Grace Ferguson looked radiant. Those glowing eyes—the hope wafting off her like a perfume—doused his tainted views of love and tempted to resurrect the romantic he'd once been.

He couldn't look away from her. He didn't *want* to look away.

He welcomed her forward with a smile inspired by much more than a business agreement, the hallowed place stamping his intentions with an even truer understanding. This *was* his second chance—his second chance to restore a hope buried beneath bitterness and grief. A second chance to discover what true love was. He'd misconstrued romance in his mind with the paltry deception of Celia Blackmore and the shallow attempts afterward to assuage his physical needs. But here? Now? Did he really have the opportunity for a fresh and beautiful start?

He didn't deserve this. . .grace. His stifled chuckle almost shook out like a sob. *Grace.* No, the more he learned about her, the more he felt quite certain he didn't deserve her. Her gaze sought his, timid, trusting. How long would it take him to sort out the color of those eyes? Sometimes dark blue, sometimes gray blue. He studied her. Such a child in a woman's body. So untouched by the darkness of his past and present. A deep surge of protection rose within him. He hadn't been able to shield his own innocent heart, but he could attempt to protect hers.

He offered his hand. With a slight hitch in her breath, she released her hold on her father's arm and slid her fingers into his, the simple action securing an internal determination. He would endeavor to give her the romance she craved, even if it meant fighting past his own demons, his mother's indifference, and the expectations of society to do so, and if love followed for them, then they'd win their fairy tale too.

Married nightclothes were very different from unmarried nightclothes.

Grace tugged the silky robe more tightly around the equally smooth gown beneath, feeling both uncomfortable and exhilarated at the touch of satin against her bare skin. In fact, the two words—uncomfortable and exhilarated—summed up the last twelve hours to perfection. A reception filled with well-wishers who attempted to sort out the "scandal" of Lord Astley's Ferguson bride, a teary goodbye at the station, a few stops along the way to tour a town here or there, and finally sharing a "room" with her. . .husband.

Her husband? What a thought!

Lord Astley—Frederick—had been the very model of an attentive groom, especially with all the guests swarming in to, as Mrs. Whitlock whispered, ascertain whether the rumors of transferred affections were true. With a touch of her hand here and a gentle smile there, Grace was inclined to believe the rumors too.

Though she knew the truth. Love rarely happened so quickly in real life, and she felt fairly certain she didn't love Lord Astley quite yet. She hadn't felt like swooning once, and she wasn't even certain what *pining* looked like.

Lord Astley sat up in bed, book in hand, without looking Grace's way, so she slipped into the berth directly across from his, separated by an aisle and a curtain, if she chose. Their conversation during dinner consisted of books and Grace's limited traveling experiences. Of course, she'd been on trains, but despite her sister's extensive travels, Grace had never gone across the ocean. She'd chosen to stay behind to care for her aging grandfather when her father and Lillias traveled, a delight that easily overshadowed any regret.

She pulled out her own set of books, one on Italian gardening and one of D. H. Lawrence's newest, called *Sons and Lovers*. It was a fascinatingly sad book, which seemed particularly interesting in her current situation. Lover? Clearly, from some of the books she'd read, *lover* meant a wealth of heated kisses, sometimes in a bedroom and other times. . .various other places, but further than that her imagination drew a blank.

She couldn't think of anything quite as lovely as spending an evening kissing Frederick, just to experiment some more. Did a kiss always bring about a swell of warmth in her stomach? A rise in her pulse? How many ways could one kiss, because she'd already experienced two very different ones. She bit back a grin. She dearly loved the mystery of it all.

Frederick didn't look up.

"What are you reading?"

He raised a brow but kept his gaze on the book. "Mrs. Whitlock allowed me to borrow *The Riddle of the Sands*."

Ah! Her suggestion. "Do you like it?"

"Yes, it's quite engaging."

Of course. That's why he kept staring at the book instead of looking at her.

She regarded her own pages but couldn't focus on any of the words. Very odd. She arranged her blankets around her, flipped through a few of the drawings in the gardening book, and then looked back over at Frederick. "Do you feel different?"

This brought his gaze to hers. "Different?"

He quickly moved his focus back to his book. Peculiar. She touched a hand to her loose hair. Did having all her hair down and wild about her shoulders shock him? Where was that beautifully endearing look he'd given her during the wedding ceremony? Perhaps it had only been a look of admiration at Lillias's gown. She gasped. Or a part he played for the crowd? Oh! That didn't sound loving at all.

She pushed away the thought. Certainly her hair was the culprit. "Now that we're *married*." She exaggerated the word, still a bit in awe at the whole notion. "Apart from having more alone conversations with you, I don't know that I feel different."

"I'm certain the feelings will come with time and. . .familiarity."

She smoothed out her blankets again, fluffed her pillow, and sighed. Why did something seem very wrong? Maybe he *had* been pretending all along. "May I ask you a question?"

He closed his eyes and grinned before looking over at her, his gaze trained on her face. "Yes, Grace."

"I'm sorry to keep interrupting your reading. I can tell you are very interested in your book."

"Not really." He narrowed his gaze as if pondering his response. "I've read the same sentence five times since you entered the room."

Well, that didn't sound like pretending. "Because I keep interrupting you?"

"Not exactly."

"Oh." She studied him. "Why?"

He sighed and placed his book down on his lap, turning to face her as much as their beds allowed. "To be perfectly candid, Grace, you are a very beautiful woman *and* you happen to be my wife. We have a future to build together, and sometimes these close quarters can make it. . .challenging."

Her smile faded. Oh dear, he didn't like her at all. "I talk too much, I know. I even talk in my sleep, but I'll try to leave you alone so these close quarters won't be unbeara—"

"Grace." He shook his head, his lips quirking into a smile that made her have kissing thoughts all over again. "The challenge is not your talking."

"It's my fidgeting, isn't it!" She sighed into a pout. "My chattering away, my distractibility, and my fidgeting. What a horrendous trinity of errors for an earl to have in a wife. Father tried to warn me that grand ladies do not—

"Grace." He held up a palm to still another excuse. His lips twitched, and then he swallowed so hard she heard it.

Look how difficult it was for him even to find the words to describe her exorbitant number of shortcomings! Poor Frederick needed much more than a Dickens Christmas miracle. He needed a fairy godmother!

"Though there are certain characteristics of an aristocratic lady that you'll learn in time, some of which you've mentioned, I was particularly referencing the fact that. . .well, simply put. . ." His pallor flushed with a red hue as he averted his gaze and waved a hand toward her. "Seeing you in your nightgown makes me wish to pull you into my bed and do. . .more than kissing."

"More than kissing?" Her eyes widened. "Better than kissing?"

"God help me." He cleared his throat. "The combination of kissing and the more make what I have in mind quite pleasant."

What an utterly fascinating idea! Sleeping in his bed? She'd slept alongside her sister before, especially during storms, but what would it feel like to share a bed with him? "I enjoy time with you, especially the kissing parts. I think I can manage whatever. . .togetherness you have in mind."

His jaw tightened. "Do you really have no idea of the intimate workings of a husband and wife?"

"Well, I know about the kissing and an occasional loss of clothing, but Lillias told me she'd share more when I became engaged."

"I see." He released another sigh.

She really was a troublesome creature, and the poor man had married her. Was he regretting it all now?

"There is more to it, but it is an intimate affair that requires, in the best cases, the mutual readiness of each party, especially if the pair wish to engage in such affections on a frequent basis."

She certainly wanted to engage in his kisses on a frequent basis. She stared at him for the longest time, trying to sort out why his entire body looked as stiff as sitting in a pew on Sunday.

"So we need to become better acquainted before we engage in such intimate affections?"

"Yes, that's it." His voice firmed as if he'd come to some sort of decision. "Exactly."

She studied him again, at a complete loss to his meaning. "Do you think it will take a long time for us to become that acquainted?"

He closed his eyes, leaned his head back against his pillows, and groaned. "Heaven help me, I hope not."

# Chapter Eleven

Grace was created for travel, even if she responded with a bit more exuberance than most of the other first-class travelers were used to seeing.

And though Frederick should likely rein in a little of her enthusiasm before they met with his mother, something in the way she filled every corner of his shadowed heart with a new perspective on. . .well, everything, paused his attempts. The world took on a ruddy glow through her eyes, and his life of loneliness came alive with colors and beauty and hope.

*Hope.*

Was this what marriage would be like to her? He couldn't even fathom it.

Of course Frederick had never been married, but he'd engaged in enough relationships to place him among the persons of interest to gossips in town. Yet this was wholly different. Whether from his own repentance from a life of recklessness in trying to sate a thirst or drown a curse or make amends for past wrongs, this connection with Grace, married and free, changed everything.

He'd watched her sleep across from him for five nights, and he wanted to span the distance between their two berths, gather her up in his arms, and discover if every part of her was as beautiful and vibrant as those eyes.

But she deserved the wooing process, the chance for affection to build toward an intimate encounter to which she was unprepared. With whom better to aspire for a fairy tale than one's own wife?

"I've never been surrounded by the sea until now, and I've always wanted to know what it would feel like since my grandfather's favorite hymn was one that mentioned God's love being as vast as the ocean." She sighed as if the thought ushered a tender memory. "Viewing all these gray and blue waves from the shore is different than being surrounded by them."

"Yes, quite different."

"Grandfather said God's love is like that. Fathoms and fathoms surrounding us so we can never escape it." Her arms stretched out as if to capture the sea. "To be loved like that must make a great deal of difference in the way we live, mustn't it?"

"Indeed." He stared out at the roiling waves dancing to the edge of the sky. Fathoms of love? Apart from his grandparents, love—if one could call it love at all—had been doled out by teaspoons, but God's love? His throat constricted, memories hammering through opened flood-gates of his mind. Grace's sentiments echoed hints of his grandmother's wisdom and called to a deep place in his heart that he'd stuffed beneath his hurt and frantic search for approval—for the love his mother refused to share and the perfection his father expected. He cleared his throat and ushered up a teasing grin. "Is this the same grandfather who taught you how to swim, ride a bicycle, and climb trees?"

"Yes, that one. He was incredibly devout, but he didn't let that impede his living life fully. In fact, his faith likely fueled a bit of his adventure because he believed God was the maker of creativity and wonder, who created life as a grand journey." She leaned back against the railing, her fiery hair blowing around her in ringlets.

His throat tightened. "My. . .my grandmother would have liked you."

She offered a wrinkle-nosed grin, completely unaware of the impact of her simple declaration. "My grandfather would have liked you. I'm sure of it."

He cleared his throat and offered his arm to her. "And why is that?"

"Because you are kind, and grandfather always told me to marry a man with a kind heart." They walked ahead on the promenade, the sea breeze blowing her scent of mint and rosemary around him. His fingers itched to capture the fiery tresses, to know their texture against his skin. They'd certainly become more comfortable with sharing space and hold-ing hands. Would she allow him the freedom of unraveling her hair?

"I'm glad you see kindness in me, Grace." He tipped his head to her. "Because I am certain you will hear different accounts when we reach Havensbrooke."

"Well, you may not have been armed with kindness in the past, but you have it now, and now is all we have anyway." She brushed a strand of hair from her eyes. "Grandfather would say, 'Kindness is your most valiant weapon. People may fight against many things, but against kindness, they fall unprepared.'" Her gaze held his, and she blinked. "But of course you have other delightful attributes, like being clever and charming." She leaned nearer, her brows raised. "And excellent company."

Her generous compliments widened his grin even more. She was much too easy to find endearing. "I must say the company has been my favorite part of the last five days. You're much better to look at than Blake and not nearly as annoying."

"What a mercy anyhow. At least *someone* is more annoying than me." She released a light laugh, continuing their walk. "But I do wonder how I might improve in my refinement. I feel certain there are probably so many suggestions you have it's difficult to narrow them down, but perhaps you could begin with a digestible three?"

It took him a full five seconds to catch up with her topic change. "Three?"

"Oh dear." Her lower lip pouted in a most distracting way as she looked up at him. "There are too many to number, aren't there? Perhaps you should just start with one."

"Right now, I only wish for you to enjoy your first transatlantic crossing."

She studied him through narrowed eyes and then turned back to the view. "Do you think I shocked Mr. and Mrs. Stein at lunch this afternoon with my thrill over the way the sunlight glowed off the ceiling in the dining salon? I didn't think her brows could rise any higher."

"Once the shock subsided, I do believe they found you quite charming."

"I hope I eventually learn how to be quite charming without shocking people senseless first."

He barely stifled his laugh.

"I do wish you'd laugh," she said as they resumed their walk. "I imagine it sounds as intoxicating as your voice."

He leaned his lips near her ear. "You find my voice intoxicating?"

"Oh." Her breath hitched and his skin heated. "One word and I'm nearly melting to the floor. Imagine how useless I'd be if you put effort into seducing me."

"My dear Lady Astley, I might terrify you if I unfurled my powers of seduction."

Her eyes widened, pulling him back to a stop. "You mean you *want* to seduce me?"

The way the woman was unaware of her own attractiveness was maddening! From the curve of her jawline to her ready humor to the tenderness in her touch. Seduce her? He wanted much more than that. "Most certainly."

"Oh, I'm so glad to hear it. I've never been seduced before." He nearly coughed his surprise at her ready response. "Why do you wait? Is it because my unladylike ways have horrified the kissing notions right out of your head?"

"That may be impossible." He drew in a deep breath and placed his palm over her hand resting on his arm, attempting to turn his wayward intentions back to cold, calm patience. He stopped their walk by the railing and glanced out to sea, his brow furrowed. "My parents did not share a friendship, let alone a—what would you say—lifelong romance?"

Her grin rewarded him.

"I should like more for us."

"I think we have excellent potential for friendship, don't you?" She looked back out at the ocean, her smile dimming a little. "Perhaps I'll have worked out my many blunders by the time Blake visits us as Havensbrooke next week, and then I'll appear the very model of an English lady."

"Did I happen to hear my name?" Blake stepped forward from the salon doorway, his gray hat tipped in its usual fashion to match his grin.

"We were just discussing my practice of becoming a proper English lady, Mr. Blake."

"Now why would you want to do that?" Blake grimaced and shook his head. "I've already told Freddie that gloomy old Havensbrooke could use a bit of your American sunshine. And you'll certainly improve the view."

"Blake." Frederick shot Blake a tempered warning, which bounced off Blake's smile like rain off a roof.

"And who would care for your little idiosyncrasies, when everyone will be so distracted by your style?" He winked over at Frederick, trying to get his back up, if Frederick knew his cousin. "Your hats have no rival, and hats are everything about status, I hear."

Grace looked from Blake to Frederick, her eyes rounding as she raised a hand to her brim. "Are they?"

"Of course. The bigger the better," Blake added, eyes brightening with a hidden laugh. "And every additional bird only proves who the real ladies are from the counterfeits."

"You really talk nonsense, don't you?" Frederick shook his head, but Grace's smile had completely faded. "He's only teasing, Grace. Blake knows as much about fashion as I do."

"Not so," Blake was quick to respond. "My mother forced such information on me since she was determined that I should have been the much longed-for daughter she failed to have until my much younger sister finally arrived." He gave a shrug. "However, Lady Astley, I feel certain you would garner attention wherever you go with such excellent fashion sense and eye-catching hair."

Grace's smile died as she absently ran her finger across the edge of her hat's brim. "Your comment about my hair just reminded me about a rather disgruntled man I saw today. He. . .he said he'd heard about Lord Astley's new ginger-headed bride but didn't believe it."

Frederick shot Blake a look before turning his attention back to Grace. "What man, Grace?"

"He passed me in the hallway as I went to our room for my scarf." She patted the blue cloth at her neck. "You remember I went back for it right after lunch?"

"I remember."

"He seemed to know a great bit about you. He said something about being acquainted with your brother and wondered if he'd run into you on the ship, but I didn't like him at all." Her brow crinkled with her frown. "There was something shifty about his eyes. I felt uncomfortable enough that I withdrew a hatpin in case I needed to defend myself. My grandfather said he knew a woman who kept two thieves at bay with a single hatpin and the heel of her—"

"What did he want?"

"Only enough to ascertain whether I was Lady Astley or not." She looked up at him rather quizzically. "He seemed rather shocked that you were my husband, but of course that may be because he expected Lillias. Her sylphlike beauty is widely known. I didn't tell him much at all and got away from him as quickly as possible."

"Very good thinking, Lady Astley." Blake's expression gave away nothing, but his eyes sharpened with their usual acuity. "Though I feel you could have taken him with your fierceness and a hatpin."

A smile burst onto Grace's face, Blake's nonchalance setting her at ease. But Blake's behavior didn't fool Frederick. Something was amiss.

Frederick attempted to match his cousin's casual response by carefully pulling Grace's arm through his to resume their walk. "Perhaps he was one of Edward's business partners. Do you recall what he looked like?"

"Well, he looked exactly as I'd imagine Captain Hook to look. Large, terrifying set of owlish eyebrows. An unruly black mane. A protruding nose just above a very unsatisfying moustache. With the size of his face, he ought to have grown it out a bit more."

Blake chuckled. "Perhaps we should listen for a ticking crocodile among the waves."

Grace flashed him a smile and then looked back at Frederick. "He tried to be sly when asking about our travel plans, but I told him it was none of his concern, to which he seemed put out. I kept my hatpin at the ready until I returned to the deck with you."

"Very smart of you, Grace." Frederick raised his eyes to Blake, an unspoken agreement passing between them to keep alert. Perhaps it was nothing, but Grace was a part of the equation now, and he'd do whatever was necessary to keep her safe, even if the "villain" proved nothing more than an exaggeration of her imagination.

<hr />

Grace had been so happy only a few hours before.

But now, as Frederick sat back in his berth and watched her riffle through three books without reading a page, he knew something was terribly wrong. Her anxiety had been growing ever since dinner, but at first he'd thought it had been her overly conscious attempt to keep from fidgeting.

Blake and Elliott had come to an agreement to keep watch outside the room for any suspicious activity, and even after a solid scout through the ship after dinner, neither Frederick nor Blake located a man fitting Grace's description. His bride may have an overactive imagination, but she was no liar, and her sense proved adept, but she wouldn't have let the mysterious man agitate her to such a degree. Truly, if anything, the presence of a mysterious man likely would have fueled her excitement.

She slipped into her bed and shifted around with the blankets, then stood, walked to the closet, and brought out a different book. But that didn't seem to suit her, so she stood back up again, wringing her hands a little as she moved.

"Grace, are you well?" The silky material of the gown brushed over her skin in a most enticing way. He squeezed his eyes closed to maintain his good intentions.

She paced the length of the row between their beds. Her brow puckered along with her bottom lip. "We arrive in England first thing in the morning, and after Mr. Blake's comments earlier today. . ."

"Yes," he answered slowly. Was she concerned for her safety?

"I—I don't know if I can do this anymore, Frederick," she muttered, pausing long enough to look over at him before resuming her pattern. "I never meant for the subterfuge to continue this long."

"What are you talking about?"

"I've not been completely honest with you." Her breath pumped with the quiver of her lip. "And I should have from the start."

Everything within him stilled. No, not her. First Celia, then Lillias, and now Grace? He couldn't have been wrong about her! "Grace?"

He braced himself for the blow.

Her rounded, sapphire eyes met his. "I don't know the first thing about fashion."

He released his held breath. "What?"

"I am well read, and I've helped Father with his house parties, so I have some understanding of being a hostess, and I can even, possibly, fake being clever, but I'm at a complete loss about fashion. All that hat talk today was terrifying."

He stared at her as her words and the intentions behind them moved through his comprehension as if they swam through thick treacle.

"You think my talking and fidgeting are bad, but I have no concept of the clothing world." Her eyes rounded in the most pitiful of ways. "All these beautiful outfits were Lillias's. I'd never know what shoes fit with which gown and what hat was meant for afternoon and—"

The pent-up fear she'd built with her introduction burst out of him in an uncontrollable wave of relief and laughter. She stopped her pacing to stare, bright eyes widening.

"I don't see what's so funny about me not knowing the proper fashion." She placed her hands on her hips. "What would your mother think if I walked into public wearing a winter dress with a summer hat? She'd be mortified. And that's an appropriate use of the word."

He couldn't answer her. He couldn't catch his breath. Her adorable concern left him useless to anything but another round of laughter.

"You're not helpful at all right now, are you?" Her pout started to slip into a grin. "But. . .but you do have a delightful laugh."

He couldn't stop himself. In one fluid motion, he grabbed her nearest hand and pulled her to him, wrapping his arms around her so she fell against him in the bed. The silky cloth of her gown slid over him until she fitted to one side, pressed against him in the small bed.

She didn't seem aware of the intimate move he'd made, because she simply pushed up from his side, hand on his chest, and looked at his face, brow peaked. "I don't see how this helps my fashion sense at all."

He chuckled, enjoying the feel of her near him, where she belonged. This was a good start in the right direction of their growing intimacy. He slipped his hand through her wealth of hair to cup the back of her head and drew her down to his mouth. She melted against him, warm, soft, each curve pressing into him with a wonderful ease.

She pursued the kiss as he turned her on her side and proceeded to move his hand over her shoulder and down her back. With an easy introduction, he slid his lips from her mouth and began a gentle descent of kisses over her jaw to her ear. She gasped, her fingers grabbing at his shirt, and nearly undoing his careful control. Slowly. Not too much— and certainly not in this tiny bed.

Her skin, smooth and warm beneath his lips, heated to his touch, carrying with it the sweet scent of rosemary. He left her ear and moved his kisses down her neck until she moaned against him, her fingers fisting his shirt in both hands. No one had ever kissed her like this. He was the first, and the realization tempered his desire with something deeper and sweeter.

He slipped his kisses back to her mouth and ended by tucking her against his side, her chest pumping shallow breaths. Her body trembled as he pushed back her hair from her face. She opened those glossy eyes, foggy from the effects of his mouth's attention to her neck.

"Please tell me that's a common occurrence in marriage," she rasped.

"I certainly hope so." He pressed a kiss to her forehead. "I think it ought to be."

"Oh yes, most certainly." She sighed against him and then, without warning, pushed back up against his chest. "Do you mean to tell me, you could have been kissing me like that from the first day?"

Her fiery hair fell around her shoulders, a shocking contrast against her white dressing gown, tempting him to finish the blaze he'd started. "I didn't want to frighten you, darling. We've gotten to know one another better since, but we are still quite new friends."

She studied his face, gaze a little suspicious, then slipped back down beside him, pressing her cheek against his shoulder and resting her palm on his chest. Close to his heart. Sheltered in his arms.

"Will you let me stay here beside you all night?"

"If you want to stay." His breath lodged in his throat. Nothing prepared him for her. For this. He wanted to keep her right there, all soft and sweet and his, for as long as he could.

She snuggled closer in answer. "Oh yes, this is much better than by myself."

*Indeed.*

"And you smell of amber. I love amber."

He reached to wrap the blankets around her, cocooning her in with him. "And I love rosemary and mint."

He could feel her smile press in against his shoulder. "You really are the most delightful man."

If she only knew the truth. Oh, he'd cling to this view she had of him for as long as possible. "I find you quite delightful too."

"Well, it will be a saving grace that you do when I show up to some social event wearing a spring dress during a winter ball."

"What would you say if I told you that your smile is always in fashion."

She smoothed a hand over his chest, completely unaware of the effects of her touch on his internal temperature. "I'd say your answer reminds me of another quote in favor of kindness."

"Of course, it does."

She yawned, but he was far from sleep. "Mm-hmm, by Jane Austen."

"Yes?" His fingers threaded through her hair, as soft as he'd imagined. Her smile grew wide, warming his shoulder. "There is no charm equal to tenderness of heart." She yawned again. "And you, my dear Frederick, are certainly charming."

The way her voice lilted on his name nearly had him kissing her senseless again. "Hmm. . .and what is it you find most intriguing about Jane Austen's heroes, Lady Astley?"

"Oh well," she murmured, her voice sluggish with growing sleep. "All of them are rather steadfast, aren't they? Beneath their fumblings, at times, all of them beat with true hearts."

True hearts.

With God's help, he'd have a true heart with her—steadfast. And hopefully she'd forgive the past when it blew into their lives.

# Chapter Twelve

Frederick kept to Grace's side the entire transition from the docks to the car to the train, Elliott and Ellie ever present nearby. Whether it was the closeness of their new sleeping arrangement or just the fact that Grace could easily get lost among the crowds and baggage of the Liverpool docks, she wasn't sure, but she rather liked having Frederick's hand on her back or her arm through his. It made the whole marriage idea more believable, as if he might actually like her.

The unpleasant Captain Hook man appeared several times in her periphery among the crowds in coal gray and bushy brows—or so she thought—which only added to the otherworldly dynamics of her present state. Every good fiction needed a villain or two. If Grace hadn't been attempting to navigate her new environment without losing her posture, she might have pointed the man out to Frederick, but as it was, she didn't even have a free hand or moment to reach for her hatpin.

The stench of smoke and dead fish gave a very unappealing introduction to England, with Grace's bright blue gown a beacon among the gray world as they transitioned from boat to car and finally parted ways with Blake at the train depot. Her aunt Caroline's infrequent letters mentioned England's general dreariness, with its shorter days in winter and narrow city buildings, but Aunt Caroline, Duchess of Keriford, had never been particularly trustworthy. From the stories she'd heard from her father, Grace had gleaned that her mother and aunt had opposite personalities, with Aunt Caroline possessing extroversion and imagination, while Mother, with her winsome elegance, happily kept to the quieter side of society.

Aunt Caroline had married a duke fifteen years earlier, during the popular days of American heiresses uniting with poor aristocracy. And though Lady Keriford proved a much more daring personality than her niece, there was something comforting in the fact that a family member lived relatively close by. In fact, the Earl and Countess of Keriford had already invited the Astleys to their upcoming Christmas party at Keriford Hall, Frederick and Grace's first public appearance in England.

It was to Grace's great relief when she and Frederick finally took their seats in their box on the train and watched the drab city buildings thin out and finally disappear altogether. Frederick released a sigh as he relaxed back into the cushioned seat and draped an arm about her shoulders.

"Look," Frederick whispered, gesturing toward the window as the landscape opened to a vast and glorious emerald countryside. "That's not so bad, is it?"

She leaned close to the window, her reflection smiling back at her. "The land of Austen and Brontë and Dickens."

"Keats, Shelley, and Doyle," he added.

She swung her attention to him, his face so close. "I love it when you speak in fiction."

The kissable grin of his emerged. "I'll have to remember to place quotations to memory with more diligence, then."

Without hesitation, she kissed his lovely lips. Something about sharing a bed with the man changed the nature of their closeness. "Will you let me sleep with you *every* night if I'm very good?"

"Darling, I enjoyed your company so well, I plan on your sleeping beside me even if you're very bad."

"That's quite gentlemanly of you, my dear Lord Astley." She attempted to curb her grin with more allure but failed miserably. "With my fidgeting and talking and insatiable curiosity, I am certain to be bad at times."

"As am I."

She squeezed his hand, a thrill running through her at the remembrance of his deliciously dastardly kisses. "Villainously bad?"

The smile waited in his eyes. "There is a distinct possibility."

"Then you shall most certainly sleep beside me, especially if your villainy involves kisses like last night." Her face heated at the thought while her whole body gravitated toward him.

"I can assure you, it's the most rewarding villainy a man can possibly commit with his wife."

She studied him, his gaze smoldering her burning cheeks. "Oh dear, I might require a distraction or I'll do something very improper and kiss you until you moan like you did last night."

His dark look heated her face even more, and her breath faltered a little in anticipation of possible villainy.

She blinked down at the bag she had in her lap, her notebook poking from the top. "What if we speak of Havensbrooke?"

"What do you wish to know?" The question emerged like a controlled growl, low and deep, doing nothing to distract her from her unruly thoughts.

She drew in a deep breath and attempted a smile. "I feel very much like Jane as she traveled to Thornfield Hall with all its mystery."

"Fortunately for you, or not so fortunately"—his gaze trailed down to her lips—"you've met the master of the hall already. So the mystery is gone."

"You cannot divert me with your underwhelming attitude. A place with as benign a name as Havensbrooke simply must harbor its own secrets."

His gaze flicked to her eyes, his features hardening. "You may not enjoy what you uncover, Grace. Not all stories are happy ones."

The sudden change in his expression evaporated the previous heat of their closeness. Wounds. Grief. They etched lines across his brow and curved his mouth into a frown that pulled at Grace's heart. "I made a promise before God and everyone I hold dear. Your secrets—all of them—are safe with me."

He offered a fleeting smile before lowering his gaze to their braided fingers. "I've been selfish bringing you here." His gaze, stormy and crinkle-browed, found hers. "But I believe your heart is strong."

"And my determination even stronger."

His gaze caressed her face in a way that appeared to have very little to do with money and much more to do with heart. She wasn't certain how to speak of secrets. Her deepest, darkest secrets involved simple things like stowing away in the back of a car to ride to town, putting vinegar in her father's coffee and regrettably having Larson take the blame, trying on her sister's clothes without asking, and reading books like *Udolpho* without her father knowing.

She gave his fingers a reassuring squeeze and sat up straighter. "So this new and shadowy home of mine. You and your mother reside in the west wing, yes? And where exactly is the servants' hall?"

"The servants' hall?" His smile tipped slightly. Perhaps he already knew it was a lost cause to keep her from learning of their employees. Smart man, and it distracted him from his melancholy thoughts. "It is referred to as the servants' wing and is positioned at the back of the house with the kitchens."

"Ah," she touched her finger to her lips, solutions, ideas, and even more questions firing awake. "So you keep social rooms in the east wing, but sleep in the south wing, yet the servants' wing is closer to the north and east parts of the house. It all sounds rather convoluted as far as efficiency."

"That was at my mother's bidding. The bedrooms on the second and third floors of the east wing were previously those of my brother, Edward, and his wife, Celia, as well as my mother and father. Since my brother's death, my mother had the rooms closed off and our bedrooms moved to the south wing."

Grace studied him a moment longer, noting the hesitation in his voice at the mention of his brother and sister-in-law. He'd only mentioned his brother died from a weak heart, but why did she feel something was left unsaid? "And you've already installed electricity in the south and east wings but haven't added extra bathrooms?"

He didn't immediately answer, his expression stalled in some unreadable way.

"What have I said?"

"I'm not sure what to make of my blushing bride when she's speaking of improvements instead of vistas and romances."

She rolled her eyes. "What do you think I'm doing with all these books on architecture and design? Merely looking at pictures? Though the pictures are nice." She shrugged and looked back out the window. "Besides, I'd much rather be at work *doing* something instead of worrying about fashion designs and house parties." She flipped her gaze back to his. "I warned you of my dramatic bent."

"I gathered as much about your dramatic bent upon our first meeting." His lips spread wide as if he harbored a laugh. "And I'm quite pleased you want to make Havensbrooke your home."

"I was reading from an article another American wrote of her work on her husband's estate, and she decided to close off some of the unused wings of the house to save money. That may be a first way to conserve space and energy toward refurbishing, don't you think?"

"Your suggestion is on the nose, and an easy remedy to lower some costs. The south and east wings showcase some of the best rooms of the house, and it makes sense to reduce costs by closing off the north tower rooms as well as the west wing, once we can renovate the east wing bedrooms."

"I'm afraid your mother won't like it."

He slid her a glance, his lips twitching. "She hasn't liked a great many things I've done, so this should prove in line with my usual course. But it is smart and in the long run will save money, resources, and time. I'm certain the servants will appreciate it." His expression gentled. "Do you always paint the world with such color? It's difficult to see the gray when you're a part of the conversation." He gave her fingers a squeeze. "You're rather enchanting."

The crinkle in his brow spoke of hardship, of regret, even. Paired with his comments throughout the last week, a vision of a man who'd lost some beautiful part of himself to a dark and dreary past resurrected. Lord Frederick Percy was a lost hero, as only the best fiction provided, and Grace felt certain God had placed her in Frederick's life to rescue him. After all, few people understood lurid backstories, strong-willed heroines, or happy endings quite as well as she.

And she'd always longed to rescue something or other. It sounded ever so heroic, even as they traveled nearer to a house with secrets, a bitter dowager mother, and a future of uncertain possibilities. Yes, it sounded very much like a novel. "I certainly hope I can continue to add color to your life, Lord Astley."

"Of this, I have no doubt."

❦

Frederick patiently endured his role as informant for the continuation of the train ride. Which proved a mercy, since Grace was notorious for questioning people into delirium.

The countryside looked familiar and strange all at once. Here and there among a vast expanse of rolling hills, a beige stone steeple—picturesque among the pastures—would dot the scenery like an unexpected find in a painting. Patches of sheep speckled the landscape, as twisty roads carved paths among emerald hills and rock walls. There was magic to it, especially as freezing fog—as Frederick called it—curled over distant mountains like a shroud, leaving behind a wonderland of icy trees and glistening towers.

A village of the most delightful conglomeration of gray brick, tan stone, and cobblestone lanes emerged among the hills as the train slowed. Astlynn Commons. People lined the way, some stringing garland along the outside of the train depot, others—it appeared—keeping watch. As the train came to a stop, the crowd increased with a great deal of commotion, all swarming toward the station, some with little banners, others waving their hats. What on earth was going on?

"Are you greeted this way every time you come home?" Grace grinned up at Frederick as he offered his hand to help her rise from her seat.

"They're not here to greet me." His lips lifted with the slightest smile. "They're here to see the new Countess of Astley."

"Me?" Her face drained of warmth. "Oh dear."

"I feel certain it will be relatively painless." He chuckled and drew her forward to the door of the train. "The older women of Astlynn Commons will send you smiles, the children will wave, the men will dip their chins in acknowledgment, and the young ladies will speak of nothing else but your fine hat and your lovely hair."

"My lovely hair." She rolled her eyes and allowed him to guide her through the train.

"It's as remarkable as its bearer."

He whispered the sentence, barely loud enough for her to hear, but she felt it spill through her with the sweetest thrill. He liked her hair. After shouldering years of unkind comments related to her scarlet locks, to have her husband find them—her smile stretched from cheek to cheek—*remarkable*? Well, that certainly meant something to her.

A young man in a driver's suit approached as they disembarked, removing his cap to reveal a wild array of curls almost the same color as Grace's. "Sir, glad to see you've arrived safely."

"Thank you, Patton." Frederick turned toward Grace. "Lady Astley, this our chauffeur, Mr. Patton. Patton, the Countess of Astley."

"My lady."

Grace offered him a not-so-demure smile. She'd been attempting to practice demure smiles, but they never failed to expand to her entire face, despite her best efforts. "A pleasure to meet you, Mr. Patton."

His cheeks deepened to match his hair color. "I pulled the car 'round to the side for privacy, my lord, but there's been a crowd out since mornin' trying to catch sight of the new lady." Mr. Patton returned his hat to his head, his gray eyes sparkling. "News of your arrival has caused quite a stir."

They followed Patton through the station, and Frederick stopped to greet a few people on their way. A Mr. and Mrs. Larson, who were from one of the esteemed families of the parish. Sir Archibald and Mrs. Elaine Withers represented another. By the time Frederick and Grace had made it to the Model T—all outfitted with fur-covered seats and several blankets to keep them warm on their drive—the carriage with Elliott, Ellie, and all their luggage had already disappeared down the road.

As they drove down the cobblestone street, Frederick's descriptions of the quaint village of Astlynn Commons and its series of perfectly lined, stone buildings came to life. She recognized the white-haired attendant who walked with a limp, and the rambling lane that led alongside a river. The bakery and butcher's shop. Frederick's beloved book shop, of which she took special note. A mercantile and millinery.

St. James of Astlynn's spires rose above the patchwork roofs, into a sky battling between clouds and sun. Everything about the village settled upon Grace like a picture show from a fairy tale.

The dark blush of dusk dimmed Grace's ability to take in all the sights, but each new curve in the road revealed another little gem of English charm and curbed the residual ache from the long distance to the home she'd once known.

"I love it all. It's exactly as you described." She turned to Frederick as he sat beside her in the autocar. "And Astlynn Commons is a part of your estate?"

"Our estate." He tipped his brow, holding her gaze for a moment before looking back out the window. "Yes, and we'll attend service at St. James this Sunday. Everyone will want to see you."

Grace fidgeted with her gloves. She looked out the window in an attempt to distract herself from the idea of people watching her, only to meet a dozen onlookers waving as the car passed. Well, at least they were friendly watchers. "And I can come to the village whenever I wish? I do so want to explore."

"Of course, though I'd suggest you take Ellie with you if I can't accompany you." He gestured with his chin toward the window. "You have caused quite a stir, Lady Astley. I believe every person in Astlynn Commons has come out to get a glimpse of you."

She raised a timid hand to greet a few children waving a holly branch as they stood in their caps and coats. Frederick had said before that the people of Astlynn Commons were the estate's responsibility. Their livelihoods depended on Havensbrooke. The idea took root in Grace's heart, and she sobered, staring at the faces with a new understanding, a purpose—caring for them.

"I hope you're not too disappointed at having to postpone our honeymoon."

Grace turned from the window. "Of course not! You must be here for your mother at present." She sent him another smile. "And this has been such a marvelous adventure already."

"You are much too easy on my heart, Lady Astley."

"Well, I'll make up for it by being hard on your peace of mind, I'm sure." She turned back to the window and waved at a little girl standing with her mother at the corner of a lane. How very strange to be the center of such attention. "Perhaps, after we've settled and brought Havensbrooke back to its previous splendor, you can take me on a grand tour of Europe."

"I give you my word. I'd enjoy filling your mind with actual places you've read about."

She grinned up at him and returned her attention to the staggered buildings, which were growing farther apart. They must be leaving Astlynn Commons, which meant their next stop would be Havensbrooke.

The road twisted and turned as they climbed a hill. In the distance, a horizon of small mountains came to her view, looking somewhat similar to her Blue Ridge Mountains back home. Home. She sighed. She'd have to start thinking very differently about home now, wouldn't she?

As they crested the hill, a wide river surrounded by evergreen forests came into view. A tower rose in the distance. Was that Havensbrooke? Just as Grace had the thought, a strange slamming noise exploded from the front of the car.

Grace turned to Frederick, assuming he'd know what was going on. He stared back as if thinking the same thing of her. Had she told him about the time she'd caused a cask of beer to explode? Or about the chestnut gun that backfired on her?

The slamming happened again. From the direction of the driver. It sounded nothing like a backfiring chestnut gun.

"Patton?" Frederick called to the front.

"The brakes, sir." He replied, his voice tense. "They're not responding."

Grace's mind slowly took in the meaning of the words as they began to descend the hill toward the bridge. . .and the river. Faster and faster.

"What did you say?" Frederick pushed closer to the front.

"The brakes." Patton pressed the brake lever. "Something is wrong with them, sir. I can't stop."

Grace glanced at the fast-approaching river as the car began to shake from its ever-increasing speed. She played out the scenario in her head like a scene from a book and reached for the laces of her shoes.

## Chapter Thirteen

Frederick could do nothing to prevent the oncoming disaster. And despite Patton's best attempts, the car continued accelerating toward North Haven River with no rescue in sight. Frederick turned to his young bride to find her with one boot off and almost finished unfastening the other.

"What are you doing?"

"Preparing for the probable," came her steady reply, before the car took a hard slide to the right.

Frederick grabbed Grace, cocooning her against him just as the car jumped the short stone railing of the bridge and pitched into the river.

The high water levels from heavy autumn rains provided some cushion on impact, but the jolt still sent Frederick crashing against the side of the door, pain shooting through his shoulder. Mercifully, the car remained upright, though tilted precariously forward and sinking even as he found his bearings. A shock of cold hit him in the back, as icy water rushed in on all sides of the windowless vehicle. He turned his body to keep the brunt of it from hitting Grace, but she was already hip deep.

"Oh!" She pushed back from his arms, wide eyes locked with his. "It was quite heroic, you know? Taking me in your arms that way."

Frederick opened his mouth but couldn't seem to utter a response. Grace took the initiative and started unbuttoning her coat. "This would have been so much better in summer. Less likelihood for hypothermia, you know?"

Frederick stared at his wife, then blinked a few times, only to find she'd completely removed her coat and was now working on the buttons of her day suit. Was she in shock? Going mad? And why was she removing her clothes? Frederick flipped his attention from trying to sort out his wife to focus on the front of the car. Patton slumped forward, head against the steering mechanism.

"Patton," he called.

No response.

"Take care of Mr. Patton." Grace's voice pitched higher as the water rose to her waist. "I'll swim to shore."

"What?" Swim to shore? "I won't leave you."

She shot him a look of utter confusion, brow crinkled into questions, her fingers moving to unfasten the buttons on the side of her skirt. "We have no time to argue. I am alert and capable. Mr. Patton is not."

His gaze followed her busy fingers as her skirt slid away revealing the white ruffles of her petticoat beneath the murky water. "What. . .what are you doing?"

"I cannot very well swim with that massive piece of cloth attached to my body, can I?" She released the most exasperated breath. "Do you want me to sink like a stone?"

"I want *Lady Astley* to keep her clothes on in public," he seethed through gritted teeth.

"Then I shall make a fully clothed corpse," she responded with as much venom.

Her words hit him with more force than the chill of the water. "I will not have you emerge from—"

"This is not one of those moments to concern yourself with etiquette, Lord Astley." The water submerged Grace almost to the chest level, covering any impropriety, but Frederick knew what *wasn't* on her body.

Patton tipped over in the front seat and with barely a sound, sank beneath the water.

"Now is the time to be a hero and rescue poor Mr. Patton from drowning." She pinned him with a look. "If you don't, I'll be forced to try, and then you'll be left without a wife or a chauffeur."

Her threat, along with a sudden rush of water up to his chest, propelled him into motion. He crawled out of his window, holding to the side of the car, and tugged the lifeless Mr. Patton out the window, resting the chauffeur's head against his shoulder. Through the space of the car, Frederick caught a glimpse of a hatless, bobbing ginger head slicing through the water on the other side. He groaned.

She'd removed her shirtwaist too. He shot his gaze heavenward in silent prayer for help. . .or patience. Maybe both.

With a shove from the side of the car, he turned Patton on his back and swam toward the embankment, the cold water stinging through his body. A crowd had gathered atop the bridge, some still running down the road from town, all ages.

What an introduction of the new Countess of Astley. He pinched his eyes closed, envisioning Grace emerging from the water in nothing but a union suit, casting decorum to the wind and loosening every scathing tongue in Derbyshire. He'd spent months attempting to avoid any possible scandal—and had curbed it somewhat, even with the bride debacle—but now, on his first day back home, he'd opened the gates with a near-death experience and an untamed bride.

As Frederick neared the shore, he searched the crowd for his wife, but she wasn't there. His breath seized, and he turned back to the river. She wasn't too far from him, but instead of emerging, she waited at chin level, moving in a peculiarly disjointed way beneath the chilly water, her lips almost blue.

What in heaven's name was she doing? As soon as his feet hit bottom, he pulled Patton onto the rocky shore and surged back toward the river, but just as he made it waist-deep, there she was, nearing the shore, completely covered in her soaking skirt and shirtwaist, as if she'd never taken them off.

He held out a hand to assist her, and she shot him a saucy grin. "I swam with them in my arms, in case you're wondering." She whispered with a wink, "I am a wild thing, but not *that* wild. Though"—they reached the edge and she pulled back her skirt to reveal stockingless feet—"I couldn't carry my boots too, but I doubt anyone will notice with all the excitement."

He stared at her. The woman was baffling. He had the strange urge to shake her by the shoulders before pulling her against him to ensure she was safe. As he tugged her forward, contemplating his next act, rousing applause sounded from the gathering crowd, followed by a few men running down the embankment to assist them.

Patton moaned, raising his head from his reclined position on the grass. A purple welt shone on his forehead. He focused his gaze on

Frederick and blinked, eyes widening. "Sir?"

"Our shop's just across the bridge, my lord." Mr. Quincy rushed forward, the shopkeeper's wife at his side with an armful of blankets. "Won't you rest there until we can bring a car around?"

"And Jimmy's gone for the doctor," Mrs. Quincy added, wrapping a blanket around Grace's shoulders like the grandmotherly sort she was. "Your ladyship."

"Thank you so kindly, Mrs.. . .?"

"Quincy, your ladyship." The woman stared at Grace as if she wanted to pull her into her arms, which Frederick, knowing the kindly lady as he did, suspected was exactly what Mrs. Quincy was thinking too. "And it's a pleasure to make your acquaintance, though I would wish not under such circumstances as these."

"You are very kind," Grace added, leaning forward to kiss the woman on the cheek.

After the near-death experience, Frederick chose to completely overlook Grace's tender breach of decorum. From the look on Mrs. Quincy's face, the moment would likely be remembered by the Quincy family line for decades to come.

He took Grace by the arm and followed the Quincys while Mr. Lorde, the baker, assisted Patton. Grace shivered against him, her teeth chattering loud enough for him to hear. He tugged her closer to his side, wrapping the blanket more tightly about her.

Frederick sent one of the lads, Thomas, ahead to fetch the carriage with their servants and trunks so that dry clothes could be brought back. The boy dashed off with a nod.

As Frederick and Grace crested the hill and reached the road, the crowd size had doubled, the faces of the familiar folks all pale and worried. Frederick drew in a deep breath and forced a smile. "I think this is proof that Havensbrooke is overdue for a more modern vehicle. Wouldn't you all agree?"

A round of laughter and a few relieved sighs greeted his response and stole some of the tension from the air. Grace shot him a look, but to her credit, she didn't voice whatever percolated in that head of hers. He'd have to remember to give extra praise to God for small favors. He could almost guess the turn of her thoughts, but he'd not allow his mind to go there. It made no sense. The car was old, plain and simple. Scandal-free.

Yet Blake's doubts crowded in, firming with more certainty. *Another "accident"?*

"Do you know what happened to cause the car to go all willy-nilly, ya lordship?" This from Arthur Lawrence, the blacksmith's youngest.

"Artie," his mother scolded, but Frederick tossed the lad a reassuring smile. These were good people. People his brother should have nurtured instead of ostracized. It had taken months for Frederick to garner greetings from the town folks when he walked the streets of Astlynn Commons after his brother's death. So many things had been broken in his absence.

"I don't know, and that's the truth," Patton defended from his place at Mr. Lorde's side. "I'd serviced the car this morning myself, and everything proved in top-notch order for his lordship's arrival."

Grace studied his profile with such intensity, it almost burned, but he'd not indulge her. Not in front of half the town.

As they passed by the crowd, Frederick couldn't help notice how the townspeople stared at his wife. He wasn't certain what they'd expected in the new Lady Astley, but a sopping wet, ginger-headed, smiling swimmer wasn't likely on the list. He squeezed her close and followed the Quincys through a door at the side of their shop into a small sitting area.

"If you'll be so good as to wait here by the fire, I'll fetch some tea." Mrs. Quincy disappeared through another door.

"And I'll take Mr. Patton upstairs to have a lie down till the doc can see him," Mr. Quincy added. "John should be over with his car in no time, sir."

"Thank you, Tom." Frederick ushered Grace closer to the fire.

Her skirts left a water trail across the stone floor.

The room fell silent except for the crackling of the fire. Grace's wet hair curled in disorganized ringlets around her face, and her purple lips trembled, but otherwise she seemed much too composed for a woman who'd just survived a car accident in the river. Perhaps she was in shock, but his shock was beginning to wear off, replaced by a deeper awareness that she could have died.

And it would have been his fault. His stomach pinched with sudden nausea. He took the blanket and used it as a towel to rub against her arms, garnering her attention. "Are you certain you're well?"

"Other than ruining this lovely gown and shaking like a leaf, I am." She pushed her hair from her face. "You have no idea how many times I've mentally planned to survive a mishap such as this." Her smile brightened. "Of course I hadn't factored you into my plan. You were a wonderful surprise."

Frederick shifted closer to her, keeping his voice low for fear of eavesdroppers wondering at his wife's mental health. Shock, certainly. "Are you saying you've envisioned driving off a bridge into a river?"

"Your lips are blue." She took a corner of the blanket around his shoulders and dabbed at his mouth. "Clearly, you've never ridden with Father. It was necessary to sort out ways to survive a great many possibilities when he was at the wheel of an autocar." With a sigh, she released the blanket and leaned closer to the fire "At least we can't blame Anthony Dixon for this mishap, can we?"

Had he heard correctly? "Anthony Dixon?"

"He may have sliced your saddle strap, but he certainly didn't follow us all the way to England to sabotage your car." She tapped her chin and stared into the fire as if she hadn't just shocked him senseless. "This must be someone much more sinister."

"Anthony Dixon sliced my saddle strap at Whitlock?"

She turned back to him, drops of water slipping from her hair and making a trail down her face. "Why are you acting so surprised? Didn't I tell you?"

"I think I would have remembered something as significant as almost dying at the hands of my former fiancée's lover." Even saying it aloud sounded so convoluted he had to replay the sentence in his mind to confirm he'd gotten it right. "How could you not have told me?"

She turned to face him, her brow pinched as if *he* was at fault. "I had planned to when I confessed everything about Lillias, but I was so distracted by the fact that you refused to accept my very polite marriage proposal, I must have forgotten."

"You must have forgotten?" His volume rose louder than he'd intended.

"It's an honest mistake, especially when a woman's been jilted."

He ran a hand through his wet hair and narrowed his eyes as his wife. "Did you know all along and keep it from me?"

"I only learned it just before Lillias and Anthony ran off together. And it was a fit of jealousy, Frederick. He never intended to kill you, only maim you a little to prolong his time with my sister whom he had been in love with for years."

"Maim me a little?" Did she hear herself?

"He was immediately remorseful and tried to dispatch the saddle but didn't have time without being caught."

"You. . .you hid this from me." He pointed his finger toward her, stepping closer. "How could you—"

"You have no right to point an accusing finger at me, Frederick Percy." The fact she'd used his full name brought his argument to a complete stop. "You have someone trying to kill you, and it's not Mr. Dixon, a fact you conveniently excluded from previous conversations with your *bride*."

He opened his mouth to contradict her accusations but couldn't. She was right. He hadn't been forthright with the possible threats because he hadn't been sure of them himself.

"Which means they'll try to kill me too. And if the scenario follows with the usual story line, I'll be the first one to die, because murderers rarely get things right the first time." Her eyebrows shot high, her lips still trembling. "Have you read *Under the Italian Sun*? It took the killer three attempts before he finally killed the right person."

Perhaps her imagination had taken an exaggerated turn, but she made her point painfully clear. He'd put her in danger once he'd made her his wife.

"Lucky for both of us, I know how to swim." She shook her head and turned back to the fire, rubbing her hands together. "Lillias hasn't the faintest idea, so if you'd married her—"

She looked up at him, the realization sobering their argument to dust.

"Patton would have drowned."

"And possibly my sister," Grace whispered, her bottom lip suddenly adding another tremble. Something in him broke. He grabbed her hand and pulled her against him, encasing her in his arms.

If she hadn't been able to swim, a man would be dead. And if the accident had been worse, Grace could have—

He pinched his eyes closed and rested his chin against her head. "I'm sorry, Grace. It's my responsibility to keep you safe, and I failed today."

"I believe, my dear Lord Astley, we have a responsibility to protect each other." She looked up, those eyes as filled with tenderness as ever. No reprimand. No blame. How had God given him someone he didn't even know his heart needed so much? "And we are both very much alive, as is Mr. Patton, so I wouldn't claim it as a failure at all."

He tugged her back against him, if nothing else to keep her from seeing the water film in his eyes. She was *with* him. *For* him. Someone who believed in him despite his failings? He couldn't wrap his mind around such sweetness.

He breathed a sigh out over her hair. He'd protect her. He'd protect *this*. With everything in him.

A short time later, wearing dry clothes and sitting in Mr. Quincy's car, Frederick offered a silent prayer of thanksgiving. They were arriving much later to the house than anticipated, but one of the men from town had gone ahead to Havensbrooke to alert Brandon and the staff of the delay without giving too many details, and Elliott had the unfortunate task of sharing the news with Mother.

Grace pressed in close by Frederick's side as they rode. She'd remained unnervingly quiet as they'd exited Astlynn Commons for the second time, even leaning her head against his shoulder. Despite the keen eyes of Mr. Quincy in the driver's seat, Frederick didn't move her. They'd earned a little indiscretion, and right now she seemed so quiet and compliant beside him, he didn't want to change the mood. Not after all that had happened.

He breathed a kiss against her hair and sighed back into the leather seat.

She stirred at his side and leaned her lips close to his cheek, as if she meant to kiss him. "Frederick," she whispered. "Do you have any idea who would want to kill you?"

# Chapter Fourteen

Frederick coughed at her question, or that's what his choked response sounded like. Why was the idea so surprising? Brakes being disabled? Someone attempting to run him over in Whitlock Village? Clearly everything was not as it appeared for Lord Astley of Havensbrooke.

"Either that or Mr. Patton isn't as adept at his job as you think."

Frederick snorted his disagreement. "Patton has been with us for five years. He's quite capable."

Her thoughts turned to Mr. Patton. No, he didn't seem the sort to engage in criminal activity, especially since he nearly died in the incident. *Facts, Grace. You have no facts to support your theory. And any good sleuth must have facts to pair with her intuition.*

"Then my next question would be if he left the car for any extended period of time while in town. Enough time for someone to tamper with it. It doesn't take long with these automobiles. I had Mr. Lance at Whitlock show me once."

"Grace." He pushed the heel of his palm into his forehead. "I know how it appears, but we have no idea what truly happened to the car. It is old by any standards, and until we fish it out of the river, we shouldn't speculate—"

"It's highly unlikely someone would wish to kill Mr. Patton," she continued. "And no one even knows me here, but"—she narrowed her gaze at Frederick—"you're an earl, so the only logical question is, what happens to Havensbrooke and all of its money if you die?"

"Darling, I think—"

"Because, people plot a murder for three main reasons: jealousy, revenge, or money. Which do you think it could be?"

"Could we forgo this discussion until a later date? It's been a rather trying day, and I'd prefer to look at this mishap as an accident until the car can be properly inspected. Malfunctions of automobiles happen all the time."

"So do murders."

"Grace."

"Fine. Yes. It's been a trying day." She nestled close to his warmth, her hair still damp. "But if another strange occurrence transpires, Lord Astley, I am bound by marriage vows to protect you as much as you are to protect me, so then we shall see."

His smile budded a little, and his fingers at her shoulder spun into her hair enough to knock off the residual chill. Perhaps he could distract her. Just out the window, sunset hues bowed to a darker shade of evening.

Frederick pointed toward a turn in the road. "We're coming in quite late, so I'm not certain Mother will be awake, but prepare yourself." He leaned in close as she searched ahead for the great unveiling, his voice tinged with his own pleasure. "Havensbrooke is just beyond this screen of trees."

⚮

Havensbrooke! Her new home. Grace's breath stalled, waiting, and in the fading light she caught her first glimpse of limestone, spires, and. . .turrets? She leaned closer as the view opened to a long lane lined with a variety of mature trees on either side, dusk shadowing the periphery.

Looming towers and jutting rooftops created a conglomeration of angles, chimneys, and pinnacles into the evening sky. Gothic. Grace's breath held with an immediate shock of mystery. Was it gray or tan. . .or a mixture of the two? She tried to scan every detail of the ornamental entry as the car approached. It was easily twice the size of Whitlock and much more Jane Eyre–esque. "It has turrets!"

His chuckle tingled down her neck. So close. She closed her eyes to embrace the lovely warmth, remembering how she'd awakened in his arms. . .in his bed that morning. Sleeping with her sister felt nothing like waking to the strength of a man wrapped around her in such a safe hold. And smelling of amber. Even with her imagination, she'd never dreamed up something so delightful.

She turned slightly, her face close to his in the dark car. "It has turrets," she whispered.

"Quite romantic, don't you think?" His gaze dropped to her mouth, and her lips answered his unspoken request by bridging the gap between them.

"I think you should kiss my neck again tonight." She whispered to avoid drawing attention from the driver. "It would be an excellent distraction from my thinking of someone plotting to kill you."

His expression took on a new look, something almost dangerous, and he lowered his lips to graze her ear, sending warmth spilling from his touch southward. "That is an excellent idea."

Her entire body hummed with such anticipation that her brain went foggy just as the car came to a stop. The door opened, and Frederick stepped out, then turned to offer his hand. She stared at him, piecing together her next actions as if picking them up off a heap on the floor. Take his hand. Put one foot in front of the other. Smile. Walk.

"Lady Astley?"

She blinked and took Frederick's hand, offering a mock glare. "How can I possibly keep my thoughts under control when you tease me with your"—she curbed her volume—"roguish ways?"

He rewarded her with one of the most unscrupulous grins she'd ever seen. Oh, she did like the idea of a rogue and a hero all wrapped into one.

Grace forced her thoughts out of the glorious haze his voice and lips conjured in her and met the greeting of a dark-haired man of medium height and build, expression as pressed as his livery.

"Good to see you, Brandon." Frederick nodded to the man.

Ah yes, Brandon, the butler.

In the fading daylight, two rows of servants waited at the entrance of the house. Four women and five men, all somber faced and focused forward. The kitchen staff stayed below stairs, of course, but Grace wanted to meet them too.

A stone-faced woman with pale blond-and-gray hair stood next to him, her round-rimmed glasses clinging to the edge of her small nose as if attempting to dive off the end. She looked even less welcoming than Brandon.

Of course Grace probably didn't make the best first impression. Even though she'd changed into a new dress, she hadn't had the opportunity to reset her hair, so her shocking spray of unruly curls was likely dangling in all directions around her face, which was still much colder than normal.

Grace's body sagged ever so slightly—partially beneath the weariness of a long journey and partially from the sudden impossibility of the task ahead. All the rosy ideas she'd conjured on the journey shook with uncertainty. This massive, foreboding house? Servants with allegiances to a dowager, and an entire staff expecting Lillias in all her refinement?

What did it matter if she could swim and solve murder mysteries if she couldn't be a lady?

She suddenly wondered what Lizzie Bennet felt like when she stepped from the carriage at Pemberley for the first time as Mrs. Darcy. Grace stiffened her chin. If all else failed, she had her faith, her fiction—she looked over at Frederick—and her extremely roguish friend. Surely that would be enough. How horrible could a dowager actually be?

"Welcome home, Lord Astley," Brandon offered with a tip of his head, his gaze traveling the length of them. He cleared his throat and blinked. "I'm sorry for your. . .misfortune, sir."

"Only a bit of trouble with the car, Brandon, but it's being seen to in the village for now. Mr. Quincy was kind enough to bring us the rest of the way, and Mr. Fawkes is following in the carriage with our trunks, along with Lady Astley's girl, Ellie." Frederick drew Grace forward. "I'd like to introduce you to my wife, Lady Astley." His introduction tapped her courage up a few notches. "I hope you will treat her with the same kindness and respect as you've always given me."

All eyes focused on her. Grace hoped she smiled.

"I would like to offer our welcome from the full staff, Lady Astley." Brandon's posture made Grace stand up a little straighter, his countenance giving nothing away. "We wish to make your transition to Havensbrooke a pleasant one."

Grace slid her attention to each face. Two of the young maids smiled. Another gentleman doffed his hat, but otherwise everyone remained stoic as statues—distrustful statues.

"Thank you, Brandon."

"Mrs. Powell will see to your maid when she arrives." Brandon turned back to Frederick. "And your mother wishes for you and Lady Astley to be brought to her directly, sir."

Frederick gave a quiet sigh beside her and offered Grace his arm, turning to her. "We can postpone our introduction until morning, if you wish."

From all accounts, this meeting with Lady Moriah was bound to be unpleasant. Nasty, even. Grace offered him a tremulous smile. "I prefer to get unpleasant things over with as soon as possible, so we might as well do it now."

His lips pinched as if to control a smile, and then he covered her hand on his arm before turning back to Brandon. "We'll see her straightaway." Frederick began to pass but paused. "Mrs. Powell, would you please have tea brought to Lady Astley's room. I'm certain, after our adventure, she's not only tired and cold, but hungry."

"Yes, sir."

"Thank you, Mrs. Powell." Grace hoped for a softening expression, but the woman wore somber like a proud hat.

"Don't worry." Frederick bent his head in her direction as they passed through the doors. "She's much kinder on the inside."

Grace's frown unfolded into a chuckle. "I hope underneath all of those frowns everyone here proves to be as charming as you."

He squeezed her hand and leaned close. "Hold that thought tight in your head, because your good heart is about to be duly challenged."

With that, he led her through the doors into a large hallway with magnificent arched ceilings and red carpet over stone floors. Two white sculptures stood as sentries on either side of the archway, and Grace stifled another frown. Not even the statues looked happy to see her. She pulled the edge of her glove into a twist. *Be brave, Grace.*

At the end of the hallway, another arched stone entry opened into a massive room, and Grace dropped the hold on her glove. Beautiful chandeliers hung high above her from a wooden ceiling and splayed soft light into the three-storied atrium of the house. A large fireplace served as the centerpiece in the room, complete with two dark red chairs on either side and evergreen walls framed in oak. Tall archways met the room on all four sides, leading away to other portions of the house, and the main feature of the space was the expansive staircase that wrapped the length of the room, climbing around and around up two levels to a ceiling framed with elaborately designed wooden molding. She couldn't help but stare.

"The Great Hall," she breathed, pulling away from him to step to the center of the room. Frederick had praised this particular part of Havensbrooke when he'd told her about the house during their numerous conversations, but his descriptions failed to do it justice. "It *is* magnificent."

"I wouldn't exaggerate such a truth, my dear Lady Astley." His smooth voice brushed away some of the fear the stone-faced servants left behind.

"But you haven't decorated for Christmas at all."

"We still have a few weeks left before Christmas." He scanned the room and then looked at her as if digesting her sentence. "So there's ample time for your handiwork."

"My handiwork?" Grace brought her hands together, spinning about as she took another look at the massive room. "Imagine all the garland, and how glorious a tree would look right here in the middle of the room."

"I happily give you free rein to decorate as you wish." He smiled down at her. "Would you enjoy that?"

"More than I can say." She rushed back to him and placed a kiss to his cheek. "Mistletoe in every doorway so you can't escape my kisses."

"I should never wish to escape your kisses."

Her smile unfurled at the very idea of Lord Astley's roguish kissing abilities as she surveyed the room again with a more Christmassy mind-set. Oh, they definitely needed an ample supply of mistletoe. "Is the ceiling oak paneled with. . .with arched windows?"

"It is and will appear much better with sunlight streaming through." He stepped to her side and pointed upward. "You see the balcony overlooking us from the highest spot?"

"Yes."

"I believe that particular room will be your favorite."

She slid her arm through his, drawing near. "Can we see it tonight?"

"Alas, it's much too late, and the room upstairs"—one brow rose in a teasing way—"I must unveil by sunlight. Particularly for you."

He turned their steps toward the stairs.

"How do you propose I sleep now?" She squinted to try and make out the place of which he spoke. "I might very well venture off to find it myself, just because of your teasing."

His palm slammed against his chest, feigning a wound. "And strip the pleasure from me, darling?"

She exaggerated her sigh. "Well, since you called me darling, I acquiesce."

"Most valiant of you."

"It sounds as though I'll need all my strength for the battle ahead, anyway. Why should I waste it bickering with you?" She pulled them to a stop and gazed at the myriad of portraits laddering the walls of the stairway. "Are these your family? Ancestors?"

"Yes, and if I can't detail all of them, my mother will proudly equip you with enough knowledge and depressing stories to create an entire library of romances."

"Now you've really gotten my hopes up."

He chuckled and led her through a long corridor on the second level. The cold and dark entry into the south wing seemed to seep gloom from the shadows. It probably didn't help that her damp hair caused an added shiver. If a house could emanate a feeling, Havensbrooke exuded hints of foreboding and. . .loneliness. Of course that might just be Grace's continued struggle between embracing her future and looking back at the very long distance between England and everyone she'd held dear for so long.

Electric lights gave a dim glow as they moved down a long corridor with arched doorways on each side, passing decorative tables with expensive vases or large paintings of vast landscapes—at one point, Grace even noticed a portrait of a dog—until Frederick finally stopped in front of one of the doors. He gave her fingers a squeeze before he knocked.

"Enter," came the faint reply.

The first thing Grace noticed was the lighting. Candle and lantern light streamed a golden dance over the room. No electric lights. An elaborate marble mantelpiece stood at the far end, almost barren except for two silver-framed photographs.

"I see you've arrived late."

The voice pulled Grace's attention to a chair by the fire where a pale, thin woman sat with a large book sitting atop a blanket covering her legs. She wore a simple cap and held herself as if the back of the chair wasn't as straight as it should be. Dark eyes—housed within a pale face—narrowed as they settled on Grace, and whatever warmth Frederick's nearness provided slipped out the top of Grace's head.

She'd never seen such lifeless eyes. She'd envisioned them aplenty. Every time she read *Dracula*, but their actual appearance proved more disturbing than fiction. Grace's heart sank lower at the dreadful realization. This was her mother-in-law.

Heaven help her. Shakespeare's Queen Gertrude may have nothing on Moriah Percy, the Dowager Countess of Astley.

"What is this I hear of you and the river?" She tapped the floor with her cane.

No "happy to see you" or "glad you didn't drown." No introductions.

Frederick took a slight step forward, partially shielding Grace from his mother's view. "There was no help for it. The car lost control and landed in the river. Thankfully, no one was seriously injured, and we swam to shore—"

"Who swam?" Beady eyes landed on Grace. "You swam?"

"And I'm grateful she did." Frederick offered. "If she hadn't been able to swim, we would have lost Patton."

"This is preposterous. What in the world can you mean?"

"Patton was rendered unconscious by the impact, and I couldn't save them both."

The woman stared at them for a full five seconds, lips parted, before she seemed to rally with another grimace, which seemed directed at Grace's unruly hair. "And you didn't think to make yourself suitable before presenting her to me?" Her voice sounded like wind scratching against the branches of trees, high-pitched and raspy. "Never mind. I am anxious to see the results of your unfortunate turn of events. Bring her forward."

Frederick turned to Grace and offered her a tender look, buoying her spirits enough to still her trembling. Grace should have prepared herself more for meeting cantankerous mothers-in-law and less in surviving autocar accidents, because her knees suddenly started shaking.

"Mother, might I introduce you to Gracelynn Ferguson Percy. This is my mother, Lady Moriah, Dowager Countess of Astley."

The woman cringed at the introduction, as if the reminder of the title relegated to her after her son's marriage added fresh sting.

"Come into the light, girl."

Frederick stayed by her side, which gave Grace a little sense of support as she stepped closer to the spindly looking matriarch. Oh dear, she had the overwhelming desire to search her mother-in-law's room for a magic mirror that talked of the fairest of them all. Grace's eyes widened. Was it possible her mother-in-law knew how to tamper with automobiles?

The woman perched on her throne and took her time examining Grace from bottom to top. "What happened to your hair?"

Grace raised her fingers to her head. "Well, my hair came loose in the river."

"Not your style, your color."

"My. . .my color?"

"Please tell me the firelight is playing tricks on my vision. It cannot be that red, can it?"

"There's nothing wrong with her hair, Mother. It's a beautiful color. Unique, like the bearer."

"Don't speak sentimentally, Son. It proves you're weak."

Grace's spine stiffened at the affront to sweet Frederick. This woman definitely harbored a magic mirror somewhere, possibly a poisonous apple too.

"You married her for the money and the heir, not for her personality and certainly not for her hair."

The words stung—both from the harshness and the blatant truth of the matter. A sudden pain sliced through her chest.

"Mother, that is quite enough. If you cannot speak civilly, then we shall take our leave." Frederick's voice hardened. He turned to Grace. "It's late, and Mother is overtired."

"It's an unfortunate color." Lady Astley waved away her son's words and set her gaze back on Grace. "But I suppose you had no hand in it, and at least your pale complexion and excellent fashion covers over some of your more unsightly errors."

Grace couldn't help it, whether from the band-like tension or the utter ridiculousness of the woman's standards. She laughed.

The woman's eyes tightened like a bowstring ready to fire, and Grace immediately covered her mouth with her hand, but it didn't help much. In all truth, Grace's most unsightly errors were exactly those, the ones no one could see. And there were dozens of them. Her propensity for giggling when nervous being at the top.

"Good heavens, Frederick, you've married a simpleton."

The laughter threatened another release, but Frederick stepped forward. "Grace is anything but a simpleton. She's intelligent, innovative, and kind." He tugged Grace back toward the door. "Good night, Mother."

His ready defense lifted Grace's chin. Oh, she'd never known the sheer pleasure of having a man defend her with such eloquence. Yes, Frederick's hero qualities were in excellent shape.

"Don't fool yourself, Frederick. Do you believe this. . .girl can bring pride to the Percy name? A name you have yet to redeem?"

Grace watched her husband, tenderhearted as he was, bend a little from the accusations. Something dark and horrible fed the bitterness in this woman, something with enough power to wilt her dashing rogue.

"With due respect, Lady Moriah. . .Dowager. . .um. . .Astley." English titles were terribly confusing. And from the glint in Lady Astley's eyes, Grace hadn't guessed correctly quickly enough. "You do not know what I'm capable of. I don't even know what I'm capable of, but I can assure you with the low expectations you have for me, I'll exceed them."

She cackled, a horrible sound. "I don't hold out a great deal of hope for you."

"Then it's a good thing I haven't hung my hope on your opinion either, isn't it?" Grace refused to break eye contact.

"You insolent child."

"That is enough." Frederick took Grace by the arm and turned her to him. "I will not have you butchered in this fashion." He walked her to the door and rang the bell. A maid appeared within moments.

"See Lady Astley to her room." He turned those dark eyes on her, his expression softened with an apology. "You should not have to bear such ridicule."

Grace forced a smile and grappled enough courage to mean it. "We'll face this together, won't we?"

He raised tired eyes to hers, his smile weak. "Indeed we will."

A sudden heaviness fell over Grace as she followed the maid back through the corridor. The young woman, one of the two who'd smiled at Grace earlier in the evening, moved quietly forward, black dress and white apron fitted to perfection.

"What's your name?"

The maid looked ahead, slowing her pace. "Mary, ma'am."

"It's nice to meet you, Mary."

Mary stopped in front of another one of the beautifully arched doorways. "I reckon you're tired after your travels, my lady." She pushed open the door and stepped inside, waiting to the left as Grace entered.

The expansive room spread wide, decorated in a French style with gold and white. Cool colors. Intricate and pristine. Elegant swans were carved into the door and oak crown molding with beautiful detail. "It's lovely."

"His lordship ordered it to be prepared with elegance." The girl folded her hands in front of her, smile soft. How much had the servants worked to prepare for Grace's arrival? Were they happy with Frederick's choice? Disappointed?

From the welcome at her arrival, she'd guess the latter.

"I see the tea's been brought up for you, my lady. Would you like me to pour out?"

"No thank you, Mary. I'll see to it myself."

With a bow of her golden head, Mary excused herself, leaving Grace to the impending silence. The fire crackled in the white marble hearth, adding flickering light to the electric ones dotted throughout the room. Despite the opulence of the space, reality pressed a heavy hand over Grace's spirit. She stepped close to the fire, leaning against the hearth, suddenly wearier than she'd felt in a long time. Her mother-in-law's words pierced through the sweetness of the last six married days like a flash of lightning in the dark. Frederick had only married her for money—her personality had little to do with it. And the heir? Was that the only reason he shared such beautiful kisses with her?

She pressed her eyes closed. It was the goal of every earl to ensure his family line, wasn't it? That seemed to be the main focus in books, anyway. That and winning at cards. She frowned. Or was it horse racing?

She sighed and slid into a nearby chair, her eyes stinging with unshed tears. How had she failed to prepare herself sufficiently for such a place, for such a feeling? Home waited thousands of miles away. The warmth of her father, Mr. and Mrs. Whitlock, and other friends couldn't breach such a distance. Would Frederick turn away from her too? Especially if she didn't meet whatever expectations society or his mother deemed necessary.

In all her life, Grace had never felt so. . .alone.

She pushed tears away as Ellie entered to help her prepare for bed.

*Oh God, please. . .please help me create something beautiful from this choice.*

# Chapter Fifteen

Frederick marched from his mother's room with a hardened edge knotting his stomach. There was no use arguing with her. To her he'd forever remain the black sheep of the family—the failure. Every decision, every choice she tore apart with her poisonous tongue, leaving him as bereft of her affection as always. At least when his grandmother lived, he'd known the tenderness of a woman's kindness.

Except now. With Grace. He'd never expected her presence to provide such a comfort, even as his mother spewed criticism and anger. Despite their unconventional beginning and her youthfulness, she fit him in a way he'd never imagined. They held easy conversations from anything related to improvements at Havensbrooke to fiction to faith. Even when they'd confronted one another during and after the car accident, they'd argued as friends—equals—her opinion as readied as his own. It all seemed too good to be true. Too sweet and right.

Over and over throughout their journey, Grace had looked at him as if he truly was capable and good and worth admiring. He rubbed his fingers against a new ache in his chest. When was the last time someone had looked at him with such genuine and unguarded esteem? Had anyone ever?

He gave the door latch a quiet turn and stepped from their shared sitting room into her bedroom. As he scanned the gold-and-white decor, he frowned. Gilded. Pristine. Regal. No, those didn't suit the bride he'd brought home. Grace's room should hold vibrancy and warmth.

Firelight provided the only light in the room as he stepped soundlessly forward and then stopped. Curled up on the bed, blankets piled to her chin and firelight flickering a golden glow across her face, lay his wife, fast asleep. She looked beautiful, her hair fanned out across the pillow, hand tucked beneath her cheek.

He slid a finger over her skin before trailing his hand to her hair, still damp from the river. . .where he could have lost her. The thought sent a visceral ache spiraling through his chest. Could the vows he made in front of God and the camaraderie they'd begun to share be enough to bind him to her in such a way so quickly?

She smiled in her sleep but didn't stir. Frederick hung his head with a resigned grin. She needed rest, especially after everything that had happened. His gaze dropped to the pillow beside hers. But he'd promised to sleep in the bed with her every night. He went to his room, dressed in his nightclothes, and returned. Careful not to wake her, he slipped into the bed.

Her gaze flickered open, long enough to give him a sleepy smile and curl up against him, murmuring something unintelligible as she did. He rolled his eyes toward heaven and offered another silent prayer. This time in thanksgiving instead of for help.

Perhaps God had sent Grace to fortify his prayer life, because it was working. He hadn't prayed so much in the past two years as he'd prayed in the previous two weeks.

With a sigh, he tucked her close and rested his head against her hair. His mother wouldn't make the transition easy—she rarely made anything easy—but one thing his mother hadn't counted on was the strength of Grace Ferg—Percy. *His* Lady Astley.

Despite the harsh and intimidating words his mother wielded like a blade, Frederick placed his bets on the ginger in his arms.

Morning light glittered through the slits in the curtain, orienting Grace to her surroundings. She blinked the gilded room into view, it's opulence and refinement reviving her last thoughts before sleep mercifully took hold. This room was meant for her sister. Its distant and distinguished beauty, pale and monochrome, fit Lillias's tastes.

But not hers.

She cringed at the negative turn of her thoughts and pushed herself up in bed. Lady Astley's words still clung to her heart, leeching to her joy like a black glove. Grace had never considered herself a pawn in the grand social game, but her mother-in-law's harshness revealed the fairy tale of the last few days in a stark light of reality.

Frederick married her for money, and Grace had never been part of the plan.

She clenched her eyes closed and dropped back down on the bed, refusing tears. She was an impulsive creature—too quick to make decisions without counting the cost, too ready to give everyone the benefit of the doubt. And here she was. She'd left home and family for this vast and cold world without a true friend among the walls.

She rolled on her side, an unruly tear slipping from her control to warm her temple before disappearing into the folds of her hair. *You know, Lord.* She'd chosen this path for all the right reasons, yet even He felt far off as the echoes of Lady Astley's criticism reverberated through Grace's heart.

Surely if God was everywhere, He could find His way to the second floor of the south wing of Havensbrooke Hall in the middle of Derbyshire, England. Could all of it, even her poor attempts, still somehow fashion into a grander part of God's plan? She'd been taught so, but everything blurred into a rumbling ache in the light of morning.

Grace blinked the bedside into view. The neighboring pillow and blanket lay crinkled from use. She smoothed her hand over the cloth, and the faint scent of amber accompanied her touch. Had Frederick joined her last night? She thought she'd dreamed him slipping beside her and tugging her against him, but here was evidence it was not a dream.

Maybe she wasn't so very alone after all. And maybe it wasn't just about money.

"Good morning, my lady."

Grace shoved her hair away to see Ellie drawing back the curtains, ushering morning light into the room. Being on the east side of the house would make excellent use of the sun's heat. As it was, Grace drew the blankets up a little closer to stave off the slight chill in the air. England felt much colder than Virginia in more ways than one.

At least the sun shone. That was a good start to any day.

Ellie's pale eyes looked tired, even her usually excellent posture waned. "Did you sleep at all, dear Ellie?"

She shook her head. "It's gonna take me a few days to get used to my surroundings, and since my bedroom is so far from yours, I got lost on the way this morning or I'd have been here earlier to wake you."

Sounded like wasted time to Grace, and all the more reason to move the family quarters to the east wing.

The young woman's gaze met Grace's. "And I beg your pardon, my lady, but now that you're a countess and we're in England, you're bound to call me by my surname."

All this title business was exhausting. Grace had already determined to call the elder Lady Astley "Lady Moriah" just to bypass the confusion. Besides, calling one's mother-in-law "the dowager" sounded a bit too intimidating for familial camaraderie. "But we're too well acquainted for me to call you Miss Moore."

Ellie's shoulders drooped a little farther.

"What about this, Ellie?" Grace stood and drew in a deep breath. "I will call you Ellie when we are in private but Miss Moore in other areas so neither of us will get into trouble."

She offered a weary smile and adjusted her white cap. "That will do, my lady."

"I think we both have a great number of adjustments to make, but we're young and smart." Grace pushed more confidence into her speech than she felt. In fact, she wanted to drop back down into the bed and hide for a few days like a weak heroine. "We'll make do, won't we?"

"If you say so, my lady." Ellie shook her head and opened the wardrobe, which held some of Grace's things. "At any rate, breakfast is served in a half hour, so we need to make quick work of getting you ready."

⌒⊰≈⊱⌒

Grace needed an en suite lavatory immediately.

When he'd found her in the hallway not an hour ago, half-clad in her nightgown in desperate search of the necessary, he inwardly flailed himself for his lack of thoughtfulness. Why hadn't he considered something so basic? Especially for a woman of means who was used to such conveniences.

Lillias would have thought him barbaric. Grace likely hadn't considered how insensitive the situation was. If Brandon or Elliott had happened by with her in such a state of undress! Frederick's neck grew warm at the very notion. Elliott, good man that he was, had only a year on Frederick and no wife of his own, and Frederick didn't like the idea of any of the male servants seeing something only he should appreciate.

Since he had to go into town to meet with the constable about the incident with the car, he'd take time to consult his local solicitor to inquire after qualified workmen to begin the necessary renovations immediately. He reread the message from the constable, which detailed how an inspector had been notified. Frederick frowned. Hopefully the inspector would do his part to keep the incident out of the public's knowledge as much as possible.

"You look very intent on something."

Grace entered the breakfast room clothed in a seafoam-green walking suit, her glorious hair, which had been down about her shoulders in the hallway not too long ago, now sat in some sort of style on her head that highlighted the swan-like curve of her neck. His gaze followed her to her seat, his grin in rebellion again.

He stood. "Good morning, Lady Astley."

Her smile brightened the entire room. "Good morning, my lord."

Her gaze landed on something across the room, and as if the dog realized he'd been recognized, Zeus charged directly toward Grace, who had lowered herself to meet him head-on. "Oh my goodness, what a beautiful dog."

Frederick met Brandon's wide-eyed expression.

Either Grace's exuberance had transferred to his dog, or Zeus knew a friend when he met one. The English setter had never grown into his thundering name and remained fairly docile except on rare occasions when provoked.

"This is Zeus."

She buried her face in his fur as if they'd been long-lost friends. Frederick refused to send a look to Brandon, who was likely shocked beyond words at his wife's response. "Is he ours?"

"He is."

"I'm so glad you have dogs." She smiled down at Zeus, who gave her a solid lick on the nose in return. "They're much easier to talk to than people."

A strange sound erupted from Brandon's direction, but his expression gave no change.

Grace finally stood, trailing her hand across Zeus's fur one last time before moving to the table.

Brandon assisted Grace with her chair. "Thank you, Brandon." She took in the dishes of fruit before them. "You have strawberries?" Grace sent Brandon a smile so bright even the seasoned butler stared entranced for a moment. "You must have miracle workers here, Brandon, to find strawberries in December."

"They're from the hothouse, milady." Brandon nodded, face impassive. "Lord Astley mentioned that you were particularly fond of strawberries."

She flashed Frederick another smile. "He's so very thoughtful, isn't he, Brandon?"

Brandon's expression flickered with surprise for a second and returned to its controlled posture. Hopefully Grace recognized the reservation of the staff as wholly English, but Frederick knew they were on their guard, anxious that the new Countess of Astley might prove as tedious and unmanageable as the last. Or as difficult as his mother. Since Grandmama's death, there had been very few kindhearted ladies of the house, and never one so very. . .ebullient.

"I hope you rested well after the events of the evening."

"I did, I think." Her gaze rose to his as she reached for a strawberry. "And I was happy to see you kept your promise."

His promise? At the twinkle in her eyes, understanding dawned. Sleeping beside her.

"I am a man of my word, Lady Astley."

"I'm glad to hear it, my lord, for I am very fond of words."

She took in a deep breath and adjusted her serviette in her lap, glancing about the room as she did. Did she notice the peeling wallpaper? Or the wooden trim in need of repair? Or the uneven tilt of one of the sconces?

"I think this is the best breakfast room I've ever seen."

He paused his glass to his lips and stared at her. The woman with a silver-lining view. He'd gotten much more than he deserved or anticipated in this botched contract-turned-hopeful-beginning. His chest expanded with a strange sense of gratitude that nearly brought him to tears. What in heaven's name was wrong with him?

"What an excellent use of morning light." She gestured toward the glass doors at the end of the room. "And do those lead out onto a terrace?"

"With a fine prospect of the river and hills beyond."

"There's so much to discover, isn't there?" She glanced about again, absently raising her glass to her lips before turning her attention back to him. "What do you like best about Havensbrooke?"

He lowered his glass to the table and sat back, pondering the novel question. "Well, I. . ." He looked to Brandon, who only raised a dark brow in response. "I love the memories I have of my grandparents here, as well as other things."

She rested her chin on one hand and wiggled her brows at him. "Like?"

He enjoyed her playful prodding so much that he refused to sully the moment by correcting her posture. "Like the gardens, especially when they are in good shape. And the Great Hall, as you well know. There's a room beneath one of the back stairways where Grandfather and I stored wooden bric-a-brac we'd attempt to create on our own, though neither of us knew much of woodworking."

Her wrinkled-nosed grin encouraged more.

"Grandfather had a tree house built for me once. I don't even know if it's still standing." He hadn't thought of it in years. "My grandmother and I used to take a walk up the hillside to the vista and talk of stories and history and God. It's a special place to me. And I love the east wing with its turrets and morning light. I'm actually rather pleased at the notion of moving our sleeping quarters back to that portion of the house. The third-floor observation balcony points toward the west for the best views of sunset."

"I want to see all of it." She sighed, turning back to her breakfast. "Every place."

"Why?"

"First of all, I think the more time we spend in your sunny memories, the more strength we'll possess to combat against the more shadowy present." She took a sip of her tea. "And if they're important to you, I imagine I'll find them charming too. Each place will teach me more about you, and I want to know you best of all. It's what special friends do, you know."

*Special friends.* He'd never imagined anyone wanting to know about such treasured and intimate things, but why did he keep expecting Grace to follow some prescript pattern? Nothing about her fit anything he'd ever imagined. "I would like to share them with you."

"Should we start today? Perhaps with the vista? Or the gardens?"

His hope deflated. "I'm sorry, darling, but I've been called away." He slid the telegram toward her.

"But we only arrived." She read over the paper, her face brightening. "Would the inspector need my testimony too? I can take very good note of details sometimes, especially during life-threatening moments."

Brandon's head shot up.

"I believe my account and Patton's should suffice, and I need to attend to a bit of estate business while I am there, but Mrs. Powell and Elliott will be happy to assist you while I'm away."

His reassurance failed to resurrect her smile. The choice was unfortunate in timing, but he'd not wait another day without putting this plan into motion for her. . .and for his peace of mind. "But I do have a very special place to show you that may keep you duly occupied during my absence."

Her frown deepened. "Please tell me it doesn't involve finding toilets or evading spiteful dowagers."

Brandon coughed.

"Not at all." He cleared his throat to cover his desire to laugh. "It's more to your particular tastes, I believe. When you're finished with breakfast, I'll show you."

Her jeweled eyes widened. "I expect an excellent diversion then, my lord, if you plan to abandon me so soon." She took a few bites of toast and finished every strawberry on her plate, then proceeded to encourage him to share the remainder of his strawberries too.

As he escorted her away from the breakfast room, she asked dozens of questions regarding each room and fixture. She oohed over the beauty of the Great Hall in daylight and expounded upon how she'd like to decorate it for Christmas, while Frederick assured her he'd ask Brandon to locate enough garland to line the entire staircase. Her happy chatter echoed around the room as they climbed the stairs, a joyful addition to this large house.

As they reached the top of the stairs, Grace rushed forward to one of the third-story windows that offered a dazzling scene of the countryside stretching to rolling hills and a fog-fingered horizon.

"This is remarkable," she whispered as she took in his land. His legacy.

His thoughts corrected. *Their* legacy.

"Is all of that part of Havensbrooke?"

He nodded, drinking in the familiar view. "As far as our eyes can see, all the way up to the vista, there."

She followed his direction to the tallest hill nearest the house, which rose up to a flattened area filled with rocky outcroppings and evergreens. "The place you would walk with your grandmother?"

"Yes and Grandfather too. It provides an excellent prospect of the house." He shook his head as he stared down at her. "I've thought of them more since knowing you than I have in years. I believe you're a very good reminder."

"Reminder?"

"Of good things."

She searched his face with such raw compassion, his throat tightened. He cleared it and tugged her within his embrace, his words near her ear. "Are you ready for your surprise?"

She immediately melted against him, resting her head back on his shoulder, shrouding his senses in rosemary and Grace. "Please say it involves kissing!"

He complied, her fingers finding their way to the nape of his neck and encouraging him to linger. Blast the investigation! He'd rather give Grace a more intimate tour of Havensbrooke instead of keeping his appointment with the investigator. The past few nights aboard ship, he'd introduced her to more familiar and liberal kisses, to which she responded with a degree of enthusiasm to encourage his imagination in all sorts of distractible directions. But making her his? That seemed to wait just out of reach at every turn. He rested his forehead against hers, reveling in the wonder of this unexpected sweetness, this right desire and design. "Close your eyes."

She feigned a look of suspicion, then acquiesced—grin growing as he took her hands and tugged her forward. The double doors to the library creaked open, but she dutifully kept her eyes closed.

"I smell leather," she said with a giggle. "And. . .paper?"

He beamed as he led her to the center of the room. He couldn't remember the last time he'd felt such excitement. Light streamed in from the windows and cloaked the entire space with a hazy glow. Perfect.

He brought her hands to his lips and stared at her face. "Open your eyes, Grace."

A slight gasp escaped her lips as she took in the rows and rows of bookshelves rising to meet the oak-paneled, arched ceiling. At the far end of the room, a similarly arched window took up most of the wall, allowing in enough brightness to overpower the electric lights. A red-cushioned bench waited in front of the window, allowing for a view toward the drive of the house and the hillsides beyond.

"This. . .this is perfect." She spun slowly, in rapt wonder, taking in the splendor of the room with her hand clasped to her chest. Sunlight glinted off her auburn locks. She giggled and ran to him, hugging him close. "I'm so glad you like books."

She was much too easy on his heart.

"Does this mean you'll forgive my absence today?"

"If you'll send Zeus for company." She tossed a grin over her shoulder. "I suppose you have provided an *almost* suitable distraction."

"Almost?"

She snatched a book from the shelf and opened it. "My poor fictional heroes have never had such delicious competition before."

He paused his retreat toward the door. "Competition?"

She smiled sweetly. "My very own real-life hero."

Was that how she saw him? The tenderness, the faith? He wanted to be that man. He left the room and closed his eyes. *Lord, help me remain a hero for her—even when she learns the truth.*

## Chapter Sixteen

Grace spent the entire morning in the library, even taking tea by the window to enjoy the scenes of varied green disappearing into pale skies. The landscape, both inside the house and without, urged her into a giddy prayer of thanksgiving for another item to counter the many challenges she faced. If she could just hide away in the library for the rest of her life, she'd be the perfect Lady Astley, invisible from the world—for an invisible Gracelynn Percy would prove much more refined than the present one.

Zeus kept her company, finding a cozy spot at her side no matter where she moved in the room, almost as if he were trying to herd her about. It was rather endearing.

Frederick had not returned by the time the dinner bell rang, so with great trepidation and a hearty tug at her necklace, she found her way to the grand dining room for her first dinner in Havensbrooke's dining hall. Thick, ornate wooden molding framed the tall ceilings. Disrepair showed through the faded wallpaper that had turned a ghastly orange, but the eastern wall lined with floor-to-ceiling windows drew the eyes away from the walls and onto the gardens. An excellent use of windows.

Grace took her place a few seats from Lady Moriah, offering Brandon a smile as he pushed in her chair. Quiet shrouded the meal, thick and heavy with lingering disdain from her mother-in-law. Grace enjoyed silence involving libraries and evening strolls, or even the whispered breaths of a handsome man asleep at her side, but this sort of quiet raked over her nerves like talons. She could practically *feel* the woman's disapproval.

Kindness—as her grandfather had always said—was one's greatest weapon.

"Have you enjoyed your day, Lady Astley?"

The older woman took a sip from her glass before answering. "I've had no company, no useful conversation, and nothing worthwhile to read."

"That sounds like a horrible day."

"I prefer my solitude, and it's rare to find something truly enjoyable to read with all the silly dime novels littering the world. Dramatic drivel."

Grace hid her gasp in her glass, but she thought perhaps Brandon heard it, if the look he sent her before focusing ahead again was any indication. "Perhaps you've not been given the right sort. They're incredibly entertaining and filled with such adventure and—"

"How old are you?"

Grace sat up a little taller. "I'll be nineteen on Christm—"

"You act much younger." Her beady eyes pinned her until Grace almost squirmed. "But that is young enough for time and proper instruction to temper your inappropriate enthusiasm."

"Have I been inappro—"

"You smile too much."

Grace blinked at the severe interruption. "Smile too much?"

"And too broadly. It's unnerving and exposes you as silly."

A laugh tickled at the back of Grace's throat. "Perhaps I'm happy."

The woman singed her with a sharp look. "Time will cure that as well."

The urge to laugh dwindled.

"You are not left to your own devices now, Lady Astley." She scraped the word *lady* from her throat. "You have stepped into the shoes of centuries, so you are no longer free to believe in your dime novels and fairy tales. It is time to grow up. You are responsible for securing an heir for this estate and ensuring my son completes his task of saving it. That is all, and it's time you faced your new reality."

Her voice nailed the words forward.

Grace refused to lower her gaze. "And where does making him happy fall into your plans?"

"Happiness is as fleeting as paper. It will neither buy a stone for this house or food for this table. The sooner you forget those fanciful ideas and turn your attentions to the purpose for which Frederick married you, the better for Havensbrooke. And Frederick."

Grace's breath puffed shallow. "How do you suppose someone came up with the idea for this beautiful home of Havensbrooke?"

The woman blinked. "What do you mean?"

"Or the oil landscapes so proudly displayed in this room. Do you suppose their creations stemmed from a lackluster indifference?"

Grace dared not reach for her glass, because her hands trembled from her attempt to maintain her composure.

"You talk nonsense, ridiculous girl."

"Imagination, fanciful ideas, joy in the beauty around us inspires creativity *and* productivity. Why can't we have both the beautiful and the practical? The fantastical and the functional? Didn't God create with both practicality *and* pleasure?"

"You'll be the embarrassment of us all with such drivel." Lady Moriah's jaw tightened, and she tossed her serviette to the table. "It is a sad reality that you care more for your daydreams than you do for others' opinions of your husband and his legacy."

"That is not true. Of course, I care—"

"And if you did care"—she stood and took the cane Brandon offered—"you would learn to keep your conversations safely between two topics—the weather and the state of our gardens. I fear that anything else you offer will cause Frederick more social harm at having such a silly wife than the remote possibility of doing him any good from your *proposed* creativity. You were an undesirable solution to a most unfortunate turn of events."

Heat slipped from Grace's face at the mixture of truth and barb in the woman's accusation.

Lady Moriah's cane beat against the glossy floors as she took her leave.

"Mother," Frederick said from the doorway.

"You've married a simpleton," she murmured in passing. "We'll be the laughingstocks of the county."

"That's quite enough."

His reprimand bounced off Lady Moriah's glare, and with scowl firmly fitted to every crinkle in her face, she left the room.

Grace's insides quivered almost uncontrollably, but she tempered her expression with a greeting smile. "The Bible says 'a merry heart is good like a medicine.'" Her gaze shifted to her plate. "But perhaps I cast too much sunshine in places where it is unwanted."

He rounded the table and took a chair near her. "I don't know if there is medicine strong enough to cheer her heart."

Grace refused the negative turn of her thoughts, holding back a sudden rush of tears for Frederick's sake. He'd had so much hurt, she couldn't bear to add her sadness to his brimming cup. "There's another verse that seems apt to the moment."

His smile crooked in question.

" 'All the days of the afflicted are evil: but he that is of a merry heart hath a continual feast.' "

He studied her and quite surprisingly took her hand. "I apologize for my tardiness. The venture in town took much longer than anticipated, and I still did not complete my task."

She stifled a whimper. "You'll be gone again tomorrow?"

"Only for the morning, and I'll make certain breakfast is served in your room to keep you out of Mother's claws. She has a great deal of helpful guidance about how to prepare you as an aristocratic lady, but her methods are not the best, so I will employ the help of my sister, Eleanor. I saw her in town, and she's anxious to meet you."

What if Grace failed with Eleanor too? She had found a book in the library titled *Beadle's Book of Etiquette for Ladies and Gentlemen*, but it was from the mid-1800s, so she wasn't sure how much stock to put in the advice. She'd flipped open *A Book of Edwardian Etiquette* and felt much better after reading, "The test of good manners is to be able to put up pleasantly with bad ones."

"Mrs. Powell has been instructed to meet with you each morning as you take over household responsibilities. Blake will be with us for dinner tomorrow evening, so she will certainly want to know how to prepare for our guest."

Grace pushed aside her worry and turned her attention to her new responsibilities. She pelted Frederick with questions about guest rooms, servants' names, previous meals, and Mrs. Powell's personality, to which Frederick had very little to add to Grace's initial assessment. It was shocking how men didn't know the answers to simple questions like when a person's birthday was or their favorite flower. Those questions seemed fairly elementary.

And Frederick had no news to add to the information about the crashed automobile. The inspector took notes, but the mechanic had not come to any conclusions yet. Clearly the men in town could use some help with this investigation, but Grace felt fairly certain the etiquette book would not support her dashing to town to unearth her own answers.

The dowager's assessment stung afresh. Maybe Frederick Percy really had married the wrong bride after all, and maybe that was why he hadn't taken Grace with him to town. Perhaps she really would be alone in this new world.

"You've left her alone for two days with your *mother*?"

Already Blake's directness had hit on points Frederick hadn't considered. "For an impeccable reason, as I told you."

"But she's a stranger here. Perhaps you should've taken her with you."

"To study bathtubs and toilets?"

"To *be* with you, Freddie. From my brief acquaintance with your dear wife, I'd say she could become interested in about anything without any motivation whatsoever."

Frederick stared at Blake and pinched his lips into a frown, diverting his attention to the car window and the passing countryside. Perhaps he should have left Blake at the train station to find his own way to Havensbrooke.

"Imagine it from her point of view. You're the only person she really knows in the whole of England, and her head is filled with fanciful notions of you sweeping her off to some castle forever. Then she arrives instead to find a dark, gloomy estate in disrepair, an evil dowager mother, and a houseful of doleful servants, with no friend in the world as her companion. I expected more from your tender heart."

"My tender heart, as you call it, was working feverishly on keeping my wife from the discomfort of walking about the hallways in her unmentionables."

"Yes, right. Those particular pleasures are reserved for her charming yet absent husband."

Frederick looked away. "Hmm."

Blake stared at Frederick for a full five seconds. "I say, Freddie. What is it? Has she refused your advances?"

Heat climbed up Frederick's neck at his friend's almost cultic gift of observation. "Blake."

"Is she unable to complete the task?"

"It's nothing like that." Frederick forced the words through clenched teeth. "She receives my somewhat chaste affections with. . .appreciation."

"Chaste?" Blake folded his arms across his chest. "She's your *wife!*"

"A young, naive wife who has only known me for a little over two weeks, and married to me only one."

"And who you underestimate a great deal, I believe."

Frederick growled. "What on earth do you mean?"

"You know as well as I that naivete doesn't mean disinterest." His friend studied him in a most annoying way. "And with her proclivity for romance, I'd imagine she has a healthy dose of curiosity. You've held your emotions in check for so long, perhaps it's time to give yourself as freely as she gives to you—as she likely needs you to do. Are you afraid she'll break your heart like Celia? Is that why you're waiting?"

"No." His cousin's words stung with a truth he hadn't considered. Was he? Did that undercurrent of fear pause him from offering her his heart freely? He cleared his throat and offered a half glare. "I'm attempting to be a gentleman."

Blake's brows shot high. "Freddie, a gentleman is all well and good in society, but the last thing a woman needs in the bedroom is a husband who doesn't know what he wants."

"I know what I want." His words sharpened.

"Then perhaps she wants the same thing."

Frederick released a long sigh as they turned up the drive for home. "You need to get married, Blake."

"No." He frowned and shook his head. "It's much less troublesome and more entertaining to criticize those who are already in the thick of it." He patted the seat of the car. "And I can enjoy the way you've put your wife's money to good use. A roadster is the car to have nowadays, I hear."

"Since we lost the other car in the river and already have an outdated Touring, I thought we might as well purchase something more fashionable and reliable."

"Lost the other car *in the river?*" Blake's palm rose with one blond brow. "What on earth did Lady Astley do with your car?"

"It wasn't Grace." Frederick stifled a groan, wishing he hadn't been so free with his words. It was already bad enough than an entire town watched the car accident unfold. The last thing he needed was another reason for Blake to worry. But there was no going back now. He proceeded to divulge the entire scene.

"Well, it was a good thing your lovely bride spent her childhood with servants and an eccentric grandfather, or you'd have been a chauffeur short." Blake released a whistle, his lighthearted demeanor cloaking a mind filled with caution, if Freddie knew his friend aright. "And what of the car? Did you discover the reason for the malfunction?"

Frederick kept his gaze forward as the spires of Havensbrooke came into view. "Patton and I met with the new mechanic this morning before fetching you from the station. His thoughts after examining the car were inconclusive. He noted possible evidence of tampering, but due to damage from the accident and the age of the car, it was difficult to ascertain a cause with certainty." He locked gazes with his cousin. "So it's all likely nothing but an accident."

"Of course it is."

"Blake."

"I wonder what your curious little wife will think of these inconclusive findings."

"I'd rather not worry her, especially with her generous imagination." The roadster slowed to a stop in front of Havensbrooke's entry. "Besides, the authorities will continue the investigation, and once they come to a definitive conclusion, I will share it with her."

Blake groaned and shook his head. "Freddie, it is preferable to keep information from other people's wives, but keeping secrets from one's own wife is being bound for destruction. She inevitably finds out."

Frederick stepped from the car, soaking in Blake's warning. Of course the man was right. With Grace's rabid curiosity, she'd likely find out before he had a chance to tell her anyway.

As they entered the house, Grace greeted them on the way to the dining room, wearing a deep burgundy evening dress with some sort of black lace overlay and looking every bit the part of the lady of the house. It was rather nice to come home to such a sight, though his bride's smile did not reach her eyes and her walk remained as stiff as a tree. Frederick's heart squeezed in response. What had happened?

"It's a pleasure to see you again, Mr. Blake."

Grace offered her hand, her posture the very picture of elegance. Ah, she'd been practicing. His grin paused. Yet something about her rehearsed movements turned his stomach. Where was the glimmer in those eyes? His gaze shot to Blake. Was the old chap right? Had he been holding out his most intimate affections to guard his heart? Had he neglected something she needed most to give her something he thought she needed more?

He was her only friend in England. And his mother wielded words like knives. How had he failed his wife so obviously?

"Lady Astley." Blake bowed over her gloved hand with exaggerated flair, encouraging the addition of a brief sparkle in her eyes to the smile on her face.

"I see you found my husband."

"Indeed." Blake flashed Frederick a glance from his periphery. "The poor fellow looked lost without you."

A rush of rose blushed her cheeks in a most fetching way but faded just as quickly. Frederick's stomach panged in discomfort.

"Dinner is waiting for us," Grace offered, chin high, gesturing toward the hall.

Blake extended his arm, sending a wink Frederick's way. "Freddie, you won't mind if I escort your lovely bride into dinner, will you?"

Frederick offered a begrudging nod and followed behind the pair into the dining room, where Mother already had taken her place.

At once, Grace's demeanor shifted. Her smile faded, and her conversation diminished to basic answers. She even made some noncommittal reply to Blake's question regarding her recent literary exploits. His mother kept the dialogue turned away from Grace as much as possible, sending subtle stings in the process.

Heat surged into Frederick's face. He'd been such a fool!

He'd underestimated his mother's influence. Whatever she'd said or done to steal Grace's smile, he'd allowed by his absence at such a crucial time in their relationship. He was supposed to protect his wife, even from his mother, but within a paltry two days of their arrival in Derbyshire, he'd nearly gotten Grace killed in an automobile accident *and* allowed his wife to endure alone the verbal attacks of his embittered mother. *God, help me make amends!*

And prove he could be the husband his wife needed.

Grace had chosen a simple, dark blue gown for her first visit to the parish of Astlynn Commons. She really couldn't top the river incident as far as memorable introductions, no matter what fashion mishap she made, so at least she faced lowered expectations. Besides, Lillias had always said Grace looked heavenly in dark blue, so why not match the place and the compliment? Surely, she couldn't fail with *heavenly* at church. The gown boasted an empire waist with delicate embroidery over the elbow-length sleeves. A close-fitting, cream-colored hat embellished with matching blue ribbons topped the ensemble.

Lady Moriah had impaled Grace with more criticism during lunch the previous day, and some of the advice in the *Ladies of Refinement* pamphlet left Grace convinced she'd never reach the heights of "refinement" expected for a true lady. Certainly if she failed at being a lady, she'd never win Frederick's heart.

She stared at her reflection. Her lips tipped downward in a sad little pout, her eyes almost. . .fragile. Lillias had been right. Grace hadn't known the harshness and loneliness of the world outside her books and fairy tales. What loneliness Cinderella must have known in a world so bereft of the ones who loved her.

Heated tears warmed her eyes. Was this what the rest of her life would be? Isolation? Expending energy to suppress herself and pretend to be someone else? Even if her dashing husband slept beside her at night, he disappeared during the day, leaving her to the gaping emptiness of Havensbrooke and the verbal poison of his mother.

Oh, what must Frederick's childhood have been like to live with such a woman!

Grace had spent a good half hour talking quite fervently with the Almighty that morning.

Lillias always considered Grace's animated and friendly prayers sacrilegious, but if the King of heaven adamantly referred to her as not only His child but also His friend, why keep to pious formality? And she desperately needed a friend.

God hadn't created her for plastic smiles and shallow relationships. She closed her eyes tight. This could *not* be her future.

She shook her head and dared her reflection to wilt. Heroines were not weak creatures. They captured their own futures. Forced fate's hand. What of Jo March, Shakespeare's Beatrice, Jane Eyre?

Grace stood taller, her soul drawing from her reserves. She refused to allow Moriah Percy's antagonistic disposition to steal any more hours or tears.

"You look lovely, my lady." Ellie stood behind her as she stared into the full-length mirror. "There's nothing to disapprove of in either your manner or appearance."

Grace's gaze shot to her shock of red hair, made all the more so by the hue of the gown. Oh well, there was no hiding it. And if God gave her this astounding color, He must have known she could wear it well—or at the very least, respectably.

With or without Frederick's attention, Grace had to find a way to live well where God had placed her. For her own heart, if nothing else.

Let the dowager countess do her worst.

# Chapter Seventeen

Sunlight filtered through leafy oaks among the quiet graves on either side of the cobblestone path to St. James. Frederick cast an apologetic look back to Grace as he escorted his mother ahead up the path to the church. The walkway only accommodated pairs. In Frederick's defense, Grace had suggested he help his mother since she wobbled precariously against her cane when she stood for long. But the shift only pinned the truth deeper that Grace lived outside their world, their story.

The chasm of an ocean between England and home tripled in size, but Grace shook off the melancholy. If David in the Psalms had to remind himself of the truth when his heart trembled with fear, Grace could do no less. *"Why art thou cast down, O my soul? and why art thou disquieted in me? hope thou in God: for I shall yet praise him for the help of his countenance."*

Her thoughts clung to the truth. *Hope in God.* Perhaps God was using these lonely moments to remind her that He was enough and that He'd made her just as she was, for His glory. Even if she'd never know which shoes to wear with a summer suit!

She drank in the sight of the beautiful old church. Its vine-covered rock walls and stained glass nestled between mature trees welcomed her with a sweet reminder—God was here, no matter where she moved among the world.

He was everywhere. Certainly He could help her find where she belonged.

"I hope you'll allow me to play escort, my lady." Blake came up behind her and tipped his head in her direction, offering his arm to walk.

"I didn't know you were attending church with us this morning, Mr. Blake."

"I'm a regular church attender, Lady Astley." He tugged at his collar and shot her a wink. "But I usually arrive late and leave early. Too many marriageable ladies desperate to entrap a single man."

Grace's smile bloomed for the first time that morning. "I can think of worse places to find a future bride than in church."

Blake shook his head, feigning a grimace. "Not to contradict your ladyship, but I've yet to find a perfect combination of devout, engaging, and somewhat easy on the eyes, present company excluded, of course."

"I see where the direction of my prayers for you must go in the future."

"Please allow me at least another year before you begin such entreaties, if you don't mind. I'm inclined to appreciate my current status for a bit longer."

It felt good to laugh.

"I hear you are in charge of decorating Havensbrooke for Christmas." Blake's brows rose in question.

"I am. Brandon and Mary searched for as many ornaments as they could find within the recesses of the house yesterday. And Elliott is helping me gather garland." It had all been a very good distraction until lunch with Lady Moriah. "I just have to find a tree."

"Might I offer a suggestion?"

"Please."

"When I would spend time at Havensbrooke as a child, Grandfather would take us to the vista to locate a proper tree for the house. We never failed to discover an excellent choice."

"The place where Frederick used to go with his grandparents?"

"Exactly."

"Thank you for the advice, Mr. Blake." Grace squeezed his arm. "And the company."

Morning birdsong and the din of voices from the church ahead quieted their walk. The morning chill in the air held the scent of snow.

"I know it's been a rough go since you arrived. And Lady Moriah, the dowager," he corrected while covering her hand on his arm, "she brings more storm than sun into everyone's lives. But Freddie will do right by you. He may not have his best foot forward in the beginning, but he'll find the steps soon enough."

Grace turned her attention back to her husband as he helped his mother through the church's entry. Grace didn't question his goodness, only his absence. And perhaps his priorities—especially since she didn't seem to be part of them. "I want things to go well between us, Blake. Truly."

His gaze softened into uncharacteristic sincerity. "I know you do, and so does Freddie, once he takes a hard look at things. To be honest, he's rather dumbstruck by you."

"By me? What on earth do you mean?"

"Your generosity of heart is an anomaly to a man who has always had to prove himself to the people who should have loved him best, only to have them reject him." Blake gestured forward with his chin. "Freddie and Havensbrooke, they're a lot alike, if you think about it. Both left to the weeds of the world and in need of patience and a tender hand to help them bloom again." He wiggled his brows. "They may even need some unexpected creativity too."

Her gaze followed his to the pair disappearing into the church. Tending hearts? What a beautiful idea.

She offered Blake a grin. "My good Mr. Blake, if I didn't know better, I'd take your statement as almost sentimental."

"Nonsense. A quote from the paper or some such, but regardless, Lady Astley, I have every faith in you. Weeds will have no power against your sunshine." He tipped his hat and paused at the church door. "Now I shall leave you to meet the honorable Reverend Marshall."

He spun away, nodding to a man wearing a white cassock and black preaching scarf as he passed.

"Lady Astley, welcome to St. James." The reverend bowed his bald head in deference. "We are delighted to have you in Astlynn Commons."

"Thank you, Reverend Marshall. What a beautiful day for worship."

"Yes, it is." The man's gray eyes creased at the corners as he smiled. "I would suspect you appreciate it more than most."

"I do. Most assuredly." A wash of gratitude nearly brought her to tears. "A familiar place among the unfamiliar can provide a great deal of comfort."

"You are always welcome. Kindred hearts find their place within these walls."

She bit her wobbling lip. Why was she so quick to doubt that God heard her? He'd placed yet another person in her wake to remind her of His nearness. "Thank you."

"Your fame precedes you." He leaned forward with a twinkle in his pale eyes. "I've heard you're an excellent swimmer."

Grace blinked back her tears, her grin swelling to proportions Charles Bingley would appreciate. "You should see me at lawn tennis."

Reverend Marshall raised a hand to his lips to brace the edges of his smile. "Yes, I think you will do quite well for Havensbrooke."

With that added vote of confidence, Grace crossed the threshold into the church's narrow entry, only to find Frederick lying in wait. Without a word, he pulled her aside into an alcove barely large enough to share, his gaze searching hers. "I know the service is ready to begin, but I had to speak with you."

She searched his sober face. "Are you all right?"

"*You* are concerned for me?" He sighed and studied her, shaking his head. "Oh Grace, I have so much to learn." He wrapped his fingers around hers for a brief embrace. "I'm afraid I've not been a very good friend of late, and I wish to make amends."

Her bottom lip dropped at his declaration before she recovered. "I've missed my friend immensely."

"And I've been an imbecile." He groaned as if her words inflicted pain. "Forgive me, darling?"

There was something disarming about a man who framed an apology with a truth on one end and a *darling* on the other. "Would you help me find a Christmas tree today? It would be a very friendly thing to do."

His quick smile smothered her previous doubt quite soundly, and he gave her fingers another squeeze. "I'd love to find a Christmas tree with you."

Just then Reverend Marshall dipped his head into the alcove, his gaze glimmering as it passed from Frederick to Grace. "We are ready to begin."

"Begin?" Grace's attention shifted from the reverend to Frederick.

"As the newest Earl and Countess of Astley, we sign our name to the family registry." Frederick offered her an encouraging nod.

"A tradition that has continued for over a hundred fifty years," added Reverend Marshall.

"And today, we add ours as the newest stewards of the people of

Astlynn Commons and Havensbrooke." Frederick offered his arm, his tender gaze pulling at her hope. "Together."

She drew in a breath, slipped her arm through his, and followed Reverend Marshall into the ancient sanctuary. Stone pillars lined the middle aisle, ushering them toward an upraised wooden lectern area bathed in variegated color from sunlight through the intricate stained glass windows. What a magical backdrop for worship!

With great pomp, Grace stood beside Frederick at the front of the church as he added their names beneath a long row of Percys. Her smile softened. *Together.*

*Frederick and Gracelynn Percy, Lord and Lady Astley.*

A sudden gravity landed on her shoulders, as if generations of unseen men and women crowded around them in the church to wager how they'd measure up.

Was this a small taste of what Frederick felt? A tiny glimpse into centuries of lives lived for this legacy?

"May God bless this newest generation of Percys of Havensbrooke Hall and Astlynn Commons for His own glory," Reverend Marshall announced to the crowded church. "Let us pray."

Once the prayer ended, Grace attempted to follow Frederick to his seat, but he stopped her with a gentle hand. "I must take a special place in the lord's box today." He nodded toward a seat framed in by a dark-stained wooden fence. "My great-grandfather began a tradition years ago that the lord of the manor would lead prayers once a month when he was in town." His gaze turned apologetic. "I asked Mother to save a place for you in our usual seat."

*Patience, Grace. You're tending a heart.*

Grace stiffened. "Of course." She moved to stand beside Lady Moriah.

Reverend Marshall's deep and exuberant voice pealed directly into Grace's heart.

"May the God of hope fill you with all joy and peace in believing, so that by the power of the Holy Spirit you may abound in hope."

Abound in hope? Her attention riveted to the man as if he'd spoken directly from heaven, and being a cleric and all, that's exactly what he was supposed to do. The Bible proved incredibly poetic and poignant at the most opportune times. Like now, when she needed poetic and poignant the most.

As the congregation stood for the first hymn, Grace stared down at the words. She'd not heard this hymn before.

> *O love that wilt not let me go,*
> *I rest my weary soul in Thee.*

Weary? She'd wrestled with weariness of spirit, but the words soothed over her fear with divine reminders. No matter where she went or how lost she felt, God's love would never let her go.

> *I give Thee back the life I owe,*
> *That in its ocean depths its flow*
> *May richer, fuller be.*

She closed her eyes, envisioning the ocean waves that propelled the *Aquitania* across an endless sea. The idea poured over her wounds. Her life, her hopes overflowed with the fathomless love of God. He cradled her dreams and her future in His care. She was never alone or lost to despair. The harmonies of voices all around swelled through her, reverberating with truth like an embrace from above.

She belonged to Him.

God had placed her here as she was, knowing exactly what Havensbrooke and Frederick needed most. She was not a victim of circumstance, and she would not kowtow to the fear. As any heroine worth her own story, Grace claimed her future—Frederick, Havensbrooke, even her malevolent mother-in-law.

It was time to begin *living* the newest chapter of her life.

Frederick's desire for a private conversation with his wife was ceremoniously thwarted by his mother's sudden need for assistance to her room. He should have known her well enough to recognize the ploy, because after taking much longer than necessary to reach her room, she turned on him as soon as the door closed.

"Did you see your wife in church? Are we to become accustomed to these fits of passion?"

His lips tilted at the memory of Grace's "fit of passion" in the church. Angelic. Her gaze to the heavens. Her smile, glowing. The unidentifiable feeling that had percolated in his chest throughout the entire service as he gazed upon his unconventional bride pearled into recognition.

Love.

He *loved* Grace.

Even if she loosened every gossiping tongue in town by swimming across a river or standing radiant during a somber service. She kept doing that. Entering his world of gray places and bringing light and. . .and he'd want her no other way. He *needed* her no other way.

"I shouldn't be surprised, with your history of fumbles and mistakes, that Mr. Ferguson fooled you into marrying his emotional waterworks daughter. And since you've no mind to control her, I'll have to take her in hand."

"Grace is not the problem, Mother." Her continual guilt-laced manipulation played a dull refrain he'd outgrown. "And mistakes? My brother made as many as I did. Look at the state of our home. If he'd loved this land at all instead of being controlled by his petty interests, then Havensbrooke—"

Her slap came without warning, a weak sting, but humiliating nonetheless. "You know nothing of it. He was twice the man you are. Always had been. We would never know of *his* illegitimate child or *his* decadent lifestyles, because he had the respectability and control to house his passions with discretion. You, however, flaunted your recklessness like a badge of honor."

"I'm not that man anymore, and whether you like it or not, Edward is gone. *I'm* the future of Havensbrooke. And we have an opportunity to start over—"

"Start over with *her*?" She released a humorless laugh. "How could this ginger-headed trinket of yours do anything to mend the embarrassment you've—"

"That is enough." Frederick walked toward the door. "I will begin seeking suitable housing for you in town—somewhere you will be close to Havensbrooke and well cared for—but I will not have you undermine my future any longer."

"You—" Her hand reached for her throat. "You would cast me out?"

"You will always be a part of the Percy family, but you are no longer mistress of Havensbrooke, and I will not allow your toxicity to continue its assault upon me or my wife."

His mother slipped down into her chair, black gown billowing around her, eyes wide. "How dare you speak—"

"I've attempted to open your heart to me. Spent years trying to make you care for me a little. You were never willing. Grace is more than willing. I will capture the happiness available to me and attempt to redeem what was lost."

Frederick's wife had disappeared. He searched her room, the library, his study, even had the vain hope of finding her in *his* room, to no avail. The thought that she might have run away flickered to mind, a notion he'd never consider for anyone else. But Grace? With his bumbling of her heart over the past few days, it was a distinct possibility, but he knew better now. Understood better now.

"My lord?"

Frederick turned to Elliott's call, Mary, the housemaid at his side by the east wing entrance. "Might you be in search of Lady Astley, sir?"

"You've seen her?"

"She asked about the footpath to the vista," Elliott offered.

"The vista?" Frederick's attention moved to the nearest window, where a swirl of flurries danced just beyond the pane.

"She waited for half an hour before dashin' off, sir," Mary added, her lips grappling with her smile. "It seems she went in search of a Christmas tree."

"Of course she did." Frederick half laughed, half coughed out the question. "By herself, I presume?"

"She took Zeus with her, sir," Elliott replied, and if Frederick didn't know better, he'd even say his valet had a twinkle in his eyes. "Though I don't think he was too keen on going into the cold."

"Clearly, Lady Astley doesn't have the same repulsion." Frederick reached for the coat Elliott offered.

"No sir. She was fairly giddy at the notion of choosing a tree in the snow." Elliot's lips twitched.

Mary's smile held nothing back. Elliott's emerged with a bit more subtlety. Both proved that Lady Astley had already worked her magic upon these two servants.

"Well then, I suppose I ought to go find my wife."

꧁ ꧂

Grace increased her pace up the forested hillside, breathing in the earthy scents of moss and hints of mint. Flurries swirled all around her, enticing her to spin once or twice out of pure delight. Zeus pranced along at her side, his golden-red coat a wonderful contrast to the frosty surroundings. What better way to brighten up Havensbrooke than with a Christmas tree? An enormous one.

The hymn at church, the reminder of the vows she'd made over two weeks ago, and the sweet look of confidence Frederick sent her in the car on the ride home all pointed to a clear choice: fall beneath the weight of her regret and lose her own story, or grasp with both hands and full heart the story God had placed before her. She may not have control over Lady Astley's sour demeanor or Frederick's willingness to spend time with her, but she had power over her own response, her own heart.

And she would choose hope instead of despair, because she refused to be anything less than a heroine in her own life.

She grabbed the front of her skirts and climbed higher up the hillside, pausing at a tree now and then to get Zeus's opinion on the matter. He seemed to understand perfectly, because he led her forward to the very spot where an elegant and enormous spruce stood regent over the trail as if it had spent its whole existence waiting for her arrival.

She tied her scarf around the tree and stepped farther into the clearing, her smile spreading so wide it pressed into her chilly cheeks. An evergreen forest framed the clearing on three sides, but on the fourth the world opened to a rocky outcropping and a magnificent view of frosted countryside for miles.

Grace ignored the frigid wind whooshing up from the valley and stepped toward the ledge. Nestled below, surrounded by white-dusted rolling hills, sat the sprawling estate of Havensbrooke. Its jutted roofs and spires spread out to form an H of gray-tan stone. Walled gardens framed the house on three sides, lifeless and waiting for a creative, loving hand. A river carved an S on the far side of the house, with icy hillsides rolling as far as the eye could see, and in the distance, Grace caught sight of St. James's steeple.

Havensbrooke didn't appear as foreboding when dusted in a wonderland hue. It was as if God had painted the world with hope just for her to make certain she'd been listening in church that morning. Grace raised her arms to embrace the beauty, wind billowing about her with enough force to unknot her hair from its clips.

"Great things are done when men and mountains meet," Grace called to the wind. Zeus's ears perked, and she offered the dog a grin. "Or in this case, women and mountains."

The William Blake quote disappeared into the snow-coated air.

"I see you found the vista."

Grace turned to see Frederick stepping from among the trees, his black coat and tall frame standing out from the frosty scene. He looked rather dashing with flurries in his dark hair. Grace wagered he'd age remarkably well.

"It's such a good place to gain perspective. . .and find a tree, I hear."

He came to her side, giving Zeus a pat on his head before slipping his arm around Grace's waist. "You are too good."

She looked up at him, searching his dark eyes as he searched hers. Oh, there was such remorse there. Such tenderness.

He lowered his forehead to her temple and sighed. "My mother is a harsh, bitter woman, and I left you alone to face the wolf. I'm sorry, darling."

"No one can be that horrid without a very good reason, don't you think?" Grace leaned into him as his lips slipped to her cheek. "How very sad she must be to cause everyone around her to dislike her so much."

"You're more generous in your assessment than I am." He turned to look over the view, his profile delightfully Grecian and angled.

Her gaze focused on his very kissable mouth. What a shame that perfectly placed lips were not written about with more thoroughness in literature. They proved deliciously attractive to her mind. Or at least Frederick's lips did. Perhaps the use of those lips had something to do with it.

He caught her staring, and his expression softened as he attempted to capture some of her blowing hair to tuck behind her ear. "I should have taken you with me to town, but I was so focused on meeting with the inspector and then securing your comfort that I didn't consider the consequences. I allowed my concerns for what I thought you needed to outweigh the true needs of your heart, and I'm sorry."

The wind tousled his dark locks over his crinkled forehead in a dashing sort of way. Oh, he looked handsomer when he was penitent than in any other posture—except maybe roguish.

"What you *thought* I needed?"

"The lavatory. The one for your room." His gaze searched hers, and he ran a palm over his shaking head. "I didn't tell you why I stayed in town so long, did I?"

"No." She replayed his words, attempting to decipher them, a steady warmth branching all through her. "That's why you were gone? For me?"

"You were used to better accommodations and privacy, something I couldn't afford before you came, but I have the resources to change that now and rushed ahead to—"

"You weren't annoyed by me? Embarrassed?"

He turned toward her, holding her shoulders. "Good night, Grace, is that what you thought?"

"I've read that some men see their wives as a regret, so they resort to escaping in their work or improvements or whatever. I just didn't imagine it would happen so soon—"

"Nothing of the sort." He framed her face with his gloved hands. "In fact, I was reminded all the more this morning how very grateful I am that you are my bride, and I wish to leave you with no doubt of my affection for you."

"Your affection for me?" That sounded very close to love, didn't it? Her smile trembled wider.

"I want you to be happy here with me. But my world is not a kind one, and you are so inexperienced—"

She touched her fingers softly to his lips, bringing his words to a halt. There was something so powerful in this man that it quivered through her with a mixture of awe and curiosity. His heart, his passions, and lifeline were somehow intricately tied to this land—just as Mrs. Whitlock had said—and in the beautiful stone walls and vast countryside pulsed her future as much as Frederick's, if she'd let it. But she would need to embrace it all and release her fear. "I'm stronger than *you* think I am. I may be stronger than *I* think I am, but one thing I want you to know is that you and Havensbrooke are my home now too, and I mean to take care of what is mine."

The faintest smile touched his mouth, his thumb tracing her chin, before he sealed her declaration by placing his lips on hers. Warm and strong, his kiss swirled pleasant heat up through her, dashing away the cold. She held to his jacket and her promise. Ready or not, she *was* Countess of Astley, and God had chosen her for this task, so she would make it her own.

❦

Gracelynn Percy presented the perfect portrait of his new beginning with her untamed hair flying around her face, his home as the backdrop. His past and future situated together. He pushed a strand of her hair behind her ear in a vain attempt to control the wind-frenzied locks, the intimate touch bringing him closer to those azure eyes.

He loved her.

The feeling, the realization filled every space in his chest with a desire to shout to the heavens.

"I see you found your Christmas tree," he murmured against her cheek as she faced the view, snow dancing about them like some magic was at work.

"You saw my scarf then?"

"Indeed. A good choice for the Great Hall."

She pressed in a little closer to him in gratitude, and he tightened his hold, their faces pointed toward the view. "I'm sorry I left you alone, Grace."

"I hope you've learned your lesson," The teasing in her voice peaked his grin.

"Yes, but I hope I'm a faster learner in the future." He unwound his scarf and tucked it around her neck before placing another kiss to her lips. He looked back to the estate, a memory she'd particularly enjoy coming to mind. "Do you see that garden on the east side? The small one near the edge of the river?"

"The one with the tall evergreen growing out of it?"

"Yes, that one." He closed his eyes, his cheek against her head. He'd never known such an unadulterated sense of rightness, such clarity in a choice. He almost chuckled out of sheer astonishment. He'd never have chosen Grace, but God knew what he'd *needed*. What his heart, future, and even Havensbrooke needed.

Frederick would make up his fumblings to Grace. He would show her a pure, faithful heart, if God gave him time. "It was my grandparents' garden. My grandfather built it for my grandmother upon their marriage as a little haven for them. Mr. Archer, our gardener for decades, said the two of them would disappear into the garden for hours together with only the sound of birdsong and laughter."

She turned her face toward him, her eyes, her lips enticingly close. "I read a book about a lovers' garden once."

"Of course you did."

"It was very romantic."

He touched her chin and tipped her face up to his, dipping to take a longer kiss than he'd taken a few minutes before. She made a sweet, contented hum in her throat as he deepened the kiss, his body warming to the taste and feel of her.

"I think that should be one of the first gardens we recover then."

He nodded and turned with her back to the scene. The snow had increased in thickness, blanketing the world in white and giving a heavenly sheen to the gray stone of Havensbrooke. A good reminder of redemption and hope. "I would wall myself up to read when I was younger. Find nooks, often in my grandparents' garden, because it made me feel closer to them."

"You were not much different than me, it seems." Her statement came with a sadness, a hint of understanding.

"In many ways I wasn't."

Her gaze asked for more information, but her lips did not. That would be for another time. The longer story. But not for today. Today was for making happy memories.

A flash of red in the distance caught his attention among the snow. A red Ford Touring, perhaps? He couldn't quite make it out, but it was leaving from the direction of the old ruins. He didn't know anyone with such a car. Why would someone be near the ruins? Especially someone with such a fine car? A chill settled over his skin.

A rush of protection shot through him as the car turned a bend and disappeared from view. It was likely a driver who'd lost his way among the country lanes. Or some tourist out to discover a grand house open for exploration. He shrugged away the concern, just as a low rumble sounded in the distance.

Grace's head turned toward the sound. "Does the train run near Havensbrooke?"

"Not near enough to hear it."

Another rumble resounded with a bit more clarity. Her back straightened with tension. "Then. . .then what was that?"

"Nothing but thunder."

"Thunder?" She spun around, her eyes wide. "But it's snowing!"

He placed his hands on her arms and searched her face. "Thunder snow is rare, but nothing untoward. I'm sure it will pass soon enough."

"Thunder *snow*?" She flinched back from him and then dashed toward the footpath. "Why on earth would England have something as horrible as thunder snow?"

Another round of thunder sounded, this time even closer. She took off at a faster pace, Zeus at her heels.

"What is wrong?"

She didn't appear to hear him, for she had taken off down the path, skirt flying.

"Grace!" He followed in pursuit.

"I'm sorry, my dear Frederick, but I cannot stop," she called behind her. "I'm rather terrified of storms. It's a ridiculous, childhood panic, but there's nothing to be done for it. I'd thought I'd escaped them in winter."

He chased after her down the path, her speed impressive. "What inspired such a fear?"

She flinched as another rumble echoed closer. "Daffodils."

*Daffodils?*

"It's a rather novel-worthy explanation, actually." She forged ahead, her words coming in broken breaths. "My mother died giving birth to my baby brother when I was seven years old. Lillias was away with Father—and the baby came early. Too early, the doctor said, but I didn't know those facts at seven, of course. All I knew was something was wrong and the terrible storm outside the house seemed to link to the conflict inside the house."

He rushed ahead to help her over a fallen log. "Thank you." She offered a brief smile before taking off again, but he kept hold of her hand. "Icicles in sunlight."

He squinted over at her, but she didn't seem aware of her off-topic words.

"Over the crushing thunder and flashes of lightning, I heard my mother's screams of pain. . .until they stopped forever."

He squeezed her fingers. "Dear Grace."

"As silly as it sounds, even now, I. . .I can still hear her screams in the thunder."

"What did you do to find comfort when you were at home?"

She shrugged, keeping her hand in his as she pulled him through the forest, Zeus leading the way far ahead. "When I was younger, Father said I would crawl into the cupboard and bury myself beneath pillows, but as I grew older, I'd sing very loudly to offset the volume of the storm—or I'd crawl into my sister's bed and have her talk me through it."

The snow had thickened, falling with impressive heaviness. Another roar boomed above their heads, louder than all the others. She released his hand and took up her skirt to move faster. "Strawberries, ice cream, ladybugs."

"Ladybugs?" He stumbled and then caught up with her. "What are you doing?"

"Distracting myself with happy thoughts." The house garden came into view, and another swell of thunder rolled close by. "Puppies, horses, babies' feet, children's laughter."

The entire situation struck an alarming mixture of humor and sympathy, but the humor was slowly winning as she continued her list.

"The smell of books, Christmas trees, cobblestone streets." Grace's hair had come completely loose and fell about her shoulders in damp ringlets.

Thunder rolled again, louder, quickening her voice pitch. "Chocolate pastries, amber scents." She turned with almost a smile on her pale face as he opened the side door of the house for her and Zeus. "Your kisses are a new one to add to my list."

And he grinned as if God had hand delivered an early Christmas gift to him directly in the middle of a winter thunderstorm. He pulled Grace against him and turned her kissing talk into action. She gasped against his lips at another round of thunder but didn't pull away. Instead, her hands slid up into his hair and held him in place. His wife was a fast and enthusiastic learner. A definite benefit for what he had in mind.

With a gentle break in their contact, he ushered her into the house.

"Oh that was wonderfully distracting. Could we do it again?"

"I have every hope we shall, but in a more private venue." He placed his hands on her shoulders as she moved in for another kiss. "Can you find your way to your bedroom? I'll be up directly."

Those fascinating blue eyes rounded as if wounded.

"I promise, darling. I need to speak with Brandon, and then I will come to you."

She nodded, her bottom lip wobbling before she started toward the grand staircase at almost a run. "Kisses, hugs, laughter, more kisses."

Frederick turned in time to see Brandon beside him, staring at Grace's retreating form, both brows raised to nearly touch the man's hairline. Frederick couldn't tame his grin. "She's terrified of thunder."

Brandon turned his attention slowly to Frederick. "I see, sir."

"With that in mind, Brandon, would you please inform the servants that Lady Astley and I wish not to be disturbed this afternoon."

His brows rose again, and he lowered his gaze. "Yes, sir."

"And once the snow has cleared, would you have someone ride out to the ruins to have a look about? Even hire a couple more men for the grounds, if you will." Frederick surged toward the stairway. "I'd like some extra eyes around the estate."

"Yes, sir."

Frederick bounded up the stairs, intent on providing a thorough distraction for his lovely wife. He could hear her frantic singing from outside the closed bedroom door and struggled to keep his laughter in check before entering. Why, oh why had he been afraid to give his heart to this authentically beautiful creature?

Her hair spun in wet ringlets around her face, and she'd already shed her gloves, taken off her wet coat, and even removed her shoes and stockings.

That made his job much easier.

As he entered, another burst of thunder sounded, and Grace ran directly into his arms, burying her head in his shoulder. "Do you think thunder snow is worse than regular thunder? What a horrible combination of two very different things. Snow is so lovely. Thunder is. . ." She shuddered and pushed her head into the crook of his neck.

With a gentle touch to her chin, he tipped her face up and took her mouth with his. She groaned into him, inciting his pulse and determination. His hand glided down her back, noting the placement of her buttons. Too many.

His palm slid up her arm and over her neck, before taking a slow detour down the side of her body.

She gasped. The thunder shook again. Her fingers dug into his shirt, fisting with more fervency, her breath a quiet whimper.

She needed something to do.

"Grace, darling, would you do me a favor?"

She looked up at him, half confused, half terrified, her azure eyes so close.

"My shirt is damp. Do you think you could unbutton it for me while I help you with yours?"

Her gaze sharpened with awareness as her pink bottom lip dropped. She nodded and slowly unwound the first two buttons of his shirt, her eyes searching his. Trusting him.

As another rumble roared around them, he kissed away her whimper and her fingers found their way to his other buttons, slowly, bungling through the movements at first, but making excellent progress. He'd never wanted to cherish anything—this moment, her—so much in his entire life.

Without breaking the kiss, he finished the work of her blouse and slid it off her arms, chasing her pearl-like skin with his lips down her neck to her collar bone. He caught her as her knees weakened and her breaths dissolved into a moan.

"Grace," he breathed her name over her skin.

She pushed his shirt from his shoulders, her palm sliding over his chest as if fascinated by the touch. Fire followed the trail of her fingers.

"Kissing is a very good distraction." Her words shook out on a shaky whisper.

He gathered her fingers into his and brought them to his lips, never breaking eye contact with her. "And a very good introduction."

Her brows rose, and he pressed his forehead against hers, his palms sliding down her arms to tug her against him. "Let me love you, Grace, as a husband to his wife."

Her lips took a slight turn, and she brought her palms to his cheeks, their breaths mingling, lips almost touching. "Please do, my dear Frederick. Love me."

# Chapter Eighteen

The fire from the fireplace doused the room with a golden glow as Grace blinked awake. Was it nighttime? She yawned and stretched, her body humming with warmth and pleasant exhaustion. Why was she still in bed? She sat up, only to realize she was perfectly naked, and then the delicious scenes from the past hours materialized in her mind and she dropped back against the pillows.

Heaven on earth. A husband loving his wife certainly exceeded anything Grace could have imagined. Gentle, passionate—all the mystery from Lillias's subtle comments and fiction's strategic wording finally emerged in this glorious act of. . .love.

She tugged the blankets up to her growing smile. What a remarkable design! A divine combination of tender, exhilarating, and wonderfully roguish. She turned on her side toward Frederick's pillow and her smile dissolved. Her swoon-inducing husband was woefully absent. She twisted the blanket up around her as she sat, scanning the room and nibbling her bottom lip.

Her father had always accused her of being overly exuberant. Perhaps she'd gotten too carried away for a proper lady, but Frederick hadn't seemed to mind at all. Although, there was the moment she'd accidentally hit him across the face, but surely he couldn't hold her accountable for that.

It was his own fault after all. Her grin slipped wide. His own villainous fault.

Heat soared into her cheeks, and she released a sigh. Perhaps she should go in search of him to apologize? She looked up at the ceiling, reasoning it out. The thought didn't feel right at all.

A click at the door alerted her to someone's approach. She tugged the blankets closer and peered around the bed curtain. With quiet steps, Frederick entered the room, tray in hand, looking deliciously disheveled in his breeches and partially buttoned shirt. He placed the tray of tea and sandwiches on a nearby table and stoked the fire, his bare forearms glinting gold in the firelight.

Her body warmed from the sight as if she hadn't seen a set of forearms before, but they were *his* forearms. And that made all the difference. She traced a finger over her grin. Perhaps *she* was rather villainous too. She held her breath, waiting to gauge his reaction to her. If he frowned, she'd apologize profusely for her own villainy, but if he smiled. . .

His gaze found hers, surprise softening to a smile. *A smile.* "Hello, darling."

She sighed as the sound of his voice left a trail of tingles across her shoulders. "I'm so relieved you came back."

A laugh shot from him. "Of course I came back. Why on earth would I stay away?"

She smoothed the blankets around her, heat rising into her cheeks. "Well, I thought perhaps I'd either failed to please you, which seemed unlikely from your vigorous response, or you were horrified by my. . .enthusiasm."

He chuckled and approached the bed. A look she was beginning to recognize as quite rascally flamed to life in his eyes. "If you continue to make such a valiant effort to please me, Lady Astley, we may never leave this bedroom."

"Do you mean you weren't offended by my fervor?"

"Offended?" He sat on the bed and leaned in to kiss her, so gently her body swelled forward to extend the delightful embrace. "If half the women in England showed love with such fervor, there would be a sudden increase of satisfied marriages."

She smoothed her palm over his shirt. "I have no point of reference, so I'm experimenting as we go."

"Then count me as a willing subject." He brushed a hand against her cheek, his thumb tracing the edge of her lips. "Experiment away." He kissed her nose, her lips, then her chin. "Despite my past, dear Grace, I am quite a novice at *loving*. And you, my darling, love very well."

A shadow passed over his expression. Hints of his past, thoughts of other women came to mind. She shoved them away. He'd never been married except to her, and in this one act, they'd chosen each other. "It's a rather fabulous invention, isn't it?"

He drew back from kissing her temple, his brow raised. "Invention?"

"Yes." She placed both of her palms on his cheeks, tracing the curve of his jawline. "When God says two shall become one flesh, I never understood, but we're one. You and me. I—I belong to you, and you belong to me."

"I feel certain I'm in good hands." He brushed her hair back from her face. "And I will endeavor to be a much better husband than I've been the past few days."

"You are a fantastic teacher at lovemaking." She snuggled against his chest, resting a kiss against his neck. "I suppose you've had lots of practice."

With a groan, he collected one of her hands and breathed a kiss over her knuckles. "Many of my mother's accusations are true. I was a broken man, trying to fill my brokenness with companionship but never belonging." He looked down at their braided hands, emotion wrestling across his angled features. "I've had a great deal of practice at physically pleasing another and being pleased in return, but not loving. Nothing like this. And there's no going back to anything else for me."

"I'm very glad to hear it, because I want your future, Frederick. All of it."

"You are too good for my heart, Lady Astley." Those fathomless eyes, dark and deep enough to send her off-balance, searched her face with an intensity she didn't understand—pleading, apologizing, exploring. "I'm not that man from my past anymore." An unfamiliar vulnerability trembled in his baritone voice, awakening an awareness of the power she had at this moment—to either build him up to become the man he was meant to be or hold him back. "My future *is* yours. Alone."

Grace had once read a quote about a husband and wife that mentioned something about "promises forged in love from the soul outward." At the time, she'd thought it sounded lovely, but the quote held a new, sweeter meaning after her newfound connection to her husband. What a tender and exhilarating way to express love with one another! Grace nodded heavenward in appreciation.

Frederick had been wonderfully reluctant to leave her the next morning, but there was breakfast to be had and bathroom installments to be finalized, so he retired to his office. While Brandon sent Reeves in search of more garland, Grace began to form a Christmas gift list for the servants and took the opportunity to explore more of the maze-like house.

Leaving the library via a servants' stair, Grace found herself in an unfamiliar passageway, so quiet it left a chill across her skin. She pushed through a nearby door, ornately carved with Havensbrooke's theme—lions—thinking it would lead her to the south wing, but instead, she entered a magnificent sitting room she'd never seen before. Designed in pale blue and white, with an air of French accents, the room gave a strange sense of otherworldliness. She turned to look through the way she'd just come and discovered the "door" matched the wallpaper so well it blended into the wall almost seamlessly.

Servants really had the most interesting entrances.

A book lay open on a settee as if recently left there, but from the faint light fanning between the half-closed shutters, enough dust coated the furnishings to suggest no one had been in the room for a long time.

What was this place?

She stepped farther into the deserted room, her feet barely making a sound across the carpeted floors. The setting teased her senses awake, and her scalp began to tingle its customary warning of a mystery. Lanterns waited, unused. Candles stood on the tables.

A broad hallway led into shadows, with a league of portraits lining the walls. The gallery showcased a portrait in which Grace recognized two of the faces. Lady Moriah stood between two men, an older man with features similar to Frederick, and a younger man, pale eyes and dark hair, with features more like Lady Moriah. A younger version of Frederick stood nearby, almost separate from the other three, his lips quirked in a smile very unlike any she'd seen in him. Bitter.

She reached to touch the canvas and smooth away the foreign expression. What must have caused such a look? Loneliness? Rejection?

She paused her gaze in his painted one, attempting to unearth the secrets she'd only heard hints of, before she moved farther down the hallway. One room opened into another room, all waiting in the same eerie anticipated silence.

One elegant suite showcased a massive sitting room separating two bedrooms—one more masculine, the other feminine—with windows looking out over the walled garden that led up the hillside toward the vista. *East.* She gasped. These must be the east-wing bedrooms. The place her mother-in-law had closed off when her elder son had died. Grace spun around to look behind her, as if someone watched. Somewhere within these walls, Edward Percy had breathed his last.

Another delightful chill shimmied up her spine.

She entered the sitting room with its rich reds and golds, the two oil portraits over the marble fireplace drawing her forward. One was of the brother Grace had seen in the previous family portrait, Edward, and the other was of an elegant, raven-haired beauty.

"Celia," Grace whispered into the stillness.

A rush of emerald gown wrapped around her, complementing the depth of her laughing green eyes. Everything about her pooled with elegance and refinement, from the sweep of her dark hair to the tilt of her chin. No wonder she had wooed the fates of the Percy men.

The more masculine bedroom boasted thick, box-like furnishings, but the most striking feature was the state of the room. A chair tipped back, lying topsy-turvy on the floor, as if someone left it in a hurry. Curtains were flung back instead of closed like the rest of the rooms. The bed waited, unmade, and the massive desk by the window stood littered with papers, with some sheets scattered across the floor.

Had this been where Edward died? Why wasn't the space tidied?

Grace stepped to the desk, her fingers ruffling the feathers of an old ink pen. A small box with gold trim and shaped like a pirate's treasure chest overcame Grace's self-control. With a careful twist of the clip holding the lid in place, Grace looked inside. Letters tied together with a ribbon. On the top, written in elegant hand was a simple phrase: *"To my darling Elizabeth."*

Elizabeth. Grace plundered her thoughts for a face in the Percy family to match the name. Wasn't Elizabeth the name of Frederick's grandmother? Grace shifted another piece of paper loose enough to make out the name on the next letter. *"My Oliver."*

Those were Frederick's grandparents. The letters were theirs. She grinned and tucked the box back into its spot. Perhaps she could convince Frederick to allow her to read them. What a beautiful introduction to two of the people he loved most in the world.

As she placed the box back in its spot, her hip hit the desk. A few of the precarious papers on the edge fluttered to the carpeted floor, and the middle desk drawer shook open. Grace rushed to set the papers right—an odd assortment of bills, ledger sheets, and personal correspondence, it seemed—but then Frederick's name among the words of one of the pages inside the drawer caught her attention.

> *I am now inclined to believe Frederick had no hand in the events that led to his exile.*

Grace took up the paper, stepping toward the window to get a better view of the words.

> *I have ruined my life and his with my quick judgment, instead of remembering he has loved this land with more commitment than either me or Father. Parks, do you see how my hand is shaking even now? I can barely breathe. How can I make amends for the sins which weigh me down? Even now my heart quakes from the ghost who haunts me.*

A shiver tiptoed up Grace's spine, and she scanned the room, looking for proof.

> *I am caught with no escape. I cannot seek justice for my wife's treachery without incriminating myself. I am ill, Parks. A sudden fatigue has befallen me—whether from the pains of my own remorse or a viler deviance, I am uncertain. I've ruined it all. God have mercy. I cannot trust her. I've stripped her of everything in hopes of finding some redemption for Havensbrooke.*
>
> *Send for Frederick. May he. . .*

The handwriting quaked to such an extent the words became illegible, scratching off the page.

Grace scanned through the loose papers for more of the letter, but nothing matched. How long ago had it been written? Hadn't Frederick mentioned something about his mother forbidding access to these rooms soon after Edward's death?

Grace's attention shot back to the letter in her hand. She'd read about letters scratching off before being completed, usually because the person was dying of some sort of poison or weakness. But hadn't Frederick said his brother had died from a weak heart?

Grace's gaze slipped up to catch a glimpse of Celia's portrait over the mantel in the adjoining room. Her eyes took on a decidedly darker glint, her smile mocking.

Grace swallowed through her dry throat and tucked the page into one of the books in her hand. Something felt unfinished here. Her lips tipped into a responding smile. She may not be fully equipped for a fashion debut, but solving a mystery? She'd been training for this her whole life.

The game was afoot.

# Chapter Nineteen

Was his wife going to disappear on him as a rule?

Frederick took another turn around the gardens, Zeus on his heels. This afternoon, they'd meet the tenants of Havensbrooke. His gaze slid toward a cottage tucked behind a screen of trees in the distance. Except that tenant. He'd save that introduction for a more private opportunity, once he'd divulged the worst of his sins to his wife.

But he wanted to hold on to Grace's look of admiration for one more day.

The Great Hall gave no indication of the whereabouts of his wife, though it did boast a twenty-foot spruce several men had brought in after Frederick gave them instruction on where to find it. He hadn't been home for Christmas in four years. He smiled as he passed, nodding to a few maids as they draped garland along the massive mantel. After being gone for six months, he was finally starting to feel at home in this house again.

As he passed his office, he caught sight of a flash of green and came to a roaring stop. Peering around the corner of the doorway, he watched as his wife walked faerie-light through the very masculine space.

Her day dress floated around her as she stepped from his desk to the globe in the corner and slid her free hand over the massive leather chair by the fireplace, her other hand clutching two books to her chest. Her beauty stole his breath.

She turned to look out the window, and he swept up behind her, catching her gasp with his lips. Their physical connection bound him to her in a new, more powerful, way. Unlike any woman he'd known, Grace took to their time together with the same voracious curiosity as she did to most things—and he harbored no complaints. In fact, he'd hadn't thanked God so much in years. Out loud. In several languages.

She giggled as his lips left her mouth to slip to her ear. "I missed you too."

"Did you?" He raised a brow and then delved back into appreciating the slope of her neck with his mouth. "You seem much more content than I."

"I'm being scandalously kissed by my roguish husband." Her breath hitched as he continued his perusal. "Why wouldn't I—"

"I know my way well enough, Brandon." A familiar voice from the entry hall ruptured their privacy. "Let me through."

Frederick hoped his ears played tricks on him. Surely his Aunt Lavenia hadn't arrived unannounced and with such poor timing.

"Where is she?" her question resounded closer, confirming his thoughts.

"Blast," Frederick muttered, tucking Grace against him behind the door.

"Who is it?" Grace peeked up at him from her place between him and the wall. His thoughts delved into excellent ways to take advantage of her position—

"Mrs. Redfern, if you would allow me to announce your presence—"

"Pishposh, Brandon. I must see this new bride of my nephew's." Her light voice rang through the corridors with purpose. "Upon my word, what a glorious tree!"

She'd made it to the Great Hall.

"Frederick?"

"It's my mother's sister," he responded, voice low.

"Oh no." Grace pouted. "I can't bear another one."

"Aunt Lavenia is nothing like my mother." He trailed a hand down her neck. "She's unique in her own right and married to a clergyman in Matlock."

"A clergyman?"

"My mother was not rich when my father met her."

One of Grace's brows pitched high.

"However, she was very. . .enticing."

"So much so that your father lost all reason and married the wrong sister?" Grace's eyes widened. "I've read about such intoxication in books, you know."

"I'm certain you have." Frederick chuckled and placed a kiss against her cheek. "And you may very well be right. I can only imagine Aunt Lavenia a better choice in many ways, but not when it comes to patience."

"Frederick!" Her call came closer.

Sending Grace an apologetic look, he rounded the door, bringing Grace along with him. He was beginning to regret not taking a honeymoon.

"There you are." Aunt Lavenia clapped her hands, her pale eyes wide beneath her large-brimmed hat. "And your bride!"

Frederick drew in a deep breath for strength. "Aunt Lavenia Redfern, may I introduce my wife, Gracelynn Percy, Countess of Astley."

Grace dipped her head. "Pleased to meet you, Aunt Lavenia."

"Oh, look at you!" She studied Grace for a second, stepping closer. "Well, I never imagined a redhead as the salvation of Havensbrooke, but if God can use fishermen, shepherds, and whales to bring about his plan, why not a lovely ginger?"

Grace shot Frederick an open-mouthed smile, her blue eyes dancing with her resident curiosity.

"Aunt Lavenia, we weren't expecting visitors."

"Family, dear." Lavenia waved away his words and took Grace's face in her hands, peering over the rim of her glasses for close inspection. "I met your sister in town this morning, and she invited me for tea on Friday." Lavenia released Grace's cheeks and stepped back with a satisfied sigh. "But I had to come over straightaway after Eleanor's glowing report from you." She raised a brow to Frederick. "Nothing's glowed in this house since Edward installed electric lights, so you'll understand my immediate curiosity."

Grace laughed. "I do prefer glowing to the alternative."

Lavenia's sharp gaze slid back to Grace, her smile growing with Cheshire style. "Ah, I see." Lavenia turned to Brandon. "Have tea brought to the Green Room, won't you, Brandon?" Her attention turned back to Grace. "I've a new niece to interview."

Grace couldn't help but like Lavenia Redfern. She broke conventions, smiled often, and didn't have one negative thing to say about Grace's hair color. The very fact she caused Frederick to battle with his grin made her even more endearing.

"I wasn't too keen on this whole idea of marrying for money, you understand." She waved a scone toward Grace before taking another bite. "I recognize the financial demands of a large estate, but I'm a firm believer in marrying for a partner, not position, and I'm not afraid to admit it."

"Grace and I are hopeful to have both," Frederick answered, glancing Grace's way long enough to send her thoughts spiraling back to his plundering kisses.

Was marriage truly supposed to be this delightful? Clandestine kisses in the study? Stormy nights of passion? Enchanting discussions about anything from fiction to architecture? She hadn't read a single book that painted a picture of marriage remotely close to this.

What a waste of unwritten words!

"You've always been the kindhearted one, Frederick. For all your disappointments in life, you never lost your goodness, did you?"

Disappointments? The unanswered questions in this house breathed in the air, waiting for release. Would Frederick ever trust Grace with the truth? She already knew enough to draw conclusions of her own that rivaled anything he could conjure up. After all, she was currently reading Dickens.

"But I see how it is. You two are well suited." Lavenia glanced between them, nodding with finality. "Yes, and I predict you will have a child by Christmas next year."

Grace laughed more at Frederick's look of shock than Lavenia's directness. "I'm only now discovering what it is to be a wife, dear Aunt Lavenia. I can't imagine managing the duties of mother too."

"You'll have lots of help when the time comes. Unlike most women in current society, I adore babies." She took a sip of tea. "And how do you find Havensbrooke?"

"It's situated so beautifully. Almost fairy-tale-like."

"Indeed it is." Lavenia studied Grace over her teacup, hesitating. "A large, lonely place in need of some young spirit to rewrite its stories and sort out its mysteries."

Mysteries? Grace blinked. "Speaking of mysteries." She popped up from her seat. Where had she placed her books? "I discovered one today."

She retrieved her books from the study and returned, tugging out the letter. "I found something when I got lost in the house this morning." She sat next to Frederick on the settee. "I think it's from your brother."

"My brother?" He took the paper from her, his face paling as he scanned the note. "You. . .you were in the east wing?"

"I believe so. We certainly didn't venture there on our tour, but perhaps the letter will bring you some small comfort. It seems your brother thought he'd wronged you."

Frederick sat back, rubbing his chin as he read the letter. Aunt Lavenia held out her hand for a turn, and Frederick offered a hesitant allowance. His expression gave little away, certainly nothing to help Grace sort out anything related to a possible murder. With their new intimacy, should she be able to read his thoughts a bit better? She pursed her lips in concentration as she stared at him and frowned when nothing materialized in her head. Oh well, perhaps it would take a little longer.

"There's more than that, Grace." Aunt Lavenia looked up from the paper. "This letter hints to a scandal about which I've pondered since Edward's death. Something is definitely amiss, and I think we've finally found direction for answers."

What did this mean?

Frederick reread the letter, his brother's handwriting a bittersweet stab to Frederick's grief. He should have been the one to discover this months ago. Overwhelmed by his new responsibilities as earl, he'd stayed away from the east wing at his mother's request and due to his own regret. He'd had an estate to rescue. It had seemed easier at the time to forge ahead into estate business. But what had he overlooked in the process?

"Was I right in bringing it to you?"

Grace's touch to his arm brought him back to the present. "Yes." He nodded. "I've needed to explore the east wing, and this proves the fact. It's only, I didn't know if I could—"

"We can do it together."

His bride. She offered such confidence, kindness. He cleared the emotions closing off his voice.

"Perhaps Parks can provide some insight, Frederick." Aunt Lavenia took another sip of her tea. "This may not be the first letter of its kind."

Frederick cringed. If his brother's best friend would even talk to him.

"You know where I stand about past sins and all that. I'm a clergyman's wife. I've heard it all, and I know you've tried to make things right." Lavenia's hand rested on his shoulder. "But there's something quite dark about your brother's words and the implications about his wife. I never liked her." She offered a knowing nod along with a wag of her finger. "And I'm quite keen on such things."

Celia. Frederick had stayed clear of Celia Blackmore ever since his return to England. She was poison, the reason for the rift between Frederick and his brother, and no doubt her influence contributed to the downward fall of Havensbrooke.

But a murderer? His gaze traveled to his wife—the very contradiction. She studied him with those intelligent eyes of hers, her imagination most likely conjuring up all sorts of scenarios.

"I'll leave the two of you to talk this over, but know this"—Aunt Lavenia pointed at him, those pale blue eyes flaming—"I'm a decent shot should things turn less than savory." Her fingers wiggled in the air. "And of course, I'll pray, especially to keep us free from the need for my shooting."

"You know how to fire pistols?"

Frederick stifled a groan at Grace's question. Introducing the two of them would probably prove catastrophic for his peace of mind.

Aunt Lavenia's grin broadened into a saucy boast. "It's not a widely known fact, my dear, as you can understand. After all, I'm a clergyman's wife, and knowledge of my use of pistols doesn't bode well with most parishioners."

Grace sent him a wide-eyed grin over Lavenia's shoulder as his aunt took Grace in another hug.

*Oh Lord, give me strength.*

Could the house manage two such personalities in the same room for very long?

"Don't you wish to see your sister while you're here, Aunt Lavenia?" Frederick diverted the conversation in case Lavenia decided to offer Grace shooting lessons on the spot. "You might do her some good."

"I'm not certain how much good I'll do." Lavenia's gaze moved to the stairway just beyond the Green Room door. "The woman drinks despair like brandy."

Grace's laugh echoed through the room.

"It's true dear. She can hold a grudge better than St. Peter could catch a fish." She shook her head and turned back to them, standing. "I'll take her some tea, and we'll see how things go."

"She's kept herself to her rooms since I threatened to find her a dower house," Frederick added.

"Ah well, I can imagine she's fit to be tied after that." She released another sigh and offered a renewed smile. "Wish me luck."

Grace took Aunt Lavenia's hands in hers. "It was such a pleasure to meet you, Aunt Lavenia."

"I believe we are to be very good friends, my dear Grace." Lavenia turned to Frederick. "Excellent choice, Frederick, and I simply adore her hair. Adds color in this world of colorless characters."

Grace's attention followed Aunt Lavenia, her smile growing until Lavenia disappeared down the hallway. "Oh, I like her. She inferred I was a character, and I do so hope I turn out to be a heroine in this story."

He slipped his arm around her waist and pressed a kiss to her cheek. "I can assure you, you are the heroine of mine."

She stared up at him with such unadulterated tenderness, he nearly kissed her much too thoroughly in the middle of the Green Room.

"So when do we set off for London to sort out what this letter is all about?" She tapped the paper in his hands. "Didn't you mention needing to travel there to meet with estate solicitors anyway?"

Her question doused the warmth her gentle look inspired. "I don't know if this is something we ought to pursue."

Grace's bottom lip dropped. "Aunt Lavenia clearly suspects something, and your brother's words were terribly—"

"It's not as simple as that." He stood, distancing himself from the onslaught of her incoming argument. "This has the potential to bring unwelcome attention, and that's the last thing the Astley name needs right now."

"But surely the truth is worth the risk."

He walked toward his office, trying to keep his breathing slow, but his pulse staggered into a gallop. After Lily, then Celia, and his brother's unexpected demise, if news emerged that something underhanded had occurred, it would only lengthen the shadows over Havensbrooke, especially with Frederick's name attached again. "It sounds as though my brother was ill when he wrote this letter. He could have been suffering from paranoia."

"Or paranoia had been induced by situations or"—she stepped to his side and paused with a gasp—"or certain liquids. I've read of a variety of soluble contents which can cause—"

"Grace." He didn't even want to consider where she learned such information. "My family name is in a vulnerable place. I have to consider the implications of drawing attention to a speculation."

"A life-threatening speculation!" She squeezed his arm. "Someone may have tried to kill us in your car last week, not to mention the attempt on your life in Whitlock Village. The last thing I want is to lose a husband I just marr—"

"We have no proof either of those were anything more than coinci—"

"Frederick, there very well could be a murderer free, and what if he strikes again?"

"I'm not willing to take this family through a wild goose chase over something that's more imagination than reality."

She snatched the letter and waved it in front of his face. "This letter is real."

"And incomplete. One does not pursue a remote theory based on inconclusive findings."

"Clearly you've not been reading your Sherlock. Every mystery starts with a remote theory based on inconclusive findings." She placed the letter back in his hand but wrapped her other hand around theirs. "Havensbrooke is a part of your story. You have to discover the truth."

"This is not a story, Grace." His resolve teetered on the edge of control. "This is real life. There are consequences and. . .and possible dangers."

"There are always consequences and dangers when you live a life. And of course this is a story." She waved toward one of the portraits on the wall nearby—his grandfather to be specific. "It's years and centuries of stories. Of people playing the heroes and heroines and villains of their own lives. It's *your* story." She pressed a palm to her chest. "Mine. You decide what part you'll play."

"It's not as simple as that." He collapsed into his desk chair. "It's

Havensbrooke's legacy too. You have no idea how scandal redirects futures in my world."

"Wouldn't the greater scandal be to allow a violent person to hurt someone else? I know enough to realize shadows follow people when you're pointing toward the light, Frederick, so we must—"

"What do you know of it, Grace?" He shook his head. "You've been here two weeks."

"I know we must pursue what is right." She stepped back from him, her brows furrowed. "You can't ensure the future of Havensbrooke if you're dead, and I mean to protect you, even if you will not protect yourself."

"And I must protect my family's reputation. My *home*." His words sliced into her argument. "You can't understand the burden I bear. The expectation to make things right. Centuries of expectations. How can you possibly understand it?" Her wounded expression dug his frustration deeper. . .at himself. "Your family is from new money. What would you know about the kind of sacrifice I must make to secure this future?"

As his accusations reverberated off the silence, the hurt in Grace's eyes hardened to steel. "You're right. I don't know what it's like to carry the weight of all those people on my shoulders. I don't know how to be a storyteller of others' adventures because I'd rather live my own." She pulled her ring from her finger and slammed it down on the desk. "And what would I know about sacrificing for family? Or risking everything to do what was right to save the people I love from *scandal*?" Her words pierced into his argument with enough accuracy to send pain shooting through his chest. "Practically nothing, Lord Astley." She leaned in, her fiery gaze demanding his full attention. "Whether you claim it or not, you were born to be a hero, not a shadow. And heroes don't hide from the truth."

With that, his joyful, innocent bride stormed from the room without one look back.

And what was worse? Everything she said was true.

# Chapter Twenty

Grace marched from Frederick's study, fury wracking her body with such force her hands quivered. Her eyes stung. Ooh, she hated getting this angry. She could think of dozens of other ways to expend energy that resulted in much better outcomes.

Stubborn man. What he needed was a good throttling. And at the moment, she'd gladly volunteer to dole out said throttling.

"I'll take my leave, Brandon." Aunt Lavenia's voice carried from the entry. "My sister is out of sorts, as usual."

"Your car is ready, ma'am."

"Thank you. And do remind Lady Astley that she is welcome at the rectory at any time."

Grace's steps faltered. Now there was an idea. "Please, wait," she called as she raced forward, finding the pair paused at the front entry. "I'd love to take you up on your offer immediately, Aunt Lavenia. If I may?"

The woman looked from Brandon to Grace, and then her gaze lingered on the hallway behind Grace for a second, before her brow rose like a question mark. "Would you?"

"Most certainly." Grace tugged at her gloves with a little too much force. "It appears my husband needs some time to realize his own place in the world, and I need some distance before I do something quite unladylike to his stubborn head."

Brandon made a choking sound to her right.

Aunt Lavenia's lips slipped into a slow slant. "Well, what do they say? Absence makes the heart grow fonder?" She gestured for Grace to follow.

"The rectory is a wonderful hiding place, and what heroine doesn't need to be pursued every now and again?"

Some of Grace's ire dimmed slightly in the light of Aunt Lavenia's generous understanding. Ah yes, she had certainly found a kindred spirit.

Lavenia tipped her head to the butler as he retrieved Grace's coat. "Brandon, I expect you to give us a healthy head start, won't you? My nephew doesn't need to be informed of her ladyship's absence for at least. . ." She glanced heavenward. "A half hour should be sufficient. Every woman needs a chance to ready herself for a heartfelt apology from her husband."

Brandon stiffened against the request, so Grace placed her hand on his arm. "Unless he explicitly asks, of course, Brandon, but he has the potential to brood for quite some time, I'm sure."

The butler's shoulders relaxed, and Grace followed Lavenia to the car. They'd not been driving five minutes before Grace shared the entire incident.

"I used to think brooding was a very romantic idea until put into practical use, and now my opinion has been vastly altered." She folded her arms over her chest and pressed back into the seat. "It is not attractive at all."

"Marriage is a difficult business, my dear. It's life amplified." Lavenia patted her hand and somehow poured a sweet solace over the ache Grace had felt for another woman's company. "When two passionate people live in close proximity on a regular basis, episodes of discontent and conflict are bound to surface."

"But that's not supposed to happen in marriage for at least the first year."

Aunt Lavenia's loud laugh shook Grace from her pout. "Did you read that in a book somewhere? Because I can assure you with certainty there are no time constraints on disagreements. Reverend Redfern and I had our first argument two hours after we married, and such an argument it was." She sighed as if she enjoyed the thought.

How peculiar. Grace found that conflict left a delightful thrill in fiction but abrasive distaste in real life. "I don't know why he was so irritable with me. I was trying to help him come to a practical conclusion. He should have appreciated that. I was very lucid. Don't men prefer logic?"

Lavenia released such a laugh she pressed her palm against her stomach. Grace wasn't certain what was so funny.

"Oh my dear, you are exactly what our dear Lord Astley needs." She swiped at her eyes. "What a perfect pairing!"

"I don't see how an argument can look at all perfect."

Her smile softened. "Conflict is a necessary component of relationships. Good and bad. We're none of us perfect, and I daresay there's a bit of pride and the natural follies of youth in both of you." Lavenia's grin widened again as if she wanted to laugh. "Conflict can help you grow if you allow it to make your relationship stronger."

"Stronger? By arguing?"

"Why do you suppose God allows conflicts in life?"

Grace blinked at the sudden question. "To punish us for our bad behavior? But I've not been bad." She replayed the last few days through her mind and the rather disingenuous thoughts she had for her mother-in-law, involving locked doors and discarded keys. "Mostly not."

"No, you're confusing consequences with conflict." She squeezed Grace's hand. "Conflict can become one of the great shapers of our lives. God uses conflict to reach the deepest levels of who we are as nothing else can. You have been placed into Frederick's life to love and encourage him. To be his greatest asset. But you are also there to make him a better person than he was without you, and the same for him to you. That's what people do when they love. They mold and shape one another into better forms of themselves. Sometimes the molding is comfortable—sometimes it's not." Her pale eyes widened. "Now I'm a part of your life, so I shall be a molder to you and you to me."

What a remarkable thought!

Would Lillias have brought conflict into Frederick's life so soon? Her elegant sister knew how to guard her tongue much better, but would Lillias have been the best person to shape Frederick? Frederick certainly seemed exasperated enough with Grace to be shaped into something or other. "He was supposed to marry my sister, you know. I felt certain they were meant to be soul mates. Do you think he wishes he'd married her now?"

"He married *you*, therefore you are exactly the right wife for him." Lavenia sniffed in disapproval. "There's no need to ponder the *what-ifs*. They steal the truth of what is. You are soul mates by choice and will. How closely you wrap your souls around one another is of your own choosing."

Grace allowed the idea to sink within her. How liberating! She was

Fredericks' wife. They belonged to one another in every way. It was time for her to step into the idea without holding back, even if it meant pushing him forward with an argument or two.

"It is not a light responsibility he bears, dear. Perhaps he does allow it to control him too much. Likely, he's afraid of failing. But in many respects, he is the last hope for a dying legacy."

Grace searched the woman's face. "I want to help him, but he doesn't have to be so snippy toward me. I'm on *his* side."

"Your Frederick has not had a great deal of experience with people being on his side, so he may find it difficult to believe." Aunt Lavenia's expression softened, her eyes growing sad. "Being loved for the sake of love itself is a novelty to him since losing his grandparents. He's been an outcast for a long time, but I feel your generosity of affection and. . .um. . .creative intelligence will be the making of him."

It was no wonder his wife had disappeared this time. He'd treated her abominably. He took the steps of the Great Hall two at a time but found the library as empty as every other room he'd searched. Even if her words challenged him beyond his comfort, she didn't deserve his attack. His thoughtlessness.

Hero of his own life? He couldn't even maintain hero status in his wife's eyes for longer than a day without bumbling something. Halfway through his second pass of the Great Hall, he found his faithful butler. "Brandon, I'm in need of your assistance."

The man's features tightened with a strange sort of wariness. "Sir?"

"Would you happen to know Lady Astley's whereabouts?"

The man did the strangest thing. He took in a deep breath, drew his watch from his pocket, and almost. . .smiled. "Yes, sir. I do. She left with Mrs. Redfern."

"Pardon?"

"Exactly thirty-four minutes ago."

Frederick stared at the butler for a full five seconds before resurrecting his voice. "My wife left with my aunt thirty-four minutes ago?"

"Yes, sir." Brandon cleared his throat. "They were leaving straight for the rectory, if I understood rightly, sir."

The thoughts finally reached comprehension and thrust Frederick into action. If Aunt Lavenia heard of his treatment of Grace, there was an excellent chance she'd respond in one of two ways. With her knowledge of his past and his attempts to make amends, she could have quieted Grace's fears and defended him as any good aunt should do. On the other hand, as a wife and defender of her general sex, she could have helped Grace concoct some scheme for his emotional demise.

*Lord, if I've ever done anything good in my life, please let it be the former option.*

It took over a half hour before Patton pulled the roadster in front of the well-manicured, gray stone cottage his aunt and uncle had occupied for the past twenty years. No one here would keep to ceremony for the Earl of Astley. He would always be simply Frederick.

And in this case, that may not play into his favor at all.

Perry, one of his aunt's two servants, led Frederick to the sitting room, where he was offered tea and cakes. So far so good. He waited five then ten minutes, and at the fifteen-minute mark almost went in search of his wife on his own, but Aunt Lavenia appeared in the doorway, blocking his exit.

"Ah, Frederick, how good of you to come visit so soon."

He drew in a slow, steadying breath. "You know why I'm here."

She raised a brow to him, her gaze measuring the length of him as if she didn't quite trust him. "Then you understand your best position right now is humility."

He lowered his head and stifled a groan. "I do."

"And humble men are prone to listen rather than speak."

His gaze raised to hers, brow tipped, waiting.

"You've told her nothing of your past, Frederick? Part of this disagreement between the two of you could have been thwarted by some forthrightness on your part."

"But I—"

Lavenia's raised finger and steely look paused his response. "Whether you realize it or not, your Lady Astley is exactly what you need. Young? Yes. Fanciful?" Aunt Lavenia chuckled. "Indeed. But also clever, kind, strong, and above all hopeful."

"I know. I see it." Frederick's shoulder bent.

"She's also devoted to seeing you succeed, but to do that she needs you to trust her."

He ran a hand through his hair, shifting his feet. "I just wanted to hold on to her good opinion of me. She has this notion that I'm a hero, and for a moment, I wanted to live as *that* man, not the one with the past I have."

"A hero is never who he was."

Frederick looked up at her.

"It's who he becomes." She clicked her tongue. "Don't demean your bride by treating her as if she can't see the man you were meant to be. If you mean to make a change in your generation of Percys, you need to start with openness and honesty."

"I. . .I know."

Her warm palm, crinkled with time, cupped his cheek. "Don't continue the family tradition of secrets. You've witnessed its poison. And don't stifle Grace's potential to be exactly who you need her to be. She is your partner and equal. Allow her to be both."

His eyes burned with uncustomary tears, and he swallowed through the emotions rising in his throat. Fear stalked his every step, but—God help him—it would not guide his future. He *needed* an ally for the journey, and he *wanted* that ally to be Grace.

⌁

Grace attempted to hit another croquet ball toward the hoop but only succeeded in shaking the wire arch with an impressive clod of grass. This sport was too much like golf to be enjoyable.

Shouldn't Frederick have shown up by now if he felt sorry for his grumpiness?

She shot another clod toward the hoop. Despite her frustration, her heart ached for her cranky husband. Had Frederick only known the harshness of his mother? The distance of his father? Rejection and ridicule?

Her mother had shown such love early in Grace's life that every memory seemed shrouded in a golden hue. And her father kept a hopeful countenance, always willing to trust quickly, which in some cases proved disastrous in the business realm. Still, he loved large.

If Frederick grew up on stingy love, which wasn't love at all, wouldn't that alter a person's views on trust and hope?

She supposed it was one thing to give kisses but quite another to give your heart.

A sound from the house pulled her attention to the rectory's back door.

Her husband wore penitent well. Shirt with loosened collar. Hair unkempt, most likely from his wild drive in the roadster to find her. She held back her smile at the thought of his desperate search. No, she shouldn't give in too quickly, as Aunt Lavenia had said. She must stand her ground for a solid apology.

He kept his distance, stopping several feet from her, but she focused on the mallet in hand, barely attending to her task of hitting the croquet balls poorly.

"Grace."

His voice pleaded the word in a whisper. She braced herself against the empathetic pang. "Lord Astley." Ah yes. Her voice didn't quaver as much as she thought it might.

"I didn't know where you'd gone. I searched the whole house."

Which was terribly dashing of him.

"You can't leave without alerting me of your plans."

And that was how he wished to start this conversation? She pulled the mallet's handle into a tighter grip, shooting him a mild glare before hitting another piece of grass—and the ball—toward him. "Then don't give me reason to."

"I'm sorry for what I said." He approached another step. "You sacrificed a great deal to leave all you knew and marry this misplaced earl."

She looked away, trying to hold to a thread of her hurt for Aunt Lavenia's sake. "I did."

"I am grateful for your willingness and kindness, and. . .and for you."

Oh, her heart melted into a puddle. It was much harder to stay angry than she'd thought.

He took another step closer, his presence so close she felt it. "Please forgive my harshness."

Tenderness proved a difficult weapon to battle against, and she'd promised Aunt Lavenia she'd hold her ground for at least ten minutes. Had it barely been three? "I know I said I found brooding heroes appealing, but they're tiresome in actuality." She raised her chin to continue her argument, moving away from him to hit the ball poorly again. "I prefer a more open-minded hero." She looked up and pointed her mallet. "One willing to consider other points of view."

"You've never played croquet, have you?" The gentle humor in his voice pearled over her skin like a magnet drawing her to him, baritone and tenderness.

She fought the tug. "No, but I was introduced to baseball last year, so I feel I have a pretty solid swing with the right target." She needled him with a look, which was a bad idea, because her gaze fell into his. Oh, she did care about him. Immensely.

His lips twitched into that crooked grin she couldn't quite sort out but found rather fascinating. "I believe there's something wrong with your grip."

"My grip?"

Before she could move away, he'd captured her left hand. "Ah, yes." He took her fingers gently into his warm ones and examined her hand with such intensity, her frustration diminished into curiosity. "I see the problem. Your hand isn't balanced properly."

"My what?"

With a quick movement, he slipped her wedding ring back on her finger and tugged her closer to him. "Forgive me?" His brow crinkled into a dozen wrinkles, his dark eyes searching hers. "I'm sorry I hurt you."

All her defenses crumbled, and she hadn't even succeeded in making it to five minutes. Oh, she'd never been very good at holding grudges. "I forgive you."

"You know, I will disappoint you again." He captured a stray strand of her hair between his fingers, staring down at it with such intensity. "I'm a broken man, an aspiring hero, at best, but hopelessly flawed."

Aunt Lavenia's words took deeper root, and Grace saw Frederick as a little boy searching for someone to love him. Pain squeezed her heart. The burden he bore took on a greater weight when viewed from the eyes of a child who wanted to earn favor from unforgiving parents.

A harrowing feat she'd never known.

"Perfect heroes are boring." She touched his cheek, bringing his attention to her face. "The only heroes worth reading about are the broken ones. They have the greatest potential because they've learned what it takes to be truly strong. And seeking forgiveness is certainly the act of a hero."

He lowered his forehead to hers. "I wanted to remain your noble knight as long as possible, but I seem adept at falling off my steed."

"That's all right." Her smile broadened as her fingers grazed his cheek.

"As I recall, I've helped you back on a steed before."

He stared at her, gaze roving her face in almost wonder. "How can you be so—" His breath caught, or was it a sob? His hands cupped her face, and he took her lips in a slow, tantalizing kiss that reverberated through her with much more than desire—tenderness.

Her dear, wounded hero had excellent potential.

"Come." He brought her hands to his lips, his expression all teary-eyed and grateful. "We need to talk." He took the mallet from her hand with a raised brow, then guided her through the back of the rectory to a small sitting room, a cheerful fire aglow.

Without releasing his hold, he led her to the couch and settled next to her. "You are very clever, so you've probably surmised my past choices have led to certain scandals for our family."

She'd anticipated this great unveiling of his past. In fact, she'd conjured up enough possibilities to write a three-volume novel herself. Secret wife? Diamond thief? Mercenary? Pirate? She fought her grin. Well, pirate wasn't so bad, but she didn't like the secret wife scenario at all. No wonder Jane was so upset.

Grace steadied her shoulders, readied for the revelation.

"I was left to my own devices early in my youth and quickly became enamored with the daughter of one of our tenants." He smoothed his thumb over her knuckles, his brow a fury of creases. "At the time, I didn't know it was her design to entrap me into a financial obligation by carrying my child."

Secret child? Oh, she'd left that one off the list. "Your. . .your child?"

"Yes." He cleared his throat. "The woman died in childbirth, to my father's relief because it averted further scandal, but the rumors were not kind, though I attempted to make amends with her family."

He wore the weight of his past with such penitence, shoulders stooped, gaze turned down toward their braided hands. Her chest squeezed with pain. "Oh Frederick, your tender heart."

"Yes," he growled, in a very un-Frederick-like way. "A tender heart is all well and good, but without wisdom it leads to folly." His eyes wilted closed. "Such folly."

Grace squeezed his hand. "And you've grown in wisdom?"

"Now?" His gaze found hers, the tension around his eyes softening a little. "Perhaps now, but not soon enough." He stroked her hand almost methodically as he spoke. "I had a weakness for women who appeared to need me and who would at least pretend to adore me." His expression hardened. "I wanted to prove myself, to feel strong and important."

*And find love.*

Grace's heart ached with pain again. For him. For the loneliness he must have known.

"Along came Celia Blackmore. She had the right connections to impress my mother and a family history to impress my father. All she lacked was money, and I had no idea she'd do anything to obtain it."

"She sounds like Milady de Winter from *The Three Musketeers*. Villainous, beautiful, and a devastating temptress." Grace shook her head. "She was able to seduce a priest, for goodness' sake. Of course you couldn't withstand such deviousness."

"And much like Athos, I thought myself in love with a woman whose heart belonged to her own chicanery. Once she realized she could gain a title and fortune through my brother, her affections conveniently transferred to him."

She thought about the portrait she'd seen of Frederick's brother, Edward, then looked back at her roguishly handsome husband. "What a poor choice on her part."

"Darling." His smile flickered, and he slid his knuckles against her cheek, eyes glistening bright again before he sobered. "It seems Father was somehow involved in the entire affair with Celia, but I was never privy to the nuances. Celia and Edward were married, and by all accounts quite happily until before Father's death. I tried to stay away in London as much as possible, but when Father became ill, I returned home. He was a shadow of his former self. Agitated. Delusional. Grabbing my hands and calling out, 'My son,' as he'd never done before. Perhaps regret tendered his heart toward me near the end, but I cannot know."

"And you had no comforting mother to help you."

His gaze gentled on her. "No, in fact, she barely left her room the last two weeks of Father's life, living like a recluse in her apartments with only her maid as company." His brows knit tightly together as he tilted his head in some sort of deep contemplation as he looked at her. "Your presence is a comfort, though."

"As yours is to me."

He kissed her hands, shaking his head as the conversation fell silent.

"What happened that sent you to India?"

His smile faded, his gaze distancing in memory. "I'd learned caution around Celia, but in my grief, I'd forgotten to keep up my guard. With the desire to be of assistance to my brother, I stayed on at Havensbrooke for a few months, and with each passing week, Celia's attentions toward me became more demonstrative."

Grace's palm came up to cover her mouth. "Oh, she is perfectly Lady de Winter."

"One night I woke, and she was in my bed. I was grieving, lonely, and when she began to make advances, I lost my senses for a moment." His gaze bore into Grace's. "But only a moment, and then I moved to get out of the bed, but Edward must have suspected something, because he arrived and saw us together."

"Poor Edward," Grace pressed her hand to her chest.

"Yes." Frederick groaned. "Of course, Celia turned the story around, claiming I'd been the pursuer."

"And Edward believed her," Grace whispered.

"She was his wife."

"Someone needs to challenge her to a duel." Grace growled. "If I ever meet her in person and learn to use pistols, I may challenge her to a duel myself."

"I appreciate your protectiveness." He offered a weak chuckle and cradled Grace's chin with his thumb and forefinger. "But I hope you never meet her. She is neither safe nor kind, and no amount of your sunshine will change her."

"Is that why you were sent to India?"

He sighed. "I joined a military outfit. I'd never gone from home for so long, and it pained me in a way I hadn't expected. This place, this land, is a part of me, and to leave in such a shameful fashion?" His shoulders sagged, feeling the weight. "I wrote to Edward several times, begging his forgiveness, attempting to explain, but he never replied. I remained in India until I received a letter from Mother about my brother's illness. He died the day I arrived. I'm the one who discovered him."

"How horrible for you." She touched his cheek.

"It *was* horrible. He must have died in such agony, from the way I found him."

Grace's thoughts spiraled back to the state of the east-wing study.

Had Edward known he was dying? Is that why he wrote the letter? "Then what happened?"

He came out of his trance-like state. "I attempted to sort out our family's finances, which had been left in ruin from both Father's and Edward's misuse. I'm still trying to place some order into their tangle of debt. Then Mother met your sister and father in London, suggested the proposal to me, and the agreement was struck."

That was all? Since she'd imagined him murdering his father, joining some slave trade in India, and harboring a secret wife, the truth proved much less shocking.

"Why were you so afraid to tell me this, Frederick? You desperately sought love because your family didn't give it and lost your heart to a vile woman who didn't recognize what a very good man she'd rejected." She shook her head. "I imagined much, much worse."

He paused, his gaze shifting back to their hands, and a sudden foreboding caught in her throat. "There is one more thing."

She braced herself. He *had* killed someone! And he was rather roguish. Perhaps he truly was a pirate, but then he wouldn't have to marry a rich woman, would he?

"I have a daughter."

"You. . .you have a daughter?"

"She's five years old. She was the child born to the tenant's daughter. Her name is Lily, short for Elizabeth, and she lives as a ward of my estate."

The idea settled through her. Frederick had a daughter. "Do you see her?"

"Regularly."

Did she look like her mother or Frederick? Oh, a little girl with his eyes would be adorable. "Does she know you are her father?"

"I cannot claim her as such, Grace. It's not the way things are done."

Grace didn't like that at all. She knew a life without a mother's presence, but to be raised bereft of both mother *and* father? She stood from the bench and paced a few steps. "We should include a nursery in our improvements."

"That's a bit premature—"

"For Lily." She turned back to him as he stood. "Surely we can bring her inside the house so she'll have people nearby to love her. You may still claim her as your ward, but no child should bear the absence of loving parents, if possible."

"What about when our children come?"

What a ridiculous question. "Then she'll have playmates."

"You wouldn't resent this reminder of my past?" He shook his head, staring at her, and a weak laugh erupted as he shook his head. "Of course you wouldn't."

She took his hands back into hers, attempting to wrap her mind around his hesitation. "We all live with reminders of the past, dear Frederick. We cannot escape them. There are plenty of regretful ones, I'm sure, so why not celebrate the sweet ones? Lily had no hand in your choices. She certainly shouldn't bear the shame in your regret."

"Grace." He took her face in his hands, thumbs trailing over her cheekbones. "Can you truly be this. . .this generous?"

His kiss caught her by surprise, slow and deliciously tantalizing. She hummed a sigh and pulled back to see his face. Dark eyes swam with a glossy luster. He'd laid his wounds bare before her, his past raw and open.

But no matter how intimidating his former life might be, she would embrace it all. All of him. The bravest of heroines love with eyes open.

"You don't need to grieve for love anymore, Frederick. I will love you." She ran a finger down his cheek and kissed him, her smile stretching with possibilities. "And I will be the best sleuthing partner you could ever imagine."

He blinked at her. "Sleuthing partner?"

"To find out what happened to your brother."

"Grace."

"What if we can do much better than Dickens's Christmas ghosts?"

His mouth fell agape and he squinted. "I don't—"

"They only changed the present and future, but what if we can reach back into the past and set things right?"

"What?"

"Your name has been maligned for years, and rumors have been left to run rampant. If we can prove what happened to your brother, perhaps your mother and others she's influenced will see you in a different light. As the hero you are *now*." She leaned close, hoping her enthusiasm softened his rather shocked expression. "And I've always wanted to solve a real mystery."

# Chapter Twenty-One

The last time Frederick had visited the east wing, he'd found his brother on the floor in his office, his face frozen in some retracted and haunting distortion, as if he couldn't catch his breath.

Frederick cringed from the memory.

Why hadn't he considered something underhanded at the time?

Because his mother had insisted his brother had struggled with a weak heart. Because he'd inherited a failing estate. Because he'd stepped into the place of earl—shoes he'd never intended to fill—and suddenly he needed to prove he could succeed at any cost.

Scandal-free.

And somehow he'd missed the clues that his brother had died alone in a way very similar to their father.

*Like Father.*

The thought slithered to life as a whisper. Frederick shook his head. No, ridiculous to even compare the two. Father had been sick for weeks. Surely they couldn't be linked. Especially with two years between them.

"Have you ever researched how much it would cost to gather coal from Creswell to provide for our glassworks? There's a chance we could make it viable again, I think."

Frederick's frown dissolved at Grace's chatter as they moved toward the east wing, her arm tucked through his. She'd talked of little else but improvement ideas since meeting the tenants of Havensbrooke. From hydraulic-powered water gardens inspired by her meeting with the grist-mill workers to orphan education encouraged by her talk with Astlynn

Commons's schoolteacher, Mrs. Jones, her creativity knew no bounds. Just the sound of her happy monologue calmed the uncertainty in his heart as they strode toward the darkened corner of the house.

"Your mind doesn't stop, does it?"

"I've watched Mr. and Mrs. Whitlock use the resources available at their estate to help create a self-sustaining property, and now I'm free to put some of my own imaginings into action. Oh, the possibilities of an evolving plan!" She chuckled. "Can you imagine all the questions I asked the dear, long-suffering couple?"

He could. And envisioned the illustrious couple thriving off Grace's curiosity and passion.

"I spent nearly two hours with Mr. Whitlock, asking questions about orchards the day before our wedding."

He released his hold on her to reach for the door. "Orchards?"

"Oh yes, they're a wonderful means of income. Speaking of income." She looked up at him with those curious eyes dancing. "I wonder why the glassworks were left in disrepair. Plenty of tenants are still interested in working there, and it's not so broken, from what Mr. Lark says."

He pulled his attention away from the door. Why had Edward stopped the glassworks? Or reduced the hours of workers at the gristmill? It was almost as if he wanted to cripple the estate.

"Frederick?" Grace slipped her hand in his, bringing him back to the present. "We can wait another day if you need more time to garner your courage. It can't be an easy feat to return here."

He shook off the melancholic turn of his thoughts and hardened his resolve. Grace was right. If something sinister led to his brother's death, then it was his duty to bring the truth to light, even if it meant facing possible ghosts from his past. He gave her hand a squeeze, attempting a bit of levity. "What do you say to a game of word making after our morning excursion?"

"Word making? Against me?" Her countenance brightened and chased his darker thoughts to the shadows. "You are very brave."

He took a taste from her pink lips and pushed open the door to the east wing. The sitting room emerged with every bit of otherworldliness he'd imagined. Streams of sunlight filtered like lamplight through the half-shuttered windows, blending into grays and golds. The quiet—as cold as the morning he'd last entered the room—chilled him, stalling his steps.

More than just the memories of his brother's death, these spaces held a storm of recollections branding him a failure. The overwhelming sense of responsibility and disappointment nearly froze him to the spot, but Grace drew him forward and threw back the window shutters so that the full rays of morning bathed the room with light.

"There! Now it's much more cheerful." She turned and examined the room, her nose wrinkling. "But yellow?" She offered Frederick an apologetic tilt of her head, drawing him further from his introspection. "Don't you think a sitting room should have a rich, dark color? Or even a pale blue?"

"This was called the Morning Room."

"Oh!" She reexamined the space.

"But I'm not fond of yellow either."

"In flowers it's positively glorious, but for a room?" She shook her head. "The sunshine should be able to do its work without competition."

She moved without the gravity of the past, flitting from one space to the next, dusting off the awkwardness. As he watched her, his pulse calmed, his breath settled. He wasn't alone to face his ghosts anymore. He had Grace.

"What was your brother like?" Grace examined trinkets on a writing desk near the back of the room. "Was he burdened by the weight of this land like you?"

Frederick offered her a half smile. "He was never burdened by much at all, which is why this letter is so peculiar."

Grace tossed a glance over her shoulder, her pale green day dress almost fairy-like in the morning gold. "From that response, you've confirmed my suspicions."

"And what were those?"

She stepped close again and touched his arm. "That somehow you've carried the weight of firstborn all your life, even before you inherited the title. And your family never valued the strong and kind person you are or the love you have for your legacy."

He tipped his head toward her, breathing in the life she brought into these dead rooms. "You think I'm strong enough for this?"

"Of course I do, but not only I. God doesn't go about placing people haphazardly into their stories. He must think you are strong enough too."

He pressed a kiss to her soft cheek. "Stronger now, I think."

"And undeniably smarter, from a clever response like that."

He chuckled and took her hand, leading her down the hallway. "If there's to be any information left behind, it would be in Edward's or Celia's rooms."

"If your grandfather made improvements to the east wing before he died, were they extensive enough to deplete the estate's funds to such an extent you were forced to marry to save it?"

Frederick paused his hand on Edward's study door. "I wasn't privy to the finances before Edward died, and I'm just now attempting to sort through them, but I never heard of financial trials while Grandfather held charge. What I uncovered when I inherited the title was a shock. It seemed impossible my brother had allowed matters to become so dire."

Frederick pushed open the door, the unexpected scent of cigar smoke hitting him with the force of a fist. His breath lodged in his lungs.

"Oh, would you mind if I confiscated your grandparents' letters?" Grace's voice pushed him back in motion. She took a small box from Edward's desk and presented it for his examination. "After all the wonderful things you've said about them, I'm terribly curious to learn of their romance."

Frederick touched the edges of the first letter, his grandfather's handwriting pricking a renewed sense of grief. "I'd like that."

"Perhaps I could read them aloud to you." She leaned nearer, her eyes twinkling. "Wouldn't that be romantic?"

A few more shadows dispersed in the wake of her smile.

They rummaged through the desk and cupboards, collecting ledgers and papers, Grace making comments here and there about the furnishings or comparing the situation to a novel or suggesting how one room or other could look different with this or that.

The longer he stayed among the halls, the warmth of the morning knocking the chill off the place, the more Frederick felt ready to make this part of the house his own.

He glanced at Grace. *Their* own.

Grace's exuberance about the turret windows in his sister-in-law's old rooms brought a grin as he stacked the letters from her desk to carry away. This room was meant for Grace—the morning light, the delicate moldings, the turrets on either side, and only a walk through an excellently windowed parlor to the room he'd make his.

A knock to the door brought his head up. Brandon entered, gaze taking in the space before approaching Frederick. "Sir, a telegram arrived for you."

"How are you this morning, Brandon?" Grace's voice lilted from the bookshelf near the window.

"Very good, miss."

Frederick stifled his smile as he looked at the butler who, if Frederick wasn't mistaken, had taken quite a fancy to the new lady of Havensbrooke. Not only had the man resurrected a sudden interest in the weather to prepare for any upcoming storms, but strawberries appeared in great abundance this year. At almost every meal.

"Dear Brandon," Grace fidgeted with the sleeve of her gown as she crossed the room. Frederick grinned at the habit of her busy finger to match her busy mind. "I'm sorry to bring up such a sad memory, but during the last week of Edward's life, were there any unexpected visitors?"

Frederick's attention shot to Grace, then to the butler, who shifted his attention to Frederick as if to ask for permission to answer.

Frederick gave an almost imperceptible nod.

"Lady Celia had a gentleman visit. A Mr. Turner, her cousin, if I recall."

"You didn't like this Mr. Turner?" Frederick had known Brandon a long time, long enough to read the man.

Brandon lowered his gaze, as if thinking. "He wasn't a pleasant sort, sir. He had a look about him."

"Did he have a protruding nose like a pirate's hook?" Grace shuffled a few steps closer, "Or a black, shaggy set of eyebrows perched above two beady eyes?"

Frederick squinted at his wife, trying to sort out her train of thought.

Brandon's brows raised northward at Grace's very specific question. "As a matter of fact, my lady, he did."

Grace sent Frederick a wide-eyed look but quickly diverted her focus back to Brandon. "And he was the only visitor?"

"Mr. Parks came to see the late Lord Astley earlier in the week." Brandon shifted his attention to Frederick. "May I ask why the sudden curiosity regarding your brother, sir?"

"We discovered information in my brother's papers that led to some unanswered questions."

Brandon nodded and backed toward the door.

"Brandon, did the late Lord Astley or his wife, Celia, share breakfast together that morning?"

He paused, his attention moving back to Grace. "No, ma'am. The lady in question left hours before breakfast and in quite an emotional state."

"Hours before? Emotional?" Frederick stood, nearing the butler. Why hadn't he asked about these things before now? "Did she give a reason?"

"She was nigh inconsolable, sir. She said Lord Astley, your brother, had cast her out."

"So she wasn't here when he died." Frederick directed his statement more to Grace than Brandon. "Thank you, Brandon."

The butler left the room, and Grace looked up at Frederick, a plan of fictional proportions sparkling behind those eyes.

"What are you thinking?"

"Oh, nothing of consequence, really." She smiled and braided her hands behind her back. "It's curious that the very day Celia leaves is the day your brother dies and you suddenly arrive. It's all too well scripted." One of her ginger brows peaked. "And now with your brother's letter? What if she knew he was trying to bring her to justice for some past crime? Or he intended to change his will? What if—"

"You've been reading too much Sherlock, darling. She wasn't here when he died, and what sort of past crime could Celia have done?" Father's face flashed to mind and paused Frederick's thoughts.

"Just because she wasn't here doesn't mean she couldn't have killed him. There are many ways to kill a person before they actually die."

He stared at her profile a bit disconcerted in the fact that she even contemplated how to kill someone, let alone knew various ways to do so. He shifted his attention to the nice, predictable telegram. "This might provide some answers. Mr. Parks has agreed to meet with me tomorrow in London."

"London? Tomorrow?" She moved to his side, taking the telegram. "Well that's all very sudden."

"I'm afraid he's away to France again the following week. If I plan to speak with him sooner rather than later, tomorrow it is. I need to meet with my solicitors at any rate."

"I'll have Ellie. . .um. . .Miss Moore pack my things at once."

"But you have tea with my sister on Saturday." He studied her upturned face. "I won't be back from London by then."

"Oh yes, that's right. Would she be terribly disappointed if I cancel?"

"She's been looking forward to meeting you since our arrival." He groaned. "And the workmen arrive in the morning for directions regarding the lavatories."

"I can see to them, Frederick! I know I can." She grabbed his arm. "I'll be here anyway, and I helped Father in his designs for Rutledge House. Besides, I've read a few books about fixtures and pipes."

"Of course you have." He rolled his eyes to the heavens with his grin spreading to a laugh. "What have you not read about, darling?"

"Rodents." Her nose crinkled in a frown. "Or drains. I've not really discovered much about drains."

"Then I'll not expect you to perform the duties of a plumber as well as wife, sleuth, and renovator." He chuckled and slipped his arm around her waist, drawing her close to place a kiss against her head. "Now I must prepare for my journey."

"I shall miss you terribly."

The slightest pucker of her forehead urged him near again. "You'll have free rein of the house without my distraction to devise how to reinvent these rooms."

"But I have a particular fondness for your kind of distraction."

He tapped the box beneath her arm. "You can spend time with my grandparents' letters."

Her lips tilted into a smile, despite her evident hesitancy to release it. "I suppose I could get to know the staff better while you're gone and collect some ideas for the gardens. And do a bit more investigating of my own."

He hoped not. "And you'll have the library with all your friends safely housed for your pleasure."

She rocked up on tiptoe and left a lingering kiss against his jaw. He couldn't remember the last time he'd smiled so much. Had he ever?

His palm slid down her back, pinning her against him. He lowered his lips to almost touch hers, reveling in the catch of her breath as he closed in. Of course, they still had the afternoon to enjoy a lengthy goodbye.

Those beautiful eyes of hers darkened. "'The sunlight claps the earth, and the moonbeams kiss the sea: what are all these kissings worth, if thou kiss not me?'"

"She quotes Percy Shelley to me."

"You know Shelley?" She slipped back an inch, eyes wide. "Oh Frederick, you have to be the most wonderful man in the world. I'm certain of it. If you confess to reading Austen, I'm fairly confident I'll reward you more valiantly than any Gothic romance Catherine Morland could ever conjure up."

No longer able to keep his distance, he claimed her lips. He would only be gone for two nights at the most. Surely she'd manage a couple of nights without too much trouble.

❧

Grace stood at the door watching Frederick's car move down the long drive on its way to the rail station. Of course he needed to meet with Mr. Parks without delay, but it seemed much too soon for an overnight separation.

The car edged farther away. It would be terribly romantic if he stopped just at the curve in the lane, hopped out, and ran back to her, coattails flapping in the wind.

She waited, holding her breath. The car turned and continued out of sight.

Oh well, what did she expect in the *real* world? Although she did hope he pined for her a little. Not enough to grow deathly ill like some men did in novels, but enough to cause the slightest discomfort in his stomach. That would be enough.

And perhaps a sleepless night.

A cavernous silence engulfed the massive house at Frederick's absence. Grace spent a few hours decorating the Great Hall with Mary and Brandon, feeling quite pleased with her design and abundant—yet strategic—mistletoe hanging. Her grin grew as the delicate plant found its way over almost every threshold in the room. No husband should ever disapprove of extra kisses. She felt certain Frederick wouldn't. He'd welcomed every one of hers from last night quite ravenously.

The thought brought a slight skip to her step and heat in her cheeks as she made her way to the servants' wing. A din of laughter tugged her down the narrow stairwell from the dining room and to the threshold of the kitchen. She peered around the doorframe.

A sturdy woman, dark hair refusing to stay beneath a white kerchief, stood by the stove coaxing a younger blond-haired woman to follow her instructions.

"May I help you, ma'am?"

Grace spun around to find Brandon standing behind her.

"Oh Brandon!" Her palm flew to her chest. "I heard laughter and wished to investigate. I'm a huge proponent of laughter."

He tucked his chin in assent but made no further response.

She leaned close, lowering her voice. "Would you mind reintroducing me to the staff?"

"Of course."

The two women at the stove had stopped their work. Two other men and women stepped in from the next room, and Mary, the maid she'd already met, waited in the hallway behind Brandon. One of the men was a footman, John, she recalled from their evening meals, and though she'd seen the other man around the house, she couldn't remember his name. Mrs. Powell emerged from the stairwell, her key ring jingling at her side, her expression as impassive as ever.

"This is Mrs. Lennox, our cook."

The heavyset woman gave a curt nod. "Pleased to meet you, my lady."

"As am I, Mrs. Lennox. You've made my introduction to Havensbrooke so delightful with your wonderful meals."

The woman's smile pressed into her round cheeks. "Thank ya, ma'am. I aim for my best." She turned to the girl at her side. "This is Amy, my help."

The young woman curtsied. "My lady."

"There is John and Laurence." Brandon added. "Our footmen, ma'am."

Grace nodded to them, hoping her smile encouraged their comfort.

"I believe you know Mary," Mrs. Powell added, stepping forward, hands folded in front of her. "With her is another housemaid, Jane. We have two more housemaids, Lucy and Alice, who are not here at the moment."

"And James is another footman," Brandon said.

"I'm pleased to meet you all again. You've all been so kind." Grace glanced to each face. "And I hope to have your input as Lord Astley and I progress with improvements."

The faces suddenly sobered.

"Oh please, don't worry. We hope to make your jobs easier. Adding bathrooms, central heating, and remodeling the east wing for our personal quarters to be closer to the servants—"

A gasp pulled Grace's attention to. . .Jane, was it? "But what about the ghost?"

"The ghost?" Grace repeated.

"Hush, girl. Don't talk nonsense," Mrs. Powell reprimanded.

Nonsense? A ghost? Grace stepped toward Jane. "What makes you think there's a ghost?"

"'Cause I heard it wailin'." The girl's eyes grew wide as saucers. "I've heard it wailin' more than once. Ever since Lord Edward died."

"Pay her no mind, Lady Astley." Brandon cleared his throat. "You know how imaginations can become excited."

"Oh definitely. I live there all the time." She turned her attention back to poor Jane. "Did the wail sound like a woman or a man?"

"Begging your pardon, my lady, but you're only encouraging her."

"Brandon, if we're going to have a ghost in the house, we should learn more about it. From what I've read, more knowledge is better than less."

He stared at Grace a full five seconds before speaking. "You're not saying you believe her?"

"I'm saying that if something is wailing like a ghost in our house, don't you think we ought to investigate?"

Brandon's shoulders sank a few inches, but Grace wasn't sure why. It seemed perfectly logical. How else would they get to the bottom of a possible haunting without embarking on a ghost hunt? Tonight.

# Chapter Twenty-Two

Mr. Mason Parks bore age poorly. Frederick remembered the man—his brother's closest friend—as a tall, intimidating sort of fellow, pale hair and dark eyes marking a striking contrast within an angled face. But the man greeted Frederick with shoulders bent and face less defined. The blond hair had taken on a silvery hue, and shadows clung to his eyes to match a past Frederick knew the man regretted—a broken family and financial decline. Only in his thirties, his misfortunes made him look double his age.

Financial strain pinched at a man's core and led to all sorts of desperation. Yet God in His ultimate act of humor and mercy salvaged Frederick's desperation by usurping his initial plans and giving him grace—in every sense of the word.

They exchanged a few pleasantries before Parks moved closer to the point.

"I was surprised you've returned from your honeymoon already," Mr. Parks sat behind his desk, hands braided before him.

Another sting of regret pierced Frederick at not giving Grace something she deserved. "I couldn't afford the additional time away from Havensbrooke, as yet."

Mr. Parks tilted his head and studied Frederick. "Is it as bad as all that?"

Understanding passed in silence.

"So your telegram said you wished to discuss your brother?" He hung his head. "Nasty business that. Too young."

"I've recently received some information which caused a few questions to be raised. I thought you might provide insight."

"I'll do what I can, Frederick, but my time is limited, you understand." He spoke too sharply for the request.

"Of course." A sudden wariness rose into Frederick's stomach. "Do you recall the last time you spoke with my brother?"

Mr. Parks rubbed his chin, gaze pointed to the ceiling. "He was in town a few weeks before he died, if I remember, attending a party. Yes, the Clarks. We spoke then."

"Did he seem. . ." Frederick struggled for the right words. "Healthy at that point?"

"Perfectly so."

"I understand you came to Havensbrooke the week he died."

"Ah yes." Parks shifted in his seat and tugged a handkerchief from his coat pocket. "He wanted my opinion on some estate business."

"Such as a change in the will, perhaps?" No reason prolonging the inevitable.

His dark gaze shot to Frederick's. "Perhaps. I can't remember."

"Of course."

"See here, Frederick, I know you and your brother left on less than amicable terms, but there's no need to question his choices." He wiped at his brow. "After your disagreement, I can see why you'd seek some consolation in your guilt."

Frederick refused to acknowledge the blame and waited until Mr. Parks met his gaze again. "I have reason to believe my brother's opinion of me had changed, Mr. Parks, and that he was not as content as you seem to suggest. Now, if you would be so kind as to revisit your memory and search again for any new information."

Mr. Parks's brow rose to the hairline, and he looked away. "He'd been anxious regarding estate costs for years, even before your father died, which was the main reason why—" He paused and reached for his handkerchief to attend to his nose. "Well, he thought the transition of power was providential."

Frederick refused to physically respond to the sudden awareness. "Are you saying Edward wanted our father to die?"

Mr. Parks cleared his throat and swiped at his nose again. "What I'm saying is that your brother was concerned about the financial status of Havensbrooke and saw the untimely death of your father as an opportunity to salvage what was left of the estate's finances. Clearly, he underestimated the cost of his actions."

"His actions?"

"I mean, his projections." He shuffled some papers around on his desk. "He'd hoped more funds would remain upon his succession, but as you know, you were compelled to marry a wealthy woman to save the property."

What was Mr. Parks hiding? The letter in Frederick's possession bled with fear but not from financial ruin. Frederick might have been away from Havensbrooke for nearly three years, but he'd known his brother well enough to doubt a desperate love of their ancestral home. For money and power? Yes. But for the welfare of a centuries' old dynasty? Not Edward. Or their father.

"And the will?"

Parks sniffed. "I advised against making rash decisions, as any good friend should do."

Ah! "So he meant to change it?"

Parks saw his blunder and gave his head a decided shake. "He didn't give details."

Frederick sat back in the chair, allowing silence a moment's gravity. "Do you have any reason to think my brother had enemies, Mr. Parks?"

"Enemies?" He coughed, a raucous sound. "What a thought! I suppose we all have people who disagree with us, but real enemies? I can't think of any."

"And what about his wife?"

"Lady Celia?" A redness deepened on the man's face. "I mean the previous Lady Astley." He cleared his throat. "A remarkable woman."

*Remarkable?* Frederick remained unmoved. "To your knowledge, did she have anyone who would wish her ill?"

He relaxed. "Celia Percy has always been the sort to garner attention, as you well know, but I can't think of anyone who'd wish her real harm." The man's grin tipped in a most unsettling way. "Unless a jilted lover, perhaps?"

Frederick didn't flinch beneath the man's suggestion. "How would you describe my brother and sister-in-law's relationship near the end of his life?"

"See here, Lord Astley, I didn't ask the man about his personal affairs. If he shared something, I listened, but I would never pry."

"Of course not." Frederick waited, the man's shifty expression deepening his doubt. Perhaps a little bait? "Disagreements between husband and wife can lead to rash decisions, of course. I'd assume if Edward was considering cutting his wife off, he may have garnered some opposition, even from someone as remarkable as my sister-in-law."

"Cut off?" The man nearly shot from his chair. "Edward wasn't the sort to allow a little tiff here and there to cause real harm." He wagged a pudgy finger at Frederick. "I can understand why you wish to console yourself, but dragging his name or that of the esteemed Lady Celia's into a scandal will not make things right between you and your brother's memory. And making these conjectures about their relationship? Nasty accusations, Lord Astley."

The malevolent glint returned to his small eyes. "Besides, weren't you the one who discovered your brother's body? And on the very day you returned to the country? Highly coincidental. Perhaps a guilty conscience has you seeing ghosts where there are none."

*Coincidental indeed.* And "esteemed Lady Celia"? In the best society, few would have referred to Celia in that way, except those who adored her. Frederick's thoughts paused to consider Mr. Parks and Celia. He grimaced.

But how did Parks know Frederick was the one to find Edward's body? Mother had written him to return to England, even included tickets for passage, with an arrival the very day of his brother's death. Either Grace's influence was starting to spark Frederick's paranoia, or something wasn't all right with Mr. Mason Parks.

"Ghosts or not, Mr. Parks, what is less known is that my brother had been dead at least an hour when I arrived. Both our family doctor and several witnesses can confirm my involvement should any unnecessary rumors arise."

"Well then, I really can't help you any further." Parks stood and marched toward the door. "I will take this conversation for what it truly was, a way for you to deal with your grief, but other than my sincere condolences, I cannot imagine being much help to you. Perhaps you should leave the sad turn of the past exactly there."

"I'm afraid, Mr. Parks, the past has an uncanny way of impacting the present, and I've no interest in being caught unawares." He tipped his head. "Good day."

Frederick moved up the steps from the District Line of the Underground, his shoes setting a steady clip as he walked beneath London's streetlamps. The lights gave off an eerie yellow hew against the fog lingering in the unusually warm December air. A festive display of garland and red ribbons adorned each lamp, cheering the gloomy cast of evening a bit. Mr. Parks's conversation unearthed more questions than provided answers, a pattern it seemed, surrounding Edward's death.

Frederick crossed the empty street toward his town house. How had he not looked deeper? All of the distractions of the estate, his own grief, and the monstrous debts created a perfect diversion from closer observation. Had that been the plan? Celia's part in a more criminal scheme emerged clearer with each revisit of the facts.

Suddenly a shadow moved in an alleyway to Frederick's right. A man—blade glinting in the light of the lamps—charged forward.

Reflexes born from his military stint resurfaced from their disuse and sent Frederick into action, shifting to the right as the blade missed Frederick's chest to slice the edge of his coat sleeve. His assailant was a tall man, sturdy but not confident in his movements.

A bit stiff. From what? Age? Inexperience?

Frederick dodged another swing and captured the man's arm, twisting it to force the weapon from his hand. A dirty handkerchief covered part of the man's face, but his dark eyes remained visible. Pale hair. Not too young, from the creases around those eyes.

The knife clinked to the ground, but the man's fist came around and slammed into Frederick's chest, seizing his breath and loosening his hold. They stumbled apart. The assailant dove for his knife, but Frederick plunged forward and captured the man around the waist, falling with him to the ground, inches away from the blade. With an unexpected twist, the man's elbow rammed into Frederick's ribs. Frederick groaned but refused to release the man's arm, twisting it until displaced. His attacker cried out and struggled to his feet, turning to land a fist directly into Frederick's upper cheek.

A couple, arm-in-arm, emerged from the next street. Was that a constable on the corner?

"Halloo!" Frederick called, but his words were cut off by another slam to the face, sending Frederick off-kilter long enough for the man to flee. He pursued his attacker toward an alleyway, but with blurred vision, he barely made out his assailant as the man escaped into the night. Frederick steadied his palms against his knees, catching his breath as the constable rushed to his side.

The constable voiced his surprise at such an act of violence happening in this particular part of town, and the steady uneasiness which had started with Edward's letter took a decided upswing. Frederick had gotten too close with his confrontation of Parks, he'd wager, and though Parks took the bait, he wasn't the attacker.

The constable accompanied Frederick to his town house and left him in the reliable care of Elliott, promising to send a patrolman to keep watch through the night.

"I think we must be on our guard, Elliott." Frederick bypassed the parlor and went directly toward his room. "Blake and Grace have been right all along. This attack wasn't random."

Elliott had been Frederick's lone confidant, apart from Blake, since Frederick's return to England. A solid mind and faithful friend. "I never liked how things ended with Lord Edward. Something seemed unfinished."

"Parks is in on it, but he's no mastermind."

Elliott stepped to the lavatory to begin drawing water for a bath. "He was quite keen on Lady Celia, if I recall."

As almost every man was who met her. Frederick winced as he rubbed a palm against his wounded ribs. "There has to be proof somewhere, but I'm going to need help. The police might bring too much attention. Perhaps a private detective?"

"I'm keen for an extra set of eyes, my lord."

Frederick nodded and peeled off his jacket.

"I've sent Alice to bring ice for your eye." Elliott gestured toward Frederick's face.

Frederick peered into the nearby mirror and frowned. A swell of purple and green darkened the skin below his right eye. "Thank you."

"I think it unwise for you to travel alone for the remainder of your trip, sir, so I shall accompany you, if I may."

Frederick steadied his gaze on Elliott. "That would be good of you."

As Frederick unbuttoned his shirt, an envelope on the desk, with *Frederick* written in a flourish on the front, caught his attention. He slid

Elliott a look, but the man was examining the slits in Frederick's jacket from the knife. With a turn of his back, Frederick slipped open the envelope and drew out the single sheet of paper.

*My dear Lord Astley. . .*

His grin tipped. Only one woman would start off a letter like this.

*For almost three weeks, I've been your wife, and already my mind and heart are filled with you. I'm still not certain how I'll manage with you away, but rest assured, my favorite fictional heroes cannot compare to the way you take my breath away with just a word.*

He cleared his throat and looked up. Elliott had moved to the dresser to lay out Frederick's bedclothes.

*I cannot know what our days or years hold, but do promise me that you'll always distract me during storms, kiss my neck as if it's the best taste, and whisper my name with enough tenderness to have the memory linger through my hours away from you like sunshine during an English rain.*

*Isn't that a lovely sentiment? It rains quite often in England, so I expect your whispers to continue with equal consistency.*

He could envision her writing the sentence with a wistful grin tugging at her beautiful lips.

*I've only belonged to you—and wish for no other. Stay safe and come back to me soon, my dear hero.*

*Yours,*
*Grace*

He trailed a thumb across her name, the words seeping through his defenses with a power none should possess.

He cleared his throat and found Elliott staring, brow raised in unvoiced question.

"You knew about this?" Frederick raised the paper.

"I did."

Frederick grinned and placed the paper into its sheath. "She's quite unexpected, isn't she?"

"If I might say so, sir. In the best possible way."

"Indeed, Elliott." And Frederick needed to solve the mystery of his brother's death before anything worse happened. Especially if the target moved from him to Grace.

⚜

What a day! First she met with the workmen with such success that even Brandon offered a smile. All right, perhaps not a smile, but a confident nod of approval. Then she sketched plans for the East Garden, complete with a meeting with Mr. Archer about the possibilities of a water garden. And now she walked up the Great Hall steps for her first official ghost hunt.

She couldn't keep her grin from spreading to impish proportions. Oh no, Lillias would never have been prepared for something like this.

Grace's candle flickered with an otherworldly glow as she opened the door into the unused wing. Vacant darkness seeped around her little light, crowding in on all sides, and a clang from the grandfather clock in the Great Hall behind her chimed midnight.

The witching hour.

If ghosts were going to visit, wouldn't it be now?

She looked back over her shoulder toward the corridor leading to the Great Hall, a faint view of the Christmas tree catching her attention. Perhaps she should have waited for one o'clock instead. That's when the ghosts came for Ebenezer Scrooge, and since it *was* close to Christmas, maybe ghosts followed a certain schedule.

She glanced back down the long corridor to the Great Room. No wonder Frederick never heard the wailing. She swallowed a growing lump in her throat at the realization. Oh dear. She was rather far away from anyone else, wasn't she? Perhaps she should have alerted Ellie to her plans. Or at least brought Zeus along as company. Of course, none of the stories she'd read had involved dogs on ghost hunts. Could dogs sense ghosts better than humans?

With hushed feet and a determined lift to her chin, she slipped farther into the Morning Room. The shadows grew especially thick toward Lord Edward's office, unless her imagination played tricks on her. Which was quite possible. When she was twelve, she'd convinced herself she'd cried hard enough to wake the dead when out of a rainstorm came a cat that looked very similar to her dear Puddles. At daylight, she'd realized the poor thing wasn't even the same color, but she'd kept it anyway.

The floor beneath her step gave a creak, and she nearly screamed. Perhaps it wasn't the best idea to have read *At Chrighton Abbey*, *Hamlet*, and Dickens's *A Christmas Carol* as ghost research before coming to the east wing at midnight.

At least Dickens's story had a happy ending.

Her candlelight flickered, moving the shadows along the floor and walls like an eerie dance. The floor creaked again, a strange, hollow, moaning sound.

No wait. Her breath caught. That wasn't the floor.

Every hair on Grace's arms stood to attention, and a chill tiptoed up her spine until it spread beneath her hairline. She pressed against the wall, sliding to a sitting position behind a massive wingback.

The sound started at a distance—low and mournful—and swelled through the room, closer. Grace blew out the candle to hide in the shadows, but then she groaned. Couldn't ghosts see in the dark? Her shoulders slumped. So basically, the only person who needed the light was her.

*What sort of ghost hunter was she?*

A flutter of white drew her attention to the hallway. Grace's air stuttered to a complete halt in her throat. She could only see an outline of a person-shaped image clothed in a flowing white gown, but the awful moan poured from the figure again, louder and more pitiful. Grace searched the space around her for a weapon. The candlestick certainly wouldn't help. The chair looked too heavy.

She pulled off one of her shoes and rolled her eyes heavenward. How on earth would her shoe stop something without a body or soul?

She paused. Well, she could give it a sole.

She stifled her snicker and peered around the corner of the chair. *Something* moved across the floor—no, almost glided—and slipped back into the darkness in the direction of Edward's office.

Grace set her jaw and stood. Perhaps she should try and talk to it. After all, the ghosts she'd read about spoke fine English.

Without a sound, she crept down the hallway, shoe raised in defense. It really was a ridiculous notion. A shoe protecting her from some spirit of the dead almost had her giggling out of sheer terror.

Only the pale light of the moon lit her way, creating a chessboard path of dark and light against the carpet. Every swish of her shoeless foot against the floor, ever wisp of breath, even the thumping of her own heartbeat in her ears magnified. Another step placed her in front of the open door of Edward's office. She pinched her eyes closed. Oh, let it be a lighthearted spirit, like the Ghost of Christmas Present.

With a deep breath, Grace squared her shoulders and crossed the threshold.

Streams of faint light filtered through the windows, bathing the study in its own spectral hue. Everything stood at haunted alert, poised in shadow and moon glow. Grace readied herself for a scream, but. . .the room stood empty. No ghost at all.

She lowered her shoe, scanning the vacant space. There were no other doors, no other means of escape except the door through which she'd entered. Her breath turned shallow, and she backed toward her exit, shoe raised again. Could this whole ghost thing be true?

"My lady?"

Grace screamed and turned to see a dark silhouette stepping from the hallway, a lit candle half revealing, half concealing a man's face.

She was going to die!

"Are you all right, madam?"

The voice bled through her hysteria into recognition. "Brandon?" A rush of relief poured over her tense muscles, and she lowered the sole-weapon. "Oh, thank heavens. I thought you were the ghost come back to exact its revenge."

"Ghost, madam?"

"Yes, I saw her, or at least I think it was a her. And she must have been a ghost, because she entered this study and didn't exit, and now"—she waved toward the room—"no one is here."

Brandon tilted his head ever so slightly, looking at Grace as if he wasn't quite certain what to make of her very logical testimony, and then stepped around her. The light's glow washed over the furniture and bookshelves as he marched to the far corner of the room and touched the edge of one of the bookshelves. Grace stuck to his side, just in case some wailing wight bled through the walls again.

"As I thought, my lady. The door is ajar."

As if by magic, Brandon pulled the bookshelf from the wall, revealing a set of stairs descending into darkness.

"A secret door? Behind a bookshelf?" She squeezed Brandon's arm. "That's brilliant."

"A servant's entry."

"Can we put one in my new room for a clandestine entrance to the library, perhaps?"

Brandon shot her a sideways glance. "Pardon?"

"Never mind." She'd ask Frederick later. "Where does it lead?"

Instead of answering, Brandon disappeared down the stairs, Grace close behind. They descended one level, followed a narrow corridor, and exited into the Great Hall. She turned and noticed their exit door was covered with a tall portrait.

"How clever." Her grin grew. "Now I don't trust a single portrait or bookshelf in this house."

Brandon bowed his head, his lips twitching again, as if he just might want to laugh. Maybe. She'd keep hoping. "Do you wish for one of the maids to escort you to your room?"

"Oh." She looked up the dark, lonely stairway. "No, dear Brandon, I'm certain the maids are happy to remain in their beds." She squeezed her palms together in front of her. "Besides, it appears our ghost only haunts the east wing."

"You believe it's a ghost, my lady?"

"Not really, but I mean to discover what it really is."

Brandon released a long sigh. "I have no doubt on that score."

"See?" She rewarded him with her biggest smile. "We're getting to know each other so well, your confidence in me is growing."

The man's lips tipped slightly. Ever so slightly, but a success nonetheless.

"Terror is extremely exhausting, Brandon." She stifled a yawn. "I slept for ten hours after reading *The Hound of the Baskervilles*. I think it's time to go to bed."

"Excellent notion, my lady."

"And Brandon?" She started for the stairs and then stopped. "Thank you for coming to the east wing tonight. It was exceedingly heroic of you."

He ducked his head in silent acceptance of her gratitude. She raised her head and slowly walked up the stairs until out of Brandon's view—then she ran down the long, dark hallway to her room.

# Chapter Twenty-Three

Grace breathed in the crisp air of the afternoon, enjoying the fresh snowfall covering the beautiful countryside with a fine dusting of powdery white. To get a closer view, she'd taken one of Havensbrooke's stallions, Dash, out for a ride. He lived up to his moniker, gliding across the lush fields and offering her a sense of celebration since successfully managing workmen, surviving a ghost hunt, and—most daunting of all—navigating morning tea with Frederick's sister.

Of course Eleanor proved the perfect example of a genteel, collected English lady. Nothing like Lady Moriah. Thank heavens! And Grace didn't seem to shock Eleanor half as much as she thought she might, even when Grace put an inordinate amount of sugar into her tea or spoke of the glassworks with such exuberance that the table shook. Perhaps Frederick or Lavenia had given her due warning. Very clever of them.

The meeting also proved providential in a most desperate of ways. Eleanor Percy Ratcliff knew something about fashion! So Grace divulged her deepest concerns and inadequacies regarding the topic, particularly with the upcoming dinner party at Lord and Lady Keriford's house, and Eleanor rose to the challenge—referring Grace to a dress shop called Rouselle's in nearby Edensbury.

The idea of embarrassing her husband and all of his progeny by wearing a summer gown on a winter evening seemed less likely than ever. Eleanor even allowed Grace to take a few fashion magazines for perusal.

Following a path along the tree line, Grace reveled in the beauty of her new home. Untouched forests, acres of farmland, and a river emptying out into a lake—with a gristmill at the water's edge. Havensbrooke was a gold mine of opportunity.

As the spires of Havensbrooke Hall rose in the distance, she felt a renewed connection. Yes, she could learn to love this place. And if God had brought her all this way under such extreme circumstances, He must certainly think she belonged here too, even with a ghost haunting, a possible murderer, and Grace's poor fashion choices.

A movement to the right caught her attention. Through the veil of trees, a rider approached, clothed in black with a scarf covering the lower half of his face. A chill snaked up her neck. She turned to a sound on her left, only to find a second rider, both in pursuit of *her*.

Well, this definitely proved that something underhanded was going on, because hooded men didn't ride around on other people's land for an afternoon excursion of delight.

The house waited up ahead, at least a fifteen-minute hard ride away. Plenty of time for the assailants to catch her, possibly kill her, and maybe even drag her lifeless body into the woods to dispose of it under freshly dampened, snow-covered earth.

She stiffened her shoulders. They'd have to outride her first.

Thankful for her billowing riding skirt, she tossed her right leg over the saddle to secure a better grip on the horse and spurred Dash into a hard gallop. Here was another logical rationale for riding astride. Escaping murderers.

Up ahead and off to her right, a cottage came into view. Not huge or elaborate, but enough to provide witnesses and possibly a weapon.

*Perfect.* She glided across the field, hooves beating close behind. With a quick tug to the strap at her chin, she flung her riding hat in the direction of the man at her right. It hit his shoulder, surprising him enough to nearly knock him from the horse.

Aha! What else? She leaned close, reaching into the saddle bag, her hand meeting something hard and metal. Wrapping her fingers around the find, she turned enough to get in a solid aim and swing. The horseshoe slammed into the short man's leg, provoking a cry of pain that spooked the horse and sent the animal galloping in the opposite direction.

One down.

But the tall man was gaining on her. She neared the cottage, urged Dash to jump the stone fence surrounding the house, and slid from the horse before he'd come to a complete stop. Without looking back, she ran to the cottage door, slapping her palm against the wood.

"Help."

She turned to see the tall man on the other side of the rock wall.

"Please." She shook the door handle. "Let me in."

Just as he jumped the fence, the cottage door opened and Grace stumbled inside to find a motherly looking woman staring at her, wide eyed.

"Two men in black are chasing me." She burst out the words. "Do you have a weapon we can use to fend them off?"

The dark-haired woman stood immobile, so Grace ran to the kitchen and began rummaging through the cupboards for a knife.

Suddenly the sound of a gunshot reverberated through the room. Grace froze and waited for death's icy grip. Most books described it that way, but on the contrary, her pulse pumped a warm stream through her quivering legs.

A child's cry sounded from the corner of the room where a little girl, perhaps four or five, sat tucked against the wall, knees to her chin. Oh dear! Had Grace gotten a mother killed?

But instead of wilting from a gunshot wound, the woman stood poised at the door with a rifle in hand. Grace paused to appreciate the fierceness of the stance. *Fantastic!*

Graced edge up behind her. "Did you shoot him?"

"No, milady." She turned, lowering the rifle to her side. "But I put the fear of God in 'im. He rode north."

*My lady?* Had Grace met the woman on the day she and Frederick visited the tenants?

"Well, you were spectacular with that rifle. I mean to learn how to use one as soon as Lord Astley will teach me."

The woman's pale gaze shot to Grace, pale brows raised. A whimper came from the little girl, so with another glance outside, the woman closed the door and made her way across the room.

"It's all right, luv." The woman knelt and rubbed the top of the little girl's head, soothing away the whimper. "The worst is over."

Grace stepped closer to them, smiling at the little girl, whose large, dark brown eyes looked strangely familiar.

"Do you have any idea who he was?" The woman tossed the words over her shoulder.

"Not at all," Grace murmured, studying the little face.

"It's curious why they'd come this far from the main house." The woman moved forward toward the stone fireplace, holding the little girl's hand. "They must have been after you specially."

"Exactly." Which tossed a kink in the idea of someone trying to murder Frederick. She paced near the round table at the edge of the small kitchen, speaking more to herself. "Ransom? Revenge?" She looked over at the woman. "I don't think I've been here long enough to offend somebody to the point of murder."

The woman's lips softened at the corners. "You must alert the authorities, ma'am."

"Oh, most certainly." Grace's breathing began to relax so she could take in her surroundings. A quaint cottage with warm colors all around, from the hardwood floors covered with rugs to the dark red curtains on the windows.

The woman gestured toward Grace. "We have a guest here, don't we, Lily?"

Grace turned her full attention on the little girl, who had quieted at the woman's side. Loose dark curls framed a pale, cherub-like face. *Frederick's daughter.*

The little girl studied Grace's face with such fascination, Grace couldn't help seeing a little of Frederick as a boy in those eyes.

"Lily." Grace melted to her knees. "That's a beautiful name." A nursery was certainly the next addition on Grace's list of renovations. "I'm Lady Astley, but I think you should call me Grace."

"I can tell already Lord Astley's worries were in vain." The woman studied Grace, the hesitance in her smile dissipating.

"Worries?"

"I think he was concerned about how you'd take to his ward." She touched Lily's head with the tenderness of a mother. "Though he wouldn't say as much outright."

"I can't imagine not falling in love with her." Grace touched Lily's nose, inciting a shy grin, and looked back to the woman. "Do you have all you need here? You'll be safe?"

"Lord Astley takes good care of us, but I've been seein' to myself for years." The woman's jaw hardened. "And my brother lives here with us."

"Oh, I'm so glad you're not in the cottage alone." Her gaze went back to the window. "Though, I may send an extra man to scout the area tonight, if you don't mind."

The woman's expression gentled as she nodded.

"Dat was a woud noise." Lily blinked those dark eyes up at Grace with renewed interest.

The sweet voice shot directly into Grace's heart. "I'm sorry, Lilibit."

"I don't wike woud noises."

"I don't either. Thunder especially."

Her nose scrunched into a frown. "It can be vewy woud."

"And terribly frightening. I try to think of happy thoughts when I hear thunder. Is that what you do?"

She nodded, bouncing those curls. "And hide in de piwows."

"I couldn't agree more." Grace brushed back a loose strand of Lily's hair and stood, finally feeling as if her pulse had resumed a normal pace. A double-dimpled smile crested the little girl's face, stealing Grace's heart forever.

Grace looked at the woman. "I cannot thank you enough for your help, Miss—?"

"Quinnly, ma'am. And you'll know my brother. He works in the stables."

"Yes, I've met him. He goes by Quinnly, yes?" Grace looked out the window, wondering how she should get back to the house without a horse.

"He does." The woman glanced toward the window, as if reading Grace's thoughts. "He'll be home soon for a bite to eat, and I know he'd feel better escortin' you to the main house."

Grace's shoulders relaxed with a sigh. "That would be wonderful."

And in the meantime, Grace could get to know the ward of Havensbrooke.

⚜

Frederick's day had gone from bad to decidedly worse, and it wasn't even teatime.

Parks didn't return to work the following morning, and his assistant had no idea of any impending travel to France, which only added more incentive for Frederick to go to the police. Frederick's meeting with his brother's solicitor proved a nasty business, especially when Frederick asked pointed questions related to certain investments. After only a half hour, Frederick left the office with all of the man's paperwork related to Havensbrooke and in search of a new solicitor.

If Frederick had only pursued the financial particulars before now!

"I'm not meaning to pry, sir," Elliott offered as the two of them sat in a pub overlooking Linton Street. "But if you're in need of someone trustworthy, might I offer a recommendation?"

"I'd be grateful for it, Elliott." Frederick sat back with a hard sigh. "Some of the finances are murky, and I need an honest, smart man to help me sort it out."

"What about Andrew Piper, sir?"

Frederick's attention shot across the table. "Grandfather's former solicitor?"

Elliott nodded, looking quite uncomfortable at a chair in the pub across from his employer as if they were comrades, but Frederick trusted no man other than Blake more than he did Elliott.

"He was a young man when your grandfather took him on, and it's not been four years since your brother replaced him." Elliott cleared his throat and reached for the cup in front of him. "He had an excellent reputation."

Why hadn't Frederick considered him at the onset? Kind but shrewd, he'd worked with Grandfather for years.

"That's an excellent notion, Elliott." Frederick rapped a palm to the table. "Do you recall why Edward released him?"

Elliott scratched at the back of his neck and swallowed. "I believe Lady Celia wasn't too keen on his financial advice."

"He probably put a knot in her plans." And how worse had it gotten when Frederick left the country? "I happened to see Mr. Piper before leaving for India, and we spoke of my grandfather. Do you think he still lives at the same London address?"

Elliott raised his cup. "It can't hurt to start there, can it?"

"Then that is our next stop, directly after we locate a detective I've heard about."

Elliott's expression sobered. "Sir, may I ask you something?"

"Of course, Elliott."

The valet's brow pinched as his finger skimmed the rim of his cup. "I don't understand what reason Parks or anyone else would have to harm you."

"I have an unconfirmed theory on that score." Frederick took a sip of tea before answering. "Money."

"But Havensbrooke has been struggling for years, hasn't it?"

"Exactly, almost as if on purpose. Which leads to the question of what happens if the estate is left without lord or heir and must then be sold."

"What happens to the money, you mean?"

"Right." Frederick's jaw tensed as his musing took on voice. "After securing my sister's allowance and a few stipends to certain staff, according to Edward's most recent will, if the estate is sold, the remaining funds are divided among the three widows."

"Three?"

"Yes." Frederick shot Elliott a knowing look. "Mother, Lady Astley, and—"

Elliott's gaze locked with Frederick's. "Lady Celia."

"Exactly."

"I think you ought to have a new will written straightaway, sir." Elliott drew in a deep breath. "Not that I expect your death, but I wouldn't want Celia Blackmore taking anything more from Havensbrooke than she already has."

<hr>

The day ended much better than it had begun. Frederick located Jack Miracle, the young and astute private detective he had read about in the papers. Miracle took detailed notes on Frederick's knowledge and conjectures, as well as interviewed Elliott. Something about knowing a detective was keeping watch put a little more confidence in Frederick's steps.

Andrew Piper was in the process of leaving his office for the day when Frederick and Elliott caught him. He welcomed Frederick like the lost prodigal, and after hearing an accounting of all the facts thus far, Piper readily took back his position as solicitor for Havensbrooke. He even made plans to meet with Detective Miracle before traveling to Havensbrooke within the week to divulge any inconsistencies he uncovered in the information Frederick left with him.

As Elliott and Frederick settled back at the town house for the night, the weight Frederick had carried since leaving Havensbrooke felt a little lighter. Blake. Piper. Elliott. Miracle. He had four allies in the messy affair now—his grin spread as he removed his coat—and Grace, of course. Who knew what she'd been up to during his absence? Knowing she'd met Eleanor and had Aunt Lavenia as an acquaintance made the idea of leaving her alone with Mother a bit easier, especially since Mother had refused to leave her rooms since Frederick had told her he was searching for a dower house for her.

The same longing he'd experienced throughout the day branched through his chest. He missed Grace.

As Frederick turned toward the desk to read through some of the documents he'd collected from the former solicitor, another envelope, like the one from the night before, caught his eye. Frederick picked up the card and pointed it toward the valet. "Did she plan this with you?"

Elliott's brows rose in faux surprise. "I assure you, sir, I only followed Lady Astley's instructions."

"Which, I suspect, were quite detailed." Frederick imagined his wife with her bright eyes regaling the valet with her secret designs.

"And given with great excitement, sir."

Frederick's smile unfurled. "No doubt."

"If I might say so, she does bring a certain light with her. It doesn't go unnoticed in the house or"—Elliott turned to place Frederick's jacket in the wardrobe—"in you, sir."

Frederick slid down into the desk chair. "Why, Elliott, you sound almost poetic."

"I shall try to refrain from future exposition, my lord."

Frederick chuckled at the man's droll reply, but the observation clung around his heart with welcome truth. "You're right, though. She does bring light with her."

"If you were hoping to add the right people to your good intentions, a higher hand chose better for you than you chose for yourself."

Frederick lowered his face with a nod, slowly peeling open the note. "It's a pity it's taken me such hardship to prefer His choices to mine."

"As my mother would say, sir, that is the beginning of wisdom."

Frederick cast him a knowing grin, embracing the awareness of God's fingerprints all over the debacle with Lillias. No, he wouldn't have chosen as well for himself. He'd have chosen out of duty and necessity, but God chose for his heart.

Once Elliott left the room, Frederick opened his note.

> *Oh, hero of mine, I'm determined to keep myself fresh in your thoughts.*

He could practically see her sitting at her desk, pen in hand, mischievous smile tipping her tantalizing lips into a grin.

> *And if you were to miss me in the slightest, I thought these notes would help me feel closer to you. I'm a sentimental girl, but I hope you don't mind it too awfully. I can assure you, it will only prove to be for your benefit, especially once you return and I can sequester you away all to myself.*

The slow rising heat associated with her innuendo scorched the inside of his throat with a rush of longing. It had taken him much too long to go to sleep last night as she visited his thoughts. The endearing minx. She would most certainly accompany him on any trip from this point forward.

> *Of course I wish for your journey to be successful, but I do hope you miss me a little bit. I'm certain I shall miss you. If you're to become my dearest friend—and we've gotten off to a very friendly start—then I shall have to find things to do to distract myself from searching the drive for your return.*
>
> *I do prefer your brand of friendliness. I must say it's my favorite kind, and I hope you will continue to be friendly with me as often as you like. Very friendly. Often.*

Good heavens, he was going to attack the poor girl as soon as he crossed the threshold of Havensbrooke!

> *Do have a marvelous time among the solicitors and architects you meet. Dear me, that doesn't sound exciting at all, but I'm sure you'll find a way to make it memorable.*
>
> *I look forward to seeing you tomorrow, my dear Lord Astley. My lips await your steadfast attentions.*
>
> *Your Grace*

# Chapter Twenty-Four

The ghost didn't appear again the next evening, though Grace searched until almost one o'clock. Aunt Lavenia joined Grace for morning tea, providing a wonderful opportunity for Grace to divulge the discovery of her ghost with someone who wouldn't become too concerned about her mental faculties.

Before leaving, Lavenia made a short visit to Lady Moriah, returning much sadder than when she'd walked up the stairs.

"Her heart is so cold, dear Grace. If anyone could thaw her, perhaps you could," Aunt Lavenia whispered, walking to the door. "How desperately she needs the warmth of love."

As Grace waved goodbye to Lavenia, guilt nudged at the corners of her heart. She'd made every effort to avoid her mother-in-law over the past two days, but was Lavenia right? Did God place Grace at Havensbrooke for more than just Frederick, but his mother too?

Grace's morning Bible reading also nudged her spirit about doing good and praying for those "that hate you. . .and despitefully use you." And *spiteful* certainly fit the dowager. Grace really ought to stop referring to Lady Moriah as *the dowager* in her mind when she felt particularly cross with the woman. It didn't encourage kindness at all.

She sighed and peered heavenward as she took the steps to the south wing.

Grace's knock was met by her mother-in-law grousing, "Come in." Now that Grace knew a little more about her mother-in-law, she noticed the tattered brocade wallpaper and the photographs of a younger Moriah with her husband, a room as lonely and weathered as the woman occupying it.

"What do you want?"

Well, perhaps Lady Moriah was more cantankerous than lonely.

Grace tempered her scowl with a smile and stepped farther into the room. "I heard you weren't feeling well this morning, so I wondered if you might like some company."

"From you?" The woman's face contorted. "I can barely stand the thought of you, let alone listen to your American accent."

Grace's hand clenched at her side, and she looked away, replaying one of the verses about love through her mind. Her gaze landed on the excellent grand piano with sheet music propped and ready. "Do you play?"

"Not in years." She tipped up her chin. "I used to be quite excellent, however."

Well, either Lady Moriah *did* play recently or cared so much for the instrument that she kept it polished and open. A weakness Grace wasn't too proud to exploit for kindness' sake. Surely God wouldn't mind.

"I've played since I was seven. I imagine I could play any piece you used to play."

A sound like a growl came from the woman. "I performed for hundreds by the time I was your age."

Ah, but she didn't say no. Grace stepped toward the piano. "Then I imagine you could give me excellent guidance on becoming a better pianist, assuming you remember."

"Of course I remember." The woman slammed her palm down on her blanket-covered lap. "I may be sick, but my mind is still intact." She waved her hand toward the piano. "Brahms's Rhapsody in D Minor is on the piano—a less technical piece, so perhaps you can play it, if you start slowly."

Grace turned her head so that Lady Moriah couldn't see her eye roll. "I shall do my best."

She'd played this piece before, but not under such scrutiny. Grace gave it her all, pouring her own little magic into the music with an added trill here and an extra note there.

"Your technique could use a firm hand, but you do not play poorly, though I doubt you are prepared for some of Liszt's work."

Grace decided then and there she was going to ignore every rude thing the dowager countess said, and if it meant she wouldn't remember one word of the conversation, so be it. "I'll be happy to grow under your tutelage."

The woman's beady eyes examined Grace's face, almost as if they wished to push her down a few inches in height. "You do not understand your place at all, do you?"

"As wife to your son?"

"As the stone in a home that has withstood centuries. You know nothing of the privilege of being part of a vast legacy." Her lips curled. "You and your new money."

Grace refused to back down. One way or another, this rivalry had to stop, and if her mother-in-law wasn't going to act her age, then Grace would be forced to. "Then why don't you educate me?"

The woman's eyes grew wide. "Educate you?"

"Whether you like me and my hair or not, the truth remains that I'm the only one who can bear an heir. If I'm to be a part of the Astley history, then teach me about it instead of judging me. Otherwise you will have no hand in the upbringing of my children, and I will be at my leisure to raise them to be as American as I choose."

"I will not be forced by you."

Grace refused to give up. "Do you know that I ride astride?"

"What?"

"Wearing trousers."

The woman clapped her palm to her chest.

Grace's grin peaked. Aha, she'd found her mark. "And I believe girls should receive an education at a university, if they want."

"How dare you speak to me of my future granddaughters and edu—"

"And the very next moment I can get our chauffeur free, I'm going to have him teach me how to drive our car."

The woman's mouth dropped as wide as her eyes. "Preposterous."

"So if you don't want an entire herd of little Americans running about your centuries-old museum"—Grace waved toward the walls—"then I suggest you take the time to introduce me to your legacy and pray I fall in love with it, because until now, you have not given me any reason to care about *your* world."

The woman backed away until she slid down in her chair again, eyes remaining wide. Oh well, perhaps Grace had gone too far with the driving statement, even though it was true. From the look on Lady Moriah's pale face, Grace wondered if the woman was still breathing. Could someone die of dislike for a daughter-in-law? Would that be considered murder or suicide?

A knock broke the volatile silence in the room, followed by Brandon's welcome, nonsmiling face. "We just received word that Lord Astley has arrived at the station and should be home within the hour."

"Thank you for letting us know, Brandon." Grace barely kept her feet on the floor as she ran to the door. "I shall keep watch from the library window."

"Tell my son to see me as soon as he arrives."

Lady Moriah could have her son, as soon as Grace finished greeting him in private.

❧

Frederick caught the first morning train to Derbyshire, each mile proving only to increase his agitation. The car barely rolled to a stop at Havensbrooke's entrance before he opened the door himself and stepped out. A rush of blue suddenly filled the doorway, and his bride came into view among the gathering servants. His breath caught as he took her in—the delightfully missed and wonderfully his, Lady Astley.

"Glad to have you back, my lord."

"Thank you, Brandon." Frederick forced his attention to the butler. "It's good to be back."

The butler's attention rested on Frederick's bruised eye. "I hope your trip was successful."

"A minor accident." He waved toward the bruise. "Besides, I have good news. Mr. Andrew Piper will be returning as solicitor and steward of Havensbrooke."

Brandon's bushy brows rose, and a light flickered into his expression. "Very good, sir."

Frederick nodded to the other servants as he passed, each step drawing him closer to the pinnacle of his thoughts the past two days—and nights. There she stood, almost bouncing on tiptoe to contain her joy, with her hands dutifully clasped in front of her. Her obvious admiration plowed over him in glorious and grateful waves. All her beautiful ginger hair sat piled on her head, waiting for him to remove those pins, and the blue shade of her gown deepened the hue of her eyes.

Had she grown more beautiful over the past two days?

"You look well, Lady Astley."

Her smile stretched wide. "I'm much better now, my lord, though I am sorry for your beautiful eye."

"It's nothing, really." He examined every part of her face, even the tiniest freckles on the bridge of her nose. Keeping his distance proved so painful his teeth ached. "I'm glad to be home."

"Might I accompany you to our sitting room? Where we can. . ." Her gaze spoke in a language his pulse interpreted perfectly. "Talk?"

"Excellent."

"There is a lot to say." Her voice dropped to a whisper. "It may take a while."

"All afternoon, I'd expect." He met her volume, ready to devour those lovely lips of hers.

"Do you wish to have tea brought up, my lord?" Mrs. Powell asked as they passed through the threshold.

"No, thank you." Frederick turned to her but did not release his hold on his wife. "In fact, I should like to rest until dinner."

He pressed his palm over Grace's hand so snug against the crook of his arm and kept an unhurried pace up the stairs of the Great Hall. The room looked resplendent with holiday decor. The tree, which had been barren before he'd left, now stood adorned in old ornaments, strings of white beads, and dashes of holly. Garland trimmed the stair rail, framing the room in evergreen and ribbons.

"I don't know as I've ever seen the hall so festive."

Grace's nose wrinkled with her grin. "Do you like it?" She leaned close as they continued their climb. "I would have you note the very strategic placement of mistletoe. I expect you to keep with tradition, my lord, publicly or privately, at your pleasure."

"At my pleasure?" He raised a brow, and as soon as they turned the corner on their private hallway away from curious eyes, he swept her into his arms for a lingering kiss. "Will that do?"

"It's a wonderful start," she breathed, tugging at his jacket. "But don't worry, I've placed mistletoe around my bed too, just in case you needed more reminders."

"I need no reminders, darling." He brought her fingers to his smile and kissed them, slowly trailing his lips over each one in such a way that his beautiful bride gasped. "I think you should write me letters every day."

"I was inspired by your grandparents' letters." Her breath shook out the words, her gaze focused on his lips against her hand. "They provide such lovely romantic inspiration."

Once they were sequestered in their sitting room, Frederick guided Grace to the window seat and tugged her down on his lap, continuing the kiss he'd started in the hallway. She tasted of warmth and strawberries—and home. Her rosemary scent wrapped around him in welcome as she melted against him, the softest breath escaping her mouth as he skimmed his lips down her neck.

"Grace," he whispered against her neck as he skimmed kisses across her skin. "I've never longed for anyone like I long for you."

She pulled back, her palms framing his face as glimmers of sunlight bathed her glorious hair in fiery gold. "That was beautifully poetic."

He kissed one corner of her mouth, then the other. "Next time you're going with me to London."

Her nose skimmed over his, teasing. "And on any of your other adventures?"

"*All* of my other adventures." His mouth took another detour down her neck.

"Since you're so agreeable for the moment."

His lips found her ear.

"I have a confession to make."

His palms found their way into her hair, loosening her pins. Cool locks of silk fell over his knuckles, and he buried his face into them. "Mm-hmm?"

"I met Lily yesterday."

*Lily?* His hands paused in her hair, his gaze meeting hers. "What?"

She smoothed her palms over the front of his shirt, a pucker forming on her brow. "I didn't plan to meet her, but I was out riding—"

"What did you think of her?"

"She's wonderful!" Her smile spread. "I fell in love with her on the spot, and the fact you named her after your grandmother—"

"You knew about her name?"

"You forget, I have your grandmother's letters, and when you've talked of them, I've listened." Grace drew so close those gold flecks hidden in her sapphire orbs glistened in the sunlight. "I see the love of your grandparents in you. Their kindness and desire to do good." She rubbed against his chest as if she was trying to wipe away a wound. "They've influenced who you are, even if the past hurts overshadowed it for a while."

He covered her hand with his, holding her fingers against his chest. "You are a part of who I am, and I should want my life no other way."

Her gaze roamed his face, pausing on his eye. "Then, if I am such a part of you, tell me what happened to your eye. Your lip is slightly swollen too."

He trailed kisses down her neck again, attempting to derail her curiosity.

"My dear Lord Astley." She framed his face with her hands and pulled his attention back up, those eyes an unyielding force. "I feel certain you want my undivided attention right now. So give me the benefit of your doubts and tell me what happened."

His throat constricted at the notion of her faithful companionship, her love. He unpinned more of her hair and ran his fingers through it until her eyes flickered closed in response, giving him time to find his voice. "I don't want you to worry."

"I'll worry more from having to conjure up my own scenarios, which will invariably be much worse than the truth."

He grinned and brushed back some of the loose tendrils from her face. "I was attacked in London."

"Attacked? At night?" Her eyes widened. "Of course it was at night. Much easier to conceal an attack." Her gaze—alive and curious—searched his. "Was it a fog-fingered night? The most likely candidate."

"Yes and only a few hours after my rather revealing meeting with Mr. Parks."

"I knew it." She patted the front of his shirt, rocking back on his lap. "There is something underhanded going on, and if this didn't confirm it, the men who chased me on horseback yesterday certainly do."

Frederick's entire body surged to alert. He took her by the shoulders. "What did you say?"

"It was all such a surprise." She'd loosened one of his shirt buttons as if she hadn't just sent his heart careening toward terror. "Two men in black came after me from the forest during my ride, almost out of nowhere it seems, but of course they had to come from *somewhere*. At any rate, they chased me across the field, and my first thought was to find other people so there would be witnesses, you see."

All the internal warmth from their earlier kisses chilled. Men chasing her? At Havensbrooke? He covered her fidgeting hand with his own to remove the added distraction. "Tell me everything that happened, Grace. Every detail so that we can share it when the inspector arrives."

"You've secured an inspector! Very clever of you, Frederick. I do believe this case is getting much too unwieldy for us amateurs." She snuggled in closer to him as if she hadn't completely shaken him from any peace.

He wrapped his arms around her, holding her against him, offering thanksgiving for her safety. "Grace, I won't leave you again, not even for an hour, until this situation is resolved." He pulled back. "You may be strong, but I'm not certain I'm strong enough to see someone hurt you."

"You are incredibly dashing when you're worried about me."

He shook his head, smile reluctant at best. "Then I must appear as the very model of a jaunty rogue." He sobered, tipping her chin up with his finger and thumb. "We must take care. This situation has become more dangerous than even you can imagine."

"I will take care, I promise." She brushed back hair from his forehead and offered a consolatory smile. "But I don't think anything could ever be *that* dangerous."

# Chapter Twenty-Five

As Grace readied for dinner, she tugged another letter from the box belonging to Frederick's grandparents, grinning at the recollection of their sweet adoration for one another. Oh, she hoped she and Frederick would create such a tender romance. They'd gotten off to a fantastic start. She skimmed a finger over her lips at the thought of their most recent romantic interlude. All afternoon.

She sighed. What a perfectly delightful man!

As her fingers skimmed over the papers, she touched paper of a different texture tucked at the back of the box. Newer. Not worn from time.

How curious.

Carefully, she removed the sheets and unfolded them. At the top of the first page, she read the words:

> *I, Edward Richard Phineas Percy, the sixth Earl of Astley,*
> *being of sound mind and mortal body, do make my last will*
> *and testament. I revoke all previous wills in my name.*

Grace's fingers clenched reflexively against the paper. The date by Edward's signature at the bottom of the page marked only one week before he died. She skimmed over the document, not fully understanding some of it, but what she did comprehend was that this will left everything to Frederick alone, bequeathing nothing to Celia or even Lady Moriah.

Grace met her own reflection in the mirror. "We have a motive."

But for whom? Celia or Lady Moriah? Or some third player in the game?

Grace turned to the next page, and a shiver slipped up her arms from her fingertips.

Two lines from a shaky hand marked the page:

*Frederick, my brother,*

*I have wronged you beyond forgiveness. Do what I could not.*

Grace stood so fast her gilded chair nearly tumbled over.

"Lady Astley?" Ellie called as Grace ran for the door. "I still need to set your hair."

"What care I for hair when there is such a discovery upon us, Ellie." She jerked open the door and peered back at her wide-eyed maid. "I must find Lord Astley at once."

Frederick stood just outside his office, speaking to Brandon and looking rather dashing in his evening tails. Grace almost lost her train of thought in order to give him the thorough appreciation such a figure deserved, but she blinked from her stupor and focused on the task at hand.

"Frederick. I found something."

Frederick's head came up, and Brandon's eyes grew wide as she approached at a pace quite unlike a countess. Perhaps her wild hair had something to do with it as well.

"Are you all right?"

She nodded and took Frederick by the hand, pulling him into the study away from listening ears. "You come too, Brandon. I think we'll need an extra pair of eyes."

Brandon looked to Frederick, who hesitated for only a moment before gesturing for Brandon to follow. As soon as the door clicked closed, Grace pulled the paper from behind her back and turned it for Frederick's view. "I found the will. Your brother must have known you'd want your grandparents' letters, so he hid it there for you to find. It's proof of what you already knew. Edward had written her out of everything." Her breath pulsed as she tried to calm down. "Not only Celia, but your mother too."

"What are you talking about?" Frederick took the paper and read over the words, his face paling. When he turned to the next page, he pressed his palm to his head and collapsed into a nearby chair.

"He. . .he wrote to me." Frederick's words emerged on broken air. He worked his jaw as if attempting to control his emotions. Oh, her dear hero. She lowered herself to her knees by his chair and rested her hand against his arm, drawing Frederick's watery focus back to her. "He called me *brother*."

Grace's vision blurred at the mingling of grief and gratefulness weaving across Frederick's features. For too long he'd carried the label of *outcast*, unforgiven especially by one of the most important people in his life, and now, painfully late and from the grave, his brother offered healing.

Frederick drew in a shaky breath and wiped a hand across his eyes. "I'll present this to Piper when he arrives and phone Detective Miracle." He sat up straighter. "But he'll be here in a few days to look at it himself." He offered the will to Brandon. "The signature looks authentic."

Brandon studied the paper and nodded. "Indeed, sir."

"I hope this will provide you some peace, knowing he thought of you at the end." Grace stood and wrapped her fingers around his. "That he believed in you."

Frederick cleared his throat. "There is a measure of solace in that."

"I'm only sorry I didn't find it sooner." She sighed. "I'd have gotten through the letters yesterday if I hadn't been so tired from another ghost hunt."

The dinner bell sounded from the other side of the door, so Grace moved in that direction, but Frederick caught her by the arm. "What did you say?"

Grace looked from Brandon to Frederick. "I wish I'd found the will sooner?"

"Something about a ghost hunt?"

"Oh goodness, yes. Brandon can attest to it." She leaned forward, the tantalizing details of the past two nights still tingling near the surface of her memory. "One of the servants said there was a ghost living in the east wing." She paused, shaking her head. "Well I suppose, it's not really alive, so it's not *living* in the east wing, but haunting the east wing. I went in search of it so you wouldn't have to be bothered when you returned home."

His eyes narrowed as she continued.

"But I'm afraid you'll have to be bothered, because the first night I saw the ghost, but it disappeared before I could identify it, and the second night, the ghost never appeared at all."

He was blinking like he had something in his eyes.

"I don't really think it's a ghost." Grace offered, trying to remain sensible. "But someone certainly walks about the east wing in a white gown, moaning at night."

"Why haven't I heard of this before now?" Frederick turned to Brandon.

"It only began during your travels to the States, sir."

"So it isn't a figment of Lady Astley's"—he stumbled over his words as he met her gaze again—"most remarkable imagination?"

She smiled her appreciation at his careful choice of words. "I do have an overzealous imagination, but I rarely see things that aren't there. I only pretend to." She smoothed her palms across her waist. "I plan to search for our ghost again tonight and would be ever so grateful if you'd join me. If not, I'll have to enlist the services of Brandon again, and I'm fairly certain he'd rather not be party to another ghost hunt."

Brandon coughed, something he seemed to do quite often, if she thought about it.

Frederick took a great deal of time to resurrect a response. "I'll be happy to take over my butler's place as your sleuthing partner."

"Sleuthing partner. It sounds much more delightful when you say it." Grace braided her hands in front of her and brought them to her chin. "But I think I've sorted out the mystery of our ghost, and I hope to uncover the truth tonight."

⁓✗⁓

Frederick had envisioned many opportunities in his life, but sneaking through the east wing in search of a ghost? He'd never even remotely imagined something this bizarre. Of course he'd never expected his life to have Grace in it, and Grace changed everything.

He held the lantern ahead of them with one hand and Grace's hand with the other as they entered the Morning Room. Whether from Grace's influence or the memory of his brother's body, a cold sweat broke out over Frederick's skin. Ghosts didn't have to float into view to impact a life. Sometimes they haunted thoughts and memories.

At the recollection of the hastily scrawled note, Frederick's throat tightened. Edward had forgiven him. Believed in him even, as Grace had said. Some lost piece within Frederick's heart emerged from hiding to make his heart whole again.

"The last time she came from the hallway."

Frederick shook away the gathering tears and looked down at his wife. "She?"

"From the timbre of the moan and the flow of the skirts, our ghost is female."

His gaze shot to the ceiling, laughter tickling to release the tension. "Of course she is."

"Doubt as you may, Husband dearest, but I can assure you I'm more educated about ghosts than you are," she whispered, her eyes glinting in the golden lantern light.

He held her gaze, hoping his touch, his expression somehow communicated how much she meant to him. "I have no doubt, darling."

"I love it when you call me *darling*." Her grin surfaced. "You always say it so sweetly, as if you like it, even when you're doubting my clearheadedness."

Despite the gloomy theme to the room, his smile spread, and he placed a kiss on Grace's head. "I like you, clearheaded or not."

"I'm ever so glad you do, since we are bound to each other for all eternity."

Being bound to her was one of his favorite activities.

They moved around the room in tandem, steps quiet. And then he heard it. A swelling moan, rising from the deep recesses of the wing. He nearly dropped the lantern, his gaze searching the shadows. The moan rose again. He pushed Grace behind him and searched the darkness for the origin of the eerie sound.

"Blow out the lantern" Grace whispered from behind him.

"What?"

"If it's a real ghost, the lantern light will keep us from seeing clearly. If it isn't, the light may cause her to stay away."

"Grace, I don't—"

"There's enough moonlight to help us." She ducked beneath his arm and blew out the flame.

The sound emerged again. Closer. His eyes adjusted to the moon's glow from the windows, and he reached back to wrap his fingers through Grace's, keeping her near. Safe. Or as safe as a ghost hunt could keep anyone.

A white flutter of cloth slipped in and out of his periphery through the room they passed to their left. Frederick's blood went cold. He pressed Grace back against the wall, shielding her as he peeked around the doorframe.

"Isn't this romantic?" Grace's whisper pulled his gaze to her face. She was almost smiling. "You're ever so good at protecting me."

Frederick drew a blank for response, so he switched his attention back to the room, but the ghost was gone.

Her moan rose from the adjoining room.

"She's saying something. Do you hear her?" Grace's question spurred him farther down the hall. "Can you make it out?"

Three syllables.

"The last word is *me*," Grace murmured, his sweet bride not intimidated in the slightest.

The words became clearer as they stepped over the threshold into his brother's office.

Frederick's breath halted. *"Forgive me."*

Icicles of awareness slid a chill of cold sweat down his neck. What sort of fictional world had Grace brought into his real life?

Bent over Edward's desk, the moonlight draping a luminescent glow over her contorted face, stood his mother. She wept as she scanned his brother's desk, shifting through the pages, eyes fixed and unblinking.

"Mother?" the word scraped over his dry throat, barely making a sound.

"She's sleepwalking," Grace's voice came near his ear. "Do you see her face?"

"Charles," her wild cry upheaved with a new rush of volume. "Edward."

Frederick couldn't move, transfixed by the scene before him, haunted by a myriad of questions. What drove his mother to such grief that she'd seek consolation in her sleep?

Her body shuddered beneath the weight of her sobs.

He'd never seen her weep, and now in the ghostly light, tears rained over her sunken cheeks, her hair a wild mass around her face. The pale light highlighted her hollowed eyes and reflected off the silver streaks in her dark hair. Mother circled the desk, blindly sifting through the papers.

"Tell me you forgive me." Pages fluttered to the floor as she continued her perusal and finally, as if defeated, quit her task. "Where? I must find it."

With those words, she stepped to the far bookshelf and escaped out the servants' entry in a wisp of white. Frederick followed her, entranced.

When they reached the dimly lit Great Hall, only the emptiness of the room greeted him. Grace's warm fingers slid into his. Had she been there all along? "I thought it was her, but I never imagined. . ."

"There's more than grief there." His voice came scratchy. "Regret?" He met Grace's gaze. "Guilt?"

She breathed out a sigh as she searched his face before bringing his hand to her lips. "Let's go to bed, Frederick. Rest. Pray. And discuss this in the morning. There's nothing to be done now that can't wait."

He looked up the stairway, fighting the inclination to run to his mother's room for immediate answers. Did she know something about Edward's death? Father's? She'd begged forgiveness for both. What did that mean?

"Let her sleep." Grace wrapped her arm through his, tugging him toward the stairs. "I doubt she even knows what she's doing, and drawing attention to it at the wrong time won't bring any answers."

"I don't understand this."

"We've uncovered something hidden for a long time, I think, and so dark it emerges in your mother's sleep. We must be very careful from here on out, Frederick. I fear we're nearing the end of the game, the darkest part of the story, and someone doesn't want us to discover the truth."

❧

Frederick sat on the edge of the bed, his naked back turned to her as he stared out the window. At the sight of him, Grace's heart squeezed with a mixture of fascination, empathetic ache, and something deep she couldn't quite name. What they'd uncovered, the questions surfacing from their discovery, weighted the room with threatening possibilities. Why would Lady Moriah beg forgiveness of her deceased husband and son?

Grace swallowed a gathering lump in her throat. Or worse, what had she done?

"You said during your meeting with Parks you felt certain he knew something about Celia." Grace pulled the duvet up around her body and scooted closer to the edge of the bed. "Did she have the sort of personality to harm your brother?"

Frederick pushed a hand through his dark mass of hair and sighed. "It seems too harsh to speak aloud, but yes. Now that I consider everything. She chose self-preservation at all cost. At one point, she even had my father wrapped around her finger. That's the only way he would have agreed to Edward marrying a woman with nothing but her charm to recommend her."

"Did she foresee the financial downfall of Havensbrooke?" She slid her palm down his back, attempting to offer comfort. "Gain some sort of widow's allowance upon Edward's death?"

"She had to have known about the finances, and yes, she received an allowance, but also"—his head came up, gaze fixing to hers—"she met someone with more money. Gavin Campbell, a businessman who'd gained his sudden wealth through industry. Or at least that's what I'd heard a few weeks before I returned home."

"I suppose she won't be a widow for long then," Grace whispered, trying to conjecture the missing pieces.

"She'd wait for at least the mourning year or fear being cast out of all good society." Frederick's brow creased.

"Which means as a widow she's still desperate to keep her financial status."

"Widow." Frederick turned. "Edward's first will, the one Celia would have known about, provided financially for her and Mother, should the entail end. And when I married you, the will included you as one of the beneficiary widows. No other family member wanted the burden of Havensbrooke."

"What does that mean?"

"Should I die without an heir, the estate will be sold, and the proceeds split three ways, between the three widows. If only two widows are left, then—"

"The money will be halved." Grace squeezed close. "Frederick, the car accident? Your attack? Someone's been after you since you got back from the States. It must be her!"

"I don't know."

"I can't imagine losing you." She pressed a kiss to his shoulder and leaned her cheek against the spot. "I've only just gotten to know you so well."

He interlocked his fingers with hers and brought their braided hands to his chest. "I don't plan to go anywhere if I can help it."

"What would lead a wife to contemplate such deviousness?" Grace shuddered and closed her eyes. "Is money really that important to her?"

"Money is a powerful taskmaster, darling." He ran a finger down her cheek. "For good or ill."

She grinned up at him. "At least in our case, it was for good."

"Mercifully so."

But with such ill-intent, a dangerous weapon. "So how did she kill him and make it look like heart failure? That's what we must sort out."

"We can't be certain Celia did this, Grace. There seem to be a number of unsavory business choices, which could have resulted in—"

"Do you have all of Conan Doyle's works in the library?" She rubbed her cheek against his shoulder again. "Maybe a book about poisons or poisonous plants?"

"You truly are incorrigible, but I'm afraid the entire situation has become much darker than I expected." He turned his head so that his lips tipped close to hers. "I don't suppose I could convince you to stay out of this nasty business, could I?"

Her eyes popped wide. "Why on earth would you want me out of it? I'm your best advocate." She placed another kiss on his shoulder, peering up at him as she did so. In all honesty, it was a ridiculous question. He wasn't as well equipped with sleuthing knowledge as she was. "And we're very good together, you know."

"I don't want you to be hurt, Grace." He slipped his arm around her, bringing her into his lap. "We're not speaking of pretend ghosts and obscure letters anymore. We're talking of murder."

"Exactly." She snuggled into the warmth and strength of his chest, his arms a powerful force around her. "And I feel certain I know a great deal more about murder than you."

"I'll not win this fight, will I?"

She shook her head and grinned. "Indeed, you will not." With a sigh, she rested her cheek against his shoulder, breathing in the amber scent of his skin. The quiet surrounded them, their breaths a gentle hush into the late morning. The unnamed emotion in her chest pinched deeper as her thoughts spiraled into the idea of someone hurting him. *Her* Frederick.

His fingers smoothed through her loose hair and down her back, his chin resting against her head. "Is it exhausting to live inside your mind?"

"Oh no, quite the contrary. It's rather energizing. Though I think living outside my head may be exhausting for others. But since we're sleuthing partners, as you've said, we should have the best of both minds. Your clarity and shrewdness, and my. . ." She looked up to the ceiling in search of a proper description.

"Imagination and somewhat terrifying fictional ingenuity."

She laughed and slapped his chest. "Which you mean in the very best way, of course."

"Of course."

She sobered. "But you must think creatively too. Is there a place we can go that might provide more information? Somewhere important to your brother or Celia? A secret place?"

He paused, his gaze locking with hers and then turning away. "Well, there are the ruins."

"The ruins?"

"Celia and I had secret rendezvous there a long time ago, but of more recent note, I noticed an unfamiliar car driving away from the place when we visited the vista."

The very thought of anyone having a secret meeting with her husband turned Grace's stomach inside out—and made her want to play Beethoven's *Tempest* sonata quite loudly and with so little restraint Lady Moriah would pale in horror. "I think we should forgo an immediate confrontation with your mother to investigate these ruins."

"I can't imagine why they'd be important."

"Is it a place where unsavory people might hide?" She wrapped her arms around his so that there was barely any space between them. "Like the men who chased me?"

His body stiffened at her words. "It's an excellent place for something like that, I'm afraid." He groaned and pressed his face into her neck. "I should have investigated the ruins before I left for London. I put you in danger—"

"I am fine, as you see." She pressed a kiss to his frown before slipping back from him. "But we have time to search them now."

"But Piper is coming to discuss finances with me." He paused and slipped a finger under her chin. "With *us* over dinner."

"That's hours away." She stood up. "Oh, my dear sleuth, you have so much to learn." His grin crooked at her fun-loving reprimand. "If something curious is happening at the ruins at just the time so many other curious things are happening to us, then I do believe it's worth our direct investigation. I'm developing quite the portrait of Lady Celia in my mind, and I feel certain she's at the heart of this mystery."

# Chapter Twenty-Six

Frederick glanced over at Grace as they guided their horses through the forest to the ruins. Introducing her to this tangled part of his past gripped him with cautionary claws. How many times had he met Celia here when they'd first begun their affair? The recollections were stained with past sins.

The tower of the ruins rose above the tree line. Oh how those past decisions haunted the present in unexpected ways. *God forgive him.* Frederick glanced at his bride. And God had—offering him a new and most undeserved beginning.

"This was the first house your ancestors built on the property?" Grace squinted as if to see through the final veil of trees separating them from the ruin.

"About three hundred years ago." Ah, he knew how to tease her. "And there are a great many stories surrounding this place, including hidden tunnels and lost treasures of Mary, Queen of Scots."

"Oh my!" She nearly turned in her saddle with her gasp. "A new place to research."

Yes, Grace's light could shine on this place and fade the old memories as she'd done in so many of the other parts of his life. "It's certainly your sort of place."

The three-story stone home emerged in the clearing, a narrow, partially crumbled, box-shaped structure.

"Is that a chapel?"

He followed her gesture to an ivy-covered church a short distance from the house—still intact with its frosted windows and small bell tower.

Almost magical, if he guessed at Grace's thoughts. "Yes, my grandparents were married there."

Grace's smile bloomed large enough to add a sparkle to her eyes. "Then I love it even more."

Oh, how could he touch her heart as quickly and freely as she touched his with the simplest of words? Frederick dismounted.

"It's rumored that tunnels were dug beneath the chapel in hopes of freeing Queen Mary during her imprisonment from—"

"Queen Elizabeth." Her eyes twinkled. "British history is so much more interesting than American history."

"Well it's quite a bit older too." He rounded his horse to stand by hers.

"And to your knowledge, no one has been here since Celia?" She peered down at him, a rebel ginger lock slipping from beneath her riding cap. "Except for the people in the red car, of course." Her teeth skimmed over her bottom lip as she fought with a smile and reached for him to help her dismount. "You remember? On the day of the storm when we first, well, found one another."

One of the best days of his life. His hands slid about her waist, bringing her against him. "I remember."

Her eyes darkened with awareness as her body glided over his to the ground. No wonder people referred to marital *bliss*. His thoughts paused on the notion. Dear Lord, he was beginning to sound like Grace in his head.

She hooked her arms around his neck and nudged his nose with hers, a caress he was beginning to realize she particularly enjoyed. "I *almost* wish for thunderstorms so you can kiss me into distraction."

Without another hesitation, he took her lips in a lingering embrace before braiding his fingers through hers. "I am the Watson to your Sherlock." He gestured toward the ruins. "Do what you do best."

"Words to my heart."

They began on the second floor and worked their way down to the first. Frederick pointed out several sets of dusty footprints in the former gallery of the home, and Grace found a cloth stained with something that appeared to be blood.

"From the rider you hit with a horseshoe perhaps?"

Her grin rewarded him. "You are beginning to think in the proper way for the surroundings, my lord."

But the real curiosities came when they reached what was formerly a main-floor sitting room. One of the few spaces with intact windows, the space held a few cooking utensils and an assortment of other remains hinting at recent occupation.

"Someone has certainly been here." Frederick kicked at a mussed blanket on the floor and stepped to the large window overlooking the entry, the road to the ruins a tangle of overgrowth. Someone would have to know where they were going to take that route.

Grace didn't respond. She was examining something by a table in the corner near a back window.

"The ash is fresh in the fire." Frederick added, which meant the occupants hadn't been gone too long. He patted the pistol he'd slipped into his riding jacket, ensuring its place should the unwelcome guests return.

"Frederick, did you alert anyone in the house of your impending arrival from India?"

What an odd question. Grace didn't face him, her attention still riveted on what appeared to be a small white flower and a medicine bottle.

"I sent a telegram when I'd arrived in London to let the house know to expect me first thing in the morning."

Her gaze came up to his. "So everyone knew exactly when you'd return."

Frederick caught the suggestion behind her statement, and his chest tightened. "What is it?"

Grace raised the flower to him with her gloved hand, her breath shaking ever so slightly. "This."

He crossed the room. "Queen Anne's lace?"

But the look in her eyes proved this little plant was something much different.

"Frederick, I believe this is hemlock. One of the most poisonous plants in the world."

❧

Everything began to come together. The ability for Celia to be absent at the time of Edward's death. The perfect timing of Frederick's arrival.

"What do you mean?"

She pushed past him and walked to the fireplace. "The purple speckles on the stem, as well as other small differences, show that it's different from Queen Anne's lace." She bent by a discarded pot among the fire's ashes. Aha. A root. She stood and returned to Frederick's side. "More possible proof. A root for making oil, I suspect. Likely hemlock oil." She raised the root so he could see it more clearly, an idea forming. "Do you recall Brandon or Elliott giving any specifics about your brother's symptoms before he died?"

"No, nothing." He shoved a hand through his hair and took another glance about the room. "Good night, Grace! Are you saying, someone made poison here?"

"It seems likely. Hemlock is extremely toxic, especially in liquid form."

A burst of air came from her handsome hero. "How do you know these things?"

"I became curious."

"About poisons?"

She looked up from her examination of the root. Why was he so surprised? "About everything."

His expression evaporated into an uncertain smile, and he crossed the room and slid his arm around her waist. "My dear, if I didn't know you had such a kind heart, I'd be terrified of you."

She rewarded his sweet words with a grin before returning her attention to the plant. "But doctors should know the signs of such poisoning. It's not so uncommon nowadays that it can't be easily detected."

"Mother was adamant about Edward's heart being weak, and I didn't have any reason to doubt her. Even our longtime family doctor agreed with Mother's assessment, though I'm not certain his age adds to his reliability." He shook his head. "But I knew something seemed odd all the while."

"Well, from the accounts I've read of people's deaths by hemlock, they could match your description of how you found your brother." She murmured more to herself. "Muscle spasms. Breathing difficulty. Horrible deaths, unless you were Socrates, of course."

Frederick studied her a moment and cleared his throat, offering his hand to her. "We need to interview Brandon. He could give an accounting of any symptoms."

"Very clever, my dear hero." She took his hand and walked with him to the door, casting a look back over the rooms as they passed. "And as you said, Celia would have known about this place because of her. . .time with you." She shook her head against the direction her imagination turned. "So it makes sense her thugs hid here."

She pulled her hand free of Frederick's, a sudden queasiness swirling in her stomach.

Celia Blackmore. The woman took up so much space in Frederick's past, so many memories, sneaking into conversations like an unavenged spirit. Frederick had spent time with her here. Likely scandalously kissing a murderer.

The thought stung. Did he still think of her kisses? On a kissing scale, were Grace's better? She felt certain she'd only improved since her first introduction. She remained quiet until they'd stepped from the building.

"Grace?" Frederick's fingers wrapped around her wrist, bringing her to a stop next to him.

She turned, sighing out her momentary jealousy. Or was it grief? She didn't even know what to call it. "There's nothing we can do about the past, is there?" She squeezed his hand. "But I think we have an excellent start at a future, don't you?"

Those dark eyes—clouded with regret—held her attention, her heart. "I love you, Grace."

The gentle whisper, barely audible, reverberated like a blast through her. She'd read those three words before. Shakespeare lathered them with drama galore, but to hear them from her wildly handsome husband? The unnamed emotion quickening through her chest swelled, catching in her throat and fogging her vision. He'd never mentioned loving her before. Shown it with great skill, but spoken it?

Her lips trembled. Her breath paused.

With steady tenderness, his warm palms smoothed against her cheeks, his thumbs trailing soft against her skin. He pressed his forehead against hers, holding her gaze. Wordless. Their breaths mingling, lips almost touching. She couldn't find her voice as the emotion swelled in at her throat. She closed her eyes, wrapped in the ethereal haven of his confession.

He *loved* her.

She leaned into him and placed the moment to memory. Love? Was that the deep stirring within her to be with him? To see him happy? To protect him? Her lips quivered into a smile. She tipped her chin in silent entreaty, and he complied, lowering his mouth to hers in silent confirmation.

With another lingering glance, he slipped her arm through his and guided her to the horses.

"Once we get home, I'll phone Detective Miracle about our findings today." He helped her on her horse.

"Excellent." She peered down at him with a grin. "And I believe I have an important meeting with your mother before Mr. Piper's arrival."

He paused as he rounded her horse to his. "A meeting with my mother?"

"Mm-hmm. She's going to explain to me the family history of the Percys through the portraits in the Great Hall and gallery."

"She's agreed to this?" Her husband eyed her with a great deal of doubt as he mounted his horse.

"Not yet, but I have a plan."

"You think you can convince her to come with you?"

"What have I told you about giving me the benefit of your doubts?" Her grin inched up as she started forward. "I will do my best."

Silence greeted her, so she glanced to her right to see her dashing hero's lips crooked ever so slightly. "My mother doesn't stand a chance."

She rewarded his confidence with a smile and drew in a deep breath, sorting out how to offer her husband a very sneaky option. "So while I'm learning about your centuries of descendants, how might you pass your time?"

"I have a strange suspicion you know exactly how I should pass my time."

"Not really." She shrugged. "With the architect's arrival next week, you could always work on estate business."

"I could." His response came slowly.

"Or you could visit that darling daughter of yours."

His eyes narrowed, unconvinced. Oh dear, he was learning her quite well. "Indeed."

"But there's always the possibility of searching your mother's room while she's out with me."

His laugh burst out. "I—what?"

"You're right." She turned her attention to the path, shaking off the temptation to plead with him. "It's probably a horrible idea, but the best sleuths resort to sneaky options in order to discover the truth."

"I am not searching my mother's room."

Grace forced her expression into wifely sobriety, or what she expected wifely sobriety looked like. "You would know best, of course."

⌇⌇

"I have a new piece for you to play today," Lady Moriah barked as soon as Grace entered the woman's sitting room. She pointed toward the piano with her cane. "Chopin."

Grace took her time getting to the piano. If Frederick changed his mind about the whole detective idea, she certainly didn't want to rush him. "Chopin? That's an excellent choice, my lady."

"Don't attempt to flatter me, girl."

"And what would you prefer I do? I have an entire wealth of abilities you've failed to unwrap. Would you prefer rude and uncouth? I'm certain I can manage it, if I really put my mind to it. My sister often complimented me on my theatrics at—"

"Chopin," came her quick order.

Grace smoothed out the pages on the piano, taking in the intricate movement of the familiar piece before beginning to play, adding in her own little trills as she went along.

"Your embellishments are not necessary to the author's masterpiece," the dowager huffed once Grace brought the composition to a close.

She didn't even flinch at the woman's harshness. The grief in Lady Moriah's voice last night as she'd haunted the east wing curbed a little of Grace's annoyance. At least enough to overlook her meanness.

"Where's your imagination, Lady Mor—Astley? Surely, as a musician, you've learned the value of whimsy."

The woman's brows rose with her chin. "Whimsy?"

Grace turned on the bench to face the woman. "Playful, fanciful, something that makes you smile from the sheer delight of it? Certainly you've experienced it in your life through romance." She waved toward the piano. "Or even music?"

The stoic expression wavered for the slightest second and then hardened. "You will never survive this world if your mind is housed in another."

"I collect a great deal of strength from a very different world so that I *can* survive this one. What do you think heaven is all about?"

Her eyes narrowed, but Grace rushed ahead without giving her time to fire another insult. "Who is the man in the portrait just left of the fireplace in the Great Hall?"

The woman blinked, completely taken off guard, so Grace continued in her plot. "The one where the gentleman's mustache looks as though the barber wasn't quite up to task."

Lady Moriah still didn't come up with an answer, so Grace grinned. "I actually appreciate paintings that are more realistic and show men and women as they naturally are. It's rather daunting trying to live up to perfection, don't you think?"

"That painting is of Sir Damien Withersby, *my* grandfather, one of the five portraits I inherited from my mother, and I can assure you there is nothing wrong with his moustache."

"How wonderful of Lord Astley to allow you to display your family alongside his." Grace stood and braided her fingers behind her back. "But I do feel as though one side of his moustache is higher than the other. Is the smaller portrait near his of your sister?"

A few carefully placed questions to Brandon had given her enough ammunition to know she'd met her mark without seeing Lady Moriah's brightened glare to confirm it.

"I will have you know that is Lord Astley, the sixth's, previous wife, *not* my sister."

"Oh well, I can only come to my own conclusions, you understand, since no one has really educated me on these matters."

"And Sir Withersby was known as one of the most fashionable men of his time. His portrait is as impeccable as the man himself."

"Of course." Grace lowered her chin in due humility. "So is his wife the one hanging by the second-level stairs? The woman with the crooked nose?"

Lady Moriah stood from her chair and drew her cane up like a sentry. "Crooked nose?"

Grace nodded, maintaining her most innocent expression. "Yes, the one in the golden frame. Blue coat."

"*That* is a *Mister* Everett Withersby. My father." Her cane hit the floor. "Impossible girl! I shall not have you embarrassing the Percy and

Withersby names with your ignorance." She marched toward the door. "Your education begins now."

⌒✦⌒

Mother's strident speech pealed through the Great Hall's quiet, shaking Frederick from his study of his brother's confusing financial records.

"You shall know the generations much better when I am finished with you. I shall not have future progeny suffer the ill effects of your ignorance."

Frederick's eyes closed. What had his wife done?

He peered out of his office door. The two women made their way up the stairs, and Mother began a detailed history of the portrait of Charles Percy. It looked as though his lovely bride had somehow convinced his mother to venture out of her rooms for an ancestry lesson.

He glanced toward the south wing. If his mother explained each portrait housed in the Great Hall, Frederick would have plenty of time to search her rooms. Nothing lengthy or too intrusive, but a cursory inquiry to help with the investigation.

Mother's back was turned, and Grace's profile stood in perfect view as she stared dutifully at the teacher. With a deep breath, he walked toward the stairs, glancing up to check if his mother had shifted her attention toward him.

Grace caught his movements and with beautiful synchrony, winked then turned her attention to the painting. "Did you say he was the one who married the blacksmith's daughter?"

"Truly girl! Are your ears full of cotton? A baron's daughter!"

Frederick covered his grin as he slipped through the entrance to the south wing.

His wife!

He'd never known such a force as this desire to protect her, this need to cherish who she was to him. Yet here he was, drawing her into an enigma of murder plots, poisonous plants, and a mother who haunted an abandoned wing of the house. But his bride didn't seem to mind at all. Rather, from the glint in her eyes, she was doing exactly as she wished—helping him, loving him, and using her unique set of resources to do so.

He'd never known love until her. He'd been a man as untouched in his heart as Grace's lips had been with a kiss.

Frederick silently slid into his mother's chambers and closed the door behind him, breathing in the scent of rosewater and honey, his mother's lotions. The overcast sky gave little assistance to light the dim room, but a faint glow from his mother's lanterns led his way.

This was ridiculous. Utterly. Yet he moved across the carpet with soundless steps, slipping through the door into his mother's bedroom.

The room's decor gave nothing suspicious away. A four-poster bed. Dresser. Ornate side table. A wardrobe. And her desk.

He peeked into her curio cabinet, examining a few of the trinkets, and scanned the spines of the books on a shelf nearby. A hush fell over the room, her crackling fire his only companion. Where would his mother hide something precious to her?

He walked to her bedside table, her sleeping draught readied for the evening. Nothing suspicious. Then he approached her desk. Stationery waited in an unused stack to one side, and two books sat propped against an ornate wooden box. Ah! He brought the shoe-sized box into his hands and unclipped the lid. A whiff of strong perfume hit his nostrils before he noticed the twine-bound letters. A dozen of them, at least. With a careful hand, he picked up the parcel and examined it.

His mother's handwriting. Air whooshed from his lungs. The letters she'd written his father during courtship? He squinted. No, it wasn't his father's name on the letters, but another man's. Rupert? He carefully peeled open one of the pages in search of a date, and air stilled in his throat. Did he read 1880? Two years after his parents were married?

What did this mean?

He shook his head and carefully returned the letters to the box, but as he placed it back in its spot, one of the books fell, landing with a thud on the floor and sending loose pages in various directions. Frederick scanned the expanse, as if someone heard his trespass, but no one appeared. With a deep breath, he knelt to collect the age-stained papers but paused, the hair at the nape of his neck rising. From within the slips of a folded sheet, the faded petals of a dried white-clustered flower emerged.

He lifted the paper from the ground, pinching the pages around the plant and then carefully opened the note to expose the entire flower.

Hemlock. Dried.

His throat closed around his anger. *No.*

But the handwriting on the page wasn't his mother's: *"A reminder of your silence."*

A threat? He fished through the other papers and came upon a letter with the same handwriting. A familiar style.

*"You understand the heavy hand of vengeance—the desperate actions one must take in order to assuage the thirst for justice. I assisted you, and now you will assist me. You shall pay your penance through silence, and I will be free."*

Frederick gripped the page between his fingers. He knew that handwriting. Celia.

# Chapter Twenty-Seven

"Thank you for meeting with us, Brandon." Frederick nodded, gesturing the man toward a chair. "Please, sit down."

Brandon paused, glancing around the private sitting room before taking a seat in the proffered wingback. It was as uncommon for him to sit in this intimate room shared by only Grace and his lord as it was for Frederick to ask him to enter, but no other room, apart from their bedrooms, provided as much privacy from eavesdroppers.

"As you are well aware, we have recently become concerned about the events surrounding my brother's death. No one is as intimately acquainted with the workings of this house. Would you give a thorough recounting of the last day of my brother's life? Was there anything unusual?"

Brandon sent a glance to Grace.

"It's all right, Brandon. You can speak plainly." Frederick held her gaze. "Lady Astley and I are attempting to sort things out together."

"I've read Poe." She placed her hand on the back of a chair near Brandon. "I can handle any dastardly details you must narrate."

Brandon's lips tipped ever so slightly as he lowered his head. The man's posture withered for only a second before he raised his head to them. "Lord Edward hadn't been himself for weeks. Quieter. More reserved."

"And his health?"

He lifted his gaze to Frederick. "Apart from appearing more anxious, I didn't notice a difference, sir."

"And estate business?"

"I cannot say, sir. It seemed his wife had a hand in a great number of decisions." Brandon looked between Frederick and Grace, his expression lost. "Their arguments had become less reserved."

"But their arguments weren't so unusual, were they?" Frederick asked, remembering the extensive rows he'd overheard at times.

"It seemed they attempted to keep their disagreements behind closed doors at first, sir. But in the last six months of the elder Lord Astley's life. . ." Brandon searched for the word. "Well, it didn't seem to matter."

"And these disagreements, were they about the estate?" At Brandon's hesitation, Frederick continued. "It's all right, Brandon, I know you'd never wish to be improper, but this is important."

The butler looked down. "As far as I recall, sir, the conversations were about the estate and funds, and at times"—Brandon paused and swallowed audibly—"his wife's. . .friendships with other men."

Frederick took the couch across from Brandon. "Any names associated with these friendships?"

"I only recall that one was the man she's been most recently affiliated with."

Ah, so they'd been friendly before Edward's death.

"And the last time you saw her was the morning of Lord Edward's. . .er, the elder Lord Astley's death?" Grace asked, joining Frederick on the couch. So many titles to sort out within this family.

"Yes, a quite memorable exit hours before Lord Astley arrived." He nodded toward Frederick. "Or Lord Edward was discovered."

"Memorable, I'd say, so no one could dispute her exit."

Frederick glanced over at Grace, whose eyes twinkled with interest. "Did you note anything about Lord Edward that morning, Brandon? Lethargy? Nervousness?"

"Actually, madam, he complained of rheumatism in his legs." Brandon sat up straighter, his face paling by slow degrees. "And his hands were trembling with his tea, so he retired to his study to recline."

"Did he regularly take any medicine in the mornings, Brandon?"

"Yes, milady. His cordial draught. For his stomach."

Grace's gaze locked with Frederick's. It was all coming together.

Frederick turned to the butler. "Were you the only one who knew of this, Brandon?"

"I mentioned it to the young doctor who came right after we found the body. We couldn't locate Dr. Ingle, so Elliott contacted the new doctor in Edensbury. He seemed highly interested in your brother's situation, but the dowager countess sent him away when Dr. Ingle arrived."

*So that she could cover up foul play?*

His attention flitted back to his wife, and her wide-eyed look let him know he'd guessed her thoughts too. A sweet warmth branched out through his chest at the wordless understanding, although it was perhaps a little unsettling that he was beginning to think like a fiction-loving amateur detective.

Then came the painful realization of his mother's real involvement.

A murky picture of longstanding deceit was beginning to come together. Deceit with two possible offenders.

Frederick thought back through the events surrounding his arrival at Havensbrooke. "This young doctor, who was he? Dr. Ingle had traveled to a neighboring town for supplies, wasn't that right?"

"Yes, sir," Brandon answered, hesitant. "Dr. David Ross was his name, if I recall."

"But Brandon, you didn't agree with his dismissal?" This from Grace. "What was it?"

"The young doctor wanted to investigate further." Brandon shifted in his chair. "He felt something was amiss. But Lady Astley strictly opposed anything hinting toward a scandal. I deferred to her, of course, but I see now that I should have approached you, my lord."

"You've done nothing wrong." Frederick sat in the chair opposite the older gentleman and leaned forward. "I could have sought clarification as well, and I didn't." His gaze met Grace's. "I think we need to meet with this Dr. Ross before we make any other inquiries."

Her smile slid from one rosy cheek to the other. "My dear Lord Astley, you are thinking like a sleuth."

"With the house party in two days and Mr. Piper's arrival in a few hours, I think we shouldn't confront your mother until we return." Grace stood near the window in their sitting room, watching her husband pace the floor, his clothes disheveled, his face drawn.

Oh how difficult all this information must be for him to consider.

"We need answers, Grace."

"But we also need as much proof as we can obtain to take into our confrontation with her." She caught his hand as he paced past her. "I have an idea."

He sighed but gave her hand a squeeze. "I'm almost afraid to ask."

"I have my dress fitting in Edensbury tomorrow morning."

He turned fully to face her. "Oh yes, I'd forgotten." Silence shrouded them, binding them more tightly together. Her family lived across the sea. His family were possible criminals. They only had each other. "And what is this idea of yours?"

She tugged him down to the window seat beside her. "I don't think your mother killed her son. Perhaps, she knew about it—"

"Why the flower, Grace?"

Grace sifted through her inventory of fictional options involving some sort of hideous corruption, perhaps from Poe or Gaboriau. "Blackmail?"

"And what sin could Celia hold over my mother to silence her from a deed this serious?"

"Something dark enough to shake the foundations of Havensbrooke, I'd guess." His face paled. Oh dear, she should have worded that a little differently. "So I suggest after my dress fitting, we pay Dr. David Ross a visit. Perhaps he's the one who can shed some evidence on our conjectures, and then we speak to your mother."

<hr />

Dinner with Andrew Piper proved a lighthearted affair. The man oozed quick wit and kindness, but when they retired to Frederick's study, the conversation took a decidedly serious turn.

Frederick, Piper, and Grace poured over dozens of financial books, a personal journal or two, and added the recent ledgers recovered from Edward's study.

"Your brother closed the glassworks two years ago," Grace said. "But there's no indication that the business wasn't viable any longer."

Piper blinked over at Grace and looked to Frederick, who couldn't help the hint of pride pushing up at the corners of his mouth. True, most women didn't usually speak of money and business affairs, but Grace was certainly unlike most women.

"But the gristmill became a point of contention years ago," Piper said, "just before I was dismissed. Mr. Rupert Cooper and your father came to blows, and in a fit of passion, your father closed it all down."

Rupert? Frederick's mind paused on the name, but he wasn't certain why.

"The gristmill closed by your father and the glassworks by your brother?" Grace shook her head. "No wonder the estate began to wane, and if Celia had taken over finances along with the natural expenses of covering the costs of such a large property. . ."

"She always seemed to get her way, if I recall correctly," Piper added, examining the ledgers strewn across the billiard table. "When I met with Detective Miracle about some of the inconsistencies in the books, he mentioned that the former Lady Astley had been married before. Did you know?"

Celia? Frederick nearly spit the drink he'd just taken. "Married?"

"It appears that your detective did a little digging and uncovered that she'd been married to a businessman with new money, nearly three times her age."

"What happened?" Grace's palm flew to her chest. "Oh, oh, let me guess."

Piper's lips twitched beneath his finely trimmed moustache.

"The husband was found dead within the first year."

Piper ran a palm over his mouth, studying Grace with a quizzically humored expression. "Very clever, Lady Astley." The man's blue gaze flipped to Frederick's. "You have a budding detective on your hands, my lord."

Frederick wasn't certain whether to smile or not.

"It's a repeated plot in many fiction books." She nodded, sending Frederick a wrinkle-nosed grin for her cleverness.

Frederick resigned his concern and turned back to Piper. "And how did Celia's first husband die?"

"It was listed as"—Piper nailed Frederick with a look—"a heart condition."

Deafening silence followed Piper's declaration.

"But what proof do we have?" Frederick gestured toward the papers on the table. "Nothing. It's too late to exhume bodies to test for poisoning, and what would Celia have to gain from it all? I was still alive."

"Money." Piper tapped the ledgers in his hands. "Or it seems as though someone is. There are large and consistent funds missing from each of your brother's former accounts, and the notes for the fund transfers are not in his handwriting. It's a close attempt but not exact."

Frederick walked to Piper's side and peered over him to review the notes. "Celia, you think?"

"She signed as your brother?" Grace came to his side.

"It seems most of the accounts for the last few months of your brother's life were managed by the lady in question. He'd given her sovereignty."

"Or she'd taken it," Grace added.

"But one would think Mother would have recognized what was happening."

"Unless someone held something over her." Grace reminded.

A fire fueled beneath Frederick's skin, pulse pumping for justice. "Can you trace these funds?"

"Miracle was able to locate that information, actually." Piper sorted through a few more of the ledgers, comparing information, and then raised his direct gaze to Frederick. "An account held by Mr. Mason Parks of London."

Frederick braced his hand against the table. The web was much worse and more prevalent than he'd imagined.

And increasingly more dangerous.

Dr. David Ross was nothing like Grace imagined a country doctor to be.

"Lord Astley." The young doctor offered his hand, his smile at the ready. He turned to Grace. "Lady Astley. To what do I own this unexpected visit."

"I've come on a private matter, Doctor, as it concerns my brother whom you were kind enough to see to earlier this year."

The man's emerald gaze settled on Frederick and then switched to Grace. "I see. Please, sit down." Dr. Ross gestured toward two chairs in his private office. "And how may I help you?"

"I've heard good things about you, Doctor. And well—" Frederick stiffened in his chair. "I don't care to shilly-shally around the point. Time is essential. I'm sorry you were dismissed from Havensbrooke in so hasty and, as I understand it, impolite a manner after my brother's death. If I'd been more present of mind, I'd have come to you sooner to discuss your findings on that day."

"It was my understanding you'd only arrived back in the country. To discover your brother's unexpected death along with inheriting the responsibility of his title? I can imagine how overcome you must have been."

"Thank you." Frederick bowed his head in appreciation, and Grace ignored the urge to take his hand in front of the good doctor. "But since then, certain concerns have come to light that have brought me to your door. Do you recall that day?"

"Indeed I do." Dr. Ross sighed and stood, walking to a shelf nearby and sifting through some papers, finally withdrawing one from the pile. "I'm afraid you'll not like my findings."

"I don't think they'll surprise us, Doctor," Grace added.

Dr. Ross took his seat and leaned forward, offering Frederick the papers. "I have all of my observations detailed here. Your brother had symptoms consistent with poisoning, and not just any poisoning, but a quite common one which most doctors would note upon a cursory examination, especially after the butler answered a few questions for me."

"Hemlock."

Dr. Ross examined Grace's face. "Yes."

Silence stained the moment with a sudden dread Grace felt to her toes. This wasn't from a story or a fantasy. Without any doubt, Edward had been murdered.

"I suggest you alert the authorities, Lord Astley." David's palms pressed against the desk. "If the perpetrator knows of your doubts, this may put both of you in danger."

"I'm afraid it already has." Frederick turned to Grace, his dark gaze holding hers. "But we believe we know the culprit. We only need prove it, and you've given us some help on that score."

The declaration sent a wonderful thrill through Grace's entire body. Oh heavens, her husband would make a gloriously dashing detective. She could almost picture him with spyglass in hand. Marriage certainly proved much more exciting than she'd anticipated, and if they survived another week without being drowned, poisoned, or attacked by moonlight, just imagine how much more thrilling it could become.

Frederick phoned Detective Miracle with the new details from their meeting with Dr. Ross when they returned home, and the detective planned to take the first train to Havensbrooke the next morning to meet Grace and Frederick after the house party. Tension tinged the air. They were hurtling toward some unseen culmination in this dark plot, and the only thing to do was prepare as best one could.

Frederick's wife dazzled the guests upon entry at Keriford Hall in a gown of midnight blue lace, silk, and beading, a sash of a paler hue cinched around her waist, enhancing curves he knew so well.

Her hair was a halo of fiery red, piled into a mass of curls on her head and decorated with a thin band of silver. He held his breath at the sight of her. And she was his. The awareness reverberated through him afresh every time he acknowledged God's gift in giving him Grace.

Lady Caroline Keriford welcomed them forward, a vision in dark rose, her expression honed to perfection. Grace must have inherited her eyes from the Rosemunds, because her aunt shared the same captivating hue.

"Aunt Caroline, your home is beautiful." Grace released Frederick's arm to embrace her aunt. "Thank you for this wonderful gesture tonight."

"I couldn't leave you to the wolves of the aristocracy without a proper introduction, my dear." Lady Keriford peered over Grace's shoulder to offer Frederick a wink. "But I daresay you're in excellent hands. Mr. Andrew Piper is a mutual acquaintance, and quite complimentary of the new Earl of Astley."

Frederick dipped his head in acceptance of the compliment. "He's the best of men."

"Yes he is." She offered her hand to Frederick, which he accepted with a bow.

"And so is Lord Astley." Grace lifted her eyes to her husband, one eyebrow winging high in a flirtatious tilt.

A smile warmed his face at her unabashed admiration.

"You're acting as if you truly like one another." Lady Keriford chuckled. "Very uncommon indeed."

"Our American counterparts do bring a shock to the institution, don't they, Lord Astley?" This from Lord Keriford who joined his wife's side in greeting. Lord Keriford had done well in his marriage, by all accounts from the outside world, and the two made an amiable pair if first impressions held any credence.

"I'm quite certain I married well."

"Of course you did. You married into *my* family." Lady Keriford ushered them forward with a laugh. "I'm pleased to have you so close, Gracelynn. It's been much too long since I've seen family."

Music filtered from the room ahead of them, a space boasting high, elaborately carved golden ceilings and a pale oak floor that glowed in the carefully placed lighting. "I should prepare the two of you, though. At the last minute, Lord Elston brought a guest not unknown to you, Lord Astley."

Frederick halted at the threshold of the doorway, tension constricting his chest with warning. Almost as if drawn by magnetic force, Frederick's gaze found the root of the aggravation. Surrounded by a group of ladies and gentlemen at the far corner of the room stood Celia Percy in her mourning gown. The very fact she'd shown up to the house party filled with some of the upper crust of English society defied every social expectation, yet from the faces of the enraptured throng, no one seemed to mind. His mother would have been horrified that Celia had taken some of the more relaxed views of mourning by wearing half-mourning attire, let alone showing up at a house party when her husband hadn't even been in the grave a year.

"I was surprised at her arrival, of course, since she's still in mourning." Lady Keriford offered a one-shoulder shrug. "But this is such a small party, and though some of the more astute members of the gentry may scoff, I felt it couldn't hurt anything really. She seemed determined to celebrate your happiness, so I overlooked propriety this once. Family, you know."

"This once?" Lord Keriford offered his wife his arm and a crooked grin. "You've been overlooking propriety since the day you stepped off the boat from America."

"You are right." She laughed and took his arm. "But I do attempt to avoid scandal, at least." Her gaze settled on Grace. "Which is the only point you need to remember in this British upper class. You're allowed a great many liberties as long as none of them end in scandal."

"Come darling, let's announce the guests of honor." Lord Keriford drew his wife away from them, leaving Frederick a few seconds with Grace.

"She's even better than I imagined."

Frederick really should have failed to be alarmed by Grace at this point.

"Raven hair, deliciously deceptive eyes, and a smile with all sorts of alluring secrets." She touched his arm. "Oh Frederick, no wonder you fell so desperately."

"Stay near me, Grace." He shook his head and leaned closer, lowering his voice. "If anything happened to you, I'd never forgive myself."

"Who's to say you won't need me to protect you, my chivalrous husband?"

As creative and inventive as her mind could be, his bride had no idea of Celia's cunning. Manipulation was one thing; murder was another.

At that moment, the music died, and Lord Keriford's voice swelled over the quieting throng of about forty people. "Thank you for joining us this evening for our Christmas celebrations. We would like to welcome our guests of honor, Lord and Lady Astley, in their first public appearance in England as man and wife."

Frederick's attention swept directly toward his sister-in-law, who didn't disappoint. Her dark eyes met his, and her lips curved into a smile as wicked as that of the serpent in the garden. His stomach curled. It all seemed so clear now, so obvious. The death of her first husband. The game she'd played with Frederick's affections. Whatever scheme she concocted in his brother's death.

Frederick forced a smile and turned to the hosts. "Lady Astley and I thank you for your generosity and kindness. And thank you all for celebrating with us this evening."

"Take up your glasses everyone!" Lord Keriford held up his glass. "To the bride and groom."

The room erupted in the expected echo of congratulations followed by an immediate quiet as everyone took a sip of their drinks—everyone except Celia.

Frederick and Grace mingled with some of the guests, Frederick taking the happy opportunity to introduce Grace to those living in Havensbrooke's general vicinity.

As Celia approached through the crowd, Frederick turned to Grace. "Will you go and speak with your aunt? Let her know we'll be leaving as soon as dinner ends due to. . ." He searched for an excuse.

"My being overtired?" She shrugged, attempting to help him.

"Would anyone actually believe that, darling?"

Her eyes brightened. "Well, I *am* a new bride."

Her beautiful smile drew him closer, his lips dropping to her cheek. "You are indeed."

With a squeeze to his hand, she retreated through the crowd until she'd made it safely to her aunt's side. Frederick's relaxed expression hardened as he turned to the scent of lilacs and the ominous presence of Celia Blackmore Percy.

"So that is your blushing bride?" She swirled the liquid in her glass, following Frederick's gaze across the room. "What a lovely *child*."

Even her voice lathered false. Frederick kept his expression stoic. "I hadn't expected to see you here."

Her dark brow angled high, fully aware of his implications at her rebellion against the social norms. "I simply couldn't refuse an opportunity to share in the joys of my brother-in-law's happiness after such loss." Her lips reflected the appropriate emotion that her eyes failed to convey. "How could I stay away?"

"A handwritten note would have appealed to convention a bit more."

She took a slow drink, biding her time. "I've never been fond of convention. Besides, I heard you were asking about me in London, so I thought perhaps"—her gaze trailed over him in a way he understood full well—"your sweet little American wasn't quite up to the task."

"Do not fear, Celia." His gaze bore into hers. "Your very thorough lesson on the value of faithfulness and honesty has ensured my fidelity."

"Fidelity?" The light in her eyes faded a little, but she recovered with a raised brow. "How quaint. I had wondered about the value of this unexpected marriage, but I see a quite profitable connection."

"For me, yes." The undercurrent in her words churned with threats. "I'm immensely grateful I hadn't conceded my heart to a lesser woman."

The sting hit its mark. Her stare faltered slightly, but she was quick to rally. "How is your mother?"

Frederick forced his features still. "She's as content as she is able."

This almost resurrected the woman's smile. "An accurate answer, no doubt, but how is her grief? To lose a husband and son in five years' time? There's no wonder what sort of stories she might concoct to appease her heartache."

"Even the most sorrow-induced stories bite with some truth."

The hitch in her smile spoke volumes. "I wouldn't attempt to dig too deeply, Lord Astley."

"A threat does not become you."

Her laugh rang false. "I don't threaten, my dear Frederick." She never moved her gaze from his. "But do remember, curiosity is a dangerous thing in the wrong hands."

Her words fired a warning shot Frederick felt to the core. There was no more time to wait. Tomorrow Detective Miracle and Frederick would present their evidence to the authorities before something more sinister led to another scar on the Percy name. Or worse, on his heart. His gaze rose to find Grace.

# Chapter Twenty-Eight

Lady Celia exceeded any expectation Grace could have envisioned for a villainess. Even her smile slid to just the right angle for deceit. She was remarkably fascinating in real life.

Romance, mystery, murderess, secret passageways, ghosts? She was living a novel and within only the first three weeks of marriage!

As soon as they returned to Havensbrooke, Frederick rang Detective Miracle, who was surprisingly asleep. But then Grace saw the clock and noted that it read two in the morning. Most people slept then, unless they were finishing an excellent book or participating in a ghost hunt, she supposed. Detective Miracle assured Frederick that he would go to the authorities with the information he'd collected and be on the first train from London in the morning.

Frederick and Grace slept a few hours, took an early breakfast, and alerted Lady Moriah that they would like to see her.

Would this encounter prove the most difficult one of all? Was her dear hero prepared for whatever they might uncover? Grace had already worked through ten possible scenarios.

"What do you think Celia has planned? She gave a clear threat to you at the party."

"I don't know, but we must keep our heads." He placed his hand over Grace's on his arm as they walked toward Lady Moriah's room. "She's not one to be trifled with."

"Clearly she has practiced this plan before." Grace shuddered at the sheer cleverness of the scheme. "She *is* Lady de Winter."

"Except, my darling, she's quite real." His gaze met hers, and for the first time, she noticed the smallest hint of fear. "And dangerous." He stopped at his mother's door and brought Grace's knuckles to his lips. "As much as I adore your cleverness, you are not Lady Molly of Scotland Yard who can survive on the page."

Poor man, he really didn't understand how very educational mass reading could be. Money-seeking murderer was not an unfamiliar archetype in fiction, and with Celia's threats from the night before, Grace knew the most dangerous part of the story happened next. Most likely someone would receive a mysterious note or be kidnapped or find that one of the servants had inexplicably disappeared, and all just before the authorities could arrive to nab the scoundrel. That was exactly when the hero and heroine were placed in the most life-threatening situation of all. Though she hadn't quite worked out what Celia might choose. Fire? No, it seemed too obvious. Shooting? Not very creative.

At any rate, Grace had already thought through three different ways to escape a kidnapping, which is why she had a pair of scissors in her pocket.

She touched Frederick's cheek and brought her lips to his, lingering in the sweet sensations of skin on skin. His arms slipped around her, engulfing her in that wonderful feel of safety she'd come to adore. She pulled back far enough to look into his eyes. "I'm not afraid."

"That's what concerns me."

"Do you know why?"

"Because you've reread Sir Arthur Conan Doyle's works often enough to calculate Celia's next move?"

Grace laughed at his exasperated attempt to reprimand her. "No, though you may be surprised at how much I have gleaned from the trials of Violet Strange or Dora Myrl. I'm not afraid, because we have each other. Two very good brains, if I may say so." She tugged him toward Lady Moriah's door. "Let's finish this so we can move on to our next adventure together."

Grace slipped her hand into Frederick's as he knocked on his mother's door, the simple touch easing the tension in his jaw. There was something infinitely dear in that sort of power to soothe some of the weariness in his world. A tenderness stole over her, hints of it she'd experienced throughout the passing weeks. Love. A caress over the crinkles of life. A hand to hold in the dark. Or lips to kiss during a storm. Yes, she loved him.

Lady Moriah's voice ushered them inside.

She greeted them with her usual impassive expression, hands folded on her lap, every wrinkle giving off a very Miss Havisham waxiness, but Grace had seen beneath the veneer. In Lady Moriah's uninhibited moments of sleepwalking, in the chinks in her stoic condescension, brokenness hovered just beneath the surface.

"We've come to speak to you about a serious matter, Mother."

One of her brows tipped. "Have you finally procured some hovel in the village where you can banish me?"

"We've come to inquire after Edward's death."

The wax melted off her expression, but she quickly recovered, straightening her spine in a defensive move. Her eyes darkened to steely coldness. "I don't see how discussing that horrific day is of any benefit."

"We've not discussed it, Mother." He stepped closer, stance as tense as hers. "I never asked the questions I should have. I never stopped to see the inconsistencies."

"I am sorry I pushed you so quickly toward finding a wife." She raised a palm, a sudden softening of her features giving off an artificial concern. "I feel certain the pressure has been overwhelming." Her gaze flitted to Grace with a grimace tagged on. "I see the errors of my haste."

"No, Mother. Grace is the best decision that's been made about my life in years."

Grace almost melted into the carpet. What a man!

"But now is the time for answers."

"There are no answers." Lady Moriah stood, faster than Grace had ever seen her move. "Death doesn't give any. Leave the dead in peace."

"Not when it impacts the living."

"We know about the hemlock."

The dowager turned those piercing eyes on Grace. "What did you say?"

"The reason your son Edward is dead."

The woman wilted back into the chair, every year of her life suddenly reflected in the lines around her eyes. "I don't know what you mean."

"Your response would suggest otherwise." Frederick placed the dried hemlock and note on the table beside his mother. "Were you involved in Celia's plot all along?"

"How dare you charge me with a desire to see Edward dead." She pushed up from her chair, garnering her strength, her teeth barred. "He was my son."

Frederick's body gave the slightest twitch from the sting in her words. "The police will be here within the hour. If you don't wish for me to name you along with Celia in this crime, you need to speak of what you know."

Her hand trembled as she pushed a strand of hair from her forehead and looked away. Her breaths shivered into the silence. "I. . .I didn't know she was killing him until I saw the signs." She walked toward the window, body quaking against her cane. "It wasn't the slow way, like she'd used with your father, but I recognized her desperation."

"Like Father?" Frederick's voice faltered.

"You wanted all the truth." The dowager speared him with a glare, her words frigid. "Your father had recently discovered Edward was not his legitimate son."

Frederick's chest deflated with a release of air. "Rupert."

Grace pieced together the news. The letters Frederick had found. The change in his father's disposition toward Frederick just before his death.

"Yes." She ground out the word, bracing her hand against the window frame. "A common man untouched by the weight and responsibility of Havensbrooke's burden." She sneered and turned away. "I thought no one knew, but Celia discovered it."

"So she threatened to make your past public?" The history began to unfold in Grace's mind.

"Unless I gave her something she wanted." She turned her attention back to the window.

"A title," Grace whispered.

What money-hungry temptress would do less?

"You helped her kill Father? To protect your reputation?" Frederick's voice broke, and Grace wrapped her arm around his for support.

"She didn't plan to kill him at first. She only wanted the social status." This time when Lady Moriah turned to face them, her red-rimmed eyes held all the remorse of her confession. Gone was the impenetrable matriarch. "I agreed to encourage Edward's relationship with Celia to secure her future in exchange for her silence about my past."

"He trusted your opinion above everyone's," Frederick whispered at her side.

"I only wanted to keep my past quiet and protect Edward's future because, don't you see, he had no one, if not for me." Her voice wavered. "Then your father somehow discovered that Edward wasn't his son. I can only imagine the witch told him. He threatened to remove the earldom from Edward and give it to you instead. But Celia would not be outdone." She tapped the floor with her cane and turned those dark eyes back to them. "It wasn't until your father's health had failed that I learned of the arsenic she'd used to weaken him."

Frederick slipped down into a nearby chair. "She killed Father to secure the title."

"She planned it from the start. I was trapped then, don't you see? She held all the cards." Lady Moriah dropped down onto her window seat. "When she became discontented with Edward and her poorly executed plans for the funds of Havensbrooke began to limit her access, I couldn't do anything, because every time I tried—"

"She would remind you of what she knew about you and that you let her kill your husband," Grace breathed.

"She could have pinned the death on me, and I would have been defenseless against her accusations. Don't you see?" Blame beat the woman's shoulders into a slumped posture. "I never thought she'd kill Edward. Leave him penniless, perhaps. And yes, I watched her convince him to pour money into the most useless of schemes. Then I heard of her dalliances, and I feared the worst."

"Yet you did nothing." Frederick shot to his feet with startling fury. "You knew what she was capable of, and you let her kill him. Both of them."

The darkness in his eyes, the rage, almost took Grace's breath. She'd never felt the flames from his anger. But what a glorious fury!

"Do you have any proof of what Celia did, Lady Astley?" Grace soothed the question into the conflict. "Anything we can take with us to the authorities?"

The woman blinked her bleary eyes, her lips trembling. Despite everything Grace had learned, something softened toward her mother-in-law, who lived as a recluse so tortured by her guilt it haunted her sleep. "N–nothing specific, only innuendos and warnings."

Grace sighed and slid her hand down Frederick's arm to link with his fingers, his breaths pumping a galloping rhythm. He needed to come back from whatever dangerous brink his brooding thoughts had taken him. "Keep your head, Frederick. We must think. Plan."

"I have lost my father and my brother because of *her*." His dark gaze met hers, almost pushing her back a step. "My entire life I've felt worthless because of *her*."

"You lost them because of Celia." He tried to pull his hand away, but she held on. "This is the time in the story where one slip from our focus can lead to disaster."

"This is not a story, Grace." He jerked away. "This is *my* life. *My* loss." He turned his ire back to his mother. "I've always wanted to do right by you. My whole life you kept the one thing I longed for most from me. Your acceptance. You've not only withheld your affections, you've stolen my brother and father from me. You've attempted to ruin me and this family."

Lady Moriah turned away, pressing a handkerchief to her face.

"Frederick Percy," Grace clapped her hands on both sides of his face, forcing his attention to her. "*You* are not ruined. *We* are not ruined. Havensbrooke may be your home, but it's not your legacy. How we live, who we love, *that* is the true legacy. *That* is who you truly are."

A knock broke into the gritty silence, and Frederick stumbled back from Grace, shaking his head, his gaze searing hers, still so lost in his indignation.

Brandon entered. "I'm sorry to disturb you, sir, but an Inspector Clarkson is downstairs to see you."

"Clarkson?" Grace looked to Frederick, who barely glanced her way. "Didn't Detective Miracle mention an Inspector Reynolds?"

"I'll be there at once." Frederick shot his mother another glare and turned toward the door.

"Frederick. I'm not certain—"

"I cannot discuss forgiveness and hope right now, Grace." His hand sliced the air. "Not now."

The door slammed behind him, shattering through the tension in the room. Grace braced herself with a palm to the back of a nearby wingback. Her husband had been dealt a blow to his soul. Perhaps time and distance from his mother would provide clarity.

Grace turned to Lady Moriah. The strong, powerful woman from days before withered beneath her admissions, her soul as frail as her body. In a few halting steps, Grace sat next to her at the window.

"Haven't you done enough?" the woman muttered. "All of this started when you arrived."

Grace ignored the remark. "I can't imagine what grief you've carried to keep this secret for so long."

The gentle answer brought Lady Moriah's attention around. She studied Grace, eyes narrowing. "What do you want?"

"I want your help." Grace stared right back. "Can you search your memory for anything to prove what Celia's done? Anything at all? For the son you do have."

Lady Moriah shook her head but paused. "There might be something." She stood and walked to her desk, cane tapping against the floor in a crescendo of anticipation. "It's half burned, though I think the intention is clear."

"Burned?" Grace followed.

"One of the maids found it in Celia's fireplace and brought it to me." Moriah raised her chin. "I promoted her to my lady's maid at that point to ensure she didn't rattle on about what she'd uncovered. But Dr. Ingle's signature is clear."

Lady Moriah sifted through a box on her desk, drawing out a crumbled, half-scorched page and handing it to Grace.

Grace skimmed over the writing, pausing on a few sentences.

> *Do not bully me. I will not be privy to another one of your schemes. Already I covered your first*—burn marks blocked the words—*death of a good man. I will not provide arsenic or anything else. I will not. There is enough blood on my hands. Threaten as you*—burns blocked the remainder of the sentence.

"This is proof of Dr. Ingles's knowledge." Grace looked up. "And Detective Miracle interviewed Dr. Ingle this morning, but Frederick and I haven't had time to discuss his findings since our return from Leavenworth." She waved the page. "If he refuses to talk, this will force his hand. Frederick will see the good of your giving this to us."

"Don't dangle your hope here," she whispered, turning back to the window. "There is no redemption for me."

"As long as you draw breath, there is a chance for redemption." Grace covered the woman's hand. "Even for you."

The woman's gaze faltered.

"Frederick and I saw you in the east wing at night. You must have been sleepwalking."

Her weary eyes took on caution. "You—you saw me."

"Grief is a powerful force."

The woman pressed her fist against her chest and looked away. "I would wake there some nights."

"You seemed to be searching for something. Can you recall what it was?"

Lady Moriah shook her head and wiped a loose tear. "I don't know." Her voice warbled. "I suppose. . .I suppose I was searching for forgiveness."

Grace's vision blurred. No novel in all of her readings had been gripped with such open wounds.

"Lady Astley." A crash came from the doorway as Mary stumbled into the room. "Ma'am, you have to come."

Grace pushed to a stand. "Mary?"

"Lord Astley"—she held her stomach, catching her breath—"they've taken him."

"Taken him?" Grace increased her pace to the door. "What do you mean?"

"Someone's taken Lord Astley." Mary's breaths pulsed out the words. "He's. . .he's gone."

# Chapter Twenty-Nine

Frederick struggled against the ropes to no avail. His arms were pressed tight at his sides, and despite his feet being free from constraints, there was little room for them to move in the red Ford Touring.

A few punches to his stomach and a slam to the head from "Inspector Clarkson" incapacitated Frederick enough for the man and his cohort to wrestle him out of Havensbrooke, bind him, and drive away.

"The chauffeur is after us." The man to Frederick's left leaned forward. The car swerved and tossed Frederick against him.

"The crazy fool." This from a woman sitting in the front. He knew that voice. Celia? "He's trying to block our path."

Before Frederick could confirm the author of the voice, the car swerved again, ramming him against the window. He blinked to clear his vision, and the second man came into blurry view. Was that Mason Parks?

"Turn here for the ruins. We'll hide there until dark."

Frederick's gaze darted to the front and fell into Celia's serpentine gaze.

Her smile curled. "Besides, it shouldn't take long for us to finish our business with our handsome and unwitting guest."

Frederick eased back into the seat, his head pounding. One eye swollen, from the feel of it.

Three men accompanied Celia. Parks, "Inspector Clarkson"—who looked somewhat familiar—and a driver. All men brainwashed and paid off by the lovely Celia, if Frederick guessed right, from the funds she'd pilfered from Havensbrooke.

"I do hate that you hit him in the nose, Turner." Celia turned from her perch in the passenger seat, red lips sliding into a smile. "It is one of his winning features."

"We've lost the chauffeur, Celia," the driver said.

"Excellent, Randolph." Her gaze skimmed over Frederick and then turned to the driver. "After ascertaining his acute attachment to his little bride at Keriford, I feel our dear Lord Astley will be quick to agree to any of our demands."

His attention shot to Celia. *Grace!* That's why she'd come to Keriford? Scouting out her plan for Grace? A chill crawled through his chest. The money. Havensbrooke's money.

He wrestled against the ropes but stopped. *No, Frederick. Remain calm. Celia wants to get to your senses. Stop. Think. Even if this scene is like something from a book.*

A book! Grace would tell him to think like a character.

Well then, what would a Sherlock sort of character do? He drew in a deep breath. Observe. Reason. Plan.

Frederick took in his surroundings with a new, more focused purpose. "Inspector Clarkson" sat farthest to Frederick's left, a tall, lean-looking man, bushy brow pulled over a set of gray eyes. His jacket looked well worn, and the hem of his pants was frayed. He barely moved, eyes trained ahead, calculated. And his nose resembled a hook.

Grace's Captain Hook! From the ship.

A glint of metal from the man's jacket hinted to a pistol. Weapon number one.

Frederick's attention shifted to Celia. Her dark gaze bore into his with icy calculation. She wore one of the smaller hats, slanted slightly to cover one side of her forehead.

He couldn't observe much about the driver except to note his broad build. Of the three men, he'd likely be the stoutest, and as the driver in front with Celia, he probably had the strongest attachment to her.

By consequence, this made him the most dangerous.

How Parks had involved himself in this messy business, Frederick had no idea, but he'd gotten his fingers in the mix before Edward died. Adoration for Celia paired with money troubles proved the likely motivators for Parks's involvement, so desperate that the man would even forfeit his friendship with Edward.

Ah, Celia—like a spider, once she trapped a victim in her web, she secured that person by whatever means necessary.

Like she'd done to his mother.

Parks fidgeted with the hat in his lap, sweat beading across his thinning hairline.

A weak link, perhaps?

"Parks, I thought you were Edward's friend."

The accusation hit its mark. Parks's fidgeting ceased, and he looked away, jaw tightening.

"What could she have possibly promised you to have you turn on your friend?" He kept his voice low. "Monetary gain, I'd suspect from the ledgers."

"The ledgers?" Park's gaze shot up. "How did you—"

"It can't last long, though, can it? Celia drained him dry. But I suppose you already know that since you are the lone account holder for this embezzling. All in your name." Frederick drew in a deep breath as if it was all a shame. "Not one cent can be traced to her. Clever, isn't it?"

Parks grabbed Frederick's collar. "Stop talkin'." He spat out the threat.

"Don't let him intimidate you, Parks, darling." Celia cooed from the front seat, her green gaze resting on Frederick in warning. "We should have gagged him as well. He's being quite a nuisance."

"But he knows about the—"

"Havensbrooke may have been penniless three weeks ago." Her poisonous gaze never left Frederick's. "But it isn't any longer. It's fed by American money now, so don't worry, Parks. You'll be well taken care of."

"I'll not give you anything, Celia."

"No?" Her smile took a devilish turn. "I believe with the right incentive, I can encourage a great deal of generosity."

The knot in Frederick's chest coiled tighter at the serpentine twist in her words.

"Yes." She raised a finger to her lips, her gaze never leaving his face. Watching. Waiting for the slightest break in his demeanor. "Once we have you securely tucked away at the ruins, I'll make my way to your home, where your darling Lady Astley will have no one to protect her. Turner isn't fond of Americans, you see. Especially women. A lady treated his heart rather ruthlessly, didn't she, Turner?"

Turner's hand fisted in response.

"And your dear little wife wasn't very forthcoming to Turner when he attempted to collect information on the ship from America. Rather snappish, wasn't she, Turner?" Celia's attention flickered back to Frederick. "So I imagine with Lady Astley at Turner's ready disposal, you'll give me whatever I want."

"That's an empty threat, Celia." He kept his gaze locked on hers, refusing to bow to the intimidation. "What makes you think the police won't arrest you as soon as you walk through the front doors?"

"They're looking for two men who fit the descriptions of Turner and Parks." Her brow peaked. "Not the mourning widow of the previous Earl of Astley."

Parks turned his head in her direction, clearly off-put by this new revelation. Turner gave a similar reaction. Ah, maybe her followers weren't as loyal as she thought. And in his favor, Celia had no idea Jack Miracle was on his way to Havensbrooke with the police even now, looking very specifically for the mourning widow.

A point he'd keep close to his chest.

"You doubt the intelligence and strength of my staff and my wife."

"Well, she has been rather tiresome, I must say. You both have." Celia sighed, her gaze raking over his face. "Though now I'm glad you didn't drown in the river, or there would have been nothing to do for my financial future, since from what I understand, my dearly departed husband rearranged things at the last. Very unhusbandly of him, wasn't it? And then to have police scouting about right after the car accident. We had to bide our time."

The roof of the ruins came into view. "Of course, Rogers didn't hear of our change in plans before he attacked you in London." She shook her head. "No matter. He was a bit overeager at any rate, so Randolph had to dispose of him." She ran a hand over the driver's shoulder, an intimate touch. "He's usually very good at dispatching people, except for this bride of yours, and she simply won't follow the rules. Swimming? Riding astride? Using a hunting rifle?"

Hunting rifle? If they all survived this, Grace could ride astride whenever she chose, and he might very well teach her how to use pistols himself.

"I had hoped that instead of you, she'd be the first from the house—to reduce the middleman." She chuckled. "We'll just have to turn the plan around. She'll give us what we want as long as we have you, and you'll give me what I want as long as I have her. It's all fairly simple."

Her words shot a shaft of fear through him. He hated to imagine what Celia and her thugs might do to Grace.

He shifted his attention back to Parks and lowered his voice. "Do you really want a crime on your head, old bean?" Of course he already had a few at this point. "Is all this worth it to you?"

"I'd stop speaking unless spoken too, Lord Astley. Or dear Randolph will have to silence you."

The driver turned enough to show a hint of a smile on his profile. Frederick's stomach curled with a wave of nausea. How could he have been dimwitted enough to fall for Celia's manipulation? When held against the forthrightness of his bride, Celia's falseness and shallow affections were revealed as the grotesque distortions they were. There was no comparison.

And he wasn't a fool anymore.

Grace's words rushed back to him. *"Remember whose you are."*

Havensbrooke held his heart and his history. A piece of him inextricably linked to the stories and soil of this earth, but he belonged to an even greater legacy. One bound to an eternal story—etched out of sacrifice and love, not stone and dirt. Facing life as Earl of Astley gave him a temporary home, but living life as a child of God gave him an identity.

A truth written on his soul.

"Pull behind the ruins, and we'll sort out the next step of our new plan." Celia's words jerked Frederick's gaze ahead.

The walls of the ruins took a golden hue in the glow of morning. How much time did he have? He needed to stall them. Give the police more time to arrive.

"People know I'm missing, Celia. They'll be looking."

"Not here. Who would even care for our little rendezvous spot?"

Perhaps her arrogance would be her downfall. Frederick could only hope. Someone had to have seen where the car turned and made a guess as to the possible location. *Lord, please. Bring help. And protect Grace.*

As Parks took hold of him to pull him from the car, Frederick rushed the man, knocking him to the ground. Without pausing, Frederick stumbled into a run and darted toward the forest trail.

His bonds hampered his escape, but he tried nonetheless, dodging one attempt by Randolph to apprehend him. Turner tackled him at the forest's edge, both falling into the moist earth. Using tactics learned through his military stint, Frederick tripped Turner to the ground and then wrapped his legs around the man's neck, squeezing with enough force to render his assailant unconscious. Just as the man's struggling began to weaken, a shadow fell over Frederick and a crash shook his skull. Everything froze. Pain ricocheted inside his head, loosening his balance, his vision blurred, and the world crumbled to darkness.

⤛⁂⤜

"Someone's taken Lord Astley?" Grace took Mary by the shoulders. "What are you talking about?"

"I heard a commotion at the front, your ladyship." The young maid shook her head. "And when I got there, Brandon was laid out on the floor."

"Brandon?" Grace rushed down the corridor toward the Great Hall.

"I saw two men shoving Lord Astley into the back of a car."

Grace's feet came to a stop, and she stared at Mary for the longest time. Was Grace dreaming? This sounded too much like something she'd actually concoct to be real. After all, *she* was the one with the scissors. "Two men kidnapped Lord Astley?" She forced her feet into motion again, meeting the stairs. *Kidnap* didn't seem right, because her strong and capable husband was anything but a kid. *Man-nap* perhaps, but that word didn't seem to fit either.

When Grace reached the bottom of the stairs, the truth crashed into her fictional world with painful reality. Elliott, Peter, and Mrs. Powell struggled to pull Brandon's still body into one of the chairs in the Great Hall, while several of the housemaids stood watch.

"Oh my! Frederick really has been man-napped." She rushed to the bottom of the stairs and joined the servants, an unexpected burn of tears threatening release. It was one thing to turn the page at such a moment and quite another to wonder if she'd ever see her husband again. "How did this happen?"

"I was just coming from the kitchens, and I heard Brandon cry out." Elliott adjusted the unconscious man into the chair. "When I reached the front hall, Brandon was on the floor, so I rushed to the door."

"That's where I was," Mary added. "Two men, one who was placing a sack over the master's head, were dragging him to a car."

"What?" Grace gasped. "A sack over his head?"

"I can't be sure," Elliott continued, as Mrs. Powell reached around him to place a cool cloth on Brandon's forehead. "But one of the men looked like Mr. Parks."

*Oh, the fiend!* Grace stepped close to Elliott, taking his hands in hers and shaking them. "Did they bind him with ropes? Gag him? Was there any sort of injection into his skin?"

Elliott stared down at her, mouth opening and closing like a fish.

"They've taken the side road." Mr. Patton ran into the room, breaths coming in spurts. "I chased them up the main drive and tried to block their escape, but the driver seemed to know the way. He turned by the rock gardens, and I lost their trail."

Grace looked to Elliott for clarification. "It goes along the river."

"The river? What's out there?"

"Nothing, your ladyship, except the old ruins."

"The ruins?" She cleared her throat and dashed away a rebel tear. What good were those at a time like this? *Think like a detective.* "It's Celia. I know it."

"What do we need to do, ma'am?" Elliott stepped forward, ready for the challenge.

Yes, the faithful valet would do excellently as a cohort. She'd have preferred Frederick, of course, but he was off being man-napped. With a set of her chin and a push of her palm against her stomach to still the tremors, she turned to the chauffeur. "Mr. Patton, the police should be on their way with Detective Miracle. See if you can meet them on the drive to direct them toward the ruins. I have a feeling we'll need their brawn before this morning is out." Grace paced from one chair to the next. "Celia must be desperate to have taken Frederick from his home in broad daylight, which means she might be desperate enough to do something much worse." The declaration pooled through Grace, reverberating with consequences she hadn't considered. Her knees weakened. She shook the thought from her mind and focused on Elliott. "Elliott, can you ride a horse?

Elliott's brows flew to his hairline. "Yes."

"Perfect. Follow me." She ran from the house and toward the stables, Elliott at her heels.

"And exactly what are we doing, my lady?"

For such an efficient man, he certainly was taking his time coming to conclusions. "We're going to rescue Lord Astley."

"Pardon me?" When had Elliott's voice pitched so high?

Grace pushed open the door to the stables, and stopped, her mind a whir. "We ought to bring a rope."

"A rope?" He shook his head, clearly faltering. Was she the only person in the house prepared for a man-napping and possible murder?

"Yes, a rope. All the best detective stories use them. I'm not sure why, but I feel certain we ought to bring one along just in case."

After the slightest hesitation, Elliott took charge, directing the stable hands to prepare two of their fastest horses.

"And maybe we should bring some extra cloths, in case someone is wounded." Grace added, taking one of the leather bags hanging nearby. "What else?" If they survived this suspense, she was going to make certain the servants had an opportunity to read a healthy share of detective books. She shouldn't be the only one equipped to rescue people in such situations.

"Wh—what about a gun?"

Grace swung around to face Elliott, her smile wide. The good valet only needed to warm up to the notion a bit. "Perfect, Elliott. Now you're thinking like a sleuth."

# Chapter Thirty

Grace slid from her horse as she and Elliott stopped just outside the clearing of the ruins. Her mind had bustled through several scenarios as she'd ridden along the trail. Would she find Frederick at all, or would he be dead? She tilted her head and studied the crumbling manor house. Perhaps he took on his attackers with the fierce and strategic maneuvers of the trained military man he was, leaving them all incapacitated at his feet. Her cheeks heated at the very idea.

"I'm going to peek inside," she whispered to Elliott. "We need to ensure Frederick is here before we make our plans."

"Peek?" came Elliott's choked reply, scurrying down off his horse to follow her. "My lady, I can't let you go in there alone."

She tugged the rope from the bag in her saddle. "Well, I'd hope not, Elliott."

With careful steps, Grace slipped through the forest edge around the side of the ruins with the fewest windows. Elliott stayed close, his feet shuffling against the fallen leaves behind her, crackling every twig. She shot him a warning look, but the intent bounced off his intense expression. Poor man, she couldn't really fault him. Obviously he hadn't had her training.

"Lord Astley would not approve of you doing this." His whisper emerged too loud in the tense silence.

"Clearly, Elliott, you have never read any of Grant Allen's female detective stories." She inched closer to the nearest half-shattered window, listening for voices. "I'm more than equipped for the task. Brawn is an excellent assistant, but brains are how real crimes are solved."

"Police solve real crimes," his voice rose, blending with a sound from inside the building.

Grace dropped to the ground and pulled Elliott down too, her nose almost touching his. "Have you never practiced sleuthing before in your life?"

His eyes rounded in answer of his utter innocence in the act.

"Have you even *imagined* it?"

He blinked.

"All right, I'll teach you." She sighed. "Lesson one, you must speak quietly or not at all. Our lives, dear Elliott, very well may be in danger, but if we're going to die, let's not be caught at the very beginning of our adventure. That's simply embarrassing." She gestured with her chin to the house. "I hear voices."

"My lady, I must protest."

"Shhh!" She waved away Elliott's complaint and slid to the window, but the lowest portion of the glass was still well over a foot above her head.

Voices blurred unintelligibly from inside. A woman's timbre among them, if she guessed from the pitch and tone. *Celia?*

"Elliott," Grace pulled at the poor valet's jacket to bring him closer. "I need you to give me a boost."

Elliott sent her entire body a look before settling his confused gaze back on her face. "A what?"

"Lift me up so I can see in the window. It's taller than either one of us, and we need to get our bearings."

Poor Elliott looked positively horrified.

"Come now. This is an emergency. Do you really want the death of your master on your hands because you refused to raise me high enough to see in a window?"

He shook his head and proceeded to approach in the most awkward of ways, his hands moving first to one side of her waist, then the next, as if unsure how to pick up a woman.

"For heaven's sake." Grace grabbed his wrists and planted his palms on her sides. "One here and one here. That will do." She tempered her frustration with a smile. "Though I am glad that you are reluctant to be inappropriately friendly with me, dear Elliott. Lord Astley would highly approve of your admirable discretion."

After a pause, most likely from Elliott trying to work up the courage to complete the task, he raised Grace high enough to see through the bottom half of the window. Despite wobbling a little, she caught sight of three people standing on the far side of what had once been a large gallery. Another person sat in a chair.

*Frederick.*

Grace gasped. Tied to a chair?

Just above where the collection of villains stood, the ceiling had collapsed into the main level, leaving a gaping hole from the first floor. She could easily spy down from that spot as she'd done in the stables at Whitlock.

"Elliott, I have the origins of an idea," she whispered, gesturing for him to let her down.

"Oh dear," came his grunted reply.

"Don't worry." She offered him a reassuring smile. "This time you won't have to touch my waist at all." She patted his arm. "I'll only need to climb onto your shoulders."

"Pardon me?" Elliot's exclamation burst out.

Grace covered his mouth with her palm and froze. So did the voices inside. She pulled Elliott back against the wall and waited. Movement skittered to life from the other side of the window.

"Don't worry. Who could know where we're hiding? It's practically buried behind this forest," the female voice hissed. "We'll wait a little longer and make our way back to the main house through the forest."

Elliott exchanged a look with Grace but only moved enough to place his arm in front of her as a guard. What a sweet man! He was terrified and a bit bumbling as a detective, but ever loyal. She'd hug him if he wouldn't become discombobulated and give away their location.

"Aren't you the least bit concerned they'll try to kill you, ma'am?" He used an appropriate whisper.

"Of course, but I'm much *more* concerned they'll kill Frederick without my having at least tried to help him when I could."

When the voices distanced, Grace slid against the stone toward a section of the wall where a two-story window hung, empty of glass and accurately placed above Frederick's position, if she guessed right. Perfect.

She would sort out what to do next, but bringing a rope was the smartest idea she'd had all day.

A few scattered stones made a wonderful perch for Elliott, and the old trellis could support part of her weight as she climbed on Elliott's shoulders to reach the window.

When she relayed the plan to the valet, his response wasn't as enthusiastic. "I simply cannot have you climbing up my person like a tree, my lady."

"I promise I won't tell Brandon. Will that suit you?"

"Lady Astley!"

"Elliott." She placed her hands on her hips and stared at him. "I admire your great propriety, but my husband is held hostage by an insane woman who has murdered at least two people and most likely has designs to murder a third, so I believe we've moved beyond the realms of propriety, don't you?"

He sighed, closed his eyes, and turned, bracing his hands against the wall for support. She slipped off her shoes to lessen the discomfort for the long-suffering man and adjusted her gown for the occupation as best she could.

Elliott would thank her for this someday. What a story to recount to his progeny!

"Just keep your eyes closed, and you can pretend it never happened." Grace shoved the rope onto her shoulder and grasped the rickety trellis. "But it would make a great scene in a book, don't you think?"

He groaned a response, or maybe it was a chuckle. She couldn't tell.

"After I'm up, I'll drop the rope for you to follow. If necessary, I'll cause a distraction so you can get into position."

"I have no doubt of your abilities to create a distraction," came his mumbled response.

At least he had faith in her.

With a bit of struggle, she made it to a full stand on his shoulders and was fairly delighted that the windowsill came to her chest. Grasping the edge of the frame, she pushed off Elliott's shoulders until her elbows hooked over the edge of the sill.

Elliott released a low grunt.

"Sorry, dear Elliott," she whispered as she clung to the frame and scraped her feet against the stone wall to gain traction.

A shuffling noise came from one corner of the house as Grace struggled through the window. Her gown billowed around her in a most unladylike way. She never imagined the female detectives in novels flapping like fish in their exploits, but in all honesty, what else could be done?

The noise came again. Closer. If the sill hadn't pressed into her stomach, stealing her breath, she would have told Elliott to hide.

She gripped the frame, her fingers pinching to the point of pain, and finally succeeded in hooking one foot into a crevice in the wall while her other leg flailed in the air. Oh good heavens, hopefully Elliott still had his eyes closed. She'd never been so thankful for pantaloons in her life!

With a final tug of her quivering arms and a push from her foot, she tumbled through the window into a quiet heap on the floor. For a second, she lay there, resting her head in her hands, breathing in and out. Her body ached a little, and the exertion proved a bit more than she'd expected, but in all truth, her other sleuthing exploits had been on the page. Perhaps she should invest in calisthenics to prepare for her next detective opportunity.

After pushing herself to a sitting position, she took inventory of her surroundings. A few pieces of broken furniture, some crumbed stone, a broken vase, and even a partially intact tapestry hinted that this space was some sort of sitting room in a previous generation. About ten feet in front of her a gaping hole opened to the floor beneath, giving more clarity to the voices below.

"I see you're finally waking, Lord Astley." A female voice rose into the cavernous space. "Don't look at me that way. If you hadn't tried to escape, you wouldn't have such a headache."

Grace's eyes widened. Oh, Lady Celia was marvelous. Exactly as any solid villainess should be!

Grace scooted on her stomach to the edge of the hole and peered down. Celia paced back and forth, the central figure dressed in a magnificent fitted purple day suit with a mummy-type skirt. Grace shook her head. The woman looked resplendent—villainously so—though Grace despised those hobble skirts. If Grace ever became a villainess, which seemed rather unlikely, she'd wear trousers as a uniform of treachery.

"Now here's what you're going to do." Celia's voice pearled with false sweetness. "You will go to London on the evening train, accompanied by Randolph and Parks. Turner and I will keep your wife and mother company. Then you'll dip into Lady Astley's substantial fortune." She named a ridiculous sum. "Transfer it into Parks's account and send me a wire that it's been done."

A muscular sort of brute stood to Celia's right, and another man, broad chested with an impressively bushy pair of black eyebrows, waited at her left with a gun in his hand. Grace held in her gasp. Oh dear, it was Captain Hook from the ship to England.

Celia had been after Frederick from the start.

"I didn't see anyone, Lady Celia." This from a man out of sight. He must've been the one snooping about outside a few seconds before. Parks, if she guessed.

Well, the odds weren't the best for Grace. Three men. One woman. But at least Elliott had a gun and Grace a pair of scissors.

"I'm not giving you anything, Celia."

Frederick's voice pulled Grace's attention back to her husband. As Celia stepped aside, Grace had a clear view of him. Air closed off in her throat. One of his eyes was swollen almost closed, blood tinged the side of his head, and ropes bound him so tightly they bunched his chest inward.

Heat scorched up from her stomach into her face. How dare they!

She shoved back from her perch, swallowing through her burning throat. This deed would not go unpunished. She searched the room, her attention landing on a broken yet heavy vase nearby. But who to aim for? Every burning coal in her chest wanted to target Celia, but the detective brain took hold. Aim for the man with the gun —she shifted her gaze back to the mastermind in purple —then she would claw Celia's eyes out.

Grace took the rope, fastened it to one of the stone pillars in the room, and peeked back out the window. Elliott waited below, so she tossed the rope over and gathered the vase in her arms. It was much heavier than she'd anticipated, which only made her choice more rewarding.

With stealthy and somewhat awkward, steps, she approached her perch directly above the place she'd seen the man with the gun. The three villains faced Frederick, their backs to Grace, but she had a clear view of her dear husband.

He looked up haphazardly but refocused his attention on her, eyes widening. Well, one eye widened, of course. The other was pitifully closed and purplish. His look of utter shock nearly distracted her from her rescue mission. Why did he look so surprised? She attempted to offer him a reassuring smile, but it didn't seem to help.

Oh well, if he'd been hit over the head, there was a good chance he wasn't thinking clearly. Before the crew of menacing man-nappers could turn, Grace nodded to her darling husband, took aim, and released the vase to its ultimate destination.

It almost hit its mark.

With a thud, then a crash, the vase slammed against the man's shoulder and maybe a part of his head, sending him sprawling to the ground and the vase crashing nearby. Grace turned to see if Elliott had made it up the rope yet, but he was nowhere to be seen.

Her plan suddenly shifted into the unknown. Where was *her* man with a gun?

The group of villains all stared up at her for a full five seconds, before Celia seemed to rally. "Parks, go get her."

Grace gasped. What to do? Her attention fastened on the rope and back to the hole, where the malevolent mistress of evil stared up at her. Footfall from the stairway alerted her to Parks's approach. Oh heavens! She had to do something.

Grace ran to the column and pulled up the rope. Clearly, Elliott hadn't read her mind about the plan. She'd have to lay it out more clearly next time.

She ran back toward the hole, rope in hand. It didn't look that far down. Her gaze came back to Frederick. Why was he shaking his head? Perhaps his vision was imbalanced because of the swollen eye and possible head injury.

Parks appeared in the doorway, rushing forward as if to grab her. With a deep breath, a mental image of what she imagined Tarzan might do, and a quick prayer, she aimed for Lady Celia and slid through the hole.

Unfortunately, the idea in her head failed to execute as fluidly. In her haste to escape Parks, she overextended her swing, and since she had no trapeze experience of any kind, her legs flew in all different directions, spinning her body in a twirl of skirts, pantaloons, and red hair. One foot slammed into one of the villains, knocking him to the floor, and in another twirl she nearly decapitated Celia before landing directly on top of Frederick with such force he and the chair flipped backward.

She was no Tarzan.

It was a good thing Elliott wasn't watching, because all sorts of propriety had just flown out the broken windows.

Frederick had just been thinking about how to protect his sweet, innocent wife from the wiles of the devious Celia Blackmore Percy, when Grace—standing as a fiery fairy in forest green —materialized above him holding a—vase?

He blinked his one good eye, but the picture stayed the same.

How hard had Randolph hit him?

He blinked again, but still she stood, a flaming glint in her eyes as she raised the vase.

He shook his head, trying to dislodge the vision, but her sapphire gaze pinned him with purpose, and she nodded, as if that would explain everything.

He must be dreaming. Yet the vase slipped from her grasp and crashed into Randolph, sending him to the ground.

Silence enveloped the room as everyone turned to stare up at Lady Astley.

Celia turned to Frederick, a look of utter bewilderment crossing her face. "Parks," she called, "go get her!"

"No." Frederick tugged against his binds, his chair shaking beneath the force. "Grace! Run."

Parks took off for the stairs. Grace disappeared from view, heeding his command.

"Turner, check outside to see if she's alone," Celia took a few steps back, her face raised to the second level, distracted.

With what strength he had, Frederick scooted the chair toward Randolph, who struggled to push himself up, still feeling the impact of the vase. One strong kick of Frederick's hard-toed shoe rendered the man unconscious.

Now how to protect Grace?

But then she reappeared above him with a rope? He squinted to decipher her plan. What was she going to do with—

Before he could process the possibilities, down swung his bride, gown billowing about her like a fast-approaching emerald umbrella. Her feet flung in one direction, her hair in another. There was nothing to be done but stare. His mind drew a blank.

She kicked Parks, knocked Celia down as the woman attempted to dodge Grace's uncontrolled spinning, and then landed with full force right against his chest.

Frederick's chair tilted backward and slammed against the floor with Grace and all her layers encapsulating him.

"Oh my goodness!" She pushed off him, slapping him in the nose as she did.

He nearly cried from the shock of pain.

"Frederick! I'm so sorry. I wasn't aiming for you, I promise." She grabbed his face in her palms. "I was hoping to hit Lady de Winter, but I'd never swung down on a rope before, you see, so I wasn't quite sure of the trajectory."

His brain and his vision failed to match. "What are you doing here?"

She paused, her brow crinkling. "Well, that's a silly question." Her eyes widened. "Oh, your ropes." She reached into her skirts and brought out a pair of scissors. "I'm so glad I brought along the rope and these scissors, but since I have no practice with guns, Elliott kept those."

"Elliott is here?" His throat barely worked out the question.

She cut at his bonds with her usual energy. "Did you really think I'd come to your rescue by myself?"

He raised a brow.

She sighed. "All right, I would've. But Elliott is such a gentleman, he insisted on accompanying me. I think he deserves a raise after this, Frederick."

One of the ropes loosened as the scissors slit through, but not in time to free him completely before a shadow fell over them.

"Grace!"

She turned too late. Parks jerked her up by her arm and twisted the scissors from her grip. With a firm tug of her body eliciting a squeal of pain, Parks pinned Grace against him, opening the scissors and pressing a blade to her throat.

Frederick struggled against the loosening bonds as Celia rose from the ground—with some difficulty—and dusted off her skirt. "Well done, Parks." She pushed back a strand of loose ebony hair from her forehead and raised her chin as she approached Grace, her smile not as quick to resurface as before. "We have all of our cards now, don't we?"

Celia stepped up to Grace, her gaze trailing the younger woman from head to toe. "I suppose you think you're clever and brave."

His beautiful wife narrowed her eyes, blue gleaming like flint. She looked stunning. "I *am* clever and brave. I don't have to hide behind poisonous flowers and hired thugs."

"But you see, dear." Celia ran a fingernail down Grace's cheek. "Your little exploit has done nothing but secure my plan. As long as I have you, your darling husband will give me whatever I want."

A gunshot exploded from outside.

"I don't need luck." Grace grinned. "I have a valet."

Grace's theatrics worked long enough for Frederick to loosen his bonds. One more thread.

Celia pushed Parks's hand away and placed her bony fingers around Grace's throat, squeezing. "Oh, but if I can't get what I want from Frederick Percy, I'll make certain he loses what he loves most in the process."

Grace's eyes widened as Celia's fingers increased pressure.

Everything within Frederick surged to attack. Breaking the last bind, he rushed toward Parks and Celia, managing to break her hold on his wife's neck. His clever wife made use of his disruption to bring her heel down on Parks's foot before twisting away in time for Frederick's fist to make contact with the man's face. Celia stumbled back, and Parks toppled to the floor. Within seconds, Frederick rendered him unconscious with a single blow.

※

Grace rolled out of the way as Frederick rushed to the attack. If she hadn't been internally shaking from her near-death experience, she'd have done something fictionally ridiculous like brand him with her lips.

But common sense and a healthy dose of feminine rage prevailed. She pushed herself to a stand in time to see Celia rushing to escape.

The woman couldn't run very fast in her fashionable outfit, but Grace's riding skirt gave her legs freedom.

"You have nowhere to go," Grace called. "The police are on their way here now." She hoped. "And I can outrun you." With certainty.

Lady Celia ran out the side door, Grace on her heels, and with a perfectly placed leap, Grace tackled Celia around the hips and they both slammed against the ground. Well, at least Celia broke Grace's fall. From the sound of it, the Villainess de Winter had her breath knocked from her.

"Ah, I see you have things well in hand, Lady Astley."

Grace looked up to find Blake staring down at her, pistol fashionably posed in his hand. She grinned. "Mr. Blake, what impeccable timing for a visit."

His lips twitched into a smile, and he offered his hand to her as he trained the gun on a flailing Celia. "I couldn't allow you to have all the adventures on your own now, could I? What sort of friend would I be?"

Grace took his proffered hand. "However did you know to come?"

His blond brows hinged. "I know too many people with too much information in various places, my lady, and I always make certain to keep informed about my friends."

"Aren't you clever to have around, then." She leaned forward, lowering her voice.

Blake's lips twisted with effort. He reached to grab Celia's arm, keeping the gun trained on her. He was quite fluid with the device, as if he used it on a regular basis.

Grace's thoughts spiraled in dastardly directions. Was Blake a secret detective of his own?

"Blake, you know you haven't got it in you to shoot me." Celia purred, jerking against his hold and sending Grace a glare.

"Actually, Celia, I've wanted to dispatch you for years." He gave her arm a tighter squeeze, and she winced. "But that would be much too easy for the likes of you and much too messy for the likes of me."

"And how is Elliott?" Grace smoothed a palm down her quaking middle. "Have you seen him?"

"He's fine, Lady Astley," Blake answered, tugging Celia away. "His boxing history came to the forefront as he took out one of Celia's brutes who attempted an escape."

Grace's mouth came unhinged. "Boxing history? Elliott?"

Before Blake answered, around the corner of the house came a rush of men in uniforms followed by Detective Miracle. "Lady Celia Blackmore Percy, you are under arrest for the murders of Davis Lockley; Richard, Lord of Astley; as well as his son, Edward Percy." Two men took her by the arms.

"And the attempted murder of quite a few others," Grace added.

Celia's face contorted into a menacing sneer as she was led away. With three murders and countless other crimes for which to atone, Celia

Blackmore Percy was likely out of Grace's life for good.

Grace held her smile in place until everyone had disappeared around the corner of the ruins. Then her knees gave way. She sank to the ground, the tension in her muscles uncoiling and leaving a shaky response. Poor Frederick had been man-napped and beaten. She'd scaled a wall, propelled from a ceiling, and been held at scissors-point, not to mention almost being strangled.

But everyone was safe now. Her emotions trembled beneath the declaration. *Thank You, God.*

"Grace."

She turned to see Frederick march through the door. His breaths shook his broad shoulders, and his eyes—or at least the one that wasn't swollen shut—fastened on her, holding her in place. Tears swarmed into her vision.

In one fluid movement, he pulled her up from the ground and wrapped her in the safety of his arms. That's when the tears came, full and free against his strong shoulder. She tightened her grip around his waist, burying her face in his neck, refusing to let go. They stood together in an embrace until their lips finally found each other—a kiss of gratitude, of near-loss, of acknowledgment that they'd fought for each other and won.

"You shouldn't have come." He drew back, his knuckles skimming her cheek, words rasped. "You could have been killed."

Her lip pouted, wounded at his reprimand. "But you needed me."

A sound caught in his throat, and he lowered his forehead to hers. "Yes, my darling. I do need you. Always."

Elliott gathered up their dishes from the small table in their sitting room, effectively taking Brandon's place as the butler recuperated from the concussion he'd received when Celia's men had taken Frederick.

Frederick welcomed the intimacy of their quarters over the dining hall, especially after the harrowing events of the day. His body ached all over, and though his eye was still sore, the swelling had reduced enough for him to see across the table to his wife.

She'd born a few wounds of her own. A scrape down one cheek. A shallow cut to her neck, and a bruise on her forehead. But in that moment as candlelight flickered across her features, deepening her flaming hair to auburn, she'd never looked more beautiful.

"How do you suppose Blake knew when to arrive?"

Frederick chuckled and sent Elliott a glance. "Blake has an uncanny way of knowing things."

"It likely helps that he spends too much idle time either being arrested or befriending police, my lady."

A laugh burst from Grace, the sound of it soothing over some of the residual pain in Frederick's chest at the idea of losing her. "Why does that not surprise me at all?"

"Because you've gotten to know my lifelong friend well enough to expect no less." Frederick answered. "And your exuberant imagination likely does the rest."

"I'm glad he went to speak to your mother," Grace added, nodding her thanks to Elliott as he took her plate.

"He's always had a way of talking with her," Frederick nodded. "But she must still be held accountable for her actions."

"Your mother has borne the penalty of her choices for years." Grace's fingers covered his. "If there's a way to extend mercy, perhaps the ending of her story will look very different than the preceding chapters."

He breathed out his frustrations and collected Grace's hand in his. "I will only do it for your sake. Not hers."

"That's an excellent place to start." She pulled his fingers to her lips and kissed them, her smile more captivating and precious with each passing minute. "You were very brave today. A true hero."

"A hero?" He chuckled. "What about you? I suspect not even Robert Louis Stevenson or Jules Verne could have posed such a rescue as we witnessed today."

"You certainly know how to compliment a lady." Her face beamed with pleasure. "But despite her superb villainous qualities, I should never wish to meet Celia again."

"According to Detective Miracle, evidence has been mounting against her for some time. All they needed was proof to connect everything." Frederick stood and brought Grace up with him. "Parks was quick to confess the entire plan, with Turner not far behind."

"Will she. . .hang?"

He almost smiled at the compassion in her question. Even with the ruthless Celia Blackmore Percy, Grace desired mercy. Would he ever plumb the depths of her generous heart?

"I cannot say." He squeezed her hand, drawing her to the window seat as Elliott continued clearing their dishes. "But she certainly met her match with you, darling."

She looked up at him, moonlight drifting through the window and draping her in a halo of white. "Whatever do you mean?"

"Celia lived for her own desires, her own happiness. She had no script for you and your selflessness."

"Actually, what she didn't expect was how we worked together. She'd anticipated you to be alone, like her." Grace settled next to him in the window. "But I'm here to ensure you're never alone."

He tugged her close to his side. "Nor I you."

"And we make an excellent team. Who's to say we might not become detectives all our own."

Tension flew back into his spine. "Grace."

"You were perfect for finding clues. The letters. The flowers. Putting the pieces together." Her eyes sparkled in a terrifying sort of way.

"I have no desire to—"

"And we can learn from Detective Miracle." She squeezed his fingers, her smile growing. "You have to admit it's rather exhilarating."

"Near-death experiences? Being held at knifepoint?"

"Scissors-point," she corrected. "And since Mr. Patton is teaching me to drive, not all the pressure would be on you for a quick getaway. I wonder if you might help improve my archery though."

"Patton is teaching you to drive?"

"I started archery once, but Father stopped lessons when I almost killed the dog."

"Grace." This time his attempt was half-hearted. She was happiest when concocting plans.

"He was a very old dog." She nodded, looking duly remorseful. "I feel I would do better now."

"I've heard that Mr. Reams, our gardener, is quite adept at throwing knives," came Elliot's addition.

Grace's mouth dropped wide to match her eyes.

"You're not helping, Elliott."

"Ever so sorry, sir." His old friend chuckled before opening the door to leave. The door closed behind his apology.

"Knives would be excellent protection, Frederick." She leaned close, drawing him into her wonder. "But what would be even better? Pistols. Aunt Lavenia has already offered a lesson or two."

Frederick shook his head, his smile unfurling at her tenacity, and he gently framed her face with his hands. All words closed off in his throat at the perplexing mixture of gratitude and fascination. He might have desired a bride more fitting for the life of an earl, but God knew what he needed most. A bride for his heart, his soul, his imagination. And Gracelynn Ferguson Percy proved beyond his imaginings.

"Darling, we'll talk about it tomorrow."

She slid her palm up his shirt to grab his collar. "I know what you're doing."

He tipped his face closer, drawn in by the light in her eyes, the scent surrounding her, everything Grace. His mouth found hers ready, soft. "And what is that?"

"You're trying to distract me," her words whispered against his mouth.

His lips trailed down her neck, inciting a gasp. "Actually I'm using my excellent skills of deduction to come to the conclusion that my wife is ready for bed."

He felt her smile more than saw it. "See what an excellent start at investigating you have already made."

He sighed and embraced her just as she was. Besides, she'd find a pistol waiting for her in two days when she opened her birthday present beneath the Christmas tree. "And how are my deductions?"

"I believe, my dear Watson, the game is afoot." She stood and drew him up with her toward his bedroom door. Her eyes glittered like the darling pixie she was. "In fact, I have a few private mysteries of the romantic variety just for you."

Merry Christmas, indeed! Frederick rolled his gaze to heaven in silent thanksgiving. He was playing for the happily-ever-after with Grace, even if it included another mystery. . .or two.

# *Epilogue*

"Sir. Madam." Elliott breathed out the response as he sent a shy gaze around the Great Hall, where the other servants sat or stood, each opening their own gifts from Lord and Lady Astley.

Grace squeezed her hands together, attempting to keep her giggle of delight in check. She'd always loved watching people open presents. It was like a marvelous mystery of the sweetest kind, even if she knew exactly what the gift was. The mystery came with the response of the recipient, and she felt confident in her choices.

Once she'd known the servants for an entire year, just imagine how excellent her gift-giving could become!

First, Elliott uncovered Frederick's chosen gift. From the folds of white paper, a golden pocket watch gleamed into the glow of soft lights around the room. "Sir?"

Frederick nodded, a look moving between the two men. Perhaps Elliott truly understood how much Frederick respected him with this gift. "Turn it over," he whispered.

Grace nearly bounded from her seat next to Frederick. She'd encouraged Frederick to leave a personal note, especially after her dear husband had shared with her some of the history he had with Elliott. Having someone rescue you from a life of boxing only to have Elliott save Frederick's life on occasion certainly deserved recognition, in her book anyway.

Elliott read the simple inscription and flashed a smile. "Thank you, sir."

Grace squeezed Frederick's hand, her teeth skimming over her lips in pure delight. *My friend.* Frederick's choice for his message to Elliott.

Elliott cleared his throat and raised a brow as he tugged a larger parcel from the wrapping. Grace's entire body stiffened as the paper fell away to reveal her choice for Elliott. Three books. *A Study in Scarlet, The Moonstone,* and *The Manual of Becoming a Detective.*

"Just imagine how much more prepared you'll be next time." Grace grinned and leaned forward to watch the man's smile brim to sparkle in his eyes.

"I have no words to express my emotions right now, my lady."

She clasped her hands together. "I'd hug you if it wasn't improper, Elliott, and I feel I've already pushed your limits for impropriety enough this week."

A coughing sound erupted from the handsome hero at her side, so she quickly reached for a glass of customary Christmas champagne and handed it to him. "Do you see how excited Lord Astley is at the very idea of you becoming more prepared for sleuthing, dear Elliott?"

Grace sent Frederick a subtle wink, chuckling a little to herself that her sweet husband was trying his best not to reveal how amused he was at her plans, but she didn't mind. She'd already proven how very helpful studying fiction could be to real-life crimes. She only needed to test the theory a few more times to prove her hypothesis, and what better way than to bring along as many knowledgeable, trustworthy people as possible in the process?

As Brandon opened his gift, Grace had to get as close as politely possible to watch him, because the man's expression remained as stoic as ever. How could anyone remain stoic while opening Christmas presents?

The first present to meet Brandon's eyes was from Frederick. A beautifully crafted fountain pen with an emblem of Havensbrooke etched in the pen holder.

"I noticed you needed a new one for all the excellent work you do for us, Brandon," Frederick offered, causing the man to nod stiffly and run a finger over the smooth, polished wood of the pen's stem.

"Thank you, sir. It's the best one I've ever owned."

"It's a small token for your service."

The man refused to raise his gaze as he continued sifting through the gift paper. The firelight played across his etched features, deepening the lines on his face into a frown. Grace began fidgeting with the edge of her sleeve, her stomach lurching in sudden agitation. What if she'd chosen poorly? They hadn't known each other a great while yet.

He raised the small bag to view first, reading the words on the front aloud. "Luden's Cough Drops?"

"I don't want you to become sick, dear Brandon, so I thought these may help with that nasty cough you seem to have so often."

"Cough, madam?" His large brows rose in wonder.

"Yes, I've heard it fairly regularly, and these are supposed to help soothe any possible beginnings of an illness."

Brandon's gaze shifted to Frederick, and then the butler's lips pinched and his shoulders seized, releasing a short-lived cough.

"See? There it is!" She gestured toward the bag. "And now you have relief."

His lips pressed even tighter, but he nodded. "Thank you, madam," but the way he said it sounded strained and tight.

Oh dear, she had chosen poorly. What would he do when he saw the second gift she'd picked?

Frederick's hand suddenly swallowed up her fidgeting one, and he offered her a smile. "Don't worry, darling," he whispered. "You chose everything with such personal care, they'll all appreciate them. I think you might be their favorite surprise this Christmas, and the gifts are just a bonus."

"What do you mean?"

"You care, Grace. And they know it." He squeezed her fingers, his gaze caressing her face with such tenderness it nearly brought her to tears. She wanted to grab his face and kiss him, but in the middle of a Christmas party in the Great Hall probably wasn't the best time for acting on those impulses. "It's been a long time since they've known such kindness from their mistress, and they may never have known kindness with such. . .generosity before."

Grace breathed a sigh and turned just in time to see Brandon pull his lovely hardbound book from the wrappings. *A Christmas Carol*, in the beautiful red cover used when it was first published. His gaze came up to hers, brow pinched with questions.

"For the ghosts." Grace shrugged. "So you'll know what to expect next time."

Then the most remarkable thing happened. Brandon laughed. Not just a simple chuckle, but a hearty, shoulder-shaking laugh that garnered everyone's attention in the room and brought out their smiles—though Mrs. Powell looked more shocked than amused.

Grace's bottom lip dropped in a wide-mouthed smile.

"Thank you, my lady." Brandon chuckled through the words, taking out his handkerchief to wipe at his eyes. "I'm honored, and this particular book is very special to me because it was one my father used to read to me when I was a lad."

It took everything in Grace not to pop up from her seat and give the sweet man a kiss on the cheek. Maybe she could later, when all the other staff weren't looking. Surely Frederick wouldn't find that too inappropriate for a countess, would he?

"I'm so glad it brings good memories with it, Brandon, considering the circumstances surrounding our spectral night of ghost hunting together."

Another cough slipped from his smile, but this time it sounded much more like a laugh. Grace blinked. Had he been laughing all along? Perhaps he wasn't in need of cough drops at all! For an amateur sleuth, she felt very silly, but the twinkle in Brandon's dark eyes as he grinned at her somehow doused her momentary frustration.

Each servant opened their gifts, and each appeared to enjoy the simple offerings. Grace had gotten the cook a new hat to wear to church, since she'd heard the woman had a fondness for hats. She'd cooed and aahed over the green felt as if she'd never seen a hat before. And with the dashes of auburn in her hair, the round-faced woman looked rather fetching wearing the lovely shade of green. Grace had chosen classy new heels for each of the maids, and she'd particularly chosen the fur-lined ones for winter, as well as a book for each person. With a few strategic questions here and there, she'd learned of interests and reading levels— some rather surprising. Who would have known that Mary enjoyed Gothic romances? She seemed like such a quiet girl.

Mrs. Powell, as reserved as the woman usually was, sat in shock for a good ten seconds before responding when she opened the teapot Grace had chosen for her. Mary had mentioned how Mrs. Powell loved butterflies and had recently chipped her personal server, so when Grace had seen the Herend Rothschild china tea set in the window of a local shop—complete with a bright flourish of butterflies—she'd snatched it up. Grace had made sure to leave her gift for Lady Moriah on a table in the woman's room so she could open it on her own. She'd felt compelled to give her mother-in-law her own beloved version of *Pilgrim's Progress*, complete with Grace's own rather whimsical notes in the margins.

After all the servants opened their gifts, the dancing began. Grace had read about the Servants' Ball, a festive time for the servants to dress in their best and enjoy dancing, merriment, and delicious food, along with their employers, that usually happened in January. But given that both Frederick and Grace were rather happy with quiet, subdued holidays—and since they'd apparently fulfilled their social duty by attending the Kerifords' Christmas party—Frederick had agreed to Grace's suggestion that they hold the Servants' Ball on Christmas Day.

After the presents and a solemn moment of Frederick reading the Christmas story from the Gospel of Luke, Grace encouraged the quiet housemaid Lucy to take to the piano, and the dancing commenced. Frederick gallantly sought out Mrs. Powell, who stood slack-jawed for the third time that evening, as he asked for a dance, and Grace encouraged the rather reticent Brandon to be her own partner. Elliott took the opportunity to ask Mary, and other partners made it to the floor of the Great Hall as Lucy impressed them all with her expert repertoire of country dance tunes.

Grace gave Lucy a reprieve from piano playing so the young girl could have her turn at dancing, which enabled Grace the opportunity to watch the others from her perch in the corner of the room. The massive tree glowed with golden electric lights, the firelight waved its toasty warmth across the gleaming wood floor, and the room hummed with the happy chatter of people who may have been different as far as society was concerned, but not so different at the heart. As Grace looked from face to face, she claimed them all as her new family. Even the grumpy footman John, who refused to dance with anyone at all.

Her eyes narrowed as she stared at him. Perhaps he waited because he had a secret engagement to a young woman in the village and felt that dancing with any other lady would betray his wholehearted devotion to his beloved.

Grace sighed as her gaze settled on her handsome hero. He was dancing with Mrs. Lennox, and the cook's rosy cheeks were a sight bit rosier than usual. His smile shone with kindness, his dark eyes lit with the glow from the surrounding lights.

A month ago, Grace never would have imagined being married to an earl. In fact, she hadn't planned on being married at all. But just when she'd thought her choice to take her sister's place would lead to her giving up on her dreams, God had used the unexpected to give her even more. How very clever of Him! She supposed He did have the very best of imaginations, since He had created imaginations from the start.

She'd not only become a wife, but a mother of sorts, even though she couldn't openly announce Lily as her adopted darling. Grace and Frederick had visited the sweet girl together earlier in the day and brought not only presents but also the grand surprise of bringing Lily and Miss Quinnly into the house once the renovations were complete.

As Frederick tugged Grace close to his side later that evening in their private sitting room, Grace nestled against him, grateful all over again that God had made her husband a wonderful combination of all the things she loved best about fictional heroes. Dashing, intelligent, kind, brave, devoted, and wonderfully roguish—in his own special way. She'd never appreciated lips as much in her life. Her cheeks heated. Lips were wonderful inventions.

And she'd never quite realized how wonderful it was to have a husband who cared about her thoughts and imaginations, but she found it one of his most attractive features of all.

"It seemed everyone enjoyed the gifts we gave them." She looked up at him from the cocoon of his arms. "Though John didn't show it, I caught him opening *Ulysses* when he thought no one was looking. I knew a fellow Irishman would be tempted by his own countryman's work."

Frederick chuckled, his fingers moving through her hair, loosening it with expert skill. He was excellent at misplacing her pins, but the feel of his hands in her hair made it worth every lost one.

"I had much more fun watching you watch them than I did seeing their reaction, I'm afraid."

She blinked up at him. "What do you mean?"

His palm slid to her cheek, and he captured her chin with his finger and thumb, placing a gentle kiss to her lips. "The sheer pleasure in your face lights up the room more than electric lights ever could. I think half the servants enjoyed watching your joy as much as receiving presents or dancing." He held her gaze. "You have been the very best gift for Havensbrooke—and for me, my darling."

Grace nearly melted into his admiration until the word *gift* surfaced in her comprehension. She pushed out of his arms. "Oh, you haven't opened your gift yet!"

She dashed to her bedroom and returned with a long package, barely able to contain the laughter bubbling up in her throat. It was unnerving choosing a gift for a man whom she'd only begun to fall desperately in love with. Well, not desperately in love. That sounded rather pathetic. And *thoroughly* in love sounded a bit too pedantic. Hmm. Shamelessly? Yes. Scandalously? Her grin took a decided upswing. Most certainly. Incandescently? Her face warmed. Oh yes.

"I know you said that I was your gift, which was terribly romantic of you, but I feel the very same way about you." She returned to her seat beside him, the firelight playing across his features and causing his eyes to take on an even softer glow. "To be perfectly honest, I expected an earl-like husband to be rather boring, a little overbearing, and thoroughly, well. . .proper."

"I know my heart holds a great number of emotions all the time and my head swirls with uncommon notions, but I do think you are the very best for me, and I can't imagine loving you more." She shrugged, hoping he caught her intention. "You've been absolutely and deliciously wonderful, Frederick Percy."

"Except for when I refused your marriage proposal." His lips twitched. "Or nearly got us killed in the river, or left you at the mercy of my mother, or behaved so idiotically you ran off to my aunt's house in retaliation, or—"

Grace's laugh burst out. "You're deliciously wonderful in all the ways that matter most." She leaned close and kissed his cheek. "Especially in your long-suffering ability to listen to your wife and in the rather adept way you have in making up after disagreements."

His gaze took the type of dark turn that incited a wonderful thrill through her body.

Her breath hitched as she pushed the gift forward. "I cannot offer you anything that could remotely equal these enormous affections I have for you, but at least I can give you something special for our very first Christmas together."

He held her gaze, his expression so tender, she nearly leaned forward and rewarded him with a kiss, but she had the sneaky suspicion that if the kissing started, it might not end for a very long time, and Christmas presents needed to be opened on Christmas, after all.

He tugged at the top wrapping, which soon opened to its contents. His laugh burst out before he sobered and offered her a look through narrowed eyes. "A deerstalker? As if I'm the enigmatic Sherlock?" He placed the hat on his head and raised his brows.

"I don't think that's for you." She swept it off his head, liking his dark waves much better. "And it's never truly mentioned that he wore that sort of hat often, but I did want to tease you a little."

He grinned and pulled the next thing from the wrapping, turning the cover around for her view. "Detective Miracle's Advice to the Amateur Sleuth?"

"Did you know he'd written a book?" She clapped her hands together, smile growing. "After everyone who needed to be arrested was arrested and everyone who needed to give testimony had given testimony, and I was able to get Detective Miracle to myself for a moment before he was swept away by the inspector, I asked him for some suggestions on how I could improve my sleuthing skills, and he told me about his book! Isn't that convenient?"

"Remarkably."

"So not only do we have a little practical experience, but we can learn a bit of head knowledge too." She tapped her head and nodded, her entire body nearly shaking. "And once I learn how to use my new pistol you bought me, think of what a pair we'll be."

"I try not to, darling." His shoulders shook from his internal chuckle. "But I'm glad it makes you happy."

She rolled her eyes at him and pushed the remainder of the gift deeper into his hold. "Oh, stop teasing and finish opening your gift."

He sent her one of his rare winks, dousing any annoyance she might have felt at his teasing, and pushed back the last remnants of paper to reveal the pinnacle of the gift she had specifically designed for him. All humor fled from his face as the wrapping revealed more and more of the painting.

"I didn't use the original letters of your grandparents. I copied them to create the matte for the painting of Havensbrooke because it just felt like they were there too, hugging you and your world through the painting, so to speak." She grinned to herself as she traced one of the signatures in the paintings' matte with her finger. "I hope you don't mind that I used a copy of the letters, only the sweetest parts, of course, but it seemed to reflect their love for you and Havensbrooke so well together." She pointed at the way the "letters" had been set around the watercolor landscape. "Mr. Poole in the village has a daughter who is excellent at watercolor, and when I asked if she could create a painting of Havensbrooke at sunset, with the glow coming from behind the beautiful stones, she eagerly agreed. The payment probably helped too, but it turned out so well. And you have a spot in your office where it would fit perfectly right over—"

His mouth took hers without warning. He kissed as if he savored her taste, her touch, his fingers trailing from her neck up into her hair, turning her face so his lips had the best access. His caress radiated the tenderest of emotions, slow, lingering, somehow leaving her teary-eyed and swooning at the same time.

"I have no words, Grace." He leaned his head against hers, fingers playing with strands of her hair as he stared at her. "It is the perfect gift to complete the very best Christmas of my life."

"I'm so glad you like it." She sneaked another kiss. "Just imagine how excellent my present choices will become as I get to know you better."

He slid a palm down her cheek and kissed her ready lips again, then slid back, raising a brow. "Now I believe it's time for *your* gifts and, if I use my powers of deduction well enough, I'd guess that my wife loves presents."

She clapped her hands together. "See how well you are at deductions already, and you haven't even read Detective Miracle's book yet."

His chuckle followed him to his room and back, as he returned with a gift that looked much too small for what she'd expected. Well, she wasn't quite sure what she'd expected, but the simple, oddly shaped rectangle didn't fit her expectations. But it held an odd book shape, which certainly couldn't be bad.

And after all, her husband had only known her for about a month.

He eyed her carefully as he placed the gift on her lap and took his place beside her. "Merry Christmas, Lady Astley."

She opened the wrapping to find a smaller square box positioned atop a book. Grace pulled the book out first and read the title. *The Rules of Croquet.* The intention slowly flared to realization as she remembered her very poor attempts at playing croquet at Aunt Lavenia's. Grace burst out laughing and wrapped her arms around her husband's neck, giggling against his lips. "Be careful, husband dearest." She sat back to wave the book at him. "If I actually learn how to play the game, I may best you at it like I will at lawn tennis this spring."

He crooked a brow, his dark eyes glimmering. "I look forward to the challenge, my lady." His gaze dropped to the smaller box. "But we may have something else to prepare for this spring."

She studied him a moment before reaching for the box. Carefully, she unclasped the simple gold clasp and raised the lid. Inside sat a beautiful ornate brass compass. She gasped and looked back at him, but he only smiled, encouraging her continued perusal. With careful fingers, she opened the compass. The internal cogs and dials shone through a clear lens, and the arrow swayed back and forth searching for north. Her teeth skimmed over her lips as she examined every part of the new gift, until she finally tipped it over to the bottom. Engraved in calligraphic style were three words and a name. *For our adventures. Frederick.*

She drew the compass to her chest and blinked back tears. "Thank you, Frederick." The words barely made it above a whisper. Perhaps he knew her better than she had guessed, because instead of giving her something finite, he'd given her a dream.

"And here is the final one." He pulled another book-sized gift from behind his back and gave it to her.

"Oh dear, I don't know that I can handle much more."

Her fingers trembled as she tugged off the simple brown paper tied with red ribbon. Yes, it was a book, and on the cover was one word. *Italy.*

Her attention flew to Frederick's face and, without looking away, he opened the front cover of the book to reveal two steamer tickets. "I think it's time to start those adventures, don't you? In the land of *Romeo and Juliet* and *Julius Caesar,* and—one of your personal favorites—*The Betrothed.*"

As she searched his face, the tears she'd barely held in spilled down her cheeks. She placed the compass and the book to the side and moved so close her face waited mere inches from his. Without a word, she framed his face with her palms, continuing to smile so wide her cheeks ached. "My dear Lord Astley, my adventures started with you the day I met you in the Whitlocks' library, and I cannot wait to continue them with you wherever they may lead."

How God could take two people's very different stories and combine them to create an entirely new tale was rather remarkable. Instead of his story or her story, it had become *their* story, and Grace was fairly certain this one would be her favorite.

**PEPPER BASHAM** is an award-winning author who writes romance peppered with grace and humor. She is a native of the Blue Ridge Mountains, where her family has lived for generations. She's the mom of five kids, speech-pathologist to about fifty more, lover of chocolate, jazz, and Jesus, and proud AlleyCat at the award-winning Writer's Alley blog. Her debut historical romance novel, *The Thorn Bearer*, released in April 2015, and the second in February 2016. Her first contemporary romance debuted in April 2016.

You can connect with Pepper on her website at www.pepperdbasham.com, Facebook at www.facebook.com/pages/Pepper-D-Basham, or Twitter at twitter.com/pepperbasham.

# OTHER BOOKS BY PEPPER BASHAM

### Hope Between the Pages

Clara Blackwell helps her mother manage a struggling one-hundred-year old family bookshop in Asheville, North Carolina, but the discovery of a forgotten letter opens a mystery of a long-lost romance and undiscovered inheritance which could save its future. Forced to step outside of her predictable world, Clara embarks on an adventure with only the name Oliver as a hint of the man's identity in her great-great-grandmother's letter. From the nearby grand estate of the Vanderbilts, to a hamlet in Derbyshire, England, Clara seeks to uncover truth about family and love that may lead to her own unexpected romance.

Paperback / 978-1-64352-826-7 / $12.99

### The Red Ribbon

In Carroll County, a corn shucking is the social event of the season, until a mischievous kiss leads to one of the biggest tragedies in Virginia history. Ava Burcham isn't your typical Blue Ridge Mountain girl. She has a bad habit of courtin' trouble, and her curiosity has opened a rift in the middle of a feud between politicians and would-be outlaws, the Allen family. Ava's tenacious desire to find a story worth reporting may land her and her best friend, Jeremiah Sutphin, into more trouble than either of them planned. The end result? The Hillsville Courthouse Massacre of 1912.

Paperback / 978-1-64352-649-2 / $12.99